BRITNEY FARR

Searching for Atonement

Book Three of The Search Series

FAITH BASED DYSTOPIAN

First published by Britney Farr 2023

Copyright © 2023 by Britney Farr

All rights reserved. No part of this publication may be reproduced, stored or transmitted in any form or by any means, electronic, mechanical, photocopying, recording, scanning, or otherwise without written permission from the publisher. It is illegal to copy this book, post it to a website, or distribute it by any other means without permission.

This novel is entirely a work of fiction. The names, characters and incidents portrayed in it are the work of the author's imagination. Any resemblance to actual persons, living or dead, events or localities is entirely coincidental.

Britney Farr asserts the moral right to be identified as the author of this work.

First edition

ISBN: 978-1-7351256-2-6

Cover art by Lance Buckley
Editing by Melinda Crouchley

This book was professionally typeset on Reedsy.
Find out more at reedsy.com

Contents

Prologue	v
Chapter 1	1
Chapter 2	15
Chapter 3	26
Chapter 4	45
Chapter 5	58
Chapter 6	76
Chapter 7	90
Chapter 8	104
Chapter 9	112
Chapter 10	123
Chapter 11	136
Chapter 12	148
Chapter 13	160
Chapter 14	178
Chapter 15	188
Chapter 16	201
Chapter 17	214
Chapter 18	229
Chapter 19	245
Chapter 20	261
Chapter 21	267
Chapter 22	284
Chapter 23	298

Chapter 24	310
Epilogue	321
About the Author	326
Also by Britney Farr	328

Prologue

Time moved slowly as the tension rose in the main hall. After several days of waiting, Eloina—Salome's friend and commander of the Hebrew warriors—convinced Aryeh to meet with Salome, Paul, and Matthias. Salome was certain they could appeal to his logic. Help him see they had no intention of ruining the order of things within the Hebrew village. They wanted and deserved a safe place to live. While Aryeh agreed to meet, his crossed arms and tight jaw indicated he had no intention of negotiation. Salome prayed Sabaoth would soften his heart and Matthias could make Aryeh come to the right decision.

"Thank you for seeing us." Matthias held his hand out. "I am Matthias Smith, head elder and leader of the Notzrim camp."

Aryeh stared at Matthias' large, calloused hand but didn't shake it. "It would appear I had little a choice. You are quite persistent." He glanced at Eloina sideways. She didn't acknowledge him, but her eyes darted away. "What is it you want? Have you come to your senses and decided to leave?"

Matthias cleared his throat. "Of course not. We intend to stay here. We've traveled a long distance and have nowhere else to go. On behalf of your humanity, we beg you to allow us to stay."

Aryeh choked at those words. "My humanity? How dare

you insult me as if I have no humanity for wanting to protect my village. Everything I have done so far it to protect them from danger. We have spent nine and a half years protected in this valley, and I am grateful. But when your people came, everything changed. It was the first time someone found us. And then Salome ran off and brought back hundreds of outsiders and who knows what other sorts of danger."

"Then you understand my desire to keep my people safe. It's been a hard nine and a half years and I don't know how much longer we will have to wait until it ends, but I'd like to do it here. Clearly, Sabaoth has blessed this valley and your people."

"I suppose, but too many people in this valley raise the risk."

"Do you question Sabaoth's ability to protect us just because it's a larger group?"

Aryeh's face reddened, but he didn't speak. Instead, he paced silently, shaking his head, debating with himself.

Salome held back a smile. Good, he's flustered. Hopefully, he would see reason. "Isn't it possible, Aryeh, that Sabaoth allowed Amina and Paxton to find the valley for a reason? Don't you think maybe we're meant to help them?"

He stared at the ground, biting the cuticles on one hand while the other rested on his hip. Quoting the Hebrew's Sacred Writings he said, "You shall make no covenant with them and show no mercy to them. You shall not intermarry with them, giving your daughters to their sons or taking their daughters for your sons, for they would turn away your sons from following me, to serve other gods. Then the anger of Sabaoth would be kindled against you, and he would destroy you quickly."

"Yes, but you take that out of context. That was toward a

wicked nation and that's not the Notzrim."

"Is not their religion different from ours?"

This is where Salome had to stop. Yes, their religion was different, but how different? Often when Paul or Mo quoted the Sacred Writings, it was the same as hers. Clearly, it was the same God and yet different because they believed Meshiakh was the Messiah already come. "Please, Aryeh. They mean no harm," Salome pleaded, but with less conviction.

Silence filled the large hall as they stood. Salome's eyes cast to the ground. The only light filling the room were the fat candles spaced along the pillars, hanging chandeliers, and the tall candelabras with six arms jutting out in a circle with a seventh candle in the center. The tiny flames of each candle flickered individually, and yet filled the room as one unified light.

Salome crossed her arms and watched Aryeh intently. This was not how she intended things to go. In her mind, bringing the Notzrim to the valley was the right thing to do, and she assumed everyone would see it the same way.

This time, it was Paul who spoke. "I understand your desire to keep your people safe and your beliefs unhindered. We are not here to convert you. I know Sabaoth is a God of compassion and acceptance. Did he not allow people like Jethro, Rahab, Naaman, and Ruth to be a part of his people? And what about the countless commands to treat foreigners with love, respect, and acceptance? This is your God, and we too worship that same God, although a bit differently."

Paul paused, watching Aryeh. Aryeh didn't move nor speak. Paul continued, "Remember what the prophet Yesha'ayahu spoke, that any foreigner who joined themselves to Sabaoth, who ministered and loved him, who chose to be his servant and keep the Sabbath. Those foreigners who hold fast to Sabaoth's word would be brought to the holy mountain and their offerings and sacrifices would be accepted, for Sabaoth's house is to be called a house of prayer for all peoples. I tell you, we do just that. We observe the Sabbath. We honor, love, and serve Sabaoth. If he accepts us, why not you? Are you to be better than Sabaoth?" Having said his peace, Paul waited for Aryeh's response.

Salome had to admit he impressed her. Paul knew his Sacred Writings well. There was no way Aryeh could deny Sabaoth's written words. Commands such as "you shall not wrong a stranger or oppress him" or "The stranger who resides with you shall be to you as the native among you, and you shall love him as yourself." Sabaoth is a God of love and acceptance. Aryeh needed to stop being fearful of the outside world.

Though everyone in the room waited for Aryeh to speak, it was Eloina who spoke first. She stepped forward and looked directly at Aryeh. Her face was as blank as ever and her tone was matter-of-fact. "The way I see it, you have no other option than to let them stay. They've stated their case clearly, they've proven they know Sabaoth's commands. If you turn them away now, it'll prove to be more dangerous than if they stayed. You and I have gone over every scenario, and you know, there is a greater risk of our being found if they leave. There's no way around it."

Aryeh glared at Eloina, his eyebrows furrowed and his hands clenched in fists. He took a step toward her. Eloina lifted her chin high, refusing to back down. "Well?"

The hairs on Salome's neck stood on end. Every muscle in her body tensed. Her eyes darted to Matthias and Paul, trying to read their faces. They too stood like statues, though she thought she saw Paul's lip twitch. Salome looked back at Aryeh and Eloina, staring one another down. If it was anyone else, Aryeh would've likely laughed in their face and thrown them out of the room. But Aryeh respected Eloina, and she knew how to get through that thick skull of his.

"Fine," he growled and turned toward Matthias and Paul. "The Notzrim can stay as long as you stay far away from us. I don't want intermingling. I don't want to even know you are here. Go live peaceably in the far corner of the valley and don't bother me again." Aryeh turned away and headed out of the room.

"Thank you, Aryeh, for accepting us into your valley," Paul called after him.

Aryeh whipped around. "I'm not accepting you. As Eloina pointed out, it's necessary to keep my village safe. If you leave, the Myriad can track you and trace your prior whereabouts to us. I don't need that happening." Aryeh tried to leave again, but Salome stopped him.

"What about supplies?"

"What about them?"

"We're going to need a little help getting started."

"We didn't have any help, and we did just fine."

"I wouldn't call losing dozens of people to starvation and hypothermia the first couple of months fine. Or did you forget all that?"

Pain pierced Aryeh's eyes, as he remembered the brutality of those first several months and the death of his wife. Salome remembered it vividly. Aryeh was broken. He wasn't the same after that. Aryeh looked at Eloina with glassy eyes. "Get them what they need," he said and stormed out.

Salome didn't mean to hurt him with such a painful memory,

but she wanted to remind him how difficult it is to start from scratch.

Six Weeks Later. . .

Chapter 1

The sun hung in the sky with not a cloud surrounding it. It beamed its rays of heat onto the peaceful valley: happy, independent, and proud. On most days, Salome welcomed the sun and its life-giving warmth, but today her clothes clung to her back and legs, damp from sweat. Salome longed for a cool breeze to cool her burning skin as she finished her morning chores. When it was hot, it didn't matter how lightweight her clothes were; she sweat.

Salome grabbed the rope dangling inside the water well and heaved it up, hand over hand, her muscles aching, until the bucket full of fresh water surfaced. She caught her reflection in the water and shook her head. Though a yellow headband held back her massive curly brown hair, it still kinked and frizzed in every direction. Other strands clung to her red forehead and cheeks.

Hiding under the strands, she gazed at the small marking on her forehead. A tattoo of a six-pointed star with the north, south, east, and west points elongated into a cross. When the image first supernaturally appeared on Salome's forehead, she was terrified and annoyed. Where had it come from? Was she marked by a demon? And why the forehead, of all places?

As she discovered more people who'd received the mark,

she realized it was special, a seal of protection for all believing Hebrews.

Salome dumped the bucket of water carefully into her own clay jar before lowering it back down for another round.

A cool breeze blew across the lake to the north and provided some brief relief. Salome closed her eyes and breathed deeply. That breeze was a reminder that fall was approaching. Soon the leaves would give way to vibrant colors and the temperature would drop to something more pleasant.

After pulling two more buckets of water and pouring them into her own jar, Salome wandered through the marketplace and toward her cabin on the south side of the village.

It didn't take long to get to her one-room wooden cabin and drop off the water jugs. Really, the cabins were more like a barracks, with long buildings divided into multiple units. Each unit contained a bed, nightstand, a table, and a small kitchenette complete with shelves, counter space, and a wash basin. It was modest but efficient. And given it'd only been six weeks since the Notzrim arrived in the valley, they worked quickly.

Salome set her water jugs in the kitchen area, grabbed an apple, and headed back out. Today was her day to teach another basket weaving class.

Salome, along with her father David, spent tireless hours teaching the Notzrim everything they needed to know to survive in the valley. Since she brought them, she felt it was her responsibility to ensure their success. When she and David started, they sought out those who knew how to construct homes, dig wells, and sew clothes to help lead the charge. While there were several to step up, there were even more who knew nothing about this life.

CHAPTER 1

As Salome reached the center of the village, she found a group of children and their mothers gathered in the modest amphitheater. They fixed their attention on an older man with long stringy black hair streaked with gray. His beard, in contrast, was short, but just as gray. Salome smiled and stopped to watch for a while.

Father Stephen, the Notzrim's holy man, was engaged in a story as the surrounding group listened earnestly. When he spoke, he flailed his long-fingered hands about and incorporated his entire body. It was hard not to be engaged while watching him.

Salome noticed her new friend Mo standing along the edge of the group, alone. She approached but didn't say anything. She didn't want to interrupt. Storytime for the children occurred daily in the Notzrim village. It gave them the entertainment they craved while offering parents the break they needed.

A gentle elbow nudged Salome in the arm.

"Do you see?" Mo whispered.

"See what?" Salome looked around, expecting to see a deer or a rabbit hiding in the bushes.

"Look closely."

The children sat enraptured with Father Stephen's boisterous story. One little boy started petting another little boy's arm and then put his head on the other boy's shoulder. The second little boy shrugged him off.

There was an exchange of words between the boys that Salome couldn't hear, but the scowl on the one boy's face let her know they were arguing. Eventually, the first little boy started crying. A mother with short brown hair hastily waved the crying boy over and comforted him. When he stood, Salome caught a glimpse of his forehead. Her mouth dropped.

The little boy clearly had the marking of the Hebrews.

"There are Hebrews in the group?" Salome said, more as a question than a statement. "How long has this been going on?"

Mo shrugged. "One day when I came to find Emily, she introduced me to her new Hebrew friend. That was just yesterday, but I imagine they've been coming for a while. It got me thinking."

Salome looked at Mo, eyebrows raised. She didn't like the tone in Mo's voice.

"We shouldn't have to live separately," Mo spoke, her enthusiasm rising. "If we were to come together as one unified family, we could really help each other."

Salome's stomach dropped. As delighted as she was to see the Hebrews and Notzrim together, she couldn't help but wonder what the other Hebrews would think. They were wary of outsiders and rightly so. Ever since the Great Desolation, persecution and prejudices were more volatile. No longer could someone choose to live outside the popular beliefs without being treated harshly. That's one reason the Hebrews fled to the mountains. Staying hidden away from judgmental eyes was safer.

"I don't know Mo. I love the idea, but Aryeh is allowing the Notzrim to stay under the agreement that we stay separate."

"Yes, but what good does that do any of us? The Notzrim need the extra help, and I'm sure we have a lot to offer them too."

She was referring to their religion. Salome knew that because Mo had made it abundantly clear to her before. And while Salome was contemplating its teachings—that Meshiakh was the true messiah—she wasn't convinced.

CHAPTER 1

"Mo, Aryeh is a finicky man. If he knew we were trying to go against his wishes, I don't know what he'd do, but it wouldn't be good. I think it's better if we stay separated." An image from her recurring nightmare brushed across her mind's eye. A blazing fire with no way out and the gloating face of Aryeh standing on the other side.

"I disagree. Unity is *always* the better option. Accepting and loving one another for our differences and working together to build on one another's strengths. That's how Sabaoth intends for us to live."

"Amen!" the group exclaimed.

Salome's head snapped toward the group as her stomach fluttered. It took a moment for her to realize the amen was regarding Father Stephen's prayer and not her and Mo's conversation.

The children dispersed, running off together in groups, laughing and playing tag. One little girl tossed a ball to the ground and started kicking it around with a few of her friends. Many of the mothers stayed to chat while their children played. It was nice to see them getting along.

In the distance, a little girl with long sandy blond hair waved at Salome and Mo. She had a big grin on her face. Mo and Salome waved back at Mo's daughter, Emily.

"I really think this is the right thing to do, but I can't make it happen without your help. Isn't this what you want, too?"

"Of course it is, Mo, but—" Salome stopped. Why was she against it? It was the right thing to do. Bringing the two groups together would only strengthen their prosperity and safety. So, why was she hesitant?

"Are you still worried about your dream?"

The nightmare flashed again in her mind. Just thinking

about it made her shiver. Salome took a deep breath. "What if it's more than just a nightmare? What if it's a prophecy or a warning?"

"I think it's just worry. Trust Sabaoth. I believe he wants unity to happen. And if so, he'll bless it."

"And if he doesn't?" Salome crossed her arms, still watching the children play.

"Just think about it, please."

Salome didn't want to turn her friend down. Mo cared a lot for her people and for the Hebrews. Salome trusted she wouldn't request anything she herself hadn't thought long and hard about first.

"No, you're right. You're absolutely right. Aryeh's request is unreasonable. We are better together. There's strength in numbers, right?"

Mo smiled. "So you're in?"

"I'm in. Let's plan something."

"Oh, that's good to hear. This is going to be really great, I promise."

At that moment, Emily shouted from across the way. "Mama, come see what we've done!" She waved Mo over to her group of friends huddling around a pile of rocks.

Mo said good before heading over to Emily and her friends.

As Salome turned to leave, something in the bushes caught her eye. A figure hunched low, staring at her. Salome's heart leaped, and she drew in a sharp breath. *What in the world?* Salome stared for a long moment as the eyes stared back. At first, she thought it was an animal, but the longer she stared, the more she realized those were human eyes watching her.

The hair pricked at the nape of Salome's neck. Slowly, she took a step closer. Her heart quickened. The figure still stared.

CHAPTER 1

She took a second small step, her muscles tightening. A branch swung in front of the prying eyes. Salome ran toward the bushes, breaking through the brush, but then stopped. The image was gone. Salome spun in a circle. There was no sign of them.

An eerie feeling trickled down Salome's spine. Someone was spying on her. But why? Salome let out a nervous laugh as she backed away. *It was probably nothing. Just some kids playing hide and seek.* She tried to dismiss what she saw, but the paranoia lingered.

* * * *

Amina lay on her sleeping mat with hands folded over her abdomen as she stared at the dingy ceiling of her tent. Dried tears stained her temples. Her mind drifted back to the garage at the capitol, replaying the dreadful scene like a glitch. The scenario played over and over with different choices, playing out what might have happened if Paxton hadn't lured the Myriad officer after him to allow her and the others to escape. In her delusional mind, some scenarios worked, but deep down, she knew they were lies. The only scenario where they made it out safe was the one that happened. The one where Paxton sacrificed himself for the sake of everyone else. Amina scowled as heat rose to her face.

Next, her mind drifted to her brother. Her stubborn pig-headed brother. What was he thinking? He's not a soldier. He's too kind, too soft to be aggressive. And yet, there was clear determination in his eyes. He wanted to bring down the evil that he saw in the capital. He wanted. . . vengeance? *No, that couldn't be. Justice. He wanted justice.*

She hated letting him go, but if she'd learned anything from her mother, it was that trying to control someone only made things worse. So, she placed her trust in Sabaoth. That he would be with Aiden and bring some sense to him. *Make my brother see that what he's doing is pointless. Bring him home, where he belongs. I don't know how you'll do it, but I know you will.*

Amina sat up and stretched the kinks out of her neck and back. Outside, the birds chirped as they flew past. How long had it been since she last went outside during the day? Time seemed to blur together. She'd spent too much time wallowing in her own misery that she couldn't remember how long she'd secluded herself from the outside world. The back of her throat ached as she swallowed.

A bright light blinded Amina and she shielded her eyes. Footsteps shuffled into the tent.

"Hello, my friend," a soft woman's voice spoke.

Amina's eyes adjusted to find two figures standing over her who couldn't be more opposite from one another. One was a tall six-foot-two man with deep-set brown eyes, black short curly hair, dark skin stretching across his clean-cut muscles, and broad shoulders. The other was a short woman with long sandy blond hair, pale blue eyes to match her pale skin, and wrinkles around her eyes and mouth. Despite their differences, they both looked at Amina with the same determined look.

In their hands, they held a basket of food, clothes, and a bucket of water. Amina groaned inwardly.

The man wrinkled his nose. "Geez, it stinks in here."

"That is what happens, Josiah, when one does not bathe or clean up messes for nearly six weeks."

Amina crossed her arms. "I resent that comment, Maya.

CHAPTER 1

I've bathed. And I've taken out my garbage, sort of."

Josiah looked around, noting the flies buzzing around half-eaten fruit and piles of clothes.

Amina's face flushed. "You know you didn't have to come in here."

Maya stepped toward Amina as if approaching an injured puppy. She kneeled beside her and smiled. "I think it's time."

"For what? I can take care of myself." She knew what they wanted. Maya and Josiah were there for a wellness check. To make sure their pathetic friend wasn't dead. While she appreciated it, she didn't need it. She knew she needed to leave the tent, but she'd do it on her own time.

"I know you can, but sometimes we need a push." Maya handed her the folded clothes. She took them. They were soft in her hands and when she inhaled deeply, she smelled a hint of rose.

"I'm okay, really. I just need some time alone," she said, not even convincing herself.

"It's been nearly six weeks," Josiah said. "You've barely come out of this tent. It's time to live again. It's the only way to get through your grief and heal."

They were very determined.

"Thank you for the clothes and food, but I'm fine."

Josiah set the bucket and food down and folded his arms. He planted his feet and lowered his chin. "We're not leaving."

Amina looked at Maya, hoping she'd be less obtrusive.

"He is most right. We go nowhere. You need fresh air, clean clothes, a bath."

Amina bit the side of her cheek as she contemplated her options. It would be nice to get some fresh air. And when was the last time she ate? Her stomach growled like an angry beast.

She put a hand over her stomach, certain the others heard it. Josiah grabbed an apple and tossed it to Amina. She bit into the fruit with a crunch as the sweet juices trickled down her chin. A smile tugged at her lip. She loved her friends. They cared about her and the least she could do was attempt to acquiesce to their efforts.

"Alright. I'll do it."

"You will feel most better cleaned, fed, and breathing fresh air. Trust me."

Josiah stepped outside a moment and brought back a large wooden tub. "For your bath. I'll get more water."

Once they filled the tub, Maya and Josiah stepped outside while Amina undressed. She stepped into the tub, sending chills up and down her body. The water was cool, but not frigid. As she slowly submerged her body, as the cleansing water soak into her skin, freeing her of all the dirt and grime she'd been carrying. While she had changed her clothes a couple of times, she couldn't remember the last time she took a dip in the river.

When Amina first returned, several visitors had stopped by. Mo to check on her wound and make sure it wasn't infected. Salome to cheer her up. Josiah and Maya with food. But even when they were here, she'd felt distant from them. Surrounded by a fog of grief that clouded her senses.

Now, as she soaked in the tub, a fog lifted and clarity return. She'd been hiding in her tent for too long and it was time to get back to a sense of living.

After soaking and lathering herself from head to toe, she finally stepped out of the tub and toweled off. She grabbed the clothes Maya picked out for her and put them on. They were simple, a pair of loose-fitted brown cotton pants and a navy blue short-sleeved shirt that fit just right. Amina pulled her dark brown hair back into a long braid before putting on the moccasins. They were comfortable, but not very sturdy. She would have to clean her boots later. Amina grabbed a small bread roll from the bowl of food on her table and stepped outside.

The sun blinded her. Amina held up her free hand to shade her eyes.

Maya held out a wide-brimmed hat for her. "You might want this until your eyes adjust. You've been in that tent a long time."

"Thanks." Amina took the hat and plopped it on her head. That's when she got a good view of the village ahead of her.

Six weeks ago, the only sign of civilization was the large group of people milling about and the large fires built at night. Now, it looked like an actual village.

From where they stood, Amina saw several wood cabins lined in rows. Off to the south was a much larger building.

"That's the barn for the animals and crops," Josiah said.

The three of them walked across the grassy field toward the barn. A slight breeze caressed Amina's skin, and she breathed in deeply the fresh air, which was almost dizzying. A hint of sweet grass filled her nose. Sheep bleated in the distance along with a dog barking as it rounded up the sheep.

"We have a sheepdog?"

"We have a lot of animals," Josiah said. "Once Aryeh agreed to let us stay, the Hebrews gave us quite a few things. And Salome and her father have been essential to teaching us how to live here."

"That's amazing." Another pang of guilt hit her. How could she be this selfish and hide away all these weeks while her people labored intensely to build an entire village?

They reached the barn and Amina noted the pigpen, chicken coop, and horse corral. The two-story barn was much larger up close.

Maya pointed to the loft. "That's where we keep the hay and animal feed. Below is where we store all the extra crops and tools for when we harvest."

They wandered past the barn toward the massive garden. Amina's eyes rounded as she saw rows of crops that had to be several acres. "This is incredible."

"Tell me about it," Josiah said.

Next, they wandered into the village, allowing Amina to see the cabins up close. It impressed Amina to see how much they had completed in just six weeks. They were thriving in this new valley and Amina's heart swelled. Things couldn't have turned out any better, and she was pleased to see that everyone was safe.

The tour continued, but Amina's mind wandered to Aiden again. He was missing so much. Here in the valley, they could forget about the Myriad and the devastated world around them. They didn't have to live in fear. If only Aiden could see where they were and experience the valley's peace, he'd change his mind. He'd have to.

Amina's heart ached for her brother. Not just for the mistake he was making, but for his presence. He and Amina were close, and his long absence was eating at her. She wasn't sure how much longer she could stand to be away from him.

A thought bubbled to the surface of her mind. The village didn't need her. They were doing just fine building a new life here, with Salome and David as their advocates. It would be easy for her to leave, go find Aiden, and bring him back to the valley.

CHAPTER 1

They came to the end of their tour and stopped in front of a barracks. "And this," Maya pointed at a door, "is your home."

Amina didn't expect that. She figured she'd live with someone else or there wouldn't be a home for her until she crawled out of her hole.

"We wanted to make sure you had somewhere else to go once we got you out of that tent." Josiah walked over to the two steps leading into the cabin and gestured at the open doorway. "Welcome home."

Amina walked into the small cabin room and took in her surroundings. A lump caught in her throat. "Thank you." It wasn't much, but it was a house. An actual structure that she could call hers.

"Josiah and I live in the two cabins beside you, and your aunt and uncle are in the other cabins across from us. We're all together."

It was true. She had her family. She had a home. And she had a community where she could finally find purpose again. It was everything she could ever desire. This place contained everything except Aiden.

Amina turned to her friends. "Thank you. Seriously, I'm not sure I would've ever gotten out of that tent without you. And seeing our people thriving is such an encouragement."

Josiah leaned over to Maya. "I feel a 'but' coming on."

"There's no but this time. I truly appreciate everything. You're both right. I need to get out of my hole, and I need to live. My goal was for us to find a new refuge and we have it." A small lump choked her. She swallowed hard. "I only wish Aiden and Paxton were here with us."

"We all do." Maya smiled sympathetically and hugged Amina. Amina hugged back, taking in her warmth and comfort.

There was family here who loved and cared for her. She needed to do the same and stop being selfish. Leaving the valley to get Aiden would be too dangerous and futile.

Amina's eyes drifted to Josiah, who stood stoic, jaw tense and arms rigid. Why was he always difficult to read?

"We must move forward. There is still much to be joyful about. Like tonight's dinner," Maya said.

Amina tilted her head, curious.

"Every Sunday night we get together with your family, Salome, and her father, and we feast. Please come. Everyone will be most happy to see you."

Amina's cheeks flushed at the thought of facing everyone again. After her return, she immediately retreated into her reclusive state. How would they respond to her now? Only one way to find out.

Chapter 2

Aiden sat cross-legged on the floor of his sister's tiny tent, staring at the small leather strand hanging from the top pole. Tiny colorful beads were knotted through the strand and at the end of it hung a paper heart. His cousin Emily made it for Amina years ago and Amina had held on to it, treasuring it.

Aiden closed his eyes and took a deep breath, breathing in the phantom smells of his sister. Imagining her still in the tunnels with him. Still poking fun at his inventions or tackling him to the ground when she was in a playful mood. It'd be easy to just leave, go find the valley, and forget about the Myriad.

Then again, who was he kidding? How could he forget what Frank did to him? What the Myriad were trying to do to everyone like him? There'd be no true peace for him if he left. Not to mention he had absolutely no idea how to find his sister. He'd likely die of starvation wandering those mountains before he ever found her.

Aiden stood, giving the tent one last look around. "See you tomorrow, sis."

He headed out of the tent and wound his way through the familiar tunnels. His feet splashed in the stagnant water, kicking up vile odors of rotting sewage. It was a wonder that there was a time when such horrific smells didn't bother Aiden.

Now, they made his stomach churn. Inside the large dome-shaped living areas, the smell wasn't as bad. But without a cleaning crew around, old sewage water seeped its way into the tunnels, forcing Aiden to wear a bandanna over his nose.

Eventually, Aiden found his way to Dwelling Two, where a large group of men and women gathered. Several ran through various exercise drills to keep their bodies fit, while others practiced their hand-to-hand combat.

Since returning from the capitol and back to the tunnels and Terrance's militia, Aiden spent his time observing. That was all his body could handle. He hadn't realized how much damage Frank's goon had done to him until the adrenaline from his escape and the whirlwind of emotion settled down.

Aiden descended the ladder, heading over to the hand-to-hand combat group. After six weeks, he was feeling better. Most of his cuts were merely small scabs or bright pink scars with his more prominent bruises, a faded yellowish-green color. As for his ribs . . . he'd make do. He couldn't keep putting things off. The Myriad weren't resting and neither could he.

He stopped beside the spectators and watched as a short, yet very strong woman took down another woman a foot taller and at least twenty pounds larger than her. After the group counted to three, the smaller woman stood and helped the other woman. The taller woman congratulated the other before walking away to grab water. The shorter woman made eye contact with Aiden. She smiled and walked over to him.

"Aiden, good to see you here."

"Hi Tessa, that was a good fight. You're getting stronger."

"I've been practicing. So, you feeling up for a round today?"

"I think so." Before he could step into the ring, a hand

grabbed him and pulled him back.

"Where do you think you're going, little Bambino?"

Aiden turned to find Evan with a toothpick in his mouth, eying him. Evan was a trainer and a real stickler. His bald head glistened and made his large ears stick out like a mouse while his dark, round eyes hid under bushy brows. And while his face had soft features, his body bulged with muscles that threatened anyone who thought of challenging him.

"I'm here to train today. I'm feeling better."

"Did you clear it with the nurse?"

"No, but I think I'd know what I can and can't handle."

"You know, the hare thought he could handle the tortoise, and look how that turned out. I'm just looking out for you. Why don't you start with PT instead of jumping right into fighting?"

Aiden huffed but yielded. Since coming back, it seemed everyone was treating him like some wounded animal. He was wounded, not weak. If being in that capitol taught him anything, it was how to be tough. They might be physically strong and know how to fight, but they'd crumble if they endured half of what Aiden did mentally.

No matter what, if Aiden wanted to stay in the militia, he needed to play by their rules.

Aiden spent the afternoon doing every exercise possible. Jumping jacks, squats, lunges, planks, pushups, sits ups, pull-ups, triceps presses, and many others. By the end of the day, his body was jelly. He collapsed on the ground and lay on his back, trying to slow his breathing. He hadn't realized just how out of shape he'd become. That would have to change.

Tessa hovered over him, dangling a canteen above his face. Aiden weakly grabbed at it and sat up. The cool water was refreshing, but what he really needed was food.

"I hope they didn't run you into the ground too hard." She smirked.

Aiden shrugged. He probably looked as exhausted as he felt.

"Anyway," Tessa continued, "we're all having dinner together tonight and trying some moonshine Terrance made."

"Moonshine? How'd he manage that?"

"I dunno. You wanna come?"

Aiden wanted to say no. All he wanted was to eat and pass out, but he also couldn't miss the opportunity to spend time with everyone. "Yeah, I'll come."

Tessa offered her hand, and Aiden took it. His whole body shook as he stood, and he wasn't sure his legs could hold his weight. Aiden took another gulp of the water before following Tessa toward the edge of the training grounds and up the ladder. He groaned, wishing for the luxury of an elevator.

* * * *

"Eight...nine..." Paxton breathed heavily, willing himself to keep going, "ten." Paxton collapsed to the ground and pressed his sweaty cheek to the cold cement. Only ten pushups. That's two less than yesterday and about ninety less than he once could.

Time in prison was taking a toll on his body. It wasn't just the lack of food or the insufficient sleep, though. About every three days, Frank would show up and resume his torturous interrogations.

Paxton did his best every day to keep himself physically fit doing a whole workout routine. He refused to let Frank whittle him into a helpless heap of flesh. And while working on the physical was something Paxton could do, something the Myriad trained him in, keeping his mind sane was not.

Bouts of depression, rage, regret, and a whole slew of emotions would take over him. He did his best to think positively. To remember Amina and his love for her. Remember his grandmother and father and their time in the mountains together. All these happy memories made Paxton feel loved and motivated. But the continual torture was eating away at him physically and mentally and Paxton wasn't sure how much longer he could take it.

Wouldn't it just be easier to give in, to fall back in line with the Myriad and follow the rules? At least there he had stability and something he could rely on. There were no unknowns because he followed orders and didn't have to question them.

But then again, after the past several months, after all he learned about the Notzrim and seeing the Myriad for who they truly are, how could he go back? He'd die before he realigned himself with them.

Paxton rolled onto his back and drew his knees up so his bare feet were flat on the floor. He slid his calloused hands under his neck and started his set of sit-ups. He'd only completed two before he heard the beep on his cell door. They weren't supposed to come until tomorrow.

The door swung open to an ordinary-looking man with no notable features standing in the hallway. It was Frank, his captor. Frank was an average five foot nine, with short black hair and dark brown eyes. His round face and medium build did not make him intimidating, but Paxton knew better. His jaw tightened as he stood, refusing to let Frank see how painful such a simple task was.

"Oh good, you're up," Frank said, as if addressing a friend.

"Come with me."

Paxton debated following his orders. Usually, when it was time for more interrogation, a soldier came to get Paxton, not Frank. Paxton's curiosity got the better of him and he followed in silence. It wasn't until they were in the elevator and heading to the 27th floor that Frank shared his plans.

"Today, I thought we'd try something different." Paxton looked at him sideways but didn't respond. "Today, I want to prove why you're making a terrible mistake by keeping silent."

The elevator stopped, and they got out, heading down a long white hallway lined with doors and security cameras. They turned the corner once and came to a door with Frank's name engraved on a placard mounted beside the door.

Inside, a light flicked on, revealing a large office filled with straight-edged metal and leather furniture. It felt more like a living room than an actual office.

Frank motioned to his left at another door. "In there, you'll find a shower and some clothes to change into. Go get cleaned up. We need you looking presentable when we tour the facility."

Paxton pressed his lips into a thin line. If the bruises and cuts all over his body were an indicator, there was no way Paxton would look presentable to anyone, but he did as he was told and went into the bathroom. A hot shower and clean clothes were a small luxury he could enjoy without regret.

Despite having not showered in over a month, Paxton's military training kicked in and he finished showering, changing into the military fatigues, and brushing his teeth in fifteen minutes. It felt good to be clean, but when he looked in the mirror, he grimaced at the reflection staring back at him. Hollowed cheeks, exhausted eyes, bruises, a fat lip, and a look of utter defeat. Paxton squared his shoulders, furrowed his brow, and willed himself to change his expression. He was a soldier, not a decrepit invalid.

Paxton turned on his heels and walked out of the bathroom and back into Frank's office. He stopped just short of the couch where Frank sat. He stood at ease with the tops of his hands resting on the small of his back and stared at the wall across from him. While his head didn't move, Paxton's eyes scanned the room. Across the walls hung award plaques, photographs of Frank with other various officials, and a shadow box of all his medals. He also showed off several statues, trophies, and books on his wide glass shelving unit.

For all Frank accomplished in his career, Paxton wondered why he'd gone to such lengths to focus on Paxton. He had people to deal with his dirty work. There was no need for him to even speak with Paxton, let alone invite him to his office and show him special attention. Then again, Frank did always like to have control.

Paxton's eyes continued to scan until they froze on one particularly familiar item. It was an old dinged-up metal compass on a leather band. Paxton's nostrils flared. He thought he'd lost his father's compass a year ago and yet, there it was, in Frank's office. Every muscle in his body tensed and he was ready to demand Frank give him back what was his, but he held his tongue.

"Well, don't you look squared away," Frank stated. "Have I ever told you, you remind me of my younger brother?"

Paxton looked at Frank but didn't answer.

"You both have that stubborn tenacity to protect others, even to the detriment of your own self." Frank shook his head. "Pitiful really. Though I don't know what's worse, your self-deprivation or my naivete that I thought I had a second chance to mold someone into a strong and ruthless leader."

"I'm not your brother, sir."

"Clearly not, and yet you are the same. That's why I took such a liking to you all those years ago. Took you under my wing, brought you alongside me as we built the Purification Unit. I thought you could be my second. But then, just like my brother, you chose the weaker side." Frank let out a puff of air and stood. "No matter, I'll get what I want one way or another, and no one is going to stand in my way. Let's go then, soldier."

Paxton followed, feeling increasingly uncomfortable. Frank's cloud of mystery was not helpful, and Paxton wished he weren't being lured into a trap.

They made their way through the building's lobby and outside, and hopped onto a golf cart where Frank drove them out to the airfield.

They pulled up to a massive hangar that was completely closed up. Frank got out and headed to the hangar door. Paxton followed, still uncertain about what Frank wanted to show him that would change his mind.

Inside the hangar, Paxton noticed nothing out of the ordinary. It was a hangar that housed a few military aircraft and at the back of the room were several tables with computer monitors alongside missiles and ammunition.

They walked to the tables and stopped in front of a voluptuous blonde with bright red lipstick that contrasted against her pale skin. When she looked up, her striking green eyes locked with Paxton, and she smiled flirtatiously.

"Hey there, handsome, it's been a while." The woman came around the table and hugged Paxton with familiarity.

CHAPTER 2

"Hi Gwyneth," Paxton said flatly.

Gwyneth took a step back and pouted. "Now is that any way to treat your girlfriend?"

"Ex-girlfriend, Gwyneth, ex."

Gwyneth waved her hand as if shooing away a fly. "Tomaeto, tomahto. Either way, good to see. We'll have to grab drinks and catch up." Gwyneth turned to Frank. "What can I do for you, Captain?"

"Well, you see, Chief Mnuchin, our private here needs some convincing."

Gwyneth looked intrigued. "How so?"

"He's got it in his head that the Notzrim aren't all that bad and that if he helps them, they can somehow win this war."

Paxton wanted to roll his eyes but steeled himself. Frank's ego and exaggeration were enough to make Paxton want to punch him in the face.

Gwyneth laughed. "Sorry Cap, I'm not laughing at you, but," Gwyneth looked at Paxton again. "Do you honestly think those hellions deserve to live? Have you forgotten all your training about who they are and what they've done?"

Paxton gritted his teeth. He knew that their "training" was all a lie, but there was no point arguing that.

"Their so-called morality is a threat to everything we stand for. They nearly destroyed the peace we now have and they're hell-bent on still trying to do so. They're trying to start a war against us, but mind you, we're ready for them. They don't stand a chance."

"And why's that Gwyneth?" It was as if the two of them were reading from a script, but Paxton stood at ease with a blank face, letting them explain and show off all their gadgets whose only sole purpose was to seek and destroy their targets.

It wasn't until Paxton saw the missile that his confidence in Amina and her people's security wavered.

"It's really quite exciting. This is a brand new, next-level type of hypersonic cruise missile. As soon as we have an estimate of at least 50 miles, this weapon will find them and eliminate them for good."

Paxton's cheek twitched, and he groaned inwardly when he realized Frank had seen him falter.

Frank stepped close to Paxton and spoke just above a whisper. "That's right son, all we need is to be within a 50-mile radius of them and they're gone. The Notzrim and your little fling, too."

Frank thanked Gwyneth for her presentation. With Frank's back turned, Paxton grabbed a ballpoint pen off the table and shoved it into his pocket. He continued to wait patiently for Frank to finish talking. Frank spoke in hushed tones, but Paxton was able to make out a couple of comments.

"This war is coming fast, this needs to be ready."

Paxton didn't understand why the Myriad were insistent on this supposed war. From everything he knew about the Notzrim they had no interest in fighting. They only wanted Meshiakh to come back. Then again, the Notzrim believed Meshiakh would bring a holy war with him. Is that what the Myriad are nervous about?

As Frank drove them back to the main building at the front of the capitol, he attempted to strike a deal with Paxton. "Now, I know how easy it is to get wrapped up in a pretty face and forget everything important. That's why I wanted you to see this. These Notzrim have no chance and there is no logical reason for trying to protect them. Eventually, we will find and eliminate them. That's always been the plan, stop fighting it.

CHAPTER 2

Stop putting yourself through needless torture for someone who's destined for death.

"Instead, rejoin the one place where you truly belong. I'll even sweeten the deal by promoting you to Major and putting you in charge of Civil-military operations overseas. What do you say?"

Paxton had desired that position for a long time, and he did miss the routine and familiarity of the military. But at what cost would he have to give in? Whose blood would be on his hands? He was already responsible for too many innocent lives. How many more would have to die because of him?

"And if I refuse?" Paxton stared straight ahead.

"Then etymtorp. But—"

"That doesn't work on me."

"Hold on, let me finish. This is not normal etymtorp. I've been having some scientists work on a stronger version of the elixir. One that can penetrate the strongest of minds, even those who are immune to the regular strength. And lucky for me, they're ready to test it out."

The golf cart stopped in front of the main building. "Last chance. Take the deal or take the etymtorp."

Chapter 3

Salome walked up and down the aisles of her outdoor classroom. She did her best to focus on the women as they continued their work on basket weaving, but she struggled. Seeing those eyes staring at her earlier had made her paranoid. Every sound beyond their classroom made her jump, and she constantly looked over her shoulder or into the bushes beyond, expecting to see someone staring at her again. There wasn't, of course, but it didn't make her feel any better.

Refocusing, Salome watched the women work. They were making good progress learning how to make baskets, bowls, and cups out of the foraged materials around the valley, such as blackberry bramble vines, tall river grass, and even pine needles.

As she observed the women's work, Salome made suggestions when she noticed someone doing a weave wrong or too loose. She enjoyed teaching and the joy it gave her when she saw someone complete a project.

Salome looked at the sky again. Class was nearly over. Salome made her way to the front of the group and got their attention. "Lovely, ladies. I really like what I'm seeing. You're welcome to stay and keep working, otherwise, I'll see you tomorrow."

CHAPTER 3

A woman with long silky auburn hair raised her hand and Salome walked over to help her out. "What is it?"

"I have the beginnings of this bowl, but it's not making the shape I want."

Salome took the partially formed item from the woman's small hands and looked it over. Immediately, she knew the problem. "Two things, one you need to keep it wet so that it bends and molds to how you like it without snapping. And second, as you weave the bramble sticks in and out, change the tension, and it forces your other sticks to move vertically instead of staying flat. Watch." Salome took the basket and undid some weaves and showed her how to fix the issue. Once she did a few, she handed it back, and the woman copied what she saw.

Salome nodded. "Nicely done."

Most of the women took off to continue their day preparing dinner or other chores, but a few stayed. Salome also stayed behind to help them as needed. She walked over to a nearby rock and sat on it. It felt good to give her legs a break.

Across the way, she noticed Matthias standing at the edge of the group. He stuck out among the group of women milling about, collecting their things, and chit-chatting before taking off. He stood several inches taller than anyone there, with his arms crossed and his stoic stare. His squared shoulders seemed to match his square head. Salome's stomach dropped. While Matthias had apologized for being harsh in the beginning, and they were on better terms, she was still uneasy around him. He was stern and blunt, not at all an easy person to talk with. Salome waved at Matthias, and he smiled as he headed over to her.

"Class over?"

"It is." Salome stood, feeling the ache in her leg muscles. "A few ladies like to stay and finish their projects, so I'm sticking around."

"It's good to see them enjoying the basket weaving. It comes in handy."

"It really does, and with harvest season coming any day now, you'll need all the baskets you can get." There was an awkward lull in the conversation. Salome glanced over at the women still weaving. They stared at their bowls, working hard to finish them.

"Right, well." Matthias cleared his throat. "I actually came to offer you something."

Salome eyed him curiously. It wasn't often that Matthias came around or even conversed with Salome. He was always busy.

"The elders and I have been discussing. You have been crucial to our development here in the valley, and we would like to offer you a more permanent role as our Hebrew advisor. You wouldn't be an elder, but you're welcome to come to our meetings and have your voice heard among our group in a more official capacity. Eventually, we hope that you'll also reach out to the Hebrews and work on a more cohesive union."

Salome's face flickered with a smile. "Wow, that's very flattering, Matthias, but I'm not sure I'm right for the job?" Despite being a part of the Hebrew leadership, Salome never felt like much of a leader.

"You've proved yourself these past weeks, and we were all in agreement that you are of great value to us."

"What about the rest of the Notzrim?"

"I'm sure they'd have no problem with our decision. Everyone seems to like you here."

CHAPTER 3

Salome nodded. It was good to know she had the confidence of Matthias and the other elders, but what benefit could she bring to their people? "Thank you, sir. I have enjoyed helping these past weeks and will continue to help with the development of the village, but—"

"Now, before you object, hear me out. You are already doing so much to help. You've offered advice and taught us most of our survival skills. You've been a liaison for us with the Hebrew people, making sure we get the supplies we need, and your devotion to our success is unsurmountable. You're already a leader, Salome, just without a title."

Salome tilted her head from side to side. He wasn't wrong. "Okay, I accept." She was still uneasy about the situation, but how could she turn him down?

"Good, we will announce it at the next town hall meeting." Matthias turned to leave, but Salome stopped him. This was a perfect opportunity to share her and Mo's idea.

"Before you go, I have a request."

Matthias turned around. This time he was the one with the curious look.

"Mo and I would like to throw a unity dinner with the Hebrews. We feel it's time to unite both groups and make peace."

Matthias frowned, but before he could say anything, Salome continued, "I know what Aryeh said, but we feel the people are ready for this. Already I've seen Hebrew mothers bring their children here during story time and they've been helpful to provide excess materials."

Matthias let out a breath as he crossed his arms. Salome watched him carefully, trying to decipher his expression. Finally, he spoke. "I don't love the idea, but I do think it's a good one. But let's keep it small and simple. Nothing outrageous that could cause problems with Aryeh and the others. You should speak to Aryeh about it, and make sure he's okay with it, too. I want to respect our arrangement with him."

Salome's stomach dropped. Of course, Aryeh wouldn't be okay with it. He was too stubborn. Salome forced a smile. "Of course, I will."

"Good, see you tonight then." Matthias turned and headed back toward the center of the village.

Salome sunk onto the rock again, deflated. She couldn't talk to Aryeh. He was too unreasonable and pigheaded. How would she ever convince him to do this?

* * * *

Salome stepped into Mo's cabin to find Mo bustling about preparing for dinner. Her auburn hair was pulled back into a low messy bun with strands falling out all over. Flour splattered her cheeks and arms. Bowls filled with vegetables, fruit, and leftover dough covered the tiny counter space.

Tonight was a special occasion for everyone. Amina was finally coming to dinner.

It tore Salome apart when Amina isolated herself and refused to see anyone. She was heartbroken for Amina and all she went through, but she also had countless questions.

When Amina came back, she delivered a letter to Salome from her daughter, Ruth. That was it. No proper explanation, just the letter.

The contents of the letter were encouraging, bringing Salome a peace about her and her daughter's relationship that

CHAPTER 3

she thought she'd never get, but wanted answers to her questions. Like why Ruth didn't come with Amina. How did they meet? Where was she living now? And others.

Finally, Amina was out of her hole and Salome could finally have that long-awaited conversation.

"Oh, good, you're here." Mo walked over to her dough and started kneading it. "I already have some ideas for our unity party. I'm thinking we meet in the big field between the two villages." Salome opened her mouth, wanting to stop Mo from rattling off all her ideas, but she couldn't seem to get a word in. "It's a good neutral zone. We can lay out blankets and set up tables for food. I'm even thinking of asking a few people to play music."

"That sounds great, but—"

"But what?" Mo stopped for the first time, her hands held out as if holding an imaginary ball, covered in sticky dough. "You don't like it?"

"No I do, but I spoke with Matthias and—"

"He's not on board?"

Salome put a hand up to stop Mo from continually interrupting her. "He is, but he wants us to keep it small and simple."

Mo's face fell and Salome hated bursting her bubble. Mo turned back to her dough and slowly formed it into a long loaf. The energy she once had now dissipated.

Salome sighed as she watched Mo put the loaf on a wooden tray. "There's more," Salome said as she bobbled her head back and forth, not sure how to share the next bit of news.

There was no easy way to say it, so Salome simply spit it out. "I have to run it by Aryeh."

Mo's head whirled toward Salome. "What?! That's outrageous! You know what he's going to say. What makes Matthias think that's in any way a good idea?"

"Considering Aryeh set the parameters for our being here. . . look I don't like the idea either. Aryeh is a pain to talk to—"

"So we don't and say we did. What Aryeh doesn't know won't hurt him." Mo turned back to her food preparations. Grabbing the bowl of green beans, she broke off the stems.

Salome closed her eyes and sighed. Someone was spying on Salome, likely for Aryeh. If she did anything he didn't like, he'd know about it and react harshly. She didn't want to risk any unnecessary hardships on the Notzrim people. Salome walked over and joined in with breaking off stems and tossing them into the compost bucket.

"Don't tell anyone," Salome started, "but I think Aryeh has someone spying on me."

"What?" Mo stopped her work and grabbed at Salome's arm. "Are you certain?"

"No, but I don't want to take that risk."

"He wouldn't hurt you would he?"

Salome shook her head. "He's likely making sure I *comply* with his request, but until I know for certain, I think I should go talk to him as Matthias requested."

Heavy-footed steps came up the steps and through the front door. Salome looked to see Paul holding a basket of fish. "Today was a good day at the river. I think they finally figured out why there were having trouble catching fish." He smiled, but it soon faded. "What's got you two down?"

Salome glanced at Mo from her peripheral but said nothing. She wasn't sure how much she'd told Paul about their plans.

"Oh you know," Mo tossed a bean into the bowl, "just Matthias being his usual difficult self."

"What's that supposed to mean?"

CHAPTER 3

Mo stopped her work. "Salome and I had a fantastic plan to unify the two villages. Women from the Hebrew village are already coming over here on their own, why not encourage it? Except, Matthias wants Salome to ask Aryeh for permission first." Mo stood and walked over to Paul. She took hold of the fish basket. "Do you agree with him?" She stared him down as if to challenge his loyalty. Salome shifted in her seat uncomfortably as she watched the couple.

"Mo, you know I love you and I love your ideas, but Aryeh did state in order for us to stay, we must keep separated. If he's changed his mind, great, let's have a party."

Mo glared at Paul and then turned away and walked to the kitchen counter. "I disagree. If we have the party, we can change Aryeh's mind. Sometimes, the only way to convince someone to change their mind is to show them the error of their ways. You agree with me, right, Salome?"

The last thing she wanted to do was get in the middle of a marital argument, but there was nothing she could do. Say nothing and Mo would assume she's taking Paul's side, say something and it would only bolster Mo's argumentative attitude. "Matthias didn't say we couldn't have a party. He just wants to make sure it doesn't cause us to be driven out of the valley."

"Exactly. I say we continue to plan it. I'm fine keeping it quieter and smaller so as not to arouse too much concern from Aryeh. Heck, we can even invite Aryeh once it's all planned. He can come and see just how good this idea really is." Mo grabbed her knife and a fish and started scraping the scales off.

Paul walked up behind Mo and placed his hands on her shoulders. He leaned in and kissed her on the cheek. "I love your spirit."

Mo cracked a half smile. "Even when I'm a little too earnest and impatient?"

"Even then."

Paul joined in with the fish scaling while Salome turned back to the green beans. While she should've felt more at ease knowing Paul was backing them up to continue planning without telling Aryeh about it until the day of, it still didn't sit right with her. Yes, uniting the groups was the right thing to do, but she couldn't help but wonder if this would start the fire from her dream.

* * * *

Amina spent the day moving what few belongings she had into her new home. It was a modest place, but it was home, and it was close to everyone. By the time she finished, she had some time to wander the village. Amina wanted to do more exploring on her own to get a feel for the layout. That last thing she wanted was to get lost all the time.

The sun dipped behind the cliff, cluing Amina to head back to her cabin for dinner. She stopped and put her hands on her hips as tried to reorient herself. In front of her was a large open space with a small stage and benches placed in an arc. That meant she was in the center of town. She knew that there were cabins straight ahead, as well as to her left. Maybe if she started to her left, she could work her way around until she found everyone.

Eventually, Amina found a long table set between the two cabins lined with benches and set for a party. They had hand-formed clay cups, plates, and silverware. In the center,

CHAPTER 3

someone had collected bright yellow, purple, and pink flowers wildflowers and stuffed the vase. Mo, Maya, and Salome were moving around the table setting out bowls of fruit, a rice and veggie dish, and bread. Uncle Paul stepped out of his cabin with a large roasted fowl, followed closely by Josiah holding a plate of fish.

Amina smiled. She knew she'd find them, eventually. Her heart warmed to see her family again. They might not be her actual mother, father, and brother, but they might as well be. Since Aiden and Amina arrived in the tunnels, Mo and Paul immediately took them under their wing and cared for them like their own children. Looking back, Amina regretted how she treated her aunt. All she showed was love and care, and Amina could barely even look at her. She reminded her too much of her mother. Now, Amina loved Mo and respected her strength.

"Amina!"

Before Amina could register who was shouting at her, a small object pummeled her and clung to her waist, causing her to tumble backward. Thankfully, the cabin door stopped her from tumbling onto her behind.

Amina looked down at her attacker and found big brown eyes and the wide smile of a ten-year-old looking up at her.

"Hi, Emily."

"I missed you."

"I missed you too." Amina squeezed back before letting go.

Emily grabbed her hand and led her to the table. "You can sit next to me."

"Sounds good."

Amina and Emily climbed over the bench and sat as the others trickled over. Emily pulled a small straw doll from her waistband and proceeded to tell Amina all about her new dolly. She and Mo worked on it together and now Emily takes it wherever she goes.

"It's a very beautiful doll."

"You can hold her if you want." Emily held the doll out for Amina to take. Carefully, she accepted the doll. It was rough in her hands, except for the soft hair and clothing. She had short black hair and a long purple dress with a yellow waistband. The face was painted on carefully, giving the doll blue eyes and pink lips.

Amina handed Emily the doll back just as a slender woman with dark brown curly hair, holding a clay pitcher. Amina smiled and got up to hug Salome.

Salome set the pitcher down, and they embraced. "It's good to have you back."

"What do you mean?" Amina looked at her. "I've been back for a while."

"Have you though?"

Amina looked away. For nearly six weeks, she abandoned her family and friends, leaving them completely in the dark. They didn't deserve that. "I'm sorry."

"Forgiven. I'm glad you're here now."

A man in his mid-seventies with gray hair and a gray beard lining his powerful jaw approached. He wore similar long brown pants as Amina's and a loose-fitting red shirt. Clearly, they had limited clothing options here.

"Amina, I want you to meet my father, David."

That's why he looked familiar. Her mind flashed back to the first time they met when she'd been desperate and defiant in her interactions with him. "Nice to see you again, sir."

"It is. I know you've been through a lot, and I'm glad that

things have worked out for your people here."

"Thank you. And I want to apologize for my behavior when we first met."

"I'd call it passion, but thank you for the apology. I accept."

Salome and David found their spots at the table, and Amina said hello to the others before sitting again. She didn't want to keep getting up and down constantly. Not to mention she was eager to embrace her aunt and uncle.

Paul stood over the bird, carving it into nice thick slices. He stopped immediately, though, when he noticed Amina standing beside him. Paul set his knife down and gave Amina an enormous bear hug. He smelled of smoke and pine needles, and his beard was longer than she'd remembered. "Decided the reclusive life wasn't for you, huh?"

"Something like that."

"Alright, Paul, stop hogging her. It's my turn."

Amina let go of Paul and crossed to her aunt. Somehow, she looked younger. Mo wrapped her thin but strong arms around Amina and squeezed. "How's your leg?" She took a step back. "Are you doing the PT exercises I gave you?"

"It's doing fine. I'm hardly limping anymore, and yes, I do the exercises."

Mo eyed her suspiciously. It was true Amina had hardly stepped outside her tent during the day, but at night she spent time in the fresh air and that's when she'd work on her PT. At first, she had no interest in doing her exercises, but one day, she could barely walk to the bathroom. That's when she knew she had to do the exercises if she ever wanted to get back to normal.

"Honest, I have." Amina stepped back and walked around in a circle, then jumped and danced about to prove to Mo she had been healing.

"Alright, I believe you. Don't overdo it."

Amina gritted her teeth as she her thigh throb. "Yeah, the jumping was probably a bad idea."

By the time everyone arrived, said their hellos to Amina and settled into their seats, the table was packed. They ended up with a group of nine and Amina beamed. She was with her family. The people she cared about the most. Except for the two that were missing.

Amina's mind turned to Paxton, locked away in a cell being tortured or dead somewhere in the capitol. After what he did to save her, he didn't deserve that. And her brother. He didn't have to be away. If he only knew what he was missing out on. Amina let out a troubled breath.

Paul stood at his seat and held up his cup expectantly. Amina shook away the thoughts and wiped her eyes, focusing on her uncle.

Once the chitter chatter quieted, he began, "Now, I know that these dinners have become a tradition for us, but tonight is special. Tonight, our beloved Amina has emerged from her tent and joined the real world again." The group laughed. "But seriously, while we don't know the details of what happened, we know you must've experienced deep emotional and physical pain, and we are happy that Sabaoth—the God who never abandons his children—has stayed by Amina's side and strengthened her enough to come join us tonight." Paul raised his cup, and the others followed. "To Sabaoth's unfailing love."

"To Sabaoth." They all repeated in unison.

"And to Amina for finding us this new home and for never giving up on her family."

CHAPTER 3

"To Amina."

"And congratulations to Salome," Matthias said before everyone clinked cups. "She has accepted the offer to be our official Hebrew adviser."

Amina's jaw dropped as she looked from Matthias to Salome. She knew Salome was doing a lot to help the village, and she was previously a leader of the Hebrews, but it was no less surprising that Matthias would have her placed in an official role this soon.

Amina was happy for Salome. She deserved to be recognized for all her help, but Amina couldn't help but feel a small twinge of jealousy. Amina secretly hoped she'd be the one to join the board. After all she did to bring them to the valley, but then again, she knew that wasn't likely given how disconnected she'd been. Maybe one day it'd happen for her, but until then, she wanted to be happy for her friend.

Amina smiled and congratulated Salome, along with everyone else. They all clinked cups and drank.

Paul gave thanks to Sabaoth for the food in prayer before everyone passed the bowls around the table.

During dinner, there was a lot of conversation about the past week. People shared their highs and lows. They discussed what new skills they'd learned and what new discoveries they'd made. It seemed that every day in the valley was a new mystery to be discovered and skill to be honed. It sounded adventurous and exactly what Amina wanted. With every story told, Amina did her best to not fall deeper in love with life in the valley.

"So how about worship yesterday morning?" Matthias asked in his deep, thunderous voice. "What did everyone think of Father Stephen's message?"

Amina's head snapped toward Matthias. "Wait, you're

having worship services again?"

Matthias raised and lowered his eyebrows as he tilted his head. "The elders and I figured it was time to restart the lost tradition. We were loosing sight of what's important, the coming of Meshiakh, and we need to get back to that."

The conversation continued as everyone shared what they thought of the service. Even Salome and David shared their thoughts. It was true that Salome and David were Hebrews, part of Sabaoth's chosen people, but she wasn't sure if they believed in the new covenant or in Meshiakh being their savior. She'd have to find out sometime.

As dinner wound down, Maya got up and went into her cabin. Soon she came back out with a large tray of mini cakes covered in fruit and drizzled with honey. Amina's mouth salivated at the delightful treat. She couldn't even remember the last time she had a dessert. This was going to be incredible.

Once everyone had their cake, Amina dove in. Her mouth filled with an explosion of sweet from the honey, tart from the fruit, and a smooth buttery taste of the cake. It delicious and Amina had to be careful not to eat too fast.

Amina looked over at Emily and she was also devouring her dessert. She had red raspberry juice on her lips and a string of honey clinging to her chin. Amina laughed. "Slow down there Em, it's not going anywhere."

"Sure it is. It's going in mouth." Emily took another bite and talked with her mouth full. "It's good and we only get something sweet on special occasions."

"All the more reason to savor it," Amina laughed.

"Savor?"

"Enjoy and make it last as long as possible."

Emily set her fork down and closed her eyes as she finished

CHAPTER 3

chewing. She swallowed and opened her eyes again, looking at Amina. She had a question on her mind but didn't seem to know how to ask.

"What is it, Emily?"

"Where's Aiden? Is he okay?" Her eyes welled with emotion. "I really miss him."

"Oh, sweetie." Amina put her arm around Emily. "Yes, of course, he's okay. I saved him from the prison he was in, but he stayed in the tunnels."

Emily twisted her face. "Why?"

"There was something he needed to do first. Once he's done, he plans to come here."

"Does he know how to get here?"

Amina shook her head. "But when it's time for him to come home, I'm sure Sabaoth will show Aiden the way." Amina bit her lip, wondering again if she should leave and get Aiden herself. The valley was concealed, Aiden could wander for weeks and never find it.

Emily's face lit up.

Mo picked up on Amina's conversation with Emily and leaned closer as she spoke. "Careful not to get either of your hopes up. You don't know if he's going to come back."

"I know, but right now, I have to believe it can happen. I have to keep that hope alive. And if at some point I need to go get him, I will."

"How would you know?" Josiah asked.

She didn't know, and she no longer had the cell phone her brother had made for her. She would have to trust that Sabaoth would give her a sign. That her twinsation would urge her to find him when the time was right.

Mo's shoulders dropped. "We want Aiden here just as much

as you do, but he made his choice, and we have to respect that."

Tears sprung to Amina's eyes. "I miss him so much. Maybe I should go now. Maybe he changed his mind."

Mo placed a hand over Amina's. "You know that wouldn't be safe for anyone. There's too much risk."

"One day, Amina," Paul spoke, his words soothing, "when Meshiakh returns, you will be reunited with your brother, but until then, find solace here and in Sabaoth."

Solace. She wanted that so badly. Often, the comforting presence of Sabaoth with her in her tent. She found joy in the Sacred Writings, but then grief would creep back in, trying to take over her thoughts and heart. Images of her brother's face, memories of their times together. She missed him, but her family was right. He made his choice, and she needed to be at peace with it. That's what Aiden would want.

Footsteps approached the group. "Matthias, come quickly. Something is wrong with the pigs!" a young man spoke frantically.

"The pigs?" Matthias stood. "What do you mean?"

"I think they're sick."

Matthias and Paul exchanged looks and immediately followed the man. Amina turned and followed as well. She had no experience with pigs, but maybe she could help.

When they reached the barn, her stomach flipped as the ghastly smell of feces pummeled her nose. Amina grabbed her handkerchief out of her pocket and tied it around her face before approaching.

"I was finishing my nightly rounds when I heard some pigs making unusual squealing noises. When I came over, this is what I found." He gestured toward the pen filled with diarrhea. The pigs were wandering around restlessly and making a sort of moaning sound like one does when they're not feeling well. A few of the pigs had yellowish flaky skin. Amina didn't know pigs, but she knew this was not normal.

"What do we do?" the man held a rag over his nose with one hand and his stomach with another. His skin was pale against his blue shirt and light brown hair.

"First, we should get them out of the pen and get things cleaned up," Matthias instructed calmly. "Then we need to get David and Salome. Maybe they've seen this before."

David walked over to the pen and hopped the fence to examine some of the pigs. He spoke to the pigs in a calm, soothing voice as he moved around and touched the pigs' skin and bellies. "Are they all sick?"

The man shrugged. "I only just discovered this."

David stood and moved just as the pig he was near unloaded another pile of smelly diarrhea. David didn't seem phased by it, but everyone else took a step back instinctively, as if getting away meant they could avoid the smell. It didn't work. Despite the handkerchief, Amina's stomach did another flip.

"What about those two pigs over there?" the man asked, pointing to the pigs with the yellowish skin.

David walked over to them and almost immediately answered, "they have greasy pig. It's a type of swine disease. We need to get them, and this pen cleaned, now. Do you have another pen we can put them in?"

"If we move the horses into the pasture, we can move the pigs there."

David climbed back over the fence; his moccasins covered in mud and feces. "We need two different areas to separate the healthy from the sick."

"I can get hay barrels, and we can separate the corral into

two different sections."

"Great. Get going on that."

Paul stepped forward. "I'll help."

David motioned for Paul to follow.

"I'll help too. The faster we can get that corral separated, the better." Matthias offered. He took off after Paul and the other man.

David stepped toward Amina. "You should get us as much help as you can gather. It's going to be a long night."

Chapter 4

Frank held the etymtorp vile to the light. It was an azure blue with tiny bubbles floating inside the liquid. He smiled and looked at Paxton. "This is going to be fun."

The scientists strapped Paxton into a reclining chair, like the kind used by the dentist. They secured his ankles, wrists, head, and chest with thick straps of leather cinched tight enough to nearly cut off the circulation.

"Now, Paxton, don't try to fight this. It's much stronger than you're used to, and it may do some permanent damage if you try to fight it." Frank pulled the dropper out of the vile while the two scientists pried Paxton's mouth open with a metal contraption. Frank put two drops in Paxton's mouth, and they fizzled on his tongue. The scientists released his mouth, and he clamped it shut.

As his saliva mixed with the elixir Paxton's mouth tingled, like it was going numb. Slowly the tingling trickled down his throat and into his stomach and continued to spread across his body. At first, it wasn't terrible, but when it reached his head, it exploded with an electric shock. His vision blurred as white spots appeared and eventually blinded him. All he could see was light.

Paxton tried to slow his breathing, to stay focused on where he was and stay present in the room. He knew the etymtorp wanted to take him into a blank space where he'd become so disoriented that whatever words Frank spoke would breech his vision and create images and scenes without control, and Paxton would speak whatever he saw. He couldn't let that happen.

He had to stay focused. He had to remember where he was. Paxton tried to wiggle his toes and tap his fingers. The movement helped him stay present. He tried to envision the lab, the scientists vigorously writing their observations, Frank standing impatiently in front of Paxton. Eventually the light faded, and Paxton could actually see the room.

"No! This can't be. He needs more!" Frank's face flushed deep red.

"But sir, that could be—"

"I said he needs more!"

"Yes, sir." The scientists moved back over to Paxton and forced him mouth open again allowing Frank to add two more drops of the elixir into Paxton's mouth.

This time, the tingling turned to tiny electrical shocks moving down his throat and into his stomach. Black spots speckled his vision, growing with each moment until they spread, blinding him. His head swirled, vibrating like nothing he'd ever experienced. Ignoring Frank's warning, Paxton fought the etymtorp, but he felt distant, as if his mind and body had separated. And though he couldn't see, the world was spinning. The intensity grew until Paxton lost consciousness, but not before he heard Frank yell, "it still isn't working!"

* * * *

CHAPTER 4

When Paxton regained consciousness, he was in his cell again. His head throbbed as if he'd been beaten over the head with a bat. He sat up slowly, holding his head between his palms and staring at the ground. He waited for the spinning to stop before he looked around.

By the door was a small plate of food and a cup. Paxton grabbed his meal and returned to his spot in the middle of the cell. At least they had the decency to give him water and actual food. Instead of the usual crackers and slop, he had a roll and a chunk of what looked to be beef. Paxton sniffed at it. Smelled safe. He picked it up and took a bite. It was cold, of course, but it was food.

By the time he finished eating and gulping the water, the effects took over. His head stabilized. He was no longer spinning but softly floating as if on a boat, and the meat slightly satisfied his hunger.

That's when Paxton recalled the events from earlier. Teivel and the Myriad would stop at nothing to find the Notzrim, and that was evident in the new technology they'd developed. How long would it be before they could pinpoint a location and destroy everyone in the mountains? What was worse, he wondered, was could that information come from him?

While he was fairly certain the etymtorp didn't work the way Frank wanted it to, he knew Frank would stop at nothing. It was only a matter of time before the scientists readjusted the serum and Frank tried it again. There was no telling what it would do to Paxton mentally, and he wasn't going to stick around to find out. Paxton reached into his pocket and pulled out the ballpoint pen he'd stolen early. The next time that door opened, he'd be ready.

Footsteps echoed down the empty corridor. Paxton sprang

to his feet, pulling out the pen. The footsteps grew louder. Paxton stood his position by the door, ready to strike whoever walked through in the neck. As the footsteps grew louder still, he counted the steps. His confidence wavered. There was more than one person coming. Paxton lowered the pen and relaxed.

The footsteps stopped, and the small window near the top of the door slid open. The soldier's voice spoke, "Paxton, visitor."

Paxton stepped in front of the door to look out of the rectangular opening to find Gwyneth standing on the other side. She wore a long sleek black dress that seemed to shimmer even with the lack of lighting. The neckline plunged down between her cleavage, teasing him with what lay below. She looked at him with thick lashes outlining her bright green eyes. Paxton felt a twinge of feeling for her. Long forgotten feelings. He swallowed.

"I thought we could go out for that drink."

"Does Frank know about this?"

"What Frank doesn't know won't hurt him."

Paxton looked down. He was still wearing his military fatigues, not exactly night on the town attire. When he looked back up, Gwyneth held up a pair of black slacks, a light gray button-up shirt, a red tie, a black suit jacket, and a pair of shoes.

While the thought of going out on the town and trying to forget his troubles was tempting, he didn't trust Gwyneth. He wanted to refuse. He couldn't allow himself to forget why he was a prisoner, who he was protecting by keeping quiet. Then again, this could be his chance at escape.

Paxton changed into his new clothes and knocked on the cell door. AS soon as Paxton stepped out of the cell, the soldier

CHAPTER 4

standing beside the door slapped an armband on Paxton's wrist. It looked like a sleek digital watch, but Paxton knew better. It was his tracking monitor to make sure he didn't try to escape.

"I guess we won't exactly be alone, will we?"

"It's just to make sure I get you back here safely."

"What, you don't trust me?"

Gwyneth stepped toward Paxton and lifted a delicate hand to fix his collar. "You look good."

"Even with the busted-up face?"

She looked his face over. Her hand traced the cut on his cheek and down to his lip where it lingered. "Even with the busted-up face."

Paxton's heart raced as they stared at one another.

A stifled cough broke their focus. "Let's go, you two," the soldier said, not amused by the situation.

The drive over to the bar in town was quiet. Neither Paxton nor Gwyneth spoke as their drive took them through the streets of town and towards the restaurant district. Paxton kept his gaze outside the window. He needed to stay focused on what mattered, not on the surreal situation he was in.

Seeing Gwyneth again and going out with her tonight felt like a life he was no longer a part of. A world he'd left behind and wanted to keep that way. And yet, his feelings and memories with Gwyneth tugged at his desires. The desire for love, stability, and familiarity.

The town car pulled up to a skyscraper where the first floor was the hottest restaurant in town, Toto Z. Windows outlined the building, making it easy to see everything happening inside the packed place.

Inside, tables or small lounge booths filled the space, leaving little room for moving around. The lighting was dimmed to set the mood, and a thin purple haze filled the bar, tickling Paxton's nose with the scent of jasmine and tobacco as soon as they walked inside.

Gwyneth took Paxton's hand and led him through the crowded room and over to a secluded corner. They sat in the plush velvet high-backed booth that was just large enough for the two of them to sit closely. The round table in front of them was small and low to the ground.

Gwyneth turned toward Paxton as she crossed her legs. Her red high heel brushed his shin as he sat facing forward, rubbing his clammy hands on his pants.

"Relax," Gwyneth breathed into his ear. "We're here just to catch up."

"Is that what you think this is?"

"What else would it be?"

Paxton shook his head, not wanting to get into it. He knew Frank was behind this evening outing. He was certainly going all out to persuade him to join his side.

The server came over at that moment, a bubbly young woman with tight curls and deep brown eyes. She smiled big, flashing her perfectly straight white teeth. "What can I get you two?"

"Cosmo," Gwyneth responded.

"Water, pl–"

"Oh, don't be ridiculous," Gwyneth interrupted. "Your one night out and you're going to waste it on water?" She looked at the server. "He'll have a rusty nail. And we'll also get the tuna tartare."

The server turned and left, her black skirt bouncing with each step.

CHAPTER 4

"Why'd you do that?" Paxton asked, unamused.

"Do what?"

"Get me a drink. I didn't want it."

"What better way to relax than with a drink?"

Paxton gritted his teeth but didn't respond. If he allowed himself to relax too much, he was afraid he'd give in or let sensitive information slip.

"What's new with you? Clearly you received a promotion."

"I did. Thank you for noticing that. I'm working with intelligence now and strategizing our defense for when the war hits. We know it's coming, we just don't know when yet. But either way, a good defense is a prepared one."

Paxton knew Gwyneth was prodding him to ask, but he wasn't going to bite. He didn't want to get into anything too serious.

"With the promotion, as you know, comes a new condo. It's massive and I love it. I share it with my two cats and my fiancé William."

At that moment, the server returned with a tray of drinks and the appetizer.

Paxton grabbed his drink and took a long sip. The scotch burned his throat and warmed his belly. It felt good.

Gwyneth took a sip of her drink and waited quietly for Paxton to respond. Paxton wasn't sure what she was expecting by laying that bomb out there. They were engaged once, now they weren't. He'd moved on. So did she.

"You sure with a pending war that getting married is such a good idea?"

"Why not? You know first-hand what happens when you wait too long."

That was a low blow and Paxton felt it. Paxton put some raw

tuna on a chip and took a bite, still avoiding eye contact.

"What about you? Have you found anyone new?"

There she went again, prying into his personal life. Trying to pull out sensitive information. This wasn't a catch-up session, it was a new form of interrogation—slow and sneaky. Frank must've put her up to this.

Paxton had to play his cards right. Play along enough not to make Gwyneth too suspicious that he knew what was happening, but not give anything away. She knew him well and knew how to read between the lines. He had to be smart about it.

"You know I have."

"Tell me about her."

Paxton's mind drifted to Amina, and a smile tugged at the corners of his mouth. "She's different from anyone I've dated. Passionate, honest. She doesn't mess around. And she's fiercely protective."

"You must really love her."

Paxton let the smile spread across his face. "I do, but that doesn't matter now, does it?"

"Of course it does. It's what keeps you strong. It's what's frustrating Frank so much. He can't break you."

"Well, there's no way I'm telling him anything."

"Because of her?"

"Because of all of them. I can't explain it, but there's just something about them I want to know more. I don't believe them to be who everyone has made them out to be."

"But mostly because of her?"

"I guess, why?"

"What if there's a way to save her?"

"What do you mean?"

CHAPTER 4

"I mean. What if there was a way to get her out of her hiding place and bring her here? So, the two of you could be together. She'd be safe, here."

"No way that could never happen."

"What if there was?"

Paxton thought for a moment. It was tempting. He wanted to be with Amina; he wanted her to be safe. But how could he live with himself if she was the only one he saved?

"Do you really think I'd sink that low?"

"For love, I thought you'd be willing to do whatever it took." Gwyneth's face flushed as her voice rose. She took a breath and leaned back in her seat and took a sip of her cosmo.

"Love isn't selfish, Gwyn." Paxton finished his drink and set it down. "I learned that the hard way."

The two of them sat in silence for a while.

Paxton people watched, noticing the slowly degrading sobriety of those around him. If they stayed in the room long enough, he might be able to slip out without anyone paying attention.

As he continued to survey the room, however, he started noticing the soldiers stationed near all the doors and hallways. They weren't obvious, with uniforms and guns, but Paxton knew a fellow soldier when he saw one. They sat in pairs, wearing civilian clothes, pretending to drink and engage themselves in conversation, but they never made eye contact with one another. Instead, they constantly kept a subtle eye on Paxton, the door, and the server. They were making sure Paxton didn't do anything suspicious or that somehow the server was in on his elaborate escape plan.

In reality, Paxton hadn't thought through his escape at all. The whole outing was completely unexpected and didn't give him a lot of time to plan. He didn't even know where he was going until they showed up.

The one thing he had going for him was that he'd been to Toto Z before, and he was familiar with the layout of the building and its surroundings. He knew that the hallway leading to the bathroom also had a side door into a second hallway leading toward storage. This hallway also led to the kitchen, pantry, refrigerator and then out to the delivery dock in the alley. He knew that the place had security cameras, but the owner rarely bothered to turn them on unless a high-profile celebrity was coming in. Thankfully, tonight, no one was.

Paxton also knew that if he went to the bathroom, one of the many soldiers would likely follow him discretely down that hall. This would give Paxton very little time to slip down the service hallway before the soldiers realized he was not actually in the bathroom. That's assuming they didn't have anyone stationed in the alley. Then again, Paxton also knew the vent shafts were large enough for him to crawl through and into the next suite.

"Do you wanna get out of here?" Gwynn asked.

"What do you mean?"

"I mean go somewhere else. Somewhere quiet where you can relax. You've been tense since we got here."

"Can you blame me?" He looked around the room at all his guards. "We're not exactly alone. Did you plant all these guards here just for me?"

"It was the only way I could convince Frank to let you out, but. . ." Gwynn placed her hand on Paxton's chest and continued speaking in his ear. "If we go back to my place, there will be fewer people and I can ensure you really get to relax." Her hand drifted down his chest and toward his waist. He caught her hand and scooted away from her.

"I thought Frank didn't know we were here?"

"Oh come now, you had to know that wasn't true. Frank watches you like a hawk."

"I have to go to the bathroom," Paxton stated and stood abruptly. He started to walk off, but Gwyneth grabbed his arm.

"Don't even try."

"Order me another drink, will ya?" Paxton pulled away from her and walked toward the hallway.

That delay she caused was too much. As soon as he walked down the hallway, someone was already in front of him, the stocky male soldier who'd been sitting by the bar. Paxton slowed, hoping the man would continue into the bathroom, but he seemed to slow down as well. The soldier stopped and stooped down to tie his shoe. Paxton wrinkled his nose as he walked past and into the restroom. There was no way he could escape now.

Paxton ducked into a stall and locked it. He heard the door open and close. Paxton scratched at his forearm anxiously, then looked down. The monitor. He'd completely forgotten he was wearing it. That needed to come off before he could try anything. Paxton turned his arm, wrist up, and studied the monitor's band. It looked completely solid, with no latches or clasps to take off. Paxton tapped on the front screen. It let out a loud beep as it emitted a red light. Paxton hugged his arm, trying to muffle the sound as he coughed to cover it up.

When the light and sound stopped, Paxton looked at it again. He checked where the band and monitor head connected. He could see a tiny metal pin that held the two together. But he didn't have any tools to take it apart. Paxton pulled the pen out of his pocket and jammed it between the band and the screen, trying to use it to pull the two apart. Again, the monitor beeped, and the screen turned red.

Paxton heard laughing. He froze. This wasn't working. He'd have to cut or force it off after he escaped the restaurant. It was riskier, but what other choice did he have? At this point, he was ready to knock out the soldier in the room with him.

Paxton flushed the toilet and stepped out of the stall. The soldier stood in front of the sink and turned it on, pretending to wash his hands. Paxton did the same. The two looked at each other and nodded politely as they tried to anticipate the next person's move. Paxton would only have a split second to act.

The soldier and Paxton both dried their hands. Paxton pushed the door open and stepped out first. Just as the soldier followed behind, Paxton flung the door with full force into the soldier's face, knocking him back and disorienting him.

Paxton didn't wait to see what happened next. He bolted to the back of the hallway and through the door on his right. He closed the door and looked to see if it had a lock. It didn't. Paxton turned and sprinted down the hallway, looking through each door as he passed by. There was an office, the kitchen, the fridge.

Paxton looked up and noticed a vent opening. He stopped and jumped up, grabbing hold of the grate. It came loose, causing him and the grate to crash back down to the floor. At that moment, Paxton heard a door fly open and someone yelling. "Don't even think about it!"

Paxton looked at the soldier running toward him. He swore as he turned and kept running down the hallway toward the back door to the alley, still holding the grate. If he made a mad dash for it and ran full speed through the alley, maybe whoever was back there wouldn't be able to catch up to him.

When he reached the last door Paxton burst through it. Just outside the door was a figure standing there. Paxton flung the grate at them as hard as he could without losing speed. He heard the clang of the grate hitting the floor and footsteps behind him. Paxton willed himself to run faster. He needed to turn the corner and try to lose them.

As he was nearly around the corner, something sharp jab into his back and an explosion of electrical current surge through his body. His whole body tensed and froze. He crashed to the floor, convulsing.

Two faces appeared over him.

"Oh Paxton, all you had to do was enjoy yourself," Gwyneth frowned disapprovingly before the soldier beside her picked Paxton up and dragged his frozen body toward a car on the street.

Chapter 5

Once inside the tunnel, Aiden and Tessa made their way toward Dwelling Six.

"You know I never told you, but I'm really glad you're back," Tessa admitted.

"You and me both."

"And you're really brave to go through what you went through. I'm not sure I could've held out as long as you did. What with the torture and all."

Aiden bit his lip. He didn't feel very brave. Sure, toward the end he sustained Frank's torture from his lackey, but up to that point, Aiden lived comfortably in the capitol. His mother made certain of that.

"And to come back here ready to keep fighting them." Tessa shook her head, her short ponytail flipping back and forth. "I would've fled and found the rest of our family."

"Why didn't you go with the others, to the valley?"

"Someone's gotta make sure the Myriad don't find more Notzrim. Terrance and Jared do a great job finding us missions to gather supplies and they send them to other Notzrim hideouts around the area. We actually have a group heading south to deliver medical supplies to a group down there right now."

CHAPTER 5

"That's amazing. How'd he find them?"

"You know, I'm not sure, but he does and it always pans out. I don't question it."

They made it to Dwelling Six and descended into the large pit. A group clustered near the fire with the sound of laughter and talking intermingling with the crackle of the burning wood.

As they made their way closer, the smell of cooked meat and char wafted into Aiden's nose, startling him. His mouth salivated as his stomach rumbled. Being in the capitol spoiled him and adjusting back to the food of the tunnels was rough. He found himself constantly hungry and everything he ate disgusted him. Not that he was ungrateful for the food. His stomach had adjusted to the higher quality of proper food in the capitol, so expired canned goods and stale boxed items weren't cutting it.

"Aiden, you came!" Terrance, a man with deep-set olive-green eyes that hid under his bushy light brown eyebrows, wandered over and slapped Aiden hard on the back, causing him to stumble forward a couple of steps. "I saw you working hard during PT today. I'm glad you're feeling better."

"Mostly. We'll see how I feel tomorrow." Already Aiden's body ached more than it should, partly from being out of shape and partly from still healing. "Well, tonight, my friend, you're in for a treat. Not only did Jared find and kill a boar, but I figured out a way to make some hooch. Tonight, we party!"

And he wasn't kidding. Everyone was in the mood to enjoy themselves. Their lives were completely focused on training, running dangerous missions, and constant fear of being caught, that when they could take a few hours to forget their troubles, they went all out. A small group gathered items to create a makeshift band and were already playing a lively beat as others danced around hooting and hollering. Aiden couldn't help but laugh at their gaiety. Those who weren't dancing yet were digging into the giant boar that had just come off the fire. The size of the animal shocked him. His stomach gurgled again, begging to consume some of that meat.

"What do you think?" Jared asked as he handed Aiden a boar kabob.

"Where'd you find it?"

"I wandered into the mountains. After your sister spoke of the place still being alive, it made me wonder if the animals were too. Sure enough. I can't believe we hadn't thought of it sooner. Sabaoth has provided."

Aiden took a bite of the meat and it practically melted in his mouth. It was tender. As he chewed, he picked up on a unique flavor he hadn't experienced before. It was almost nutty.

"Make sure you grab some of Terrance's moonshine to wash it down."

Aiden nodded but didn't head to the drink. After the last time he had alcohol, he wasn't sure he wanted to dabble with the strong liquid again. Aiden wandered over to a bench and sat. Tessa was soon beside him.

"There you are. I got caught up talking to someone and I lost you."

"Oh sorry. I hadn't realized."

"Gee, thanks."

"No, I mean—look at this scene. Everyone enjoying themselves. It's how things should be. I was caught up in the moment and my hunger. Have you tried this meat?" Aiden held his half-eaten kabob toward Tessa. She held hers up and smiled. "I guess so."

"I also have this." She held up a tin cup. "Try it. It burns, but it's pretty good. I think he mixed some of the berries into it, the ones that our scientists could grow."

Aiden took the cup and sniffed it. It smelled sweet, but also made his eyes water. He knew it was going to be strong. He handed it back to Tessa without taking a sip. "No thanks. Too intense for me."

"Suit yourself." Tessa took another swig of her drink, contorting her face as the strong liquid went down. Tessa took another bite of her meat as she watched the dancers. "That looks fun."

"It does?"

"Yeah, don't you like dancing?"

"Kind of." Memories of his evening out with Mimi flooded his mind. His time with her in the capitol felt more like a dream than reality. How was she doing? When would he hear from her again?

After she helped him and the others escape, she promised to help Aiden take down the capitol. But she also said she needed to return to the capitol so as not to drudge up suspicion. It'd been five weeks and still nothing. He was worried.

Aiden shoved another bite of meat into his mouth and chewed. Across the way, he spotted another close friend of his, Mitchum. They made eye contact and Mitchum barreled his way over to Aiden, scooping him up into a giant bear hug, swallowing Aiden with his massive body.

"Aiden, my boy!" Mitchum's voice was as large as his body. As Mitchum squeezed Aiden in his embrace, Aiden winced.

"Mitchum, I'm surprised to see you here."

Mitchum set Aiden down. "All my tools and materials are here. I couldn't part with them to become some farmer."

Tessa leaned over toward Aiden. "Not to mention Jared

begged him to stay and help build robots and other gadgets."

"What can I say? I'm an engineer, an inventor. This is where I belong."

"I'm glad you're here. You'll be of help to me too, I'm sure."

"Oh? Do you have a project you want to work on?" Mitchum's eyes lit up under his bushy brows.

"Let's just say I have big plans." He wasn't sure he was ready to reveal his idea to anyone other than Jared and Terrance. Though having Tessa and Mitchum on his side would be helpful.

"Plans to take down the capitol?" Tessa asked.

Aiden looked at her sideways. "How'd you know?"

"What else would you want to do after escaping that horrific place? It's risky, but if we can execute it well, I think it'll really cripple Teivel and the Myriad."

Aiden looked at Mitchum, who stared back with wide eyes. "I'm not sure that's necessary, Aiden. And it's far too dangerous for such amateurs."

"You don't know what they're planning. I saw it, Mitchum. I saw the weapons, the war machines—they're—they're going to destroy us all."

"My boy, you've lost your focus. We're not meant to fight this war alone. Meshiakh will be here soon. Then we can fight. Then, we'll have the real victory."

"But what if we're meant to start now? Help prepare the way?"

"You're talking about one capitol in a sea of capitols around the world."

"But if that one capitol had Teivel in it when we take it down, then it'll mean something."

"It's risky, but I think it can be worth it." Tessa chimed in.

CHAPTER 5

"Help take care of one part of the evil that is surrounding us. Maybe it'll even give us some relief while we continue to wait. I hate how we're all hiding and waiting like prisoners. I don't want that anymore for anyone."

"I don't think we'll have to wait much longer."

Tessa tilted her head, staring at Mitchum with curiosity.

Mitchum looked around, becoming very mysterious. "Come with me." Mitchum turned toward the far end of the dome. Aiden and Tessa looked at one another before following.

No one spoke as Mitchum led them through a series of tunnels until they reached the most southern entrance. Mitchum checked the security cameras before climbing up and out. The three of them stood in the pitch black, still in silence. A cool breeze caressed Aiden's skin, sending chills all over. Compared to the tunnels, it was cold outside in the open air.

Aiden crossed his arms. "What are we doing out here? This isn't safe."

"Look into the sky, to your left. Do you see it?"

Aiden stared at the nearly empty. Early in the Great Desolation, many of the stars went out and even the moon lost its luster. The sky was now a black abyss with just a few faint dots.

"What are we looking for?"

"That light. The one that looks like a UFO."

Aiden kept searching the sky, wondering if Mitchum was imagining things, but then he saw it. A small elliptical-shaped light fading in and out like a distant lightning storm. Aiden's mouth fell open as he stared, awed by this mysterious dancing light.

"What is it?" Tessa asked in wonder.

"I believe that's Meshiakh with his angels, battling it out. A sort of heavenly holy war. I've been monitoring it. It's getting larger."

Aiden looked away. No, it couldn't be. When Meshiakh comes, it's going to be big and sudden. There's going to be a loud trumpet, thunderous hooves, and a sudden wave of shouting warriors as they come in and destroy Teivel and all his followers. It wasn't this tiny light, slow and subtle. "No way, Mitchum. That can't be."

"Why not? The first time Meshiakh appeared, it was not how the Hebrews expected. What makes you think we know any better?"

"Because we have the sacred writings."

"So did they."

Aiden shook his head, feeling his mind fighting what he was hearing and what he believed to be so. "I appreciate your optimism Mitchum, but you're wrong. And I want to move forward with my plan. Tessa, you'll help me convince Jared and Terrance, right?"

"Uh-huh." Her voice was distant while she continued to stare at the light in the sky.

"Will you help me too? Even if that is Meshiakh, we can still do something now to help. Please, Mitchum. I need you."

Mitchum looked at the light for a long time. He seemed to contemplate everything. As if the answer to his concerns were in the sky. Slowly, he looked back at Aiden.

Aiden waited anxiously, hoping his friend would side with him on this. That he would be there for him like he always was.

Finally, Mitchum said, "I'll make whatever you need."

"Thank you." Aiden's body relaxed. He looked around again. Standing in the dark made him anxious. Anyone could be out

CHAPTER 5

there watching them. "We need to get inside before we're seen."

Back inside, Mitchum secured the manhole before the three of them wandered back to the party.

"You really think that's Meshiakh up there?" Tessa asked as they walked.

"I really do."

"That's amazing." Tessa's voice turned from wonder to excitement. "It's really happening, isn't it? He's really coming."

"Yes, he is, and soon. It'll be any day now."

"Will it though?" Aiden asked skeptically. "I mean, how long was the Holy Star in the sky before Meshiakh was born on earth? And how long did the Hebrews have to wait to enter the Promised Land?"

Tessa agreed, sounding disappointed. "Sabaoth's timing is often longer than we expect. That's why I want to help you, Aiden. Who knows, it might be another year before he gets here."

"I hope not," Mitchum mumbled.

Before descending back into the sector where the party was still raging, Mitchum said his goodbyes. He was too old for late-night parties and wanted to be alone.

"Let's go dance," Tessa suggested as they approached the crowd.

"Tessa, I'm way too tired for that. You go."

"Your loss." She turned and skipped away, finding herself a dance partner in the crowd.

The dinner party continued for what felt like hours. Aiden was content to sit and watch as he processed what Mitchum showed him. He wanted to be hopeful and believe Mitchum, but he struggled. They'd already waited longer than anyone had predicted, but with each passing day his anger toward the Myriad overshadowed his hope.

Occasionally, people joined him on the bench, making light chit-chat before taking off again. As the crowd thinned, Terrance hollered for Aiden to join him and the others by the firepit. Aiden's eyelids were heavy. All he wanted to do was sleep, but he wouldn't miss this chance to spend with Terrance and Jared. He needed to be on their good side.

Aiden moved to the group and sat. Someone handed him a small cup of moonshine, but he shook it away.

"Why won't you take it?" Terrance asked. "Don't you like my creation?"

"I don't drink."

"More for the rest of us then," Jared said, grabbing the cup meant for Aiden.

The group sat around joking and making small talk for a while, and Aiden continued to listen and observe. He was too tired to take part, but when the conversation turned to him, he had no choice.

"So, Aiden, what was it like?" One guy in the group asked.

"What was *what* like?"

"The capitol. That's where they took you, right?"

"Well, I don't know. I was underground in their prison most of the time," Aiden lied.

Sure, he'd told them a good amount of what happened, but he left out a lot of details surrounding his work for the capitol and living in a luxurious suite. If they knew the truth, they'd never trust him again. They'd cast him out, leaving him to fend for himself. If that happened, he'd never get his chance to destroy the capitol.

CHAPTER 5

"I thought you said you saw the place."

"Once."

"So? What was it like?" Others coaxed him to share.

"Deceptively great. They have all the technology, luxury, and food you could ever want. But it's also a prison. People work there completely unaware of what Teivel and the Myriad are actually up to. They think they're doing humanitarian work, but really Teivel is preparing for a war."

"That monster," Jared snapped. "He would have to lie to get that many people on his side. I'm looking forward to the day when he gets crushed like an ant."

"If I ever had the chance," Terrance chimed in, "I'd take him out. He doesn't deserve to breathe."

Aiden didn't plan on sharing his plans tonight, but he hopped at his chance. "What if we could?"

Everyone looked at Aiden, perplexed.

"Could what?" Terrance asked. "Kill Teivel?"

"Not exactly. What if we could cut off a limb?"

"And how exactly would we do that?" Evan asked skeptically.

Aiden glanced at Jared, who was glaring at him, warning him. He knew Jared and Terrance rejected him once before, but if Aiden could get others on his side, Jared would have to go with his idea. Aiden ignored Jared's stare and went on. "By taking down the capitol?"

The group stared silently, processing what Aiden was suggesting, and then erupted in laughter.

"Getting in there is a pipedream," Terrance laughed. "We'd never get in and out alive."

"What if we could, though? What if I had a way for it to all work?"

"Yeah, okay sure," Terrance said sarcastically. "If you could figure out how to get an entire militia group through three sets of security into the most dangerous part of the city, blow it up and get us out, yeah, we'd join you."

"You would?" Aiden knew he wasn't serious, but he latched onto the opportunity, anyway.

"It's never gonna happen, Aiden," Jared argued. "There's no way. You have no training, no experience with this kinda stuff." Jared turned his head to talk to the others in the group, trying to brush off and move on from Aiden's conversation.

Aiden stood. "If I can find a way, will you help develop the plan?"

Jared looked at Aiden with a straight face. His eyes glazed over with a far-off look. He was drunk, but Aiden didn't care. If he could get Jared to agree to help, he'd hold him to his word.

The group was silent, waiting for a reply.

"Don't you want to see them taken down? To see them weak and defenseless. They've done so many horrific things, we deserve justice."

A painfully pregnant pause forced Aiden to wonder if Jared was even listening or if in his drunken stupor he'd zoned out. Finally, he answered, "Sure. You find us a way and I'll help." He didn't sound completely serious, but Aiden didn't care. Jared had agreed to help, and Aiden was going to make certain he kept his word.

* * * *

Back in the valley, Amina and the others went to work helping wherever they could. They did their best to move the giant pigs out of the pen and over to an area where they could wash them with buckets and rags.

The pigs were stubborn enough in not wanting to do what they were told, but they seemed even worse due to not feeling well. At one point, Amina was in the pen trying to get a large sow to move. She refused and plopped into the mud mixed with feces and proceeded to roll in it. When Amina tried to get the rope around the sow's neck to drag her out, she buried her nose in the mud and flung it at Amina, spraying her right in the face. Amina froze, shocked and appalled at the stubborn animal. Beside her, she heard a stifled laugh.

"I'd like to see you get this dumb animal out of here." Amina tossed Josiah the rope and wiped her face with her handkerchief.

"Watch and learn." Josiah walked over to the pig and slipped the rope on it. As he pulled the pig with all his might, the pig seemed to dig its heels in harder, refusing to move. Soon she let out a few loud snorts before lying down and rolling onto her side.

"Come on, you stubborn pig." Josiah gritted his teeth and tried to pull again. His feet sunk into the mud deeper. Eventually, the pig slid forward. He continued to drag the pig inch by inch. When he got about a foot away from the entrance, the pig stood and walked at the same moment Josiah gave a big tug. The unexpected movement of the pig combined with his forceful tug sent him flying face-first into the mud.

Amina couldn't help herself. She let out a loud belly laugh. She walked over to help Josiah up. Wet mud covered his scowling face.

"She got you good."

Josiah grunted as he rolled onto his behind and let Amina pull him up. He looked over at the sow he'd been trying to get out of the pen, walked past them, and over to the cleaning station. The sow was about to walk by it, but Maya grabbed the rope and easily guided her over to a water bucket.

It took most of the night to clear out, wash, and sort the pigs. By the time they could clean all the mud and feces out of the pen and lay a fresh layer of dirt, Amina was certain the morning was upon them. Amina plopped onto a barrel of hay and flung herself backward. The hay poked through her thin shirt, but she didn't care. She closed her eyes, letting the exhaustion of the night wash over her. All she wanted to do was sleep.

"How do you suppose they got sick?" Amina heard Matthias ask.

"They likely have E. coli or dysentery, and a couple of them have what's called greasy pig. Both can happen from having a dirty pen. Either way, we need to give them lots of fluids, and whoever you have in charge of keeping the pig pens clean needs to be retrained. We don't want your pigs dying and we don't want the other pigs or any of your people getting sick. Make sure to tell everyone to go take a warm bath and scrub hard. I'll see if I can track down some natural antibiotics as well."

"Thank you, David, you've been a great help."

Amina heard the men part ways.

"Go wash up," Matthias instructed Amina and Josiah. "We need to make sure everyone gets all the germs off them, so they don't get sick as well."

Amina sat up. "Are they going to be okay?"

"I believe so. It's odd that this would happen. Everyone has been doing such a good job of taking care of everything. I know everyone is being diligent and doing their jobs properly."

CHAPTER 5

Matthias stared off into the distance, thinking.

"You don't suspect foul play, do you?"

Matthias broke out of his thoughts and looked at Amina again. "I'm not sure how that'd work with the pigs, but this isn't the first peculiar thing that's happened." Matthias sighed. "But that's for me to worry about, not you."

Amina bit her lip, her curiosity piqued. Surely, things were bound to go wrong. Life on a farm is unpredictable, especially when you have a bunch of novices running things, but Matthias suspected something. And that made Amina uneasy. If something was awry in the village, Amina wanted to find out who was behind it and put a stop to it. Her people had gone through too much to be mistreated now.

* * * *

Salome sat at her small wooden table, biting the inside of her cheek as she mulled over the letter from her daughter. The tear-splattered paper was worn along the folded seams and the ink was smudged in spots. She'd read the letter more times than she could count, admiring the handwriting and analyzing the meaning behind the words:

Dear Mom,

I know we didn't leave on the greatest of terms. I was bitter and angry at you. I blamed you for dad leaving. I blamed you for ruining your relationship with him, and in return, I ruined our relationship. Instead of accepting the truth, that dad was a liar and a cheat, I wanted to believe the lie, that you and your faith pushed him away. But now, I've realized that I was wrong.

Your faith is what made you strong and what held you together when you found out that the love of your life left you for someone else. It was your faith that sustained you night after night when I refused to call or come home.

I am so sorry, and I hope you can find it in your heart to forgive me. I should've listened to you when you told me what was going to happen. And I should've come with you when you asked me to.

I love you and I miss you terribly. Please know that I am okay and that I think about you every day.

Your loving daughter,
  Ruth

It took Salome months to come to terms with her daughter's decision to stay behind. And even longer for her not to blame Sabaoth. Eventually, she'd moved forward, or at least suppressed the pain and guilt long enough that she could move forward, as long as she didn't think about it too much.

But now, re-reading this letter, the past ripped her wounds wide open. While there was peace in the letter and in knowing her daughter forgave her, there was still guilt and a deep longing to have her daughter with her. If she could just speak with her, she'd be able to have some closure and finally move past her mistakes.

Looking over the letter, Salome was certain her daughter wanted to be with her. That she'd willingly come if she had the chance. The clues were obvious: "I miss you terribly, I think about you every day, your faith is what made you strong." Weren't these showing Ruth's own desire to be with her mom?

Salome set the letter aside and picked up the feather lying on the table next to the small piece of parchment. Dipping the

CHAPTER 5

feather in some ink, Salome wrote,

My dearest daughter, Ruth,

It thrilled me to receive your letter and to know that not only are you alive, but you forgive me. It has been my deepest regret in life, pushing you away, and to know that you forgive me brings me peace. But I also miss you terribly. I worry about you and pray for your safety every day. Knowing that you've contacted some friends of mine, I have a request. Please come to me.

A knock came on the wall, and Salome looked up just in time to see Mo push back the curtain and waltz in. On a normal day, Salome wouldn't have cared. It was normal for people to come into others' homes without waiting. But today, Salome didn't want to be disturbed.

"Hey Salome, what are you up to?" Mo walked over to Salome's side.

"Nothing." Salome's heart quickened as she tried to hide the parchment. There was no place to hide it, and it was too late.

"Is that a letter to your daughter?"

Salome sighed. While she didn't want to talk about it, she knew Mo well enough at this point that she wouldn't give up the topic easily. "Yes. I plan to send it with Amina when she leaves."

Mo sat in the adjacent chair. She placed a hand on Salome's and gave her a concerned look. Salome tried to avoid eye contact. "I know what you're going to say," she said, trying not to roll her eyes. She and Mo had this conversation enough already. She didn't need to hear it again.

"Then why are you doing this?"

"I need closure."

"Isn't her letter closure enough? Salome, you can't keep punishing yourself with all this guilt. That's not what Sabaoth wants for you. That's why Meshiakh sacrificed himself for you and me. To rid you of the guilt and shame of your mistakes and sins."

Salome stood and walked toward a window. It was early morning, but the clouds blocked the sun's light, casting a gloomy shadow over the valley. "I'm not punishing myself. I just. . ." Salome sought to find the right words to convince Mo that she needed this. "I know my daughter, and this letter is a woman begging to be with her mother again. We need to be together. You're a mother, you should understand that."

"I do," Mo answered slowly. "But what if that never happens? What'll you do if she says no, or the letter never gets to her? How will you move on?"

Salome gently touched the letter from her daughter, staring at the handwriting. She hadn't stopped to think about that. She was stuck on believing her daughter wanted to come and would come. Was she clinging to an unfounded hope? No, that can't be. *Ruth wants to be here.*

Mo continued. Her tone was soft, but the words hurt. "Didn't she already have the opportunity and instead she chose to give Amina the letter?"

Salome bit her lip, fighting back the urge to believe Mo's negativity. "She must've had a reason."

"I'm sure she did. And that reason probably hasn't changed."

Mo was known for her bluntness and while Salome generally appreciated it, she didn't want to hear it right now.

CHAPTER 5

"Thank you, Mo, for your opinion, but I know my daughter. I know this letter may never get to her, but if it's meant to be, it'll be." Salome wiped the tear that escaped from her eyes before turning around. "Now, why is it you came over?"

Salome gently tried to stop Mo from prying further and making her feel any more confused. She knew what she wanted and what she needed to do. Write the letter and have Amina deliver it to Ruth if she went to go retrieve Aiden. End of story.

Mo didn't answer at first. She stared at Salome, analyzing her with empathetic eyes. Finally, she answered, "I wanted to join you for your class this morning. You are teaching again today, right?"

Salome nodded. "I was about to head over there."

Mo stood and headed to the door. "Good. We can walk together."

Salome glanced at the letter on the table. She wanted to get it to Amina as soon as possible.

"Amina is likely helping with the pigs. You can give it to her after class."

Salome grabbed the letter, folded it up and placed in her bag. "You're right, let's go."

Chapter 6

Amina made her way up the hill and toward the barn. Though the clouds did their best to hide the sun, Amina felt its morning warmth. Amina thanked the clouds for their coverage today and the relief it brought. Yesterday, she wasn't sure how she'd manage another day of draining heat.

Amina admired the trees and bushes brimming with life all around her. Tiny pops of yellow, red, and orange leaves played hide and seek among the mostly green trees. Fall was coming, and it was a welcomed change from the dreary landscape over the past nine years. The rest of the world was dead, nothing wanted to live. In the city there were flowers and life, but concrete and glass surrounded it. Whereas the valley was all Sabaoth's creation. Natural, earthy, and warm. Amina breathed in deeply and caught a whiff of the sweet-scented wildflowers in the grass. This was home.

A bug buzzed in her ear, and she swatted at it. She couldn't remember the last time she had to swat at a bug. It oddly made her smile. Like the bird, it meant there was life here.

As Amina approached the pig's temporary pen located to the right of the barn, she could see the pigs lounging around in the dirt. The ones they'd deemed sick were in fact looking livelier than before and Amina didn't notice as much feces.

CHAPTER 6

An elderly man with leathery skin and graying hair stood by the pigs, pouring a bucket of slop into the trough. It was the same man from last night who'd informed them about the situation.

"Good morning, Henry," Amina greeted him as she walked over.

Henry looked. His brown eyes were puffy and red.

"Did you sleep at all last night?"

"Not much. Been watching after the pigs. They're my responsibility and it's my fault they got sick. I need to make sure they recover, and we don't lose none." Henry's forehead creased with regret and concern.

"What can I do to help?"

"That burlap sack has a couple of bottles. David brought them over from some of the Hebrew families with little ones. The pigs aren't drinking water on their own. We need to feed it to them. They're already full of water mixed with watermelon juice, cucumber juice, and antibiotics to help the pigs rehydrate. Grab a bottle and start feeding."

She was unsure how to accomplish this task. After last night's fiasco, Amina didn't think the pigs would comply, but she'd try it.

Henry walked into the barn with his empty bucket, leaving Amina alone with the pigs. She threw on the tall boots that were by the bottles to help protect her pants from mud, grabbed a bottle, and climbed over the fence. Once inside, she looked around for a pig that seemed friendly. It was hard to say. They all looked calm and easy to handle. On Amina's right, however, she spotted a smaller pig standing alone and staring at her.

"Hey there, little one. Are you thirsty?" Amina approached

the pig calmly. When she was close enough, she squatted down and reached out her hand.

The pig walked up and pressed its nose into her hand and sniffed. Amina giggled as its long hairs tickled her hand. Once the pig finished investigating Amina's hand, it walked closer and started sniffing her shirt and face like a puppy. Amina laughed and tried to get up, but the pig moved closer, still causing Amina to lose her balance and fall on her behind.

That's when the pig noticed the bottle in Amina's other hand and moved toward it. Amina held it up and the pig immediately suckled the bottle's nipple. Amina gripped the bottle, tilting it just enough to keep the liquid flowing as the pig slurped it all up.

The bottle was about halfway when Amina felt a nudge on her left side. She looked over to find a much larger pig with a brown spot around its eye, standing beside her, trying to squeeze its way over to the bottle.

"Woah there, big guy, you need to wait your turn." She firmly pushed the pig back, and he snorted at her. "I know you're thirsty, but this is not your bottle. You can have the next one."

The pig stepped back and watched, as if understanding Amina. As soon as the first bottle was empty, Amina went over to grab the next one. When she turned around, the same large pig with the spot around its eye was standing directly behind her.

"You really are thirsty, aren't ya? Alright then." Amina sat and held out the bottle. The pig didn't hesitate and started sucking on the water. The bottle made squeaking sounds as the liquid squeezed its way into the pig's mouth.

"Look at you, the pig whisperer."

CHAPTER 6

Amina looked and found Josiah standing on the other side of the fence.

"Yeah, I seem to have more luck today than I did last night."

"Well, of course, you're giving them something they want instead of trying to force them to move."

"Grab a bottle and help. They're in the sack over there."

Josiah did as told and soon, they were both sitting in the pen, feeding pigs with bottles. It wasn't long before Henry came back and joined. He took the empty bottles and refilled them with more of the water mixture and then helped feed the pigs.

"Did you ever think you'd be living on a farm, feeding pigs?" Josiah asked.

"Nope. Definitely not. There was never the opportunity. I don't even think I'd ever seen a pig in real life until last night."

Josiah's eyebrows raised. "Really, never?"

"Never."

"Huh. My grandpa lived on a farm. We'd go visit him sometimes during spring break. So, I've had my fair share of pigs, horses, chickens, and goats. You name it."

"So, should I start calling you Farmer Josiah?"

"I wouldn't go that far, but I know my way around farm animals."

Matthias, Paul, and David approached the pigpen, and they did not look pleased. Matthias appeared ashen and had deep bags under his round eyes. Paul and David didn't look as sickly, but they did look exhausted, and both wore the same concerned look on their faces.

"How are the pigs this morning?" David asked.

Henry looked from the pig he was feeding. "They're drinking the mixture you gave me, and I hardly had to clean up any feces in the last two hours. I think they're slowly getting better."

"Have any of the well pigs gotten sick?" Henry shook his head. "Good. Let's just keep feeding them and keep them separated until we know for sure they're better. I don't want to risk contaminating the others."

"You got it."

Paul looked at Amina and Josiah. "I'm glad to see you two helping out."

"Of course," Amina said, "I'm part of this community too and I want to make sure the pigs get better."

"I'm sure this is just another learning curve. Most of us are not familiar with this style of living."

David nodded in agreement. "It took well over a year to really feel like we were getting the hang of it here and even then, things would come up."

Matthias wiped his forehead with a handkerchief and grunted. "This seems like an exorbitant number of issues. I'm not sure we can handle too many more."

"Nonsense," Paul disagreed. "Nothing too crazy that we can't handle. Honestly, I think the pigs have been the biggest upset. Everything else has just been minor issues."

"If you say so. Come, gentlemen, we have more rounds to make."

Paul waved goodbye. "See you two around."

Amina waved back before standing to grab another bottle. Amina sat quietly, listening to the sound of the pig sucking its water and grunting in gratitude. While she sat quietly, her mind was far from quiet. Once again Matthias had her thinking. Could it really be that there's something more going on than just a learning curve?

"Hey Josiah," Amina said, "what else has been going wrong

here?"

"What do you mean?"

"Well, your dad hinted that there's been a lot of issues."

"Nothing too crazy. We've been having trouble catching fish the last couple of weeks. The traps keep breaking." Josiah thought for a moment. "And about a month ago, someone mixed the pesticide up with something else that resulted in killing a good amount of the crop. We had to start over again. But like Paul said, they're all learning curve issues. Nothing to be worried about."

Amina bit the inside of her cheek. It's expected to have learning curves and mistakes, but something just didn't feel right. Maybe if she spoke to Salome about it, and got her input about some issues her people ran into when they first started, she'd feel better. After living for years paranoid and distrusting everything, it was a hard habit to shake. Amina needed reassurance that it was all in her head.

By the time Amina and Josiah finished feeding the pigs and washing the two greasy pigs with a special soap, the sun was high in the sky and Amina's stomach rumbled. It was nice helping and doing something new. Amina enjoyed not having to think about or worry about anything except the task in front of her. And it helped to have good company. Josiah had been a friend since high school and while he was closer to Aiden than her, they still got along well.

As Amina and Josiah cleaned, carried their supplies back into the barn, and washed their hands, Maya appeared with a picnic basket.

"I thought all of you may be hungry. I bring food. Henry, you join too." Maya insisted.

"Yes, ma'am."

They made their way to a small table outside, shaded by the tall barn, and sat. Maya pulled out leftover rolls, meat, and fruit from last night's dinner.

"Bless us Sabaoth for the food we are about to eat. May it nourish our bodies as much as you nourish our souls. Meshiakh come quickly. Amen." As soon as Maya finished her prayer, they were devouring the food. Amina's hunger pains subsided as she indulged in the fresh food.

As they ate, they filled Amina in on as much information as they could about their time building the village and gaining supplies. It hadn't been an easy task for them. Aryeh gave them a few things to start, but that was all.

"Whenever we needed something else, he'd refuse," Josiah explained, "but then Salome would jump in and argue with Aryeh until he gave in."

"That or things would just appear," Henry said, wiping his mouth with the back of his hand. "Like the pigs and horses."

Amina looked at him sideways. "What do you mean?"

"I think there are some Hebrews who want us to stay and be successful, so they've been helping secretly when they can."

"Yeah, but not everyone wants us here," Josiah contested. "We've had our share of disputes already with some of the Hebrews when we've supposedly gone too far out of our area." Josiah rolled his eyes and shook his head. "It's stupid, really."

"They will calm down eventually," Maya interjected optimistically. "Or we will not be still here."

"What do you mean?" Amina asked.

Maya pointed to the sky. "I mean, Meshiakh comes very soon. I have seen it. The holy war in the sky. Eventually, that will come down here."

Amina stared at her skeptically. How could she have seen

it? Weren't they taught it'd come unexpectedly? Maya must be mistaken, but Amina appreciated her hopefulness. Amina needed more of that in her life. When had she allowed herself to drift so far from the hope she knew to be true?

* * * *

Salome sat among the group of women she'd been teaching over the past two weeks about weaving reeds to make household items. In her hands was a half-weaved curtain where she took the long skinny reeds and weaved them over two and under two, creating an expertly twilled two pattern. It was a simple yet fun styled pattern that gave the women something more interesting to look at than the typical weave.

Some of the other women did the same, while a few watched intently. Salome spoke as she weaved and occasionally stopped to let the women look at the curtain before beginning again.

While she spoke and watched, seemingly focused on helping the women, her mind was far away. There were so many thoughts swirling in her head about the letter to her daughter, that she finally finished putting together a unity gathering without it blowing up in her face, and now this new, daunting responsibility of being the elder's official Hebrew advisor.

It took a moment for Salome to notice Amina standing in front of her. She forced a smile. "Hi there, what brings you here?"

Amina looked at the other women, who were now curiously staring at her. When she spotted Mo, she waved. "How long until your class ends?"

"Not too long. There's no real end time, though. Do you

want to join us?" Salome nodded toward a pile of brown reeds. "Grab a handful and sit. I'm showing them how to make curtains for their windows."

Amina hesitated. "I don't know. The last thing I ever made was in elementary school when I attempted to make a dog out of clay. There hadn't been enough water, and the proportions were all wrong. After it came out of the kiln, an ear and a leg fell off. The thing looked like a mutant rat more than anything else."

Salome couldn't help but laugh as she pictured Amina's clay dog-rat. Amina didn't strike her as a crafty person, but she wanted to offer nonetheless. "This is easier than that, I promise."

Some ladies motioned for Amina to sit and insisted she learn with them. Eventually, Amina gave in, though she still had a concerned look on her face.

For the next few hours, Salome taught Amina the basics of weaving and then watched Amina attempt to make her own curtain. Amina seemed to struggle the most with getting started. It was the hardest part about weaving, after all. The poor girl kept pulling too hard on the reeds and breaking them. Salome had to show her several times what to do to avoid the breakage and on what seemed to be the hundredth try, Amina finally completed her first full row of weaving.

"I see why you enjoy doing this. Once you get past the initial difficulty, weaving is pretty relaxing." When Amina finally finished, she laughed, showing off her lopsided curtain. Apparently, as she weaved, she didn't stay consistent with the tension and eventually her curtain turned from a straight-edged square to a wavy rectangle that was wider on the upper left corner than anywhere else like an overstretched and worn-out sweater.

"I think it'll still cover your window," one woman said, trying to sound encouraging.

Mo looked through one of the gaping holes. "I'm just not sure it'll keep all the rain out." She poked her finger through the hole, causing the others to laugh.

"That's to let the sun in so I don't oversleep."

The entire group burst into laughter along with Amina.

Once the class finished, Salome and Amina wandered away from the group and toward an open space away from anyone else.

"First, I want to apologize. I gave you that letter, but never an explanation or a chance for you to ask questions. I'm sorry," Amina said.

"Thank you, and I forgive you. You had a lot on your own mind."

"Yes, but I'm sure you did, too. How are you feeling about the letter and everything?"

"I'm glad that my daughter forgives me and that the letter found me. I'm still sad that she wouldn't come with you to see me. There's a lot I'd like to say to her, to let her know how I've changed. Tell me, how did you find my daughter?"

Amina swallowed hard, as if the words caught in her throat. "She works at the capitol." Amina paused, watching Salome's reaction.

"I figured as much. She'd always wanted to work there."

"She's not bad, though. Not like the others there. Somehow Aiden knew her, and she helped us escape. If it wasn't for her, I don't think we would've made it out alive."

"That's amazing. So she got you out of the capitol and back to the tunnels."

"Pretty much." Amina's eyes drifted to the ground as she grabbed at her elbow. A look of disappointment filled her. Was she thinking about Paxton? Salome could only imagine what terrible thing had happened to him. It was clear Amina had no choice other than to leave without him, but it was eating at her.

Salome reached out and touched Amina's arm in comfort. "I'm glad she helped you. She's always enjoyed caring for other people. I'm glad to hear that hasn't left her. It's too bad she didn't come here with you. I was hoping she would."

"I think she wanted to come with me, but if so, she wouldn't be able to."

Salome furrowed her brow. She was excited and confused all at the same time. "Why not?"

"She has the mark."

"The mark?" Salome had left the city before Teivel truly rose to power as a dictator, which made her unaware of this term.

"Everyone was required to take the mark of Teivel. It's a computer chip embedded into the skin used for money and documentation. I believe they have GPS trackers on them, too."

Salome opened her mouth and closed it again. It hadn't occurred to her that Ruth would have something hindering her from coming. A physical obstacle. She didn't want to put her daughter or the people of the valley at risk.

"I didn't know. . ." Salome pressed her hand against her left pocket where the letter sat. The letter she couldn't give her daughter.

A letter that would only bring guilt upon her daughter for not being here. That was the last thing she wanted.

CHAPTER 6

"I guess I'll just have to be okay with her not being with me."

"We both have to trust Sabaoth is protecting Ruth and Aiden."

It was silent for a moment. Salome took a deep breath, letting go of her hope. Amina was right. Sabaoth was still with her, watching over her, protecting her. Because of that, she felt a small bit of peace. Salome smiled. "So, what else did you want to speak about?" she asked, changing the subject.

"Right. I wanted to ask about how things are going here. Is everything running smoothly?"

"You've seen the place." Salome gestured around her. "Wonderful progress has been made. And things are going as smoothly as you can expect when you know nothing and have to be taught everything by only two people. The Notzrim are quick and eager learners."

"I agree. The place looks great, but has there been anything that seems off?"

She crossed her arms, rolling her shoulders back uncomfortably. "Like what?" She didn't like where this was leading.

"Like unnatural issues. Matthias made a comment that things seemed to go wrong a little too much and that there might be foul play at hand." Amina ended her statement, almost like a question.

Salome swallowed hard, heat flushing to her face. This was the first she was hearing of any concerns, and it worried her. Sure there were a lot of mishaps, but everyone had those in the beginning, right? There's always a learning curve, but could it be something more?

"Look, when I first arrived with the Hebrews, there were a lot of issues, too. Things that we thought couldn't possibly go wrong did. It took us several years till we were in a groove. I'm sure the same thing is happening to the Notzrim. This is undeveloped land we're talking about. There needs to be a symbiotic relationship between the Notzrim and the land, which takes time," she explained, hoping to both encourage and convince Amina. At the same time, her own doubts crept up.

Amina shrugged, though she didn't look convinced. "I guess. It's just, Matthias really got me thinking that maybe Aryeh or someone else was up to no good."

Those were dangerous thoughts floating in Amina's head. She knew Aryeh was making it difficult for them to get supplies and build a village, but he wouldn't go as far as to sabotage. He knew it was in the best interest and safety of the Hebrews to keep the Notzrim in the valley. He wouldn't do anything to jeopardize that.

Not to mention, these were Salome's people Amina was accusing. Sure she was banished from the Hebrew's village, and she wasn't sure she still believed the same as they did, but they were still her people. She spent nine years surviving with them. Salome's was not about to turn on them so flippantly.

If Salome intended to bring about unity, she needed to squash Amina and Matthias' suspicions before they did anything rash, and it completely disrupt her plans. "Be careful not to jump to conclusions too quickly. That could cause a whole lot of trouble for all of us."

"I know that. That's why I'm coming to you first. I know Aryeh was adamant about not having us here, and suddenly he's okay with it. That doesn't sit right with me."

"Look, Aryeh talks a big game, and likes to flex his authority sometimes, but he's smart. The elders and I convinced him that it's safer for us to stay here instead of wandering about, risking the Myriad finding the Notzrim and the valley. Please don't worry, I'm sure it's nothing."

Amina's face reddened as her hands curled into fists. "Not worry? I've spent nearly a decade worrying because my family was constantly under attack. Excuse me for being concerned."

"Sorry. I meant no offense. I just mean, you're safe here," Salome tried to reassure Amina and herself. She was still paranoid about the spy she saw yesterday. At first, she thought it was Aryeh keeping tabs on her, but Amina's suspicions of sabotage made her wonder if that spy was there for some other reason.

Amina took a breath and let it out. "I didn't mean to overreact, it's just. . . old habits die hard."

Salome stepped forward and hugged Amina. She could see the worry creases in her forehead and the bags under her eyes from lack of sleep. Amina took on too much.

A chilling sensation that someone was watching them. She looked around subtly but saw nothing.

"You alright?" Amina asked, also looking toward the trees behind her. "Is there something over there?"

"I'm fine. Something caught my eye, but it was nothing." Salome shook her head, trying to refocus. Telling Amina about the spy would only rile her up again.

Chapter 7

Salome marched her way into the village and over to the main hall, where Aryeh was likely conducting whatever sort of business he did on any given day. Salome's face was flushed. Whether it was from running or the rage building inside her, she didn't know. And really, it didn't matter. The more she dwelt on the spy, everything Aryeh had done in the past to keep them out, and now Amina's concerns, the more livid she became. She was tired of being watched like an caged animal. By the time she stepped into the familiar wood hall, she was ready to explode.

Salome stopped in the middle of the aisle of benches and looked around. The room that Salome had once occupied during leadership meetings was now empty. It once held proud memories of Salome's past, but they were now tainted with all that'd transpired the day Amina and Paxton walked into her life. That was the day she saw the flaws in their leadership and in the Hebrew's way of living. They were too unwelcoming, too exclusive. Salome didn't like it. That was part of the reason she willingly left to help Amina. She didn't believe in condemning anyone to die just because they weren't part of the "elite Hebrew culture."

A door opened at the front of the room and Salome watched

CHAPTER 7

as a tall, muscular man with dark olive skin and sun-bleached brown hair stepped out of the room. He wore a tan sleeveless shirt and loose linen shorts. As soon as he noticed Salome, he stopped and stared at her with hazel eyes. The fury drained out of Salome, and she questioned her motives. Only she couldn't turn back now. He spotted her.

"Salome, what a pleasure." Aryeh smirked as he walked closer.

Salome shifted uncomfortably, uncertain whether or not he was being sincere. Aryeh was always smug, and it made her cringe. "We need to talk," Salome said, trying to keep the lack of confidence out of her voice.

Aryeh motioned toward the back room. "By all means, please."

Salome couldn't put her finger on it, but there was something that made her uncomfortable with Aryeh. He had seemed unpredictable over the past year as if at any moment he'd snap.

"We can stay here."

"Suit yourself. What is it?" He leaned casually against a table and crossed his arms.

"Why are you sending people to spy on us?"

Aryeh's eyebrows raised. "Well, you don't beat around the bush, do you? Straight to the point. I've always liked that about you."

"That's not an answer."

"No, it's not, but it's all I have to say. I haven't sent anyone to spy on you. After our last interaction, I allowed the Notzrim to stay. I gave them land, a few supplies, and allowed those who were willing to share animals and food. My only request was that they stayed away and didn't converse with us. Why would I send a spy?"

Salome crossed her arms. He sounded certain and convincing it made Salome feel like a petty child. "I don't know. Maybe to check in and see how we're progressing, or to check in and make sure we're staying away."

"I couldn't care less how they're progressing. Their success doesn't concern me and it shouldn't be a concern to you either. You should be here with your people, where you belong."

"Their success *is* my concern since I live there. You banished me, remember?"

"I know I did, but I've had a change of heart. I realized that it was silly of me to banish you and your father to live with *those* people. You belong here with your people, your *real* family."

"You are *not* my family."

"Like it or not, we are bound together by Sabaoth. We are his people, a national heritage passed down since the time of Abraham. You were born a Hebrew. It's in your blood."

"Maybe, but it's only my nationality. I'm not sure it's my religion anymore."

"What do you mean? Have they converted you? Brainwashed you?"

"Brainwashed? Of course not. They've simply pointed out some very crucial things about Meshiakh, making me rethink if he truly is the messiah we've been waiting for and somehow missed centuries ago."

Aryeh threw his head back and walked in a circle. "Unbelievable. Don't you see? This is all the more reason why you need to come back home here where you belong. Their religion is confusing you."

"No, I think it's completing me." Salome shook her head as if brushing away the rising frustration. "Look, that's not why I'm here. I'm here to tell you to leave the Notzrim alone.

CHAPTER 7

You don't need to send your little spies or create any more dissension between the two people. If the Notzrim discover that you're keeping tabs on them, they will retaliate, and it'll make things worse. The best thing for all of us is peace. If anything, we should be working together to build a stronger community, not two separate communities."

"Oh please, if we combined forces, they'd drag us down. They don't know what they're doing over there, and no unified gathering is going to change that."

Her head drew back sharply as her eyebrows raised. "And how would you know? I thought you weren't keeping tabs on us."

Aryeh stumbled over his response. "I mean—of course, I don't *know*, but I can assume. And you just said you wanted us to work together."

Salome crossed her arms and stared at Aryeh for a moment. She wasn't buying it, but he was too stubborn to confess the truth. There was no point continuing to badger him.

"Just stop sending your spies and trust us." Salome turned and headed out of the hall. Her body shook, and she had to take slow deep breaths to return her heart rate back to normal. Not that Aryeh scared her, but she got flustered easily, and standing up to anyone was a challenge to her at times. She didn't like confrontation, but she was wise enough to know that sometimes it was necessary.

As Salome stepped out of the hall, she noticed her friend Eloina coming toward her.

Eloina saw her and stopped. Her long hair was pulled into a braid, revealing her stoic face. "Salome, I didn't expect to see you here."

"I needed to talk to Aryeh. He's been sending spies over to

keep tabs on the Notzrim."

A look of admission flashed in her eyes but was gone in an instant. "Can you blame him?"

Salome furrowed her brow. "I'm sorry what?"

"You bring these strangers into our home, those who aren't Hebrews, and expect us to be okay with it. The world out there is dangerous, and we don't know these people."

Salome's mouth dropped. She expected this from Aryeh, but not her best friend. "If you felt this way, why did you help in the beginning?"

"I didn't think Aryeh would let them stay."

"Eloina, they're not that different from us. The Notzrim offer something I've never experienced before with our religion. They're not about rules and regulation, they're about grace and faith."

"We're about faith. Abraham had faith, Moses had faith. But don't forget that it was non-Hebrews who throughout history have tried to annihilate us."

"And the same with the Notzrim. Throughout history, they too have been persecuted and rejected. Don't you see? We serve the same true God. It's just that they see Meshiakh as the Messiah while we still wait for ours. What if this Meshiakh is the real messiah? You should come with me Eloina and hear what they have to say and spend some time with them."

"I don't think so." Eloina put a hand on Salome's shoulder and looked her in the eyes. "Just be careful over there." Eloina climbed the steps and disappeared into the hall, leaving Salome alone.

Thoughts swirled through her mind, and it all felt so confusing. While on the one hand, she was certain this was where Sabaoth was leading her, now she started to doubt. She'd always had such firm beliefs in the Hebrew faith, in Sabaoth and the law he'd given them. Why was everything suddenly feeling jumbled? She wanted both. She wanted the beauty of her culture and traditions, but she loved the idea of Meshiakh and the acceptance he offered.

* * * *

Paxton sat in the laboratory, strapped to the same chair as before. Frank paced slowly in front of him, lecturing him about his behavior in the restaurant earlier. That Paxton couldn't stay put disappointed Frank.

"Although it's not surprising that you'd try to escape, that's why we had so many people ready for you. But I still held out hope for you. At least we still have you and now you're here again, and I have some good news. Our scientist friends here have been working day and night to fix the etymtorp. They've assured me that this time it will work on you." Frank narrowed his eyes at the two trembling scientists. "And it had better."

Paxton was relieved to hear the etymtorp didn't work the first time, he was even more apprehensive about today's experiment. These scientists worked in the capitol for a reason. They were good at what they did. They worked hard to keep their jobs, and failure was not in their vocabulary.

The scientists pulled Paxton's mouth open with their contraption, although he didn't fight it. He allowed Frank to put the drops in his mouth.

Soon, the same tingling sensation hit him and overwhelmed all his senses. It was much stronger than the last time and while he was ready to work at fighting off the etymtorp's power, he felt as if a metal claw was raking its way across his brain, scraping it open layer by layer.

Paxton screamed inaudibly as it dug deeper and deeper until it revealed a picture of the valley. Paxton had a bird's eye view of the valley that he and Amina traveled to. Then, that bird swooped down into the valley and gave an intimate view of the entire village. The open fields, the buildings, the cave, the river, and the waterfall. The bird sped along, following the river out of the valley and toward the direction of tunnels.

Paxton fought hard to block out the images. He couldn't let Frank see how to get to the valley. He had to stop it. Paxton worked on every strategy he knew to fight off the psychological drug, but nothing worked. The images grew brighter and clearer.

"No, please stop."

Paxton felt his mind growing weak. He was tired. As he lost control, the light grew brighter still, blinding him. Paxton thought his whole body was vibrating with electricity. Paxton's eyes rolled in the back of his head as the light blinded him again. The electric pain was so excruciating that Paxton thought his body was on fire. A white fiery flame burst from his chest, arms, and legs. Paxton tried to fight the image. Tried to refocus.

Through the white fire, Paxton saw golden laser beams shooting all around. Paxton's body went limp, as if falling. Falling into the light. He tried to look around but could see nothing but gold lasers and white fire. As he kept falling, he heard a voice. It sounded like Frank and yet softer and more calming. It asked him about his mission and why he defied orders. Then it asked him about how they found the new hiding place, and where Amina and her people were located.

Paxton's lips moved involuntarily as he pictured Amina's

CHAPTER 7

face, their time in the hospital together getting to know one another, the incident when she found out the truth about him, and how he convinced her to let him stay with her when he found her again in the mountains.

No, stop. You can't tell them. A voice commanded Paxton, breaking him from his vision. Paxton was back in a fiery white space. He looked around for the voice. Someone was in his head with him.

"Go on, Paxton. Tell me more about your time with Amina. It's okay." The smooth voice of Frank continued.

Paxton imagined Amina again when a violent crash deafened Paxton, breaking his thoughts. Looking around, he still couldn't find who this other person was in his head. In the distance, two figures fought. One was a glittering black, while the other was pure light.

Paxton watched as they wrestled and fought. He didn't understand what was happening or who they were, but eventually, the light overpowered the other being, shattering the glittering black being into a thousand pieces, sending shards of glass through the space and directly toward Paxton. When they hit Paxton, tiny sharp cuts pierced his entire body, and he cried out in agony. The light grew brighter as he cried until it exploded. Everything went black.

* * * *

When Paxton came to, he was back in his cell. A sharp pain split open in his head worse than before, and the darkness did nothing to relieve it. Paxton pressed the heels of his hands to his forehead, willing the headache to go away. And yet it persistently kicked back with a vengeance. Paxton winced as he tried to recall why a war raged in his head. A flash of memory came to him. An image of two figures, one of pure light and the other, a glittering black. They wrestled and fought with one another, but it made little sense. What did they have to do with him?

Then, Paxton remembered the etymtorp. He sighed. If he couldn't remember what happened, it likely meant he'd given in to the serum. Frank had gotten what he needed. Paxton yelled out into the darkness, his disappointment in himself echoing against the icy walls. How could he be so weak? He let everyone he cared for down. Their blood would now be on his hands. Hot tears surfaced and burned his eyes. He pounded his fist on the cement as hard as he could as he sniffled and held back the tears. *Failure. You don't deserve forgiveness for this. You belong in this hell.* The lies whispered like a snake slithering its way through his mind and deep into his heart.

Paxton lay still, letting the pitch black envelope him like a cold blanket. Allowing the lies to burn into his mind. He had nowhere to go now. No reason to leave.

You should just go back to your duty as a soldier. It was all you were ever good at. The lie taunted him.

An unfamiliar voice spoke, soothing and peaceful, and it told him a different story. *There's no proof they're gone yet. No proof that you failed.*

Paxton knew the voice was right, and yet, he was tired of fighting. It was just easier to believe the lie and succumb to the inevitable.

* * * *

Aiden's shoes squished in the mushy unidentifiable sewage as

CHAPTER 7

he moved through the tunnels. After weeks of silence, Mimi finally sent word about meeting. After getting Jared to agree to help if Aiden could find a way into the capitol, he'd grown more and more anxious. He'd spent endless nights wracking his brain with how to get in and out of the capitol safely, but with every new idea came new obstacles. He had concluded the only way they could do this was with Mimi's help. She'd promised to do so, but he hadn't heard from her. Not until earlier today. Finally, after nearly losing all hope of her helping, Aiden's cell phone went off with a text message: Stinkers, moonrise. Aiden knew it was Mimi wanting to meet.

Now, Aiden headed through the empty sewer tunnel toward the exit. Every so often he stopped and listened, making sure no one was following. When he reached the exit, Aiden peered at the security monitor to make sure there was no unwanted movement above ground. When he was confident the coast was clear, he climbed out of the sewer. It took him longer than he wanted to, to make his way across the open field to the highway and toward the convenience store. He had to stop every so often when the pain in his ribs became too much.

As Aiden approached the convenience store, a sound caught his attention. Aiden stopped and listened. Nothing. He moved again slowly. Then he heard it again, the scuffling of feet. Aiden whipped around behind him. No one. *You're just paranoid. There's no one there.*

Aiden crossed the highway making his way inside the store. Mimi was already there, standing in the back behind the shelves to hide from the windows. She wore her typical gray pants and zip-up jacket with her thick curly hair pulled back into a ponytail.

A smile tugged at the corner of her mouth, but then faded.

"You made it."

"Of course, I made it."

"And no one followed you." Aiden hesitated. "Aiden?"

"No one followed."

Mimi stared at him suspiciously.

"No one followed me."

Mimi kicked a large duffel bag at her feet. "This is for you and your people. It's food and water."

"Thank you. I know it must've been a lot for you to sneak this out." Aiden kneeled and looked inside the bag that was filled with fresh bread, fruit, jerky, and several MREs.

"You have no idea." Mimi crossed her arms. Something was wrong.

He slowly stood back up. "How have you been? When I didn't hear from you. . ."

"It's been rough, Aiden. Really rough. As soon as I came back, I was taken in for questioning. They cleared me, but I'm being watched like a hawk. There's constantly a Myriad soldier watching me at a distance. I know they said that I was no longer under suspicion, but it sure as hell doesn't feel like it. At the same time, all this is happening. I for sure thought I would've gotten in trouble for the plane crash and been fired or demoted, but nothing. It's like it didn't even happen. Which I guess is good since I'm helping you, but it makes me wonder. I don't want to lead them to you or get either of us killed."

"Sorry, Mimi." Aiden put a hand on Mimi's arm. "I don't want you getting hurt, either. I know this is dangerous, and you don't have to help if it's too much."

"I didn't say that. I just have to be careful and stay alert. Maybe even stay low for a while."

Aiden dropped his hand from her arm. "What do you mean,

CHAPTER 7

stay low? Like you can't help anymore? I thought you wanted to see them go down just as much as I did."

"Yes, but that was before. When I thought I was going to lose my job. I was caught up in the rush of it all, but now. . ." She stopped, trying to find words. "I don't want to get arrested or, worse, die. And with your mom constantly popping up—"

"Wait, you've talked with my mom?"

"Yeah, she's pretty certain I know what happened to you and where you are. She has no proof, of course, and I keep denying it, but whatever."

"Look, I know you're risking a lot, but Mi—I mean Ruth—"

"Don't call me Ruth."

"Fine, Mimi, don't you want to see justice for what they've done to millions of innocent people around the world? They can't keep getting away with this genocide."

"Of course, I do, but—"

"Then help me with this." He needed Mimi's help. It was the only way his plan would work. He couldn't fail. Teivel couldn't win. "If you don't, you're just like them." He instantly regretted his words, but it was too late.

Complete betrayal and anger washed over Mimi's face. "How dare you. You know very well that I am not like them. Sure, I went about my life ignorant of what they were doing and afraid for my own life, but most people are. Do I regret joining Validus Technologies? Maybe a little, but staying with them doesn't make me a murderer." Mimi held up her wrist. "They own me Aiden. Don't you get that? One little button and they could cut me off from everything or worse, kill me. There is no escaping them anymore. All I can do is comply and live. I already risked so much getting you and your sister and friends out of there for the first time. I don't know if I can do it again."

Aiden walked away, fuming. He wanted to punch something. Two steps forward, one step back. How was he ever going to complete this mission if he couldn't get into the capitol safely? He needed Mimi's help on this.

Aiden took a slow, deep breath before turning back to Mimi. "Please reconsider. I need you."

He placed his hands on her shoulders and pleaded with her. He needed her to know how important she was. "We'll make sure you get out of there safely. I have a friend who's great with technology. We can figure something out, I'm sure of it." He watched Mimi carefully, trying to read her face.

She didn't respond.

He lowered his hands and took a small step back. "At least think about it."

"Have you talked to your group yet?" Mimi bit her lip and crossed her arms.

"Kind of. I pitched the idea, but half of them were drunk. I don't think they took me seriously, but I got the leader to agree to help if I had a plan. But I only have a plan if I have you to help Mimi. This won't work without you."

A motor rumbled outside. Aiden and Mimi instinctively ducked, ensuring they couldn't be seen through the windows. Aiden pulled out his mylar emergency blanket and threw it over both of them in case the Myriad had an infrared drone flying overhead. They sat in silence, listening as the motor grew louder and then quiet again. Once Aiden was certain the car was gone, he waited even longer in case there was a second car dragging behind. Finally, he threw the blanket off of them and folded it back up. "Let's meet again in a week. It'll give more time for things to cool off at the capitol and for you to

CHAPTER 7

think about it."

"Aiden I—"

"Please. Meet here again in one week. At least give me that." He hoped she'd reconsider and come with information, but if not, Aiden would have an alternative plan ready to share with her in a week. He hoped, anyway.

Chapter 8

Amina made her way back to her cabin, slipped off her boots, and laid on her new small bed with a mattress filled with grass or hay of some sort that poked through the fabric and into her back. While it was softer than lying on the floor, it scratched at her skin, refusing to allow her any comfort.

As distracting as the sticks were, her mind was even more of a distraction from sleep. She lingered on the conversation with Salome, her distraction from something, and the itching feeling that Salome knew more than she was letting on. Surely Salome had her suspicions already. Salome was smart, but Amina couldn't understand why she didn't want to bring Amina into her confidence. Either way, Amina was not ready to give up. She'd keep an eye out herself and see if she couldn't come up with a plan to capture the culprit. No one was going to ruin her people's progress. *Sabaoth, show me what you want me to do. If there is something going on, show me. I want justice and I want everyone safe.*

Amina closed her eyes, trying to calm her mind with slow deep breathing, but the sticks poking her back were relentless. Giving up, Amina jumped out of bed and grabbed her hammock from her backpack. She examined the room, trying to find the best place to hang it. She looked up. Ceiling beams ran exposed and were sturdy enough to hang a hammock. After some finagling, she finally got the hammock to hang securely, and she hopped in.

Amina stared at the ceiling with her hands folded on her abdomen, slightly swaying like a baby in her mother's arms. Amina took slow, deep breaths, relaxing her body and mind. She didn't know when she fell asleep, but at some point, she woke to a soft but urgent-sounding voice coming from outside. She was still half asleep, but she could tell the voice was distressed. Amina tried to drift off again, telling herself it was nothing she needed to worry herself about, but then she recognized the voice.

Mo spoke, louder than before, "Emily, Emily, what's wrong, baby girl? What's hurting you? Paul, wake up. Something's wrong with Emily."

Amina gasped, and her heart quickened. She immediately flung herself out of her hammock, nearly falling onto the floor as it twisted and swayed beneath her. Barefoot, she dashed across the pathway and into Mo and Paul's cabin out of breath. Frantically, her eyes darted around the room, surveying her surroundings. There, inside, she found Mo sitting on Emily's bed with a wet cloth and a bucket. Emily was ghost white with strings of wet hair matted to her face.

"Is she sick?" Amina asked, rushing to Emily's side.

Mo looked abruptly, her eyes swollen with tears. "I think it's more than that."

Paul was out of bed and pulling a shirt over his head. "I can go get someone. Who do you need?"

"Go wake Vanita, tell her that Emily is feverish, dry heaving, headache, and stomach cramps. Her abdomen is hot to the touch and seems to be inflamed. She'll know what to get me from the medical ward."

"Got it." Paul kissed both Mo and Emily on the head. "I love you, baby girl. Daddy's gonna go get help."

"What can I do?" Amina asked. She knew little about sick people, but Mo was a nurse and knew enough. Amina would do whatever she asked.

"Get me another wet rag."

Amina rushed into action, grabbing a small rag and pouring some water from a jug. She soaked it and wrung it out into another open bowl that acted as their sink. She went and handed it to Mo. Mo gave her the old rag and pressed the new rag to Emily's forehead and neck. Emily moaned but said nothing. She kept her eyes closed and one hand clutched tightly to Mo's dress.

Amina stood a distance, bouncing on the balls of her feet while anxiously wringing the rag in her hand. She hated to see Emily this sick. As a baby, Emily would get sick a lot. She had a compromised immune system, so Mo and Paul always had to be extra careful with her. As Emily got older, her immune system strengthened and her bouts of sickness subsided significantly. Then, when they went underground, Emily seemed to never get sick. As if Sabaoth were protecting her health. If that were so, what was wrong with her now?

"Did she maybe get food poisoning or is it the flu?" Amina asked nervously. She didn't understand how Mo could be so calm.

"Not the flu. Her stomach is swollen and hot to my touch. That's not the flu. And I don't know how she would've gotten any poisoning—she eats the same things we do. Unless. . ." Mo stopped talking, but Amina knew she had to be thinking something. Maybe something far worse than she could bear to say in front of Emily. But Amina couldn't take not knowing.

"Unless what?"

Mo shook her head as if to shake the thought from her mind. "Nothing. It's probably just some new virus or bug from this area. Help me check her body." Mo lifted Emily into a seated position as Amina came to their side. Together they stripped Emily and scoured her body for any sort of bite marks, bumps, or poke marks. Other than a few scratches, she looked clean.

Mo put Emily's gown back on just as Emily leaned toward the bucket and dry heaved again. Nothing came out of her, but it was agonizing to listen to her. Her whole body convulsed as she attempted to expel what obviously did not want to come out.

Sabaoth, please help her. Heal her little body. She shouldn't have to go through this.

Amina sat at the edge of the bed and stroked Emily's back until the heaving fit stopped.

Emily laid back on her pillow, exhausted and crying. "Mommy, it hurts," she moaned weakly.

"I know, baby girl. We have some medicine coming soon. Just hold on."

An eternity passed before Paul and Vanita finally arrived with the supplies. Amina jumped up and crossed the room to Paul, leaving Vanita and Mo to do their thing.

"How are you doing?" Amina asked Paul, who was standing with one arm crossed over his stomach while he chewed on his fingernails.

"It's never good to see your little girl sick. I don't understand it. She hasn't been sick like this since she was one. She must've picked something up."

An hour passed before finally Emily seemed to calm down

and fall asleep. Whatever Vanita gave her was at least subduing Emily's symptoms, hopefully enough to allow her body to rest and heal on its own. While the Notzrim attempted to bring as much of their medical supplies and medicines with them as possible, they were limited. And they didn't have any of their equipment to perform large procedures if needed. Amina prayed it didn't come to that.

Mo and Vanita left Emily to her sleep and joined Paul and Amina, who were now sitting at the small table.

"She consumed something, I'm certain. While it may not be deadly in most people, it is toxic, and with her known history. . ." Vanita paused. She didn't have to say it, but they all knew. "Let's just keep a very close eye on her for the next twenty-four hours and go from there."

Vanita explained the medicines she'd brought over and how frequently to administer them. She gave instructions to check her temperature and the pressure on her abdomen every hour.

"Thank you, doctor, for your help," Mo said as she hugged Vanita.

"Of course. Mo, you're an excellent nurse with great instincts. Trust them."

Mo nodded and said goodbye before Vanita wandered back to her own cabin. That night Paul, Mo, and Amina took turns staying up to watch Emily and do their hourly checks on her.

It was a long and difficult night. Just when they thought Emily was getting better, she'd dry heave again, or get the chills so badly her whole body shook. There was no way Amina was leaving until she knew Emily was okay.

By late morning, Emily's temperature had gone down, and she was no longer dry heaving, but she was still weak and much too pale.

CHAPTER 8

"Do you think it passed?" Amina asked as she, Mo, and Paul ate flatbread smeared with freshly smashed raspberries and a side of salted pig jerky.

"It's hard to say," Mo spoke. "She's only been symptom-free for about an hour and a half. That's not long enough to know for sure, but it is a good sign." Mo took a bite of her flatbread and chewed as she stared at her sleeping daughter.

"Let's be sure to keep a close eye on her and continue to pray," Paul added.

"You know it's funny," Mo said. "Last night I had a dream. Probably my subconscious trying to figure out what's wrong with Emily. Anyway, I was back in nursing school, reading through a botany book, when I came across these particular symptoms. And, I think Emily has baneberry poisoning."

"How would she have gotten that?" Paul asked.

"It's possible we have baneberries growing in the area, and Emily and her friends ate them. I don't know."

Paul eyes narrowed as his mind processed the information before he spoke again. "Tomorrow, we need to do some investigating, find out if any of Emily's friends also got sick, or anyone in the village, for that matter. We also need to look for these berries. If they're poisonous, we need to get rid of them, and fast."

A sinking feeling washed over Amina as her heart rate sped up. Could it be that whatever Emily consumed wasn't by accident?

Paul hit the table with a hard bang of his fist as he stood up. He crossed to the window, and Amina was sure she heard him swear under his breath.

"Paul, honey, what is it?"

"The elders and I were just discussing our concerns about

what's been happening around the village."

"What's been happening?" Mo asked. "I thought everything was going so well."

"Mostly, yes, but there have been some very off-putting situations that I'm beginning to believe are more than just coincidences."

Mo's eyes went wide. "You think the Hebrews have something to do with this?"

Heat rose in Amina's face and her hands trembled. It was one thing when the sabotages were against animals and crops. It was a whole other issue when it started risking the lives of her family.

"We need to do something," Amina said.

The three of them pondered their situation. This was just as much their new home as it was the Hebrews. They had every right to be there, and they wouldn't allow anyone to scare them away, that was certain.

"Well, we can't cause any trouble with the Hebrews," Mo stated.

"They're the ones causing the trouble," Amina argued. "We need to defend ourselves and let them know we won't let them walk all over us."

"Of course not. Just be sure that when you do, it's done without causing a war," Mo retorted.

Amina crossed her arms. She had no intention of starting a war, but she also wanted the Notzrim to be firm and stand up for themselves. They needed to take drastic enough action to stop the Hebrews from thwarting their success.

"We don't even know for certain it was them."

Across the room, a small voice cracked, "Mama."

Mo jumped from her seat and rushed to Emily's side. "Yes,

baby girl, what is it?"

"I'm thirsty."

"Okay." Mo nodded. She grabbed the small cup of water from Emily's bedside and helped the young girl take small sips.

Emily coughed and gagged as she tried to drink. Most of the water seemed to end up on her blankets.

"I can't swallow," Emily cried. Tears poured down her face.

Mo pulled Emily tightly to her chest to soothe her. "You'll be okay, sweetie. This will pass."

Amina and Paul looked at one another with a knowing look. They needed to act fast before things got worse.

Chapter 9

There was no need to wait long. Later that morning, Matthias called an emergency elder meeting in his home. It was not the usual location for elder meetings, but as soon as Amina and Paul walked into the cabin, she understood why they were there. Matthias reclined on a pile of pillows on his bed. Beads of sweat dotted his forehead, ready to trickle down his ashen face at any moment. He looked over to Amina and Paul and nodded as if speaking took too much effort at that moment. The poison must've found Matthias as well.

Amina sat on a small round pillow in the middle of Matthias' cabin with the other elders. There were nine of them squeezed tightly into the small cabin only meant for four: six elders, Salome's father David, Salome, and Amina herself.

She sat quietly as the elders shared what information they knew about last night's mishap.

With Matthias being sick, the responsibility of leading the meeting fell to the second in command, Paul. "How many do we have in the medical ward?"

"I believe there are forty-six, most of which are the children," a woman with long gray hair, spoke. "Vanita and the others are caring for them and believe everyone will make a full recovery, but we must continue to pray for them."

CHAPTER 9

Paul agreed and led the prayer before moving forward with the meeting. They continued to discuss what else needed to be done and how to keep the people calm during this time.

"We don't want a riot or mass fear seeping through the village. Let's reassure people we're taking care of things and that this won't happen again."

"How *did* this happen?" Matthias asked.

At once, all eyes turned to Salome and her father, David.

"There are a lot of things that could've caused it," David answered calmly. "Do we know the source of the illness? Was it food, water, airborne?"

"While at the medical ward, I learned it was likely in the water," the long gray-haired woman shared.

"Thank you." David looked back at Matthias. "Then we can't know for certain what was in the water without proper testing and that's not possible here."

"I'm so sorry this happened. For now, everyone should boil their water thoroughly before drinking it," Salome said.

Amina flushed. *How could they be so calm about something so serious? Wasn't this proof that something more serious was at play in their village? Something that could be their demise if not stopped.*

"May I speak?" Amina said, trying not to sound annoyed. Matthias nodded for her to continue. "Thank you. Paul and I both have a growing concern about the various mishaps going on around the village. And I know Matthias does as well because it is he who first put the idea in my head." Amina paused, looking for reassurance to continue. What she got was a stony stare. "I just mean, I'm not the only one concerned. With so many people suddenly sick from the water, I am pretty certain that there is someone or a group of someone's who are purposely sabotaging our village. I don't know who yet or why, but I believe they're from the Hebrew village."

"That's quite the accusation," David spoke. His voice was calm, but with a hint of warning in it.

Amina knew to be careful about how she spoke. She'd made the mistake before of speaking too abrasively and it only caused more problems. "I know," Amina continued, "but there are some things that just can't be explained with natural occurrences." Amina glanced at Salome subtly, curious of her reaction. She sat silently; her lips pressed into a straight line as she stared at the wall across from her.

"And you think it's the Hebrews doing this?" David asked.

"Yes. Not all of them. Likely a small group who are still unhappy with our being here. And while I don't want to cause any wars against your people, we can't let it keep happening."

"Oh come now, we know who's doing this," an elderly man with a bald head, spoke, "it's that leader, Air-ay or however you say it. He never wanted us here in the first place, and he's making sure we know it."

"While part of that is true," Paul said, "Aryeh changed his mind and allowed us to stay. Not only that but he's given us supplies to help establish our village. Why would he then go behind our backs?"

The bald man blew out his cheeks. "I'd hardly call what he provided enough supplies to establish ourselves. We barely made our barn with what he gave us. Either way, he did it to give us false hope. To lure us into false security and then wipe us out. I don't know." He waved his hands in the air, flustered.

"I understand," David said, "that you have spent many years being hunted by the Myriad, but I can assure you that Aryeh is not like them. He just wants safety for his people like we do, and he wants to be left alone."

****

Salome sat listening to their arguments and accusations. Her heart quickened. She knew Aryeh was sending spies to keep tabs on the Notzrim. And while he was the most plausible choice for all the sabotages, that did not convince her he had a motive. Not yet anyway. If he felt threatened by the Notzrim, then maybe, but the Notzrim were keeping their distance and staying in their space.

"I agree with my father. I don't believe Aryeh has a good reason to do this," Salome said. "He wants us apart and as long as that stays the case, he's content. It would be foolish of him to do anything that might cause an uprising among the Notzrim and potentially a war of any sort."

"Well, someone's doing this and it's someone who doesn't want us here," the bald man argued.

Salome straightened in her seat. "What makes you think they're not natural occurrences?"

Amina jumped into the conversation again. "For one, everyone who got sick recently from the water. That was not a natural issue. Our water has been pure and drinkable for months. Now suddenly, it's bad? I don't think so. I think it was poisoned."

"It could be a dead animal in the water or bacteria." This was exactly what Salome didn't want to happen. The Notzrim turning against the Hebrews. The Hebrews had their flaws, but they were still her people.

"Amina is right," the long gray-haired woman spoke, "I had Maya test the water. It had traces of baneberry."

Amina raised her eyebrows at Salome as if to say, I told you so. "Then there are the pesticides that were switched out for concentrated salt water. And, while it's hard to prove, I think the same Hebrew group had something to do with the pigs' illnesses."

"So, what are you proposing?" a woman with a pointy nose and narrow face, asked. She looked pompous without even trying.

"We stop the Hebrews from being able to get in. Create a perimeter of guards or even a wall."

Salome's head snapped back over to Amina. How could she suggest such a thing? It was too extreme. Surely the elders wouldn't go for it.

Another elder, with round cheeks and even rounder eyes, spoke, "A wall is a bit severe and would take a lot of supplies and manpower. We still have several homes to finish."

"Then a night watch," Amina said. "I can help recruit people to patrol our perimeter at night to make sure we don't have any unwanted visitors."

The elders quietly thought over her idea for a long moment.

Salome wrung her hands anxiously. She needed to say something before this went too far. "While I'm all in favor of stopping these horrible things from continuing to happen." Salome swallowed hard. "I don't believe a wall is the right answer. We need peace and unity."

"Peace is a noble cause," the pointy-nosed woman said, "and eventually one I believe we should and can reach. But right now, I fear that may not be the swiftest course of action. I vote we work towards building a wall."

"Thank you for your thoughts," Paul said. He rubbed the back of his neck and tilted his head from side to side. "I love the idea of peace. It's important, and I know my wife is on your side with that as well, Salome. But I also want to respect Aryeh's conditions. I believe quietly looking for this vandal is the best course of action. I don't want to raise suspicion and fear among our people or cause any more dissension between us and the Hebrews."

"What difference does any of this make?" Matthias asked quietly.

"What do you mean?" Paul asked.

"I mean, how long do we expect to even be here? Have we forgotten that Meshiakh is coming back and we'll be going home to his kingdom?"

Salome perked up. While she didn't fully understand what Matthias was referring to, she hoped he was on her side about making peace.

"Of course not, Matthias, but we also want to ensure people are safe while we wait."

Matthias nodded. "Of course, but we can't lose sight of what's to come or how we are to live right now. The Sacred Writings teach that we live in unity, loving others with compassion. Are we doing that?"

The room fell silent as Matthias' words pervaded the tiny room, until they rested on the ears and minds of each person.

"A wall may be too drastic," Paul said, "but I'm not opposed to a perimeter watch. Do I have a second?"

"Second," the round-cheeked man agreed.

"All in favor?" Paul asked, looking around at the other elders.

Every hand went up.

Salome squeezed her eyes shut in defeat. If they started building defenses, the Hebrew mothers would surely get scared and stop coming. Then the plan she and Mo devised would crumble. The group outnumbered her, but she couldn't give up. She had to think.

Matthias dragged himself to a seated position on his bed. He looked weak and ashen. "We must call for a town hall right away." Matthias took a breath. "With this new poisoning, there will be a lot of talk and a lot of emotions. I want to get this under control." He took another slow breath and let it out. "Paul, you run it."

The grimace on Paul's face appeared as quickly as it disappeared before he said, "Yes, sir, I'll take care of it. Let's spread the word to have a meeting this evening after dinner and before the sun sets. We can also announce Salome as our board adviser."

* * * *

Amina watched as Salome stared at the floor, defeated. Her heart empathized with Salome. She understood Salome's desire for peace and unity, but someone was destroying that chance. They had to cut out the cancer before it spread.

"Amina, you're in charge of recruiting volunteers. Start with the former coalition. The idea is to patrol. Keep a vigilant watch. If they spot anyone, they are to stop that person and detain them if possible," Paul said.

"Anyone?" Hector asked. "Including Notzrim?"

"Yes. I want to enforce a curfew as well, just until we find this person. No one is allowed beyond the cabin neighborhoods after dark. We can't rule out anyone as a possible suspect right now."

Hector opened his mouth but then shut it again, keeping

CHAPTER 9

whatever objection he had to himself.

"Where will we put them?" Amina asked.

"There's a cave near the northeast area of the village. Also, be sure everyone is in pairs. That way, if they captured someone, one can guard them while the other comes to get me. Understood?"

"Yes, sir."

Paul moved on. The rest of the meeting they spent going over updates with the building, learning, and the general morale of people in the village. They discussed their needs and concerns with the medical ward and discovering more supplies and medicines. They discussed how many families still needed homes, and how the food in the storage barn was vastly undersupplied for the coming winter.

Amina admired these men and their dedication to the safety and well-being of the village. A twinge of embarrassment hit her as she thought back again to her prior meeting with them. She'd been so prideful before. It humbled her, knowing they'd let her come today. Maybe they'd eventually realize she'd make an excellent addition to their team more permanently.

Once the meeting adjourned, Paul and Amina headed over to check on Emily together. Salome joined as well.

"Salome," Paul spoke as they walked, "given the new situation, I don't think you should move forward with the unity gathering."

"What gathering?" Amina asked, looking between Paul and Salome.

"Some of the Hebrew women have been coming to Storytime. Mo had the idea of doing a unity dinner to help bring the Hebrews and the Notzrim together and show that we're stronger than one village."

"I agree with Paul. I don't think that's a good idea."

As they arrived, they found Mo sitting on a crate with her head leaning back on the cabin wall and her eyes closed. When she heard them approaching, she opened her eyes and smiled.

Salome waved at Mo and continued talking. "Given this new accusation against the Hebrews and this overreaction to the water issue, I feel that unity—"

Amina stopped in her tracks, nearly losing her footing. "Overreaction?" Amina snapped. She couldn't help herself. Salome was too calm about such dangerous issues happening in the village. "My niece is lying in a bed with a compromised immune system, and we don't know if she's going to survive because of something one of your people did. I wouldn't call this overreacting but being smart. We have to protect ourselves."

Salome's face softened. "Oh! I'm sorry I didn't know that about Emily. I pray she and all the others recover. I really do, but what I mean is that there are other things we can do besides shutting the Hebrews out. These Hebrew mothers bringing their children to the lessons of Father Stephen, I believe, are open to having a welcome lunch where we can start a positive relationship between our two villages. If Aryeh sees that, he'll be forced to soften to the idea as well."

"That's great and all, but now is not the time," Amina felt the heat rising in her face. She was reverting to the overprotective mode, wanting to control the situation, wanting to keep everyone safe. Joining up with the Hebrews while there's a wolf in their midst was dangerous.

"I'd argue it's the perfect time to do this," Mo said, joining the group. "We need to make everyone realize we're not so different from each other—that we are better together than

CHAPTER 9

we are separate. If we can do that, I believe it would make those who are out to get us rethink what they're doing."

"A little party is not going to solve this issue."

"Most things can't be solved in just one try, but it'll move the pin forward. We must step out in faith and trust the One who's in control of everything."

"What if I do some digging? Try to ask around and find out who might be doing this," Salome said. "Could we have our unity get-together then?"

Paul rubbed the back of his neck as he responded. "If you can find whoever's doing this and get them to actually confess it was them, then I don't see why not."

Amina was skeptical that Salome could do this on her own, given she wasn't even supposed to be going to the Hebrew village. At the same time, she wanted Salome to be successful. Whatever it would take to stop these things from happening was worth a try. Amina admired Salome and Mo's conviction to have this party. It was the ideal and best solution to their time in the valley, but at this moment it seemed impossible.

There was a long pause before Paul finally said, "Okay, you do what you can to find this person, but in the meantime, we are still going to set up a night guard around the village. We want Sabaoth's will done, and I believe he'd want unity among all of us as well. But if there's fear among our people, it won't happen."

"I have confidence in Salome. She'll find the person." Mo patted Salome on the back.

"No pressure." Salome gave a half smile.

"I'm going to move forward on the planning, then," Mo insisted.

Paul gave Mo a look. "That's not what we agreed on."

"No, but it's what I need. I need a distraction and I need something to look forward to. So I'm going to do this." Tears welled up in Mo's eyes and Paul pulled her in for a hug. "How's our baby girl?"

"Sleeping for now."

"I heard, Mo," Salome said, her expression changing to one of empathy. "I'm so sorry. I pray she gets better soon."

Salome hugged Mo as she responded, "You and me both."

"She's strong," Amina said, "and will pull through." She had to pull through. Amina couldn't lose someone else.

Chapter 10

Days passed, maybe even weeks. Paxton didn't keep count. And while the first several days of defeat enveloped him, the longer Frank ignored Paxton, the more curious Paxton became. If he'd given Frank what he wanted, wouldn't they have killed Paxton by now? And if they didn't get what he wanted, why weren't they still interrogating him? What was Frank waiting for? It was torture waiting and not knowing. At least give him some sort of answer. Let him know whether he'd caused the death of an entire faith group or not.

While the first few days Paxton did nothing but wallow, eventually, his own inability to feel lazy took over and he went back to his routine of working out and meditation. While he was meditating, he heard footsteps and the door open. Paxton turned his head to find Frank smugly standing in the doorway.

"Put your boots back on and come with me," Frank said before turning and heading back down the hallway.

Paxton stood and followed. This was it. He was finally going to learn what Frank knew. He was finally going to find out if today was, in fact, his last day on earth. No matter what he learned, however, Paxton would not go down without a fight.

"You must be curious what the results of our last experiment were."

"I'm not sure you'd call it curiosity."

"Well then, I have good news."

"For who?"

They walked through the lobby and out to a nearby golf cart. Once again, they headed out to the airstrip. The entire way there, Paxton's mind reeled. Frank shared no more information, and it drove Paxton crazy. The only thing he could think of was the fact that the scientists got the etymtorp to work and that he'd shared the location of Amina and the Notzrim. What else could it be? Without Paxton's intel, it was near impossible for the Myriad to find the Notzrim. And while Paxton's mind was sharp, there was only so much one could take from mental torture. Or maybe it's good news for Paxton. Maybe they haven't found the Notzrim location. But then why were they heading to the airstrip?

The golf cart pulled up again to the hangar, whose door was open, and the plane was being prepped for flight. Paxton took a deep breath, trying to calm his nerve. *Sabaoth, I don't know if you'll listen to me, but I am so sorry. Protect your people.*

Frank led Paxton to the back of the hangar and toward the command center.

"Are we all set?" Frank asked Gwyneth.

"Just about, Captain. We're doing our final safety checks and then we'll need to input the final coordinates." Gwyneth pointed toward a large screen. "As you'll see here, we have the drone hovering over the area now."

Paxton moved toward the screen and tried to keep a straight face. His worst nightmare was coming to fruition right in front of his face. Slowly, as if in a trance, Paxton moved toward the screen to get a closer look. The drone's camera showed an aerial view of the mountains. Paxton's heart sped up,

CHAPTER 10

drumming in his ears. He was certain where in the mountains it was. He swallowed hard, his mouth dry as the desert. His eyes scanned every inch of the screen for any clue that could tell him this was not the right place.

In the center of the camera was a valley. Heat rose to Paxton's face. He kept looking. He saw a tall cliff that had once been a waterfall, but now nothing fell. Large boulders mixed with dilapidated skeleton trees filled the area like trash after a festival. A flood of relief washed over Paxton. Wherever that drone was, it wasn't Amina's valley. A smile tugged at the corner of his lip, but he fought hard to keep a straight face.

Paxton glanced at Gwyneth. She looked back at him with an expression of pity mixed with, "I told you so." Paxton gritted his teeth but said nothing. He needed them to believe that he thought they were in the right location. If he could pull that off, maybe they'd stop looking so hard and Amina and the others would be safe for good.

A static white noise come over the speaker and a voice spoke. "We're over the area and have locked in on the target. Your orders?"

Gwyneth gave Paxton one last look before she leaned toward the radio and clicked a button. "You're cleared to drop."

There on the screen, a tiny black dot dropped, followed by a gigantic explosion that spread miles across the mountain terrain. A plume of smoke blotted the view of the fire and the mountains. The black smoke of death.

All his training as an undercover police officer, and all those years of playing spy in the Notzrim hideouts, now needed to be used to protect the ones he cared for. Paxton looked away from the screen, clenching his jaw. He thought of the day he left Amina behind and how it felt, hoping that would produce the right feelings for this moment. His eyes stung as tears fought to the surface. He held them back, but one slipped out and trickled down his check.

Frank turned to Paxton and smirked. "Thank you for your assistance in this mission. You will be rewarded despite your resistance. This is a big win for us."

Paxton cleared his throat. "I don't want your blood money."

"Oh, I didn't say anything about money. You'll be rewarded with your life. You see, Paxton, I'm not going to kill you. I'm going to put you back in to serve again. You're going to live out your days working for the Myriad and living with the torment and grief of knowing what you did." Frank turned away and went over to another commanding officer.

Perfect. Paxton was safe. Now he could work on a plan of escape.

A gentle hand squeezed Paxton's shoulder as a soft voice whispered into his ear. "It was for the best Paxton." Paxton didn't look at Gwyneth. "Even so, I'm sorry. And if you ever need comfort, you know where to find me." Gwyneth slipped a piece of paper into Paxton's pocket before walking away.

Frank drove Paxton over to the military dormitory and led him to his new, tiny room. While it wasn't much larger than the cell he'd lived in for the past month or so, it had a bed and a bathroom. With no longer being confined to a cell, Frank was practically handing Paxton an escape plan.

"You report at 0600. You're still on a probationary watch, so another soldier will be by to escort you."

"If I'm still a prisoner, you might as well put me back in my cell," Paxton droned, still playing his role.

"Don't smart mouth me, soldier. I can make your life a living hell."

CHAPTER 10

"It already is, so what more can you do to me?"

Frank stepped forward, getting into Paxton's face. Paxton refused to back away as he stared him down, daring him to do something.

"Don't test me soldier or you *will* regret it. I'll make sure of that." They locked eyes for a while longer. Frank, ensured Paxton knew he was serious before he turned away and left. The door locked behind him.

* * * *

The training room was in more of a frenzy today than ever. Aiden wandered into the training sector, and toward the large crowd gathered near the center. There, the returned team regaled everyone with their adventure.

"It was one of the smoothest missions we've ever experienced," one woman said, beaming with pride. "It shocked me, but I thank Sabaoth we could deliver supplies to this group. They were thankful to us and enjoyed our company. It was a very small group of eighty."

"Why so small?" someone asked.

"They survived a Myriad raid a year back."

The group was quiet for a moment, letting the gravity of that comment sink in. Aiden silently fumed. *This can't keep happening.*

The woman continued sharing about their time there and their return home. Just as she wrapped up her tale, Evan barged in and broke the group up.

"Alright, everyone. I know we're glad they're back, but we have training to do. There's already another mission to prepare for, and Jared and Terrance have asked me to pick the new crew. So today, we're going to do some tests."

Several in the crowd cheered while a few groaned.

"Hey, you don't want to be a part of something great. Fine by me. You can leave anytime. But those who want to be here follow me."

No one stayed behind. Reluctant or not, no one wanted to appear uncommitted to the cause.

Aiden meandered through the group and toward Evan. He wanted to speak with Terrance and Jared today. After taking several days to work out a plan, he finally had something that looked promising, so long as he still had Mimi to help.

"Hey Evan, where are Jared and Terrance? I need to talk to them."

"They're busy, kid." Evan stopped and made everyone form a circle around the fighting mat. Evan pointed to a man six foot wearing loose shorts and a sleeveless black shirt to show off his muscular arms. He eyed Aiden. "You're up first."

Wide-eyed, Aiden looked at his opponent and then back to Evan. "I thought you said I wasn't ready. That I needed to get cleared first."

"You want to be on this mission, right?"

"Well, I mean—"

"Look, not everyone you fight will be your size, so get over it and get in there."

Aiden looked back at the guy who was several inches taller than him and clearly more skilled. He took off his maroon sweatshirt and put on his sparring gloves.

The opponent stuck his large hand out, and they shook before starting. Aiden planted himself and watched carefully as his opponent moved about. Wisps of blond hair blocked his eyes, but Aiden kept eye contact, waiting as they silently challenged one another to take the first shot. Patiently, Aiden waited it out. The last three days of PT had left him sore but feeling stronger at the same time. However, this guy was bigger and stronger than Aiden. It wasn't a good match.

With a quick lunge forward, the other guy took the first swing. Aiden ducked, but just as he came back up, a fist landed on Aiden's jawbone. It stung. A second blow came quick and hard to his stomach, knocking the wind out of him. He doubled over but had to react quickly so as not to lose this fight. Aiden kicked his leg out and swept the guy's feet out from under him, bringing him to the ground. Aiden scrambled, but not fast enough. His opponent rolled onto his stomach and popped back up like a spring. They continued to spar, each getting a few hits in here and there, but when Aiden took a blow to his ribs, pain exploded through his body. Black specks blotted his vision as he stumbled. The other guy saw his chance and took Aiden down and pinned him. Aiden didn't even try to fight back. The pain paralyzed him.

Evan praised the winner as he climbed off Aiden.

Aiden continued to lie on his back, wincing at every slight breath he took. Evan held his hand out. Aiden took his hand and allowed Evan to pull him up, but before Aiden could let go, Evan gripped Aiden's hand harder and flipped it over, revealing the tattooed barcode. Evan's expression switched instantly from friendly to enraged. "What is that?"

"It's nothing. Just a tattoo they forced me to get." Aiden had completely forgotten about covering his tattoo. He'd been so good at wearing a sweatband around it all these weeks, but today he must've forgotten.

"You mean it's the mark? You took the mark."

"No!" Aiden pulled his arm away. "I told you when they

took me captive, they forced me to live there as if I were one of them. They put a tracker in me, and they gave me the tattoo, but they didn't implant me, and they didn't force me to take the vow. It's just ink. Nothing more."

All eyes were on him, and he could feel them searing into him, judging him. Did they believe him? The tattoo was pretty incriminating. And yet, he'd lived in the tunnels with the Notzrim for years. They knew him; they knew his loyalty to Sabaoth and to them.

"I know what you told everyone, but can I believe it? How do I know you're not lying?"

"I have no reason to lie to you. Why would I escape and come straight here?"

"Because you're a spy, just like that Paxton guy."

"You're paranoid, Evan. I'm on your side." Aiden walked away, uninterested in continuing the argument. He'd been home for six weeks. Why was Evan so resistant to him now?

"I saw you with that woman, one of them," Evan called after Aiden.

Aiden stopped and thought for a moment. How could he have seen? Aiden thought he'd been so careful.

"You snuck out the other night to meet up with some woman at the convenience store. I saw you. Were you giving her intel so the Myriad could come after us?"

Aiden closed his eyes. He remembered the sound of shuffling feet. So, he hadn't been paranoid after all.

"Come on Evan, that can't be true. Aiden would never do that," Tessa said.

"But he did. I saw it. They turned him."

Aiden looked at Tessa, grateful for being on his side. She looked back, hesitantly. "Is it true?"

CHAPTER 10

"It's true I met with someone I know from the capitol, but it's not what you think. She's the one who—"

"See, he just admitted to meeting with the enemy. He's not on our side."

Before he knew what he was doing, Aiden turned to Evan and shoved him. "What is your problem with me, huh, Evan? I'm here to help."

"My problem is you thinking you can waltz back into this group as if nothing happened. As if we didn't lose good people on that raid or our entire community wasn't forced to leave. I can't help but think that somehow you had something to do with it."

Aiden's mind flashed to that night. The attack. The gunfire. Seth's dead body. He swallowed hard. "I'm well aware of how much we lost that night, but Evan, you're being ridiculous," he said, keeping his voice even-keeled. "I'm leaving Evan. You can stay away from me."

The group parted to let Aiden through as he headed out of the sector. Now he really needed to find Jared and Terrance before Evan went and filled their heads with doubt. Two hands grabbed his arms and put him in handcuffs.

"We're going to Jared and Terrance to sort this out."

"Evan, I told you, I didn't turn. That woman is on our side."

Evan pushed Aiden toward the tunnels. "We can let them decide that."

They entered the coalition office. The office was small and dull. Cement walls, metal desks, and chairs lined up in rows around the open space. Toward the back were two smaller offices and an interrogation room. The place had once been a bunker, long abandoned and then reoccupied when the Notzrim came to inhabit the tunnels nine years ago. No one knew why the bunker existed or how long it'd been there, but it proved to be beneficial to the Notzrim.

Now the prior law enforcement office was Jared and Terrance's own militia headquarters. The two of them hovered over a table with a large map on it. They seemed to argue about something, but stopped when they noticed Aiden and Evan.

"What's this all about?" Terrance asked. "Take those off him." Terrance pointed at the handcuffs.

"Apparently, he doesn't believe why I'm back," Aiden snapped.

"I have good reason." Evan shot back. He took the handcuffs off. "Go on, show them."

Aiden cringed. How could he have been so careless? And today of all days. He'd avoided showing anyone the tattoo markings to this point, but now he had no choice.

"Show us what?" Jared asked, looking annoyed at the interruption.

"This is ridiculous. This proves nothing." Aiden turned his wrist up to let Jared and Terrance see the tattoo.

Before they could even respond, Evan spat out. "Aiden is no longer on our side. He's a traitor."

Aiden gritted his teeth. "A silly tattoo proves nothing. I still have the mark of Meshiakh. That was what you should believe." Aiden held up his other forearm to show the incandescent cross glowing from his skin.

"Why do you have that?" Jared asked.

Aiden put both arms down. "They took me captive and forced it on me. It's just ink. That's it. It means nothing."

"But you were in the prison the whole time, right?" Jared mulled over his own words. "Why would you need a barcode tattoo unless you were trying to fit in?"

CHAPTER 10

Aiden chose his words carefully, trying not to make the situation worse than it already was. "They tried to turn me. They wanted me to work for them, but I refused. My beaten body proves that. I thought if I told you, you'd think what Evan thinks."

"Of course, we don't." Terrance slapped Aiden on the back. "Is it a little suspicious? Sure. Are we pissed you didn't tell us sooner? Absolutely. But we still believe you. I can't even imagine the kind of trash you had to go through while you were in the beast's belly. I'm just glad you made it out alive."

"This is unbelievable," Evan snapped.

"No, Evan," Jared barked. "What's unbelievable is you thinking that someone as loyal and dedicated to Meshiakh as Aiden here would flip sides."

"What about the secret meeting he had?" Terrance and Jared both looked at Aiden while Evan continued, "Someone tipped off the Myriad about that raid. After seeing Aiden taken and then his secret meeting the other night, what else am I supposed to think?"

This was not exactly how he wanted to share his news about Mimi, but here went nothing.

"My secret meeting was with someone I met in the capitol who is on our side. She's the one who helped me escape, and she's going to help us get back in."

Jared stepped away from the desk he was leaning on, his arms still crossed, and his eyes furrowed. "You figured out how to get us in?"

"I spent time in the capitol. They store dozens of military planes, weapons, and intel. We blow that place up, we significantly weaken their defenses."

"You're a crazy bat," Terrance said. "But I like it."

"No way," Jared said gruffly.

"You said as the party that if I found a way in, you'd help with the plan."

"I was drunk. You can't take anything I say seriously when I'm like that. No way, it's too risky."

Aiden knew it was a risk taking Jared's word that night at the party, but he had to keep pressing. He couldn't give up. "Everything we do is risky. Our existence is risky. Why not take that risk and do something good with it?"

"We are doing good."

"Not enough. You're playing it safe. Look, the wheels are already turning. My meeting was to discuss how to get us in. Once we're in, it's up to us to get the job done. I'm confident we can do this." Aiden prayed Mimi wouldn't make a liar out of him.

"We'll need blueprints."

"She's bringing them next time we meet."

"And we'll need our crew to work on the right type of explosives with either detonators or a timer."

"Preferably a detonator in case things go sideways you don't have control with a timer," Terrance suggested.

"Good. Yes."

"So, you're in?" Aiden asked hopefully.

"Not even close. I don't know this woman you seem to so blindly trust. I also don't know how big this place is, but I assume it's large, and we likely don't have enough materials to make enough explosives. Not to mention it's a suicide mission and I'm not interested in that."

"But I've got it figured out. I can—"

"I'm not interested. So, why don't we focus on some good we can do rather than a suicide mission? There's a Notzrim group about fifty miles southeast of here that needs help to set up their communications system. I'd like you to go on that mission and help them. Without it, they're completely isolated and we can't get them the necessary assistance."

"We could be of even more help to these groups if we stopped the capitol from hunting them down altogether."

"Drop it, Aiden. It's not going to happen. Now, are you in on this mission or not? Otherwise I'll have to send Mitchum, but he's not in great shape."

The longer they waited to take down the capitol the higher the risk of more Notzrim being found and killed, but what other choice did he have? "How long will it take?"

"Why, you got a hot date later?" Terrance jabbed Aiden with his elbow as he playfully winked at him.

"No," Aiden sneered. Sometimes Terrance could be so obnoxious. "I'm supposed to meet up with Mimi again in five days. I can't miss my meeting."

"Cancel it. There's no need to meet with her if we're not breaking into the capitol," Jared insisted. His eyes narrowed, and he crossed his arms.

"Fine. When do we leave?" Aiden gritted his teeth. He wasn't giving up on his plan, but if he had to go on a few missions to get Jared on his side, he would.

"Tonight. We have a team meeting in an hour to finalize the plan."

Chapter 11

After a conversation with the Hebrew village's local gossip, Salome discovered a man named Hamman was her biggest suspect. She didn't know him well, but she knew who he was.

Trying to find Hamman, however, was difficult. Salome had to sneak around the village, hiding every time someone drew near, while also keeping an ear out for clues that would help her find Hamman. She knew he was likely with the sheep, but when she found the herd, he was nowhere in sight. She wandered to the shearing shed, but still no Hamman. After wandering around the barns and other animal pens, she gave up and headed toward Hamman's home. The more she looked and couldn't find him, the more she convinced herself he was up to no good.

By the time Salome tracked down Hamman, the sun was beyond its peak and descending behind the cliff. There was a lot of daylight left before Salome would struggle to see clearly. Although, it may also be the perfect time to discover Hamman's next plan. Evil deeds are often seduced by the night.

He was, in fact, sick at home. At least he appeared to be sick as he lay in bed with a cold rag over his head and the covers pulled to his chin. His wife stood over the stove stirring a pot.

CHAPTER 11

The smell of beef and barley stew wafted over to Salome and her stomach gurgled, but she ignored it. She was too close to Hamman to give up now, just to satisfy the pangs of hunger.

For the next hour, she crouched, watching the wife make dinner, their young daughter play with her dolls, and Hamman sleep. Eventually, the wife and daughter ate. Then, as the little girl got ready for bed, the wife went to Hamman's side and fed him soup. There was very little conversation and nothing of any significance.

Salome glanced at the sky. She was afraid she'd have to abandon her post to get over to the town hall meeting. Maybe Salome could leave. The more Salome watched, the more it convinced her that Hamman had been sick for a while, proving the opposite of what she wanted. He couldn't possibly be the culprit.

The wife set the bowl on the small nightstand and kissed Hamman on the forehead. "When will you be able to go back to work, my love? It's been several nights, and I know the men miss you during the night shift."

Hamman cleared his throat. "I think by tomorrow. I am feeling a bit better."

"Good. Here, drink some more water." She handed him a clay cup as he sat up to drink. "People were starting to wonder if—"

Salome didn't hear the rest. Someone grabbed the back of her shirt and pulled her away. Salome silently fought the attacker off as they continued to pull her several yards away from Hamman's house. When the attacker let go, Salome spun around and found a red-faced Eloina scowling at her.

"What do you think you're doing here?" Eloina hissed.

"That's none of your concern," Salome snapped back. All

the pain from their last conversation bubbled up inside her and wanted to burst.

"You're in my village spying on one of my citizens. Therefore, it's my concern. What issue do you have with Hamman?" She stood tall like a soldier and showed no empathy for Salome.

Salome crossed her arms. "I don't need to tell you that."

Eloina stepped closer, challenging Salome. Everything, from the way she spoke to the way she stood, intimidated Salome. "And I don't need to tell you what would happen if I turned you in."

"You wouldn't."

Eloina stepped away and paced, letting her guard down slightly. "Salome, you are making things very difficult for me. First, you talk of wanting peace and bringing our villages together in some big gathering. Then you talk—"

"Wait, how do you know about that?" Salome, looked Eloina in the eyes, fearful of the answer.

Eloina sighed. She didn't have to answer. The look on her face told Salome everything. She was the spy. Salome closed her eyes and turned around in a circle, completely beside herself.

"What am I supposed to do here? I don't want to see you get hurt."

"Too late for that."

Eloina stopped and stared at Salome with an apology in her eyes. "I'm only trying to look out for you and the interest of both villages. No one's ready for what you want."

"I think they are. Maybe not everyone, but many are." Salome took this as an opportunity to open up to Eloina again. She knew it was a risk, but she wasn't ready to believe that Eloina would completely betray her. "I think someone has been purposefully sabotaging the Notzrim. A lot of unusual things have occurred."

"A lot of strange things happened to us too, when we first started out."

Salome shook her head. "This is different. Pesticides were switched, and the well was poisoned. Those don't happen on their own."

"Why are you so quick to believe it's one of our people? Couldn't there be a disgruntled Notzrim who wants everyone to leave?"

"I have my sources. It's someone in this village."

Eloina motioned toward Hamman's cabin. "You mean Hamman? You think he's been doing this? He's been sick for the last week. It's not possible."

"Then he has a partner. I have good reason to think it's him."

"And what of your peace-making ideas? Not sure how spying on us fits into that."

"If I can find and stop whoever is doing this, then peace will be possible because the Notzrim won't be so scared anymore. You know how one rotten apple can spoil the whole barrel."

"Maybe, but I'm telling you, it's not Hamman."

There was a door creak and scuffling of feet in the distance. Eloina and Salome ducked behind a group of large rocks. Salome peered around the rocks to see who was out there. As she looked, she saw Hamman leaving his cabin and heading toward the edge of the village. Salome looked at Eloina, whose eyes showed just as much surprise and confusion as Salome's. "You were saying?"

"That only proves he's no longer sick."

"And lying about it. I just heard him talk to his wife about still not feeling well. That he needed another day to recover. Clearly, that was a lie and I'm going to find out what he's up to." Salome stood and headed in Hamman's direction. She didn't want to lose him. She needed to know what was happening. Salome partly expected Eloina to stop her, but she didn't.

It didn't take Salome long to track Hamman and follow him at a safe distance through the clusters of cabins. Unlike the Notzrim village, where their cabins sat in rows, the Hebrew village created circular clusters of cabins for each of the different family sets. As Hamman weaved in and out, Salome continued to follow until he came to a cabin and stopped. Salome crouched behind a crate of vegetables and watched. Hamman looked around anxiously before knocking on the door. Salome was right, he was working with someone.

The door opened, and a woman poked her head out. She smiled slyly, checking her surroundings before pulling Hamman into her cabin eagerly. Salome's body tensed and her blood boiled. Hamman wasn't who she was looking for. He was just a disgusting liar and a cheat. It took everything within her not to charge into that cabin and put them both to shame. Hamman's actions hit too close to home, and she couldn't take it. Salome stood and headed back toward Hamman's cabin.

Standing at the door, hand raised, Salome was ready to knock and let the wife know everything she saw. But her fist froze. No, it wasn't her place to tell Marjorie, not to mention the risk she took if seen in the Hebrew village.

Instead, Salome pounded hard on the door just long enough to hear a voice mumble, "just a minute." That was Salome's cue to sprint away and hide. Maybe the discovery of her missing husband would be enough to spark suspicion.

CHAPTER 11

* * * *

The small amphitheater at the center of town filled with curious faces. Amina, Josiah, and Maya sat together in the front row. Despite knowing what the meeting would be about, Amina was anxious. Anxious for the other Notzrim's reactions, along with their acceptance of Salome. Throughout the day, Amina spent her time recruiting others to join her watch team. She went to Josiah and Maya first, and they agreed immediately. By the time the meeting rolled around, Amina had found eleven other people to help. It wasn't as many as she'd like, but it was a good start.

Amina watched her uncle standing on the stage, bouncing on his heels as he nervously looked around. Keeping still was not his strong suit. The other elders sat on a bench on the side of the stage. All except Salome.

After their conversation earlier, Salome was eager to start looking for a potential suspect, but she wouldn't miss a town hall for that. This was too important.

Paul held a hand in the air as a sign that he wanted to begin.

It didn't take long for everyone to stop talking and focus on Paul. The news of poisoned water spread quickly, and everyone was impatient to hear what the elders had planned. "Thank you for coming. I know everyone has a lot to do and a lot on their mind this evening. Let us pray and then I'll begin." Paul bowed his head as he let out a heavy breath and then prayed.

When he finished, there was a resounding "Amen" from the crowd.

Paul looked at the crowd. "Before we get to the pressing matter at hand, I want to announce some good news. After much prayer and consideration, we are excited to let you know that Salome, our Hebrew friend, and mentor, has taken on a more official role as the elder board's Hebrew Advisor. Her wisdom and dedication to our people has been evident over these past weeks, and we respect her input in our endeavors as we continue to build a new life here."

Paul paused, anticipating a reaction. At first, only a few mumbles of opinion seeped through the crowd, but then the applause began. Slow and quiet at first, but then swelled as more joined in until it died out again like a crashing wave.

"Thank you for the support. The elders and I are certain that her knowledge of the valley and the Hebrew people will be invaluable.

"Moving on, to the families and people who got sick this morning, I pray that you and your loved ones heal quickly. Thankfully, everyone should make a full recovery, but nonetheless, I know it has put a hardship on all affected. We tested the water and we discovered traces of a very toxic berry called baneberry."

Quiet whispers and gasps rose from the crowd.

"We've disposed of all the baneberry bushes in the area, and the well is being purified. We should have it back and usable again in a few days."

More chatter came from the crowd. A lot of "I knew it" and "I told you something was wrong" were being whispered.

Someone voiced loudly, "How did this happen?"

"Thank you for asking. I know everyone is concerned about this." Paul took a deep breath. He scanned the area one more time as if looking for someone before he continued. "We believe it happened on purpose. By someone who doesn't want us here."

A cacophony of opinions and outrage burst from the crowd.

CHAPTER 11

Accusations, questions, and suggestions flew in every direction from every person. The sound rose into a roar that Paul struggled to get under control.

Paul placed an animal horn to his lips and blew. A deep but loud noise sounded from the horn for as long as Paul could blow.

Slowly, the crowd quieted down.

"I know this is distressing news, but we as an elder board wanted to tell you this and to reassure you we are doing everything we can to stop this. The first step is to set up a watch team to help guard our perimeter at night. Having a constant presence around the village will hinder whoever is doing this from being able to move about freely at night. We find and stop whoever is doing this."

"We all know who's doing it!" A woman shouted from the crowd. "Those nasty Hebrew people."

"Probably even Salome and David!" another shouted from the crowd.

Amina spun around, snarling at the crowd. Who would dare say such a thing?

"Come now. I understand you're afraid, but Salome and David have done nothing but help us. They are on our side."

"If that's the case, where is she?" The first woman shouted again. Amina still couldn't find the face to match the voice.

Amina stood, unable to contain herself. "She's out looking for the person doing this. Salome wants it to stop, just like the rest of us."

"I doubt that." Amina spotted the woman in the middle of the crowd. It was a short woman with deep blue eyes and fiery red hair. She crossed her arms. "She's probably out there hiding, planning her next move."

"You know you can leave anytime you want. You don't have to stay here."

"Enough. Amina, sit down!" Paul scolded from the stage.

Amina cheeks flushed as she turned to look at Paul. He glared at her sternly. She was only trying to help. Amina jumped down and sat.

"Now, as I was saying, we are setting up watch around the perimeter. If you'd like to join the team, you can speak with Amina. The more eyes we have, the faster we can find the culprit."

"We should send those Hebrews a message that we won't tolerate their childish schemes." A man argued back.

Several others from the crowd shouted in agreement.

"Violence and retaliation are not the answer! We must live in peace here, show kindness to all, even if they are our enemies, as Sabaoth has taught us."

"Forget that!"

Paul drew in a sharp breath as he combed his hand through his hair. Amina stood, wanting to help. He was flustered, and no one seemed to care. None of the elders came to his side. Paul and Amina made eye contact, and he shook his head no. Why wouldn't he let her help? Just because she wasn't an elder didn't mean she couldn't be useful.

"Have you truly forgotten what Sabaoth teaches about loving our enemies despite what they've done? The only way we ever survived in the tunnels all those years was because you all trusted the wisdom of the leadership along with trusting in Sabaoth. We worked together and committed to living in peace no matter what and that needs to happen now. We cannot start violence and distrust. It'll only make things worse."

"Except those Hebrews never wanted us here in the first

place," The short woman shouted back.

Amina fumed. Her hands clenched into tiny fists, and she was ready to jump on that stage and defend her uncle. Before she could, a large hand snatched her forearm. Josiah warned her silently to stay put.

"True, there is someone out there who doesn't want us here. They want us to run like cowards. But we're not cowards." A small affirmation rose from the crowd. "We're also not brutes. Let's not forget who we serve and how he's protected us all these years. Remain faithful to him in your conduct. Let's work together like we always have and stop this rotten apple."

The crowd was quiet for a moment, silently mulling over Paul's words.

Josiah and Maya started clapping and cheering loudly in hopes to bolster the rest of the crowd. It worked. Slowly, those around Amina clapped and shouted their affirmations until it spread across the entire crowd like a tidal wave.

"Good. Now, I am also putting in place a curfew in order to keep anyone from unnecessary suspicion. No one, unless on guard, is allowed beyond their cabin's neighborhood after dark. Pray for peace, pray for justice, and pray that Meshiakh comes quickly. Meeting adjourned."

* * * *

Salome sprinted back to the Notzrim's village in hopes she'd make it to the meeting in time, but she didn't. When she arrived there, only a few people lingered around the amphitheater while Paul and two elders stood on the stage chatting. Salome groaned, instantly feeling the disappointment. She didn't mean to miss the meeting, but watching Hamman was important. Or so she'd thought.

As Salome approached the stage, she felt as if people were staring at her, judging her. When she glanced at the small group still sitting in the amphitheater, a couple of them scowled and she could've sworn she heard the word "rat" whispered. Salome shook it off.

When she approached the stage, Paul looked over at her. "Salome, where were you? Are you alright?"

"I thought I had a lead. It didn't pan out."

"That's too bad, but I really wish you'd been here. It kinda looks bad when we announce a new position in our community and that person isn't there."

"I was doing important work, honest. I tried to get here in time."

The other elders stared, silently reprimanding her. Didn't they want her to find the culprit? Why were they all so upset about this?

"How'd the meeting go?" Salome asked.

"Not as I'd hoped. People were pretty up in arms when they heard our suspicions about someone purposefully causing problems in the village. They immediately blamed the Hebrews, but we assured them we were taking care of it and that they had nothing to worry about."

"I'm guessing they didn't like that answer?"

Paul shook his head. "They're pretty upset. They want a face. I can't say I blame them. I want to know who's behind it too."

"I'll find the person. I promise."

"Don't promise something you can't keep." Paul ran a hand through his short hair and sighed. "There's more."

"What?" Salome asked, fearing the worst.

CHAPTER 11

"They tried blaming you and your father for the problems."

Salome's mouth dropped. So, she wasn't imagining things.

"I promise you, I will help fix this."

Chapter 12

When there's nothing to do but pace back and forth along that same hundred-yard stretch, it's easy to get lost in your own mind. That's exactly what happened. Amina still didn't understand why Salome missed this important town hall meeting. She wanted to give her the benefit of the doubt, but she couldn't help but feel that Salome wasn't taking things as seriously as she should.

Amina did her best to not linger too much on her thoughts. If she did, they'd like to fester into contempt, and that was the last thing she wanted. She continued to walk her path between the market and the medical ward, moving in the opposite direction from her partner, Josiah. It was a horrendously boring job, but Amina was glad to do whatever she could to protect the village.

The stillness of the night was unsettling. All those years of living constantly on edge, it was hard to trust the calm. Amina breathed the cool air, filling her lungs and trying to settle her agitation.

She listened to the crickets chirp slowly and the owl hooting in the distance. That's what Amina needed to focus on—the beauty of her surroundings. She needed to take in the strong and lush trees surrounding her, the rocky dirt beneath her feet, and the stars twinkling above her. All around was Sabaoth's presence and the reminder that she was where she needed to be.

Amina approached Josiah again, and she nodded. "Still looking good."

Josiah stopped and looked behind around. He pressed his fingertips to his chest. "Who, me?" He grinned.

Amina rolled her eyes. "No, dodo, the area. There's no sign of anything out of the ordinary."

"Oh," Josiah said in an exaggerated and mocking realization. "Sorry, my mistake."

Amina shook her head and kept walking. *What a goofball.*

The two of them continued their march and on what must've been their hundredth pass, Josiah smiled and said, "Oh hey, fancy seeing you here. You come here often?"

Amina stopped, thrown off by his random comment. Josiah shrugged and kept walking. Amina chuckled to herself.

On the next pass, Josiah pretended to tip his hat and with a southern accent said, "Howdy, ma'am. Fine night, ain't it?"

"About as fine as a puppy with a bowtie," Amina responded with an equally thick southern accent.

From that point on, Amina and Josiah couldn't help but make goofy comments to one another on every pass. It became a competition to see who could come up with something even more ridiculous to make the other laugh. At least they were staying entertained, and there was enough anticipation to hear what the next person had to say on their passing to keep them awake.

Amina passed Josiah again, laughing so hard, she was practically crying. As she wiped tears from her eyes, she noticed a shadow standing at the well ahead of her. Amina slowed to observe. Who needed to be at the well at this time of night? Sure, it could be someone who needed a late-night drink, but Paul was clear about a curfew. Could it be someone sleepwalking?

As Amina continued to watch, she saw them lift something long and skinny in their hands. Amina moved toward them and, as she approached, she realized it was a sledgehammer. "Stop!" Amina sprinted toward the shadow.

Startled, the shadow dropped the sledgehammer and took off running toward the open field. Amina sped up, hoping she could catch up and tackle them. The intruder slithered like a snake, darting around the trees and bushes expertly. Amina moved faster, afraid her feet wouldn't keep up, and she'd fall on her face. She maneuvered between the bushes and trees, but the intruder weaved about with such ease Amina could barely keep up.

"Hey you, come back! Stop! Josiah, come help!" she yelled, hoping someone would hear and cut the intruder off before she lost them.

Instead, Amina's toe caught a rock, and she went crashing face-first into the dirt. She threw her hands in front of her body to brace her fall. Pain shot through her hands and chin as she hid the hard dirt. By the time she recovered, the intruder was gone.

"No!" Amina punched the ground.

Josiah ran up to Amina, huffing. He put his hands on his knees. "What's wrong? Are you okay?"

"No, I'm not okay." Amina pushed herself off the ground and wiped the dirt off her pants. Her hands still stung and when she looked at them, tiny red scratches and bits of rock covered the heels. Amina carefully brushed the rock out, wincing each time. "I saw someone, and they got away. Where were you?"

"I came as soon as I heard you shouting. You saw someone? What were they doing?"

"They were about to smash our well into oblivion. When they heard me, they dropped the sledgehammer and took off. They know this area well. It had to be the same person who's causing all the other problems."

"We'll get them next time. Come on, our shift is over. Let's get you cleaned up."

They headed toward the medical ward, while Amina tried to pick out the rocks embedded in her scratches. The blood pooled in her palm and even trickled down her wrist. Her mind swirled with frustration, replaying the scenario over and over in her mind. Why didn't she sneak up on him quietly? Why didn't she have a weapon? No matter how much she blamed herself or mulled over what she could've done, it didn't change the fact that the person got away. Next time, she'd have to be more prepared.

* * * *

The team joining Aiden for this mission comprised two other people. Marvin, a beefy guy with curly black hair and even darker eyes. Aiden had came across Marvin a couple of times before, but not nearly enough to know him well. What Aiden knew about him was that he was incredibly smart and could assemble just about anything you asked him to. The second person on the team was Tessa. Aiden was relieved to have someone he knew and trusted on his team. She was the scout. She had the map and was responsible for getting them there safely.

Aiden's body trembled with nerves as he finished packing his bag. Flashbacks from his last raid clouded his mind, drudging up emotions he wished he could forget. Seth's death. Being taken hostage. Seeing his mother. Aiden pushed the nightmares away and tried to focus as they made their way toward the tunnel's exit. He needed to stay present and focused.

Tessa led them in a quick prayer of safety before she went first up and out of the tunnels. Aiden followed with Marvin behind. They made their way out of the manhole and dashed over to the first crater. No one spoke as they trekked their way across the open field and toward the highway.

While it wasn't ideal to follow a highway when the Myriad still occupied it, it was the surest route to get them where they needed to go. If any vehicles or drones approached, they were ready with their mylar thermal blankets to block them from the drone's infrared as well as they could easily dart into a car or building to hide from vehicles.

"We only need to be on this highway for five miles, then we'll veer west and take trails from there until we reach our first safe house," Tessa said as she led the way.

Aiden didn't like the idea, but he followed anyway, trusting that Tessa had done her homework.

They traveled swiftly and silently, not wanting to waste any time on their travels. The trip would likely take them two days, which meant they'd have to make it to their first safe house and squat there during the day until they could travel again.

In the distance, Aiden heard the familiar rumble of a car engine.

"We need to hide," Tessa said before he could get the words

CHAPTER 12

out. They all looked around for a good hiding place. About twenty feet ahead of them was a tipped-over semi-truck. Tessa ran around the back of it, while Aiden and Marvin followed.

The trailer door stood ajar, and they climbed in. They waited silently as the car engine grew louder. As a scavenger, Aiden was used to hiding every time a patrol vehicle rolled by, but it didn't lessen his anxiety. The vehicle was right beside them now. Any moment it would pass, and they'd be clear to keep moving. Except, it didn't pass. It slowed and then stopped. Two car doors opened. Aiden stiffened. He glanced at Tessa and Marvin, who'd already drawn their handguns. Aiden squeezed his eyes shut and whispered a prayer. The semi-truck was empty, likely raided by scavengers years ago, but that made them sitting ducks. If whoever was outside that truck looked inside, they'd be spotted.

The traveler was quiet. The only sound was the scuffling of their boots as they walked. The footsteps drew closer as a large male body stumbled past the open truck door and out of sight. Aiden heard what seemed to be water trickling. It took a moment before he realized what was happening.

"Hurry up over there! We can't be out here much longer, or we'll get caught."

"I'm coming!" The body passed them again and soon the door slammed shut. The engine started and they drove off.

Aiden let out a sigh. Tessa shook her head as she chuckled to herself.

"He walked right past us and didn't even see us here," Marvin said, dumbfounded.

The group laughed, relieved. They waited a few minutes just to ensure the car was far enough away before they continued their journey south along the highway.

They made it about halfway to their destination before coming across their first pit stop. It was an old campground. And while it once was a lush, secluded campground with giant trees, thick bushes, and a creek running through it, now it was rundown. Most of the trees and bushes stood scorched with black spindly branches like boney fingers. Potholes and trash riddled the gravel road that once led campers in and out of the grounds. By the look of the number of tents and campers left behind, all badly burned, the fire that ripped through the area must've been fast and sudden.

"Do you think there are any dead bodies around?" Marvin asked with a sort of sick interest.

"It's possible," Tessa said. "It looks like a fire came through here at some point. I'd like to believe everyone made it out safely, but—" She didn't finish her thought, and she didn't have to. They knew what she was thinking. "Well boys, this is home for the day. Let's pick a spot to camp out."

They settled on an empty campsite right next to the bathroom with a vaulted toilet. They each pulled out their hammocks and did their best to find trees sturdy enough to hold their body weight. Aiden had little luck and the one spot he found, he gave to Tessa. Eventually, he settled with sleeping on top of the concrete table, while Marvin slept in the back of a pickup truck.

Exhaustion overtook Aiden's body, and though the sun was coming up, he had no problem falling asleep.

* * * *

It was no surprise to Paxton how easily he fell back into the

CHAPTER 12

soldier's routine. He went through the motions of physical training drills, weapon practice, and tactical drills fluidly. He did his best to blend in and make sure he was forgettable. After weeks of being confined to a tiny cell and constant interrogations, the training was exhausting. By the end of the day, he was so depleted of energy he could barely make it back to his room for a five-minute shower before he passed out on the bed until the next morning. He was thankful, however, for the training and the food. Regaining his strength would only make escape easier. Paxton couldn't wait for the day he left. It's too bad he wouldn't get to see the look on Frank's face.

After a week, Frank determined Paxton was no longer a flight risk and let up on his supervision. Paxton could now move about freely, but he rarely did. He didn't converse with others and refused to do anything that appeared leisurely.

Paxton walked into the gym and over to the treadmill. He turned it on and started at a fast walk to warm up. Slowly, he sped the treadmill up to a light jog. Running was the one thing that really helped Paxton think.

Now that Frank was letting up on Paxton's supervision, and Paxton felt physically strong and well nourished, it was time to put an actual plan of escape together before Frank decided Paxton was ready for a mission of some sort. The last thing he wanted was to get deployed.

Paxton pressed the button on his treadmill to speed up his pace to a run. He took slow, even breaths. As he kept his quick pace, he thought through how to escape. He wasn't allowed off the property, so walking out the front gate wasn't an option. He also didn't have an access key, so he couldn't use the elevator to go down to the sub-level tunnel leading to the subway system. Not to mention the only clothes he owned were his military fatigues or his bright red workout clothes. He'd stick out like a sore thumb in either of those, so he'd need different clothes.

Paxton's legs burned with lactic acid, but he kept pushing forward. He needed a way out, but he couldn't do it alone. And he certainly didn't trust anyone in the capitol, except—a light went on—Mimi! He'd forgotten all about Aiden's friend Mimi, who helped them escape the first time. He'd need to find her and see if there was something she could do to help. That was, if she still worked at the capitol. Paxton had no idea what happened to her, but at this moment it was all Paxton had. He'd make his way to the laboratories and see if he couldn't track her down.

Paxton slowed the treadmill to finish his run with a ten-minute cooldown. As he finished his run, the door opened, and a young soldier walked in. Paxton grabbed his things and headed toward the door.

"You don't have to leave on account of me," the newcomer said casually.

Paxton looked over at the young soldier standing near the door. He had jet-black hair buzzed in the same cut every soldier wore. His dark olive skin popped against his orange sleeveless shirt and orange workout shorts.

"I'm not. I'm done." Paxton grabbed his water bottle and towel and headed to the door.

"You're Paxton Agnelli, right?"

Paxton eyed the kid. "Who's asking?"

"The name's Keetey, Jason Keetey." The kid stuck his hand out for Paxton to shake. "I've heard a lot of good things about you coming up through training. I'm a big fan."

CHAPTER 12

Paxton reluctantly stuck his hand out and shook it. Either Jason truly knew nothing about Paxton's latest endeavors, or he was a good liar. "You must be new."

"Just got out of boot camp two days ago, sir."

"Right. Well, it's nice to meet you, Keetey. Good luck with everything."

"Thanks. You know I'd love to pick your brain sometime. I hope to get in with the Purification Unit, and they say you're the best."

Paxton cringed inwardly. "I'm not in that unit anymore."

"But you were, so you still know a lot."

"Sorry, I can't help. You'll just have to wait until your AIT and let them teach you." Paxton walked out of the gym, not wanting to continue. It was bad enough being back with the Myriad, but to have someone praise him for being a murderer was a whole other issue he didn't want to deal with.

Paxton crossed the courtyard and headed to his room. A cool breeze flew between the buildings, swirling several brown and red leaves about until they found their way to the ground. The sun was already low in the sky despite the time on Paxton's watch.

Just as Paxton approached the front entrance to the Myriad sleep hall, a golf cart pulled up. Paxton didn't turn his head. He just wanted to get to the shower. From his peripheral, however, he noticed Frank walking toward him. Out of duty, Paxton stopped, turned toward Frank, and stood at attention, loathing to find out whatever Frank had to say.

"At ease, soldier."

Paxton saluted Frank and then shifted his feet shoulder-width apart, with his hands folded and resting on his lower back. "What can I do for you, sir?"

"I have an assignment for you."

Paxton's stomach did a somersault. "Already?"

"Nothing in the field. I don't trust you there. But you're too skilled to be wasting it doing grunt work. So, you'll be in a classroom, training."

"What sort of training, sir?" Paxton asked, afraid to hear the answer.

"You'll be training the new recruits who'll be heading into the Purification Unit, specifically the undercover side of things." Frank stood, smug, watching for Paxton's reaction. Paxton refused to give him the satisfaction.

"And what makes you think I'd ever do that?"

"Duty. The will to live. The desire not to go back to that rat-infested hole. Pick one, I don't care. Just report to the classroom on Monday at 0800."

Paxton squeezed his hands behind his back. It made him sick to think he'd have to teach such horrendous things. To help others become killers, but what choice did he have? If Frank threw him back in his cell, the chance of escape would disappear. Before he left Amina, he made a promise to escape. That he'd do whatever it took to get back to her.

"Yes, sir. I'll be there, sir."

The two stared at one another for a long moment, hatred blazing in their eyes. Finally, Paxton asked through gritted teeth, "Is that all, sir?"

"Dismissed, soldier," Frank snarled.

"Yes, sir." Paxton saluted again and then turned to enter the building. Paxton wanted to lash out. He wanted to yell at Frank, tell him he was a sinister man, to find joy in someone else's agony.

Frank knew exactly what he was doing, making Paxton teach

this class, and it sickened Paxton. He wanted nothing more than to punch Frank and humble him, but he knew that would get him killed. Not to mention Frank enjoyed getting a rise out of him. So he refrained. He was determined to not let Frank get to him. He'd be an obedient soldier. *Whatever it takes.*

Chapter 13

A trickle of light extended through the branches and onto Aiden's face. Keeping his eyes closed, Aiden smiled as the warmth caressed his cheek like a mother's touch. He could lie there all day, forgetting where he was. Aiden took a deep breath. As his lungs expanded, his back pressed into the hard bumpy concrete, which refused to let him forget where he was. Reality swirled around him and settled on him, squeezing like a boa constrictor. He slowly opened his eyes as he sat up and stretched out the kinks in his body. To his left, he noticed Tessa was already up. Her hammock was put away, and she was smoothing out her hair with her fingers before pulling it back into a tight ponytail.

"Morning sunshine," she said.

Aiden looked around at the disheveled sight. He hadn't realized how truly run-down everything was. It was a graveyard. The sun's rays bounced off the clouds and cast an eerie shadow across the ground with tiny spider-webbed shadows that swayed with the breeze. The only sound was the vague rustling of dead branches or the scraping of trash dragging its way across the ground like zombies.

While before, in his stupor of half awake, half asleep, Aiden thought the sun was rising to welcome him to a new day. Now he realized it was actually setting with a fiery red glow that burned across the horizon ominously. Soon it'd dip behind the hills and the dull moon would awaken. Another night of darkness shrouding them with its cold and heartless touch. Its deep shadows of untold danger and its mysterious eyes are all around. Aiden shivered. He was tired of the night and the dark. He was tired of living in the shadows and was ready to come out of hiding for good.

"It's about time to go. Better get some food in you. I want to reach our destination by sunrise." She tossed him a bag of Fritos.

Aiden caught the bag just as his ears pricked at another sound. Footsteps. Aiden spun around, ready for a fight. It was only Marvin. Aiden relaxed. "Where'd you come from?"

"The bathroom." Marvin pulled out his own bag of chips and started eating. "It's still pretty decent in there, and there's toilet paper."

"Really? That's surprising," Tessa said before shaking the remnants of her own Fritos bag into her mouth.

"Right? Most places ran dry years ago. I wonder what happened here."

Aiden looked around at the charred wood and black soot marks left on the cars. "Judging by the looks of things, likely a very unexpected fire."

Marvin rolled his eyes. "I know there was a fire. I meant what kind of fire? Was it on purpose?"

"Could've been a meteor hit the area nearby."

"Alright, enough speculation, boys. Let's discuss routes." Tessa pulled out her map and spread it over the concrete table. As they munched on their chips and some trail mix, Marvin pulled out to share.

There were two options to get there, and both were equally dangerous. One route took them up and through the small, mountainous terrain. While this was the most direct route, it was full of unknown obstacles, from steep rocky hills to drifters living in the caves. The other route took them around the mountain but required them to follow the highway, constantly being on watch for Myriad patrols.

"I vote the highway," Tessa said after explaining their two options. "We can finish this trail all the way down as far south as we need to go, but then we can hop on the highway and cut west."

"But it's not the most direct, and with all the Myriad patrols, it could end up taking us much longer than we want," Aiden protested.

He wanted to get there and back as quickly as possible so he could get back to what really mattered. Sure, helping Notzrim was important. He wanted them to be safe, but that was just a temporary fix. His plan would make things more permanent. Plus, he was still hoping to meet with Mimi. While Jared told him to cancel the meeting, he didn't. As long as they made it to and from this mission quickly, he'd be back in time to meet with Mimi, assuming she showed up.

"Don't worry Aiden, I'll keep you safe," Marvin assured Aiden with an arrogance that rubbed Aiden the wrong way.

"I'm not worried about safety. Both routes are unsafe. I'm worried about time."

"True, it's a longer route and we have the Myriad patrols to contend with," Tessa said, "but I think it'll still be faster since the highway is flat and easy to follow. My job is to get us there in a timely manner. This group of Notzrim is counting on us to help them. The longer we take, the higher the risk it is for them to be where they are."

"I thought they were in a safe place." Aiden looked at Tessa, confused. "I was told they were there to set up communications."

"Yes, but we were also asked to take them to a new and safer location. They're in an area that's still occupied by nomads."

"Woah, wait a minute," Aiden spat out, irked by this new information. That would take too long. He wasn't prepared for this. "Why weren't we told this? I didn't sign on for transporting Notzrim."

"Your reaction is why you weren't told."

"This is messed up," Marvin said, sounding just as frustrated. "If Jared is going to send us on missions, he should trust us with the whole truth."

"Maybe, but what are you going to do about it now?" Tessa asked, her hands on her hips. "You going to bail?"

"No, of course not. I just like to be trusted with the whole truth, ya know?"

"We all do, but that's not how Jared operates. Let's get our things and head out. These are our brothers and sisters, followers of the faith, and they need our help." Tessa locked eyes with Aiden. "It's the right thing to do."

Aiden knew she was right. They were part of the Notzrim family, and they deserved their help. He'd have to miss the meeting with Mimi if she showed up. Aiden would have to beg for forgiveness later.

"Wait, we still didn't agree on a way to go," Marvin said.

"We're taking the highway, Marvin. It's the best route."

"I don't know about that. Is that really our best option? I mean, sure, I can bust some heads if I need to, but they've got drones and bigger guns. I want our best chance of survival and the highway doesn't seem to be it."

Tessa rolled her eyes. "I beg to differ. If we travel through those mountains at night, it'll take longer and there could be a lot more unseen dangers. One misstep and you could slip down a cliff or fall into an old hunter's trap."

"That's what flashlights are for. We'll take our time and move carefully."

"That'll take two more nights. And they don't have that kind of time."

"It's better than the risk of getting shot."

"What happened to 'I'll protect you Aiden?'" Aiden teased.

"Shut up. I can protect you and all of us. I just want to be smart about this, too."

The wind picked up, and a gust scooped up the map. Tessa slammed her hand on it and held it tightly. "Aiden, please say you agree with me."

Aiden took a deep breath. He didn't like either option, but he agreed faster was better. "Tessa has a point. The less time above ground in the open, the better. We need to get there quickly and following the highway will allow that. We can handle hiding from the Myriad, but we run into nomads in those woods or fall into one of their hunting traps. Who knows what they'll do? I've heard some of them are cannibals." Aiden shuddered at the thought.

Marvin shook his head. "Fine. Let's just go."

The group walked in silence along the trail, downhill. Tessa kept a brisk pace, so Aiden had to watch where he was going so he didn't stumble. The night was crisp but felt good on Aiden's warm skin.

It took them what seemed to be several hours before the trail flattened out and Aiden could see the edge of the dead

CHAPTER 13

trees. Beyond was an open wasteland and a highway. Aiden always found it odd how easy it was to go from wilderness to desert in just a few miles, but it made for great diversity and fun adventures. There was always something new to explore.

At the edge of the brush, Tessa stopped. She pulled out her night vision goggles, scanning the open space before deeming it clear for them to move forward and make their way west along the highway.

Tessa was right. The walk was flat and easy, but it was also completely open. There were no buildings and very few cars or boulders. If a Myriad patrol came through, they wouldn't have anywhere close to hide.

The wind whipped around them, blowing sand in their faces, pricking them like thousands of tiny needles. Aiden looked at the sky. The clouds swirled around them as flickers of light bounced inside. "I think a storm is coming," Aiden shouted over the wind.

"What?" Tessa looked back, her hair flailing around in all directions.

Aiden pointed at the sky. "A storm."

A giant drop of water plopped onto Aiden's arm and rolled off. Then another. It didn't take long before the sky opened, and a deluge of plump raindrops showered them. They picked up their speed, pushing against the wind and rain. Aiden squinted, trying to see through the rain that was quickly becoming more of a curtain. They needed to reach a building to take cover.

Lightning struck overhead and a loud crack of thunder followed before Aiden even had time to count. The wind howled, turning the rain sideways, and blowing into his eyes. Another crack of lightning hit. Sparks flew to their left like fireworks. Aiden jumped, startled by the noise.

Tessa stopped and turned toward the others. "There's a building ahead. Let's take cover there."

"We'd better run. That lightning is too close for comfort," Marvin hollered back.

Tessa and Aiden nodded as they took off running blindly down the highway.

By the time they reached the building, the rain had soaked them through to the bone, and they were shivering. Inside, they shed their backpacks and jackets while scouring the place for towels. They found themselves in an old gas station convenience store. The place was pretty picked over, but they found some old rags in the back.

"That storm came out of nowhere," Marvin said as he shook the water out of his curly fro.

"So much for getting there tonight." Tessa kicked an empty box as she swore.

Aiden didn't like being stuck waiting any more than she did. "It'll be okay Tessa, we'll still get there."

After stepping outside to fill their canteens with fresh rainwater, the group settled in on the floor to wait out the storm. Outside, rain pounded the windows as the lightning and thunder put on their musical performance. The lightning danced while the thunder sang. Aiden couldn't help but enjoy it.

"You know," Aiden reminisced, "my family, we used to sit in the garage on days like this with the door open and just watch the storm. It didn't matter that we'd get misted. My dad always loved the power of it all. One time, the tree in front of our house got hit and caught fire, but the rain was so intense it put the sparks out. It was amazing. I can still see the sparks flying when that lightning hit, and the tree caught." Aiden sat imagining, the scene vivid in his mind.

"I bet you like fireworks, too," Marvin said.

Aiden looked at him, coming out of his imagination. "Yeah, I guess I do."

"I love the rain." Tessa smiled as she leaned against an empty shelf with her hands wrapped around her knees. "But the best part is when the rain is done, the sun peaks out and the rainbow appears. Rainbows have always fascinated me. My sister and I would try to chase them, jumping through every puddle we could find as we attempted to look for the rainbow end."

"Did you ever find the end?"

Tessa looked at Aiden and laughed. "No, of course not. But it made for some grand adventures."

"I didn't know you had a sister," Aiden replied.

Her expression changed as her eyes took on a distant look. "I did. She died in a fire."

"Oh geez, I'm so sorry."

"Thanks. It was right at the beginning of the Great Desolation. My sister and I lived together with my grandmother. I still don't know what caused the fire. It was such a whirlwind that night. There was so much smoke and confusion. I thought my sister was behind us, but when we got out, she wasn't there. I wanted to run back in, but my grandmother wouldn't let me. When the firefighters arrived, it was too late. The house was old, with wood floors. Her foot got caught in a hole or something."

Aiden sat silently in horror. The Great Desolation brought everyone nothing but tragedy. He understood why it was happening—that it was Sabaoth's way of bringing judgment to the sins of the world and resetting it back to its original perfect state. But he didn't understand why there had to be so much suffering for Sabaoth's people, too.

Tessa took a deep breath and wiped a tear away. "Anyway, it's probably for the best that she's not here. She was a type one diabetic, and I don't think she would've survived long in hiding without her insulin."

Aiden wanted to say something comforting but was at a loss. They sat quietly, letting the sound of the rain drown out their thoughts.

"Well, I hate the rain," Marvin grumbled, breaking the silence. "My school was old, and it leaked. So whenever it rained, there'd always be puddles of rainwater on the slick tiled floors or dripping on the desks. And then, I'd usually end up having to walk home in the rain because my parents worked and couldn't bother to find anyone to pick me up. It was miserable."

Tessa and Aiden looked at one another, unsure of what to say to his comment.

Outside, a bright light shone through the window. At first, Aiden thought it was more lightning, but then he heard car doors slam shut.

Aiden looked at the others anxiously. Without a word, they grabbed their things and scurried to the back of the store and into the back storage room. Aiden closed the door, leaving it open just a crack so he could see down the hallway toward the front entrance. He felt a tug behind him but didn't move. He wanted to see who was coming in.

The front door opened, and through the curtain of rain stepped two Myriad soldiers. They stopped just inside, shaking off the rainwater.

CHAPTER 13

"Holy misery, it's raining cats and dogs out there," one soldier complained. He was tall and very large, built like a tank. His thick neck poked out of his military fatigues just enough to hold up his large head. "Remind me why you didn't want to stay in the vehicle."

"I like to check out these places and see what I can find. Sometimes there's good treasures left behind. Once I found a safe still filled with money."

"Suit yourself. We can't drive anywhere right now, anyway." The soldier gestured with both hands toward the front counter. "Have at it."

The second soldier, who was smaller than the first but no less intimidating, wandered over to the counter while the first went off in the opposite direction. Aiden took that as his cue to close and lock the storage room door silently. He turned and looked at Tessa and Marvin, who waited anxiously.

"Well?" Tessa mouthed.

"Myriad." Aiden mouthed back.

Tessa flung her head back, clenching her jaw. Aiden could tell she wanted to yell in frustration.

They looked around the room for a place to hide. If those soldiers were interested in raiding the place, it was only a matter of time before they tried to make their way back into the storage room. The storage room was small and scant. While there were some empty boxes lying about, there wasn't much else. Across the room, Aiden noticed another door. He motioned the others to follow. They quietly made their way through the door and into the refrigerator area.

Aiden looked to his left and could see through the glass doors into the store where the one soldier was wandering around. He took a step back into the shadows. With so many drinks missing, it was easy to see through. They found their way behind the extra drink racks in the back of the fridge and waited like sitting ducks.

Aiden's heart pounded in his ears louder than the thunder outside. He continued to watch the one soldier wander up and down the aisles until he came to the drink aisle. He perused the refrigerator, and then stopped.

Aiden sucked in air and held his breath. The soldier looked directly at Aiden. Aiden didn't dare move, praying that they were far enough back. Yet, they seemed to lock eyes. The muscles in Aiden's fingers twitched. Every instinct within Aiden made him want to run. He didn't dare. The display door opened, and the soldier squatted and reached his hand in to pull out some off-brand energy drink. He stood and walked away.

"Hey look what I found," he said as he let the display door bounce close.

Aiden's knees went weak. He had to grab Tessa's arm to keep from falling. Tessa's hand covered his, and she squeezed with reassurance.

They continued to wait in the muggy refrigerator for the better part of an hour, not knowing where the soldiers were or what they were up to. Aiden's legs grew stiff and tired from standing still. He wondered if the soldiers were even in the store anymore. Tessa had her eyes closed and was leaning against the wall. He nudged her with his elbow, and she slowly opened her eyes.

"Should I go check things out?" Aiden said, barely audible.

Tessa shook her head no.

He looked at Marvin. Sweat dripped down his forehead and his face flushed.

CHAPTER 13

"You okay?" Aiden asked.

Marvin nodded, but Aiden wasn't convinced.

Aiden looked back at Tessa. "They might be gone."

"No Aiden, if the storm is still going, they're still here. We need—"

The door to the storage room shuddered violently. A gunshot echoed and the door crashed open, banging against the wall.

"And that's how you do it," the second soldier bragged.

"What do you expect to find in here?" The first soldier asked.

"I dunno. That's why I'm exploring."

The soldier walked in like a bull in a china shop, stomping his boots about as he tossed boxes around.

"Everything's empty."

"Of course, it's empty. What'd you expect after nine years?"

The second soldier poked his head inside the refrigerator and looked around. He laughed. "Look what I found."

Tessa squeezed Aiden's hand again, and Aiden squeezed back. He watched, unable to look away from the soldier.

"It's the refrigerator to the drink display cases. It's all one giant room. I had no idea."

"It's probably empty, just like everything else here. Can we go now? The storm is letting up."

"Hold on, I want to see." The soldier stepped into the room and made his way deeper into the fridge and closer to Aiden and the other's hiding spot.

The sound of static followed by a beep made Aiden nearly jump. "Unit G1-5-8 do you copy?"

The soldier grabbed his walkie-talkie and responded. "Unit G1-5-8 here. What is it, Connie?"

"Your unit was reported stalled out on Highway 2 for almost an hour. Everything okay?"

"Just fine, Connie. We ran into a nasty storm and were waiting it out. We're continuing our route now." The soldier turned and headed out of the refrigerator.

Aiden was so relieved he thought he might cry. The group waited another five minutes before daring to move from their spot.

When they finally moved, Aiden's body hurt, cracking and popping like the tin man in need of oil. He looked over at Marvin, who went from being flush to looking like a ghost. Sweat dripped down his face.

"Marvin, it's okay, we're okay now."

Marvin slowly nodded, but then spun around and vomited on the floor behind him.

Aiden stepped away so the splatter wouldn't get him.

Tessa walked out of the room and returned with a rag. She looked at Aiden, motioning for them to give him some space.

Aiden couldn't blame Marvin for getting sick. Aiden was queasy about the whole situation too, but he was relieved beyond belief that they were ok.

"Praise Sabaoth for protecting us," Tessa breathed once they were in the main store.

"No kidding. That was way too close. I don't even know how they didn't see us."

"Sabaoth made us invisible."

Aiden smiled. A miracle like that was the only way to explain it.

Soon, Marvin joined the others.

"You good now?" Tessa asked.

"I'm fine. My trail mix must've been bad. That's all," Marvin explained defensively. "It wasn't 'cause I was scared."

Tessa put her hands up. "Ok, whatever you say."

CHAPTER 13

Marvin sneered but said nothing more.

The rain was now just a light drizzle, and the lightning had passed.

"Time to get going again," Tessa ordered.

Knowing the worst of the storm was behind them, the group grabbed their things. As they headed to the door, Aiden stopped. On a rack just by the door were plastic ponchos. "Hey, look what I found." Aiden grabbed three and tossed them to the others.

With their ponchos on, they headed back out onto the highway. It continued to drizzle most of the night, but at least they had the ponchos to protect them. By the time Aiden could see the first glimmer of dawn, the rain had completely stopped and the clouds dissipated. While it was good to have the rain gone, a new problem was about to present itself: sunlight.

"Are we getting close, Tessa? We can't be out here much longer?" Aiden asked.

Tessa pulled her backpack around and grabbed the map out. She continued to walk as she studied the map, determining where they were. "I'd say we're still about eight miles away."

"The sun'll be up before then," Marvin complained.

"Then we better walk fast." Tessa folded the map up and put it back in her backpack while picking up her pace.

Marvin grunted as he mumbled something about being exhausted before following behind.

They moved quickly, wanting to beat the sunshine. Aiden's legs burned, but he kept moving. The less time in the sunlight, the better.

The light expanded across the horizon and into the sky, blotting out the night. When the sun finally poked its head out, Tessa veered to her left, off the highway and toward the wilderness. The same wilderness they could've gone through to avoid the highway.

Aiden didn't question, he just followed. As they reached the edge of a large rock pile, Tessa stopped and looked around. The rocks piled one giant boulder on top of another, reaching high into the sky with large crevices for humans and animals to crawl around. The rocks were precariously leaning on one another so much it was a wonder they didn't all come crashing down.

"Is this it?" Aiden asked.

"Somewhere near here. I'm just not—this doesn't look like the description." Tessa moved along the bottom of the rock formation before settling on a place to climb.

"We're going up?"

"Yes, Marvin. Up and into the rocks. There's a cave in here where they're living. I don't recall Jared mentioning this many rocks, but I'm sure we'll find it."

They each took hold of the rocks and made their way up. For as loose as the rocks looked, they were firmly jarred into place allowing for easy climbing. Each time Tessa found a concaved section, she'd stop and look to see if it was a cave opening. When there wasn't one, she'd move on.

Aiden made his way to his right. "We should spread out."

"Good idea. Marvin spread out to our left and I'll keep going up."

They each took their time weaving in and out of the rocks like ground squirrels playing hide and seek. Each crevice was a potential for a large opening into a cave, but so far, nothing. Aiden looked as he climbed. He was getting closer to the top and still nothing. Was Tessa sure they were in the right place? Maybe she'd gotten turned around.

CHAPTER 13

"I think I found it!" Marvin waved his hand for the others to come. He was nearly to the top and hanging on the edge of the rock precariously.

Aiden and Tessa cautiously scaled their way over toward him and into the crevice. Beyond the outer layer of rock, there was a rock jutting out of the side like a natural balcony just large enough to fit the three of them. Beyond that was an opening into the side of the mountain and then darkness. They each pulled out their flashlights and flipped them on before venturing into the cave.

"Do we need to announce ourselves?" Aiden asked. "I don't want them attacking us, thinking we're dangerous."

Tessa agreed and called out. "Hello? We're not here to hurt you. We come with supplies and food. The Spirit sent us as fellow brothers and sisters."

They continued to creep into the cave's narrow passageway, but still, no one answered. Aiden didn't like this. Where was everyone? Eventually, they came to a fork, and the tunnels split in two different directions.

"Now what?" Marvin asked.

"I don't know. Someone was supposed to meet us by now to show us through. I was told it's like a maze in there."

"I don't want to get lost."

Tessa whipped around. "Obviously neither do I, Marvin. You know what, why don't you just stay here because honestly, I'm sick and tired of your attitude." Tessa turned back and marched through the tunnel to her right. Aiden followed, happy to be rid of Marvin as well.

They continued to walk deeper down the winding pathway into the cave. The walls were tight around them, but the dark insides of the earth were cool. Soon, the pathway split again.

Tessa stopped and looked at Aiden.

Before she said anything, Aiden chimed in, "I don't think we should split up. We don't know what's in here."

Tessa opened her mouth to object, but closed it again. She pulled her canteen out of her backpack and set it down at the mouth of the tunnel from where'd they'd just come. "So, we don't get lost," she explained before continuing right again.

This particular tunnel's path was flat. As they walked, the floor to their left dropped away, leaving them a narrow pathway. Aiden shone his light into the black beyond to discover beautiful rock formations—some were short and jagged like teeth and others long and smooth like sinew.

"It's gorgeous in here," Aiden awed. He pointed his light down into the open space. "Hey look."

"What is it?" Tessa stopped and followed Aiden's light with her eyes.

Below them, the floor of the opening wasn't far at all. It was a large rounded space filled with sleeping mats, blankets, and wooden bowls.

"This must be where they stay." Aiden flashed his light around, looking for a way down without jumping the ten feet. He spotted a broken ladder. There were a couple of rungs at the top and as Aiden followed with his light down the side of the rock, the ladder stopped abruptly. At the foot of the rock wall was the rest of the ladder, broken into several pieces.

Tessa let out a startled yelp. Aiden turned to where Tessa's light was pointing and immediately knew why she yelled. There, some five feet away from the ladder, was a pile of multiple dead bodies. Aiden stared in disbelief. *What happened to them?* Aiden moved along the pathway, getting closer to the area below him where believers just like him lay in a cold, desolate grave. As he drew closer, he noticed the river of dried blood flowing out from under them. The bullet wounds scattered over their bodies and the burn marks on others. This was not a natural death.

Aiden shook with rage as he clenched his jaw so tight it hurt.

"How did they find them?" Tessa spoke with a shaky voice.

Aiden couldn't answer. Rage engrossed him. He clenched his fists, ready to kill someone. Such inhumane beasts. No compassion. No heart. They were of the devil, no doubt. Aiden turned and headed back to the entrance. "It's time to go."

"Aiden, wait. What if there are others still alive in here?"

"There aren't," Aiden said through gritted teeth.

Back at the entrance, Aiden didn't stop to fill Marvin in. He continued out of the cave and down the rocks. He had only one thing on his mind. Blow up the capitol and stop the Myriad.

Chapter 14

Paxton walked into the empty classroom, loathing what he was about to do. Rows of high-end school desks filled the rectangular room. Each egg-shaped chair had a colorful cushion, while the desks folded up and down for easy access in and out of the seat. At the front was a digital whiteboard the size of the wall and on the desk up front was a tablet. Paxton picked up the tablet and turned it on. There was only one file on it titled, *Purification Unit 101: Philosophy and Guidelines.* Paxton's skin crawled.

Was he really about to do this? Teach these eager soldiers the lies someone had once fed him about the Notzrim. Convince and brainwash the soldiers into believing that it was for the good of humankind to rid the world of the Notzrim faith, and if they failed, another world war would break out.

Paxton swiped through the pages of his handbook. In it were all the images, charts, and text he'd need to show the class. It was a step-by-step guide to exactly what Paxton needed to teach. Any dummy could teach this class. Frank didn't need Paxton's expertise for this.

He reached a page that had pictures of a bombing. As he looked through the images, Paxton came across one image that made him drop the tablet as if it were on fire. He closed

CHAPTER 14

his eyes tight and opened them again. The bombing was from the first raid he'd even been on, and there was a picture in the document of him with Frank. They were standing in front of a large dump truck, smiling. Paxton shuddered.

The door opened, and Paxton's head shot up. It was Frank.

"I see you found your course curriculum. Everything you need is on that tablet."

Paxton stared at the metal desk, images from his past resurfacing. "I don't know if I can do this."

"But you must. Your life depends on it."

Paxton made a fist and twisted it into the desk. He knew the class was going to be hard enough—having to teach lies—but he hadn't expected all the memories to come flooding back so vividly. He took slow, deep breaths in and out. To fight against the surfacing panic attack, he focused on his surroundings. The cold metal beneath his fist. The smell of lemon cleaner, and the sound of footsteps coming closer.

Paxton looked over to find the young soldiers filing in to take their seats.

"I think I'll sit in on this first class just to make sure things go ok for you," Frank said.

"That's unnecessary."

"Oh, but I think it is." Frank turned and headed to the back of the classroom and took a seat.

Paxton looked at his class of twenty. They each had their tablets out and stared at him expectantly. One soldier, in particular, caught Paxton's eye. It was Keetey. Paxton grimaced inwardly. Slowly, he picked up his tablet again, walked to the front of his desk, and cleared his throat. "Good morning. I'm—" Paxton paused for a second. He didn't know how to introduce himself. Technically, he'd been demoted to

Private. At the same time, privates didn't teach.

"Go on, Corporal," Frank prompted Paxton while answering his question.

"Right. I'm Corporal Agnelli. Some of you may be familiar with my name. I was a charter soldier of the cleansing unit and the first in the unit to go underground. Over the next sixteen weeks, we will go over the following..." Paxton flipped a switch and went through the motions of the class. He read what he needed to read and showed what he was required to show without emotion. He taught through the material as best he could, without letting it affect him. He just hoped there wouldn't be questions at the end of class about his personal experience.

As he lectured, the soldiers listened and took their notes. Frank stared daggers at Paxton the entire time. Paxton did his best to ignore him, but he could feel his eyes on him the entire time.

Toward the end of class, Paxton gave the class their first assignment before dismissing them. Paxton was relieved that he'd made it through the first class without questions, but his relief was short-lived. With just five minutes left in class, Keetey raised his hand.

"Private?"

"Keetey, sir. We met in the gym yesterday."

Paxton motioned to him to continue, uninterested in being friendly. He knew whatever came next was going to be uncomfortable.

"Is it true that you were the one who actually came up with the idea to infiltrate the Notzrim in order to get rid of them?"

Paxton shifted uncomfortably. He looked from Keetey to Frank, who was watching him carefully. Paxton swallowed.

"Yes."

Another hand shot up.

Paxton looked at the muscular soldier who could barely fit in his seat. "Yes?"

"What gave you the idea? And how'd you know you'd be successful?"

Paxton looked at the clock on his tablet, hoping the class was over. It wasn't. He still had two minutes. Close enough, though. "I think that's a question for another day—"

"Answer him, Corporal," Frank ordered.

Paxton looked and challenged Frank silently, but knew it was pointless. "Before joining, I was an undercover police officer. Since I'm familiar with how to fit in undetected among dangerous groups, I figured the same could apply to the Notzrim. Up to that point, we had no leads on their whereabouts." Paxton looked at his tablet. 0930. "And that's time. You're dismissed."

Paxton could tell they were antsy to ask more questions, but they'd have to wait. And the deeper they got into the class, the harder it would be for Paxton to answer their questions. He was certain of that.

Paxton put the tablet down and was ready to dart out of the classroom. He disgusted himself and needed a shower to wash off the stink of deception, but then he remembered Frank was still in the room. He looked over at him expectantly.

"That was pathetic, soldier. Your job is to convey the seriousness of this unit and get them to believe the dangers of the Notzrim."

"If that's what you want, you've got the wrong person teaching and you know it."

"You did this to yourself, soldier. If you'd just been obedient from the beginning and followed your training and not gotten involved with the enemy, you wouldn't even be in this situation. You only have yourself to blame for your pain and guilt."

"That may be, but you don't have to twist the knife."

"Then what fun would that be?" Frank smiled. "Your next class starts in twenty. I'll be back then." Frank turned and walked out.

Paxton walked over to the front desk and sank into the seat with a groan. One class of this was hard enough, how many more would he be tortured with? Paxton slammed a fist onto the top of the desk. This wasn't what he signed up for, none of it was, and yet Frank got some sick pleasure out of watching Paxton betray his own convictions. It was true Paxton once bled these lies. They were so ingrained in him. But now? How could he stand to teach this curriculum as truth to others?

Paxton grabbed the tablet and opened it again. The book automatically loaded, but Paxton closed it and tried to poke around to see what else was on his tablet. Maybe there was information somewhere about employees that could help him learn when and where Mimi was working in the capitol.

Paxton continued to poke around, but there were only more textbooks for other classes. Eventually, he ran out of time and students were trickling into the classroom along with Frank. Paxton reopened the textbook on his tablet and stood, staring at his new students until they were all seated and ready to listen.

The second class wasn't as uncomfortable as the first. They didn't seem to be as curious or eager to learn about Paxton and his history. For that, Paxton was thankful, but he still hated teaching them the garbage that he did. And Frank continued to

CHAPTER 14

listen intently to everything Paxton said, as if waiting for him to trip up. Paxton made sure he kept strictly to the textbook and nothing beyond that. He'd teach what he needed to comply with, but nothing else. No personal anecdotes or extra intel that he knew was not inside the books. He didn't need these soldiers to become too enthusiastic about this job.

By the end of the day, Paxton had taught four ninety-minute classes, and he was exhausted. He never realized teaching was so mentally demanding. As the last student left the room, Frank walked to the front. Paxton hoped he would leave without saying a word, but that was too much to hope for.

"Better, but still abysmal. Your lackluster attitude better change on its own or I'll make it change. I want you to make me believe that you want to be here."

"But I don't. I'd rather do any other job than this one."

"Too bad. This is your assignment. So suck it up, soldier. See you tomorrow." Frank turned to leave.

"Are you seriously going to babysit the whole time? You have nothing more important to do at your rank than watch me? Or were you demoted?" Paxton couldn't help it, he had to poke the bear.

Frank whipped around and got in Paxton's face. He turned beet red, and a vein bulged from his neck. "Believe me, I would love nothing else than to send you away for good. I tried to get rid of you. Put you in the unit that's set to deploy overseas next week. But someone higher up decided you were the most qualified to teach this class. So now I'm stuck dealing with your insolent ass instead of dealing with things that really matter." Frank took a step back. "But don't you worry. I'm going to keep a close eye on you. One tiny little slip-up and you'll be outta here in a body bag." Frank stormed out of the room in a fury.

Paxton waited a moment to give space between the two of them before he took off toward the gym. While agitating Frank gave him some satisfaction, he needed to burn off the stress and anger that was boiling inside of him. He had no intention of slipping up in front of Frank and seeing his threat become reality.

* * * *

Aiden reached the bottom of the cliff and headed toward the highway. He didn't care what time of day it was or who saw him. Secretly, he hoped someone would see them so he could let out some of his anger.

"Aiden, wait! Where are you going? We can't go back now!"

Aiden ignored her.

"Aiden, stop!" A hand came down on Aiden's shoulder and pulled him to a stop. Tessa was out of breath. It took her a minute to talk. "Let's take a minute here."

"For what? The Myriad found them, they're dead, end of story. It's time to go back."

"It's also daytime. We can't head back till dark."

"I don't care. You and Marvin can stay if you want and wait, but I'm going back now. I'm going to tell Jared and Terrance what happened and I'm going to move forward on my original plan."

At this point, Marvin had rejoined the group. "You really think blowing up the capitol is going to solve this issue? Because it's not Aiden. No one is going to solve this problem except Meshiakh. He's the one who can win this war, not us."

"And where is Meshiakh, huh? How do you even know he's

coming because I sure don't!"

Tessa pulled her hand away from Aiden. Her face dropped. "What happened to you? You used to be the most optimistic person I knew."

"Reality set in, that's what happened. I saw who we're up against, and I don't like what I see. They need to be stopped. We can't keep letting innocent people die while Sabaoth does nothing."

Tears sprung to Tessa's eyes, but they didn't fall. "He's not doing nothing, and you know it."

At that moment, a car engine roared in the distance. Aiden spun around and saw a Humvee making its way toward them. Tessa grabbed Aiden's arm and tried to pull him behind an enormous pile of rocks. Aiden ripped his arm out from her grip and walked into the middle of the highway and stood there, staring at the vehicle. There needed to be justice for what happened to those Notzrim in the cave.

As the Humvee drew closer, it slowed to a stop. The soldier driving lowered his sunglasses and looked at Aiden, dumbfounded. He leaned over and said something to his partner, who got out of the vehicle.

"Now what in the world do you think you're doing?" He was a bowlegged man and as he came closer, Aiden recognized him as the smaller soldier from the convenience store earlier. "You know you're not supposed to be out here."

The man continued forward, slowly reaching for his handgun. Aiden lowered his head as he let out a yell and he ran full speed at the soldier—tackling him to the ground. The two of them hit the pavement hard, knocking the gun out of the soldier's hand. Aiden didn't wait to throw punches, blinded by his rage. The soldier fought back and overpowered Aiden, throwing Aiden off him and onto the ground. Aiden rolled onto his stomach and pushed himself to his feet.

He and the soldier noticed the gun on the pavement. They glanced at one another and both dove for the gun. Aiden threw an elbow hard into the soldier's cheek before picking up the gun and rolling onto his back, pointing the gun at the soldier who was about to come after him again. The soldier stopped and held his hands up in surrender.

The second soldier, the larger of the two, now stood outside the Humvee with his gun drawn. "Drop your weapon or you're dead."

"Hold on now," the first soldier said, still staring at Aiden.

The soldier grinned as he egged Aiden on, "C'mon. Do it. You know you want to."

Aiden's finger was on the trigger, ready to squeeze. His face contorted in rage and dripped with perspiration. He wanted so badly to give him what he deserved, but something stopped him.

"We don't have time for this," the second soldier said, raising his gun. "We're already—"

Aiden watched as a bullet ripped through the front of the second soldier's skull. The man's face went blank as he crumpled to the ground. The first soldier looked behind him and he too took a bullet to the head and fell on top of Aiden. Startled, Aiden pushed the dead soldier off him and scrambled to his feet. His breaths were shallow, and his hands shook fiercely. He looked around and saw Marvin jogging toward him.

"Help me with them." Marvin motioned to the two dead soldiers. He hooked his arms under the armpits of one and started dragging him back to the pile of rocks. Aiden stood there, his legs not working, his head blank. All his rage turned to shock. Marvin just killed two people. There they were, dead, just like the Notzrim in the cave. Lifeless bodies never to walk the earth again.

When Aiden didn't move, Tessa grabbed the second body and moved it for Aiden. When Tessa and Marvin returned, Aiden was still standing there. Marvin smacked Aiden upside the head. "What were you thinking, man?"

"You killed them," Aiden stammered.

"Well, you weren't going to and if I hadn't, you'd be dead. So, yeah, I killed those slimeballs."

"But—you shot them, they're...dead."

"What'd you think was going to happen when you went all crazy and threw yourself out there? That'd you'd throw a few punches and be on your way?"

"No, but—"

Marvin shook his head. "You're lucky I'm an excellent shot."

Tessa moved to the driver's side of the car. "We can talk about this later. Right now, we need to get out of the open. Get in the car."

"What?" Aiden and Marvin both looked at Tessa.

"Get in the car. We just got ourselves a free ride home." Tessa hopped into the driver's seat of the still-running Humvee and shoved her hand under the dashboard. Feeling around, she yanked out a small GPS tracker and tossed it out the window.

Chapter 15

Salome popped into Mo's cabin to check on her and Emily. It had been five days since the water poisoning incident. While most of those who'd gotten sick were now better, Emily still lay in bed, weak and struggling to keep food and water down.

Mo looked up from her book and forced a smile on her face as Salome entered.

Salome came over, hugged Mo, and sat. "How's she doing?"

"She ate an entire roll earlier and hasn't thrown it up yet."

"That's progress."

"It's a marvel to me how Emily did so well all those years in the tunnels with her weak immune system, but this. . . she can't seem to fight it and—" Mo stopped, unable to finish her sentence.

Salome placed her hand over Mo's and looked at her. "She'll pull through. Sabaoth will pull her out of this."

Mo nodded, her eyes glistening. "I hope you're right," she whispered, trying to hold back tears.

The women were quiet for a moment as Salome silently comforted Mo. Eventually, Mo cleared her throat and asked, "How's the search going?"

"Horrible." Salome put her elbow on the table and rested her cheek in her hand. "I have no new leads and no way of finding one without raising suspicion in the Hebrew village and getting Aryeh mad at me again."

"Don't give up." Mo looked toward the door before asking her next question. "And how goes it with this spy of ours?"

Salome frowned. "Now that one I did figure out."

"Are they going to stop?"

"I think so." Salome closed her eyes. Her heart ached at the thought of Eloina and the rift between them. They once were so close, but now, she feared they'd never be able to reconcile.

Mo placed a gentle hand over Salome's. "Who was it?" She spoke with deep concern.

"Someone I was once very close to, but not anymore."

Mo leaned over and hugged Salome, soothing her. Changing subjects, Mo pushed some papers over toward Salome. "Look at this."

Salome looked over the paper. It was a diagram and notes scrawled across it. It appeared to be the list of items needed for the party, along with a layout of the party's setup. Mo had tables for the food, an eating area in the grass, and an area for games.

"This looks amazing." Salome was in awe of Mo's work. Even with Emily sick, she was still working toward this party. "So, things are going well, I take it?"

Mo's lips pulled into a straight line as she bobbed her head from side to side with an uncertain look. "Kind of. The planning is going well, and we'll have plenty of food, but there's been a lot of talk and many of the people I originally convinced to come are rethinking."

"What? Why?"

"Rumors spread fast. People are mad. They believe that if the Hebrews can't make nice, why should they?"

"But it's not all the Hebrews, it's just one or two people."

"I know that, and you know that, but people like to exaggerate and lump everyone together as a whole. I'm afraid more will drop out if we don't reassure them fast."

It was as if everyone was against her and Mo in this. They were the only two who wanted and believed in this, but how can two people change the fearful minds of hundreds?

"What do we do?"

Mo placed a hand over Salome's. "We pray and we trust in Sabaoth. If he wants this, he'll make it happen."

Salome pulled her hand away and crossed her arms. "I'm wondering if he does want this. So many things keep going wrong. Maybe it is best to keep everyone separate."

"Have faith, Salome. It'll all come together."

At that moment, David entered the cabin. "There you are, Salome. I've been looking for you."

"Hi, papa. What's going on?"

"I came to tell you that Aryeh has sent his warriors to surround our village again."

Salome's nostrils flared as she stood and pounded her fist on the table. "He *what*! Why would he do that?"

"I'm not sure. Maybe you can talk to him."

"Oh, you bet I will." Salome stormed out of Mo's cabin and up the hill toward the open field. She gritted her teeth as heat flushed her face. This was the last straw. Salome was sick of everyone trying to make life so difficult. Why couldn't everyone just make nice and live peaceably? It was as if they'd forgotten everything they learned in preschool about making friends and being kind to one another.

* * * *

CHAPTER 15

At the top of the hill, Salome stopped. Her leg muscles twitched with adrenaline. In front of her stood a long line of statues stretching across the field between the Hebrew and Notzrim villages. It was sad that they so blindly followed Aryeh and his lies. How was it they thought it was okay to keep everyone separate? To treat these people like prisoners? Salome felt so small against this daunting task of unifying two peoples who seemed to want nothing to do with one another. Two peoples who had more in common with one another than they realized.

Salome didn't want to give up hope, but today, outrage bubbled inside her. She needed to focus on finding and cutting out the cancer in the Hebrew camp. The largest and most destructive tumor was whoever was causing all these sabotages. But today, she needed to focus on stopping Aryeh and his ludicrous decisions. Deep down, Salome believed Aryeh wanted peace, but a separated peace. Where the two villages could live as if the other didn't exist. It was an impossible dream, but maybe a good bargaining tool to get him to pull back his warriors.

Salome headed to the line and stopped in front of a man with long black hair and dark, deep-set eyes. The deep pox marks and the scowl on his face made him intimidating. Salome took a deep breath and let it out.

"Camden, I need to talk to Aryeh."

Camden scoffed. "You couldn't possibly have anything to say that he'd want to hear."

"That's for him to decide, not you. Now, go get him."

Camden chewed on his tongue for a moment as he glared at Salome. She refused to break eye contact with him, despite his demeaning stare. Camden hawked and spat on the grass next to Salome, nearly hitting her shoe. "You and your leeches should leave."

"We're not going anywhere. We have just as much right to be here as you do."

"They don't belong here and they're an endangerment to our valley."

"I'm not here to debate. I need to speak to Aryeh. Now go get him, or I'll go into the village myself."

After another moment of silent arguing, Camden turned and headed toward the Hebrew village.

Salome turned away from the others and let out a shaky breath as adrenaline pulsed through her veins.

An hour passed, and Salome still waited. She wondered if Camden was actually getting Aryeh or not. The wait was long and tedious, but at least it allowed Salome to calm down. Finally, she saw him returning, alone.

"Well?" she asked anxiously. "Where is he?"

"Come with me." Camden turned and headed toward the Hebrew village. Salome followed. They silently walked to the village. Camden didn't bother to look back to make sure Salome was following, either. He hastened, and Salome had to nearly jog to keep up.

As they approached, something seemed off. An ominous silence seeped through the community like a fog. Salome couldn't put her finger on it, but as they continued down the headed toward the main meeting building, she discovered what had happened. The place was a wreck as if a tornado had torn through it. Carts were pulled over and damaged, crates were smashed into pieces, and pottery shards were scattered among smashed fruits and vegetables. Salome's hand flew to her mouth as she looked about. All around her, she found something else destroyed and even damaged by fire.

CHAPTER 15

"What happened here?" Salome asked, afraid to know the answer.

Camden didn't respond, he just kept walking. Salome continued to follow. The few villagers she saw outside cleaning up stopped and glared. She could feel their hatred toward her. Salome's breaths grew shallow as heat rose in her face. *Please don't let this be what I think it is.*

When Salome stepped inside the large wooden building where she'd been so many times before, tears rose to her eyes. The entire inside was in shambles. Benches were thrown around, candelabras were broken, and the front altar was smashed to pieces.

"Quite a picture, isn't it?" Aryeh spoke from a bench in the middle of the room.

Salome slowly approached. "Yes."

Aryeh's eyes were red and swollen, but they had a look of rage in them. He clasped his hands tightly as he sat leaning on his knees. "I told you to stay away. I told you that keeping separate was the best option, and yet you ignored that."

"You think this is my fault?"

Aryeh's head snapped toward her. "I know it's your fault. It was the Notzrim who came in here and destroyed this place."

"You don't know that. There's no proof."

Aryeh snickered. "Proof? What proof do I need other than knowing that no one here would destroy their own home?"

"The Hebrews have been sabotaging any possibility of success for Notzrim. Did you ever consider that maybe that person framed the Notzrim?"

"Not possible." Aryeh shook his head. "My people know better."

"And yet they don't. Do you even know what they've done?"

Aryeh stood and walked away from Salome, toward the broken altar. "I should've never let them stay."

"Why are you fighting this so much? Do you realize that you have Hebrew families who want unity with the Notzrim? Who've already brought their children over to the Notzrim village and have been mingling with them? There could be such a benefit to us being together, but the problem is you keep making the Hebrews think the Notzrim are horrible people. You've put hatred in their hearts so much so that there are some who want to hurt the Notzrim. They even went as far as poisoning their well."

Aryeh slammed his fist on the altar beside him. "That's a lie!"

"Why would I lie? Aryeh, I want nothing more than for all of us to live in peace, but some people make that impossible and you're not helping the situation. This vandalism from the Notzrim is their warning that if things don't change, there will be a war. Now, I don't agree with them doing this, but I can understand it."

Aryeh walked toward Salome and stood close, towering over her. He could be intimidating, but Salome refused to allow herself to cower.

"My, how you've changed. Once so loyal to your people, and now you're nothing but a rebel."

"I've always been on the side of following Sabaoth, and that's what I'm doing."

Aryeh wrinkled his nose briefly. "What did you come here for, anyway? To gloat?"

"Of course not. I came to request you to remove your warriors and help put a stop to all this animosity."

"And why would I do that? Your people clearly need to be

contained."

"If you know what's good for your people, you'll do this. This vandalism is a warning to you. Whoever is causing these sabotages in the Notzrim village needs to stop. The only way for that to happen is if you help."

Aryeh crossed his arms. "I already told you, I know nothing about these sabotages."

Salome wanted to rip her hair out. He was being so stubborn despite seeing the evidence of what happens when two groups don't live in peace. "You honestly can tell me that with all your warriors standing guard, none of them have seen a Hebrew sneaking through into the Notzrim village to wreak havoc?"

"Like I said, I know nothing. If it were a Hebrew, I would know. Maybe it's one of your people trying to get the Notzrim to turn against the Hebrews. Ever thought of that?"

She had considered it, but she wasn't about to admit that to Aryeh. "It's not."

"I can't help you."

Salome flung her hands in the air in frustration as she walked away from Aryeh. "You're being stubborn, as usual." Salome turned back around and crossed her arms. "What do you have against the Notzrim people, anyway? What did they ever do to you?"

"Only a lifetime of ridicule and persecution."

"Really? To you personally? *All* the Notzrim of the world ridiculed you?"

Aryeh snickered. "Of course not. But they're all the same."

"What makes you think that just because you had an awful experience with one person that they're all bad?"

"It's been more than one." Aryeh's face softened as he remembered his past. He sat on a bench and stared at the ground. "Any Notzrim I've ever met growing up did nothing but make fun of me. My nose was too big, and my hair too curly. I talked funny. I'd get tripped in the hallway, never picked for projects or teams." Aryeh's face hardened as his eyes darkened. "And when one of them vandalized our home just because I went to Hebrew school, I vowed never again to trust a Notzrim." Aryeh looked up at Salome, the hate in his eyes tangible now, "or anyone who defends them."

Salome swallowed hard. Being bullied is a horrible thing to go through. She felt sorry for Aryeh, but to hold on to that hatred for so many years was wrong. "I'm sorry that happened to you, I really am, but that—"

"You can leave now." Aryeh sniffled, stood, and turned away from Salome.

"No. I need your word that you'll help find who's sabotaging the Notzrim village, so things don't get worse."

"Camden, get her out of here."

Camden came forward and grabbed hold of Salome's arm. He pulled, trying to get Salome to move, but she rooted herself to her spot. "Aryeh, don't you see you can get what you want? The Notzrim will leave you alone if you only help find this person hurting them. That's it, that's all you have to do."

Aryeh walked away while Camden continued to pull at her. Eventually, Salome ripped her arm away from Camden and left on her own. Aryeh was so stubborn, and it drove her mad. She'd done what she could on her own. Now, she prayed he'd change his mind.

* * * *

After the near capture of the intruder, the week was quiet, yet

CHAPTER 15

Amina felt unsettled. She wanted to believe that whoever was behind all the mishaps finally realized the Notzrim wised up and were now taking action to stop them. After all, nothing bad had happened since the last incident. Yet, Amina couldn't help but have a nagging feeling about it all. She was antsy. They needed to find this person.

With so little happening, Amina set to help build the cabins. She needed to keep herself busy and keep her mind off Paxton, Aiden, and anything else out of her control.

Josiah had joined the build team as well and the two of them worked together clearing bushes, leveling and compacting dirt, and prepping the area for cabins to be built.

"Amina, Josiah," a man called out. He was the head overseer of the building project. "Go get us more lumber. It's on the outskirts of the town. Take the donkey and wagon with you to haul it."

Amina and Josiah did what they were told. And after a good five minutes of coaxing the donkey to walk, they finally headed toward the far west side of the village where they kept the lumber.

It was a mild day, but with all the hard labor, Amina was sweaty, and her face flushed.

Josiah handed her a water jug. "You look terrible."

Amina took a swig of water. "Gee thanks. You don't look so great yourself."

"I just mean, you look tired. Do you want to rest while I go get the lumber?"

"No. I don't need to rest. Thank you very much. I'm fine, just hot."

Josiah shrugged. "Suit yourself."

They walked in silence for a while, not feeling the urge to

fill the void with menial conversation. But then Josiah spoke up. "How's Emily doing?"

"Okay, I guess. She'll live, which is good, but I don't know how long she'll be like this."

Another pause.

"My dad isn't doing well at all."

Amina looked at Josiah, both startled and confused. "He's still sick?"

"Yeah, and it only seems to be getting worse."

"That's awful. I'm so sorry."

"He's talking about putting someone else in charge as if he's never going to recover."

"You mean he wants to put you in charge?"

"No, thankfully. I think he's finally learned that I am not the leader type. I've tried and I kind of suck at it. He knows I'd rather be doing other things to help. Things that don't require having the weight of an entire village on my shoulders." Josiah's face dropped and his eyes glazed over. "Anyway, he's talked about Paul being in charge. I think she'd be good at it. At least until my dad—" Josiah stopped and swallowed hard. Amina could tell he was holding back tears.

They walked in silence again.

Amina and Josiah broke through the tree line and could see the pile of logs ahead of them. She also noticed several Hebrew warriors standing six feet apart in a line, guarding. Amina's face twisted, feeling both shocked and angry.

"What is going on?" Amina asked Josiah.

He shook his head, his mouth agape.

Amina stormed over to the warriors and demanded to know what was happening, but she stopped when she saw Salome coming toward the village and through the warrior's line.

CHAPTER 15

She'd been over at the Hebrew's village, but why? Salome stopped, and said something to the warrior escorting her. Amina furrowed her brow. *What was she up to?*

Salome took off, heading back toward the village. Amina took off toward her. She needed to get to the bottom of this.

"Salome!"

Salome stopped mid-stride and slowly raised a hand in greeting, but she didn't look pleased to see Amina.

"What is all that?" Amina asked, motioning her hand toward the wall of people.

"*That* is Aryeh being paranoid." Her voice was curt.

"About what? We've kept away, haven't we?"

Salome put a hand on her forehead and looked away. "Someone vandalized the Hebrew village. Of course, Aryeh thinks it was the Notzrim." Salome shook her head. She put her hands on her hips and continued. "You know, I'm trying really hard to keep the peace around here." Salome ran her hands through her hair, looking down at the village and then back up to the warriors. "Your people are making it impossible."

"There's no way it was Notzrim who did that. Our guard would've seen them leave. Likely, it was our sabotaging friend who's trying to pin this on the Notzrim and turn everyone against each other." Amina's muscles trembled as the heat rose in her face. She tried to take a step away, to even her breathing. How could Salome jump to such a harsh conclusion? "And what do you mean, *we're* making it difficult? It's *your* people who are encouraging prejudice."

Salome's nostrils flared as she held back the tears welling in her eyes, but she said nothing.

"I know tensions are high right now," Josiah spoke softly, "but let's not turn against each other. We're all friends and we all want what's best."

Amina whirled around. "What's best is stopping this sabotager and keeping to ourselves."

"No, what's best is putting this in Sabaoth's hands and stop trying to force a solution. It's only making things worse."

"Well, maybe if Salome had taken my concerns seriously sooner, we could've found and stopped this person before it escalated to this."

"I can't do everything on my own," Salome shouted. "Stop putting all the responsibility on me to find this person. We're supposed to work together."

"I'm doing my part. What are you doing? Cuz it doesn't look like much to me. Can you even handle your job?" Amina seethed.

Salome stood straight and let out a deep breath, calming herself. "I'm leaving before we both say anything worse to one another. Goodbye Amina."

Amina watched Salome head down the hill and toward her cabin before spinning around toward Josiah and letting out a shout. Her hands clenched and unclenched. What was happening? Josiah still stood, watching her, his arms crossed. Amina's stomach dropped and she looked down at the grass. Salome was her friend and Amina had said terrible things. How could she let her anger get the better of her?

"You're right, Josiah," Amina said, looking at him. "I am making things worse." She threw her hands in the air and let them drop to her side. "So what do I do?"

"We keep doing the things we're doing to protect the village, but we do it with prayer and trust that Sabaoth will bring about justice."

Chapter 16

Aiden sat silently in the backseat of the Humvee as it bounced across the highway. The tiny backseat smelled of tobacco and sweat. Aiden stared out the window, replaying the scene in his head. Regretting every second. How did he allow so much anger? He'd lost all sight of logic and wisdom. If it hadn't been for Marvin, Aiden would be dead. Aiden was thankful for Marvin, and he truly regretted his action, but it didn't take away the fact that the inhumanity of the Myriad outraged him.

Aiden wrung his shaking hands and buried his face in them, trying to slow his breathing. It didn't work. He pulled his hands away to find blood on them. Looking into the rear-view mirror, he saw the blood streaked across his cheeks. Aiden frantically looked around for a rag, a shirt, anything. He'd just watched someone die. It had happened so fast, but it was no less terrifying. Aiden found a jacket. Grabbing it, he frantically rubbed at his cheeks, hoping the blood would come off, but it was already dry. He rubbed harder until his skin was raw. Then he grabbed his backpack and pulled out his canteen. He shook what little water he could into his palm and splashed it on his face and scrubbed. The blood came off easier but still left red lines.

Aiden looked into the rear-view mirror again and noticed

Marvin watching.

"What happened in that cave?" Marvin asked.

"The Myriad killed all of them."

Marvin whistled. "Dang. That's awful. I knew we should've gone through the mountains."

"Shut up Marvin," Tessa snapped. "It wouldn't have mattered. They'd been dead for days."

"How do you know?"

"I just know." Tessa looked in the mirror. "So, what happened to you? Were you trying to get yourself killed?"

"No, of course not. I don't know, I just kinda lost it."

"Yeah, you did," Marvin smirked.

"Seriously, Marvin, if you don't shut up, I'm kicking you out of this car."

"I know this could happen," Aiden spoke, trying to process everything. "But they went into that cave like dozens of other hidings and slaughtered innocent people, all because they refused to give up their faith. It's not right, and we can't keep letting them do this."

For nine years, Aiden had lived in hiding. He knew what was happening, but it was distant knowledge, unreal to him. It wasn't until he'd spent time in the capitol and the Myriad headquarters that things became real. And now, seeing that mass grave, reality settled in. He could no longer choose to live at a distance. He couldn't live disconnected from the surrounding horrors.

"Maybe not," Tessa said, "but we have to be smart about it, too. And what you did, was straight-up stupid."

"I know." Aiden's face flushed.

"I'm all for taking down the Myriad," Marvin chimed in casually. "I'll help you do whatever you want to take them down."

"Thanks, Marvin. What about you Tessa?"

Tessa bit her lip. Not looking at Aiden, she continued to stare at the road.

"She's too gentle for that," Marvin said quietly over his right shoulder as if Tessa couldn't hear him.

Tessa slammed on the brakes. The Humvee skidded to a stop as both Marvin and Aiden braced themselves. Once the vehicle stopped, Tessa stared at Marvin with daggers in her eyes. "Get out," her voice was cold and quiet.

"Oh, c'mon Tessa. Lighten up. I was kidding."

"I told you to keep your mouth shut, or you'd have to get out. You didn't listen, so get out."

Marvin stared back, challenging her. "Make me."

No one moved. Tension and frustration permeated the Humvee. Aiden awkwardly sat there, wondering if Tessa was serious. Everyone dealt with the shock of death in their own way, and at the moment, Tessa's fuse was short.

When Aiden couldn't handle the tension anymore, he said, "We really should keep going. Tessa, you know it wouldn't be smart to make him get out. And Marvin, you should apologize."

Marvin spoke through gritted teeth. "Sorry."

Tessa narrowed her eyes. "I don't believe you, but I forgive you. Just stop with your arrogant and snarky remarks, and we'll be good."

Tessa hit the gas, and they continued on their way.

"As for your questions, Aiden. I'll help, so long as you have a smart plan, and we don't just run into the capitol, guns blazing."

"I can promise, this will be very thought out."

Aiden leaned back in his seat, satisfied. He would gather a team. It didn't matter if Jared said no. So long as he had enough followers, he would move forward. Who cares what Jared and Terrance think?

* * * *

Jared's expression, when he saw Aiden and the others enter the office, said he already suspected the worst, and Tessa confirmed it as she retold what happened. Jared swore and punched the table.

"How did they find them so fast?" Terrance asked.

"There are a lot of possibilities for that," Marvin said. "Someone might've slipped up and gone outside at the wrong time. The Myriad have new technology or they have a mole, who knows."

"We can't keep letting this happen. They can't win!" Jared yelled in frustration.

"This has happened recently?" Aiden asked, shocked by his comment.

Tessa turned. "About three weeks ago, we went to find another small group of Notzrim hiding out east, deep inside an old mining shaft. When we got there, all their things were there, but they were gone."

"Maybe they survived and just fled?"

Tessa shook her head. "Those on that mission said, about five miles southwest, they found the bodies strung up in a tree, torn to shreds."

Aiden winced at the thought, his stomach churning. "This is why we need to act. The Myriad are constantly one step ahead. How long before they realize we're still hiding here? How long

CHAPTER 16

before they find our families in the mountains? Whether or not you like it, we have to take down the capitol. I know you think—"

"I'm in," Jared interrupted. "You're right, they're gonna keep developing more tech and they're gonna keep searching until we're all gone. I don't want that to happen. Let's do this. Let's take down the capitol."

Aiden blinked, unsure of what to say next. He'd been ready for an argument, to give all the reasons this was their only option, but Jared so easily agreed. Now what? "Okay, good. I guess we should start putting some plans into action. Um... so..."

"Aiden, you and Tessa should go talk with Mitchum and start working on explosives. We're going to need a lot and they have to be powerful. We can send a team out for supplies. I know a group of nomads would be happy to give us whatever we need."

Nomads were the few non-Notzrim citizens who refused to take the mark. They lived in The Beyond, forced to roam and scavenge. The Myriad didn't hunt them like they did the Notzrim, but if caught, they still faced arrest unless they could thoroughly bribe the Myriad.

Aiden nodded. "Of course. I can also reach out to Mimi and let her know we're ready to move forward. She'll need to arrange transportation for us."

"And get us blueprints," Jared added. "Once we have those, Terrance and I can put together an entry plan. Do you think Mimi would meet with us?"

Aiden tilted his head from side to side, debating. He wasn't even sure she'd changed her mind about helping. Her mark would make coming into the tunnels unsafe for everyone.

"Probably, but only if you meet at our neutral location."

"Done. Just set it up." Jared turned to Terrance. "Go talk with Evan and put a team of at least together."

"More than that. There are three different areas to hit. Two main buildings plus the air hangers at the far end of the property. If we're going to do this, we need to take down every location where they have weapons."

Jared paused, unhappy about the new information. "Alright, we'll probably need twelve people, and they should know this is a high-risk op. It's not likely they'll come back."

"Oh, I'm on it like white on rice." Terrance high-fived a reluctant Jared before darting down the tunnel.

Jared studied Aiden with an unreadable expression. "That's more than a third of our people. This better be worth it."

* * * *

Aiden stood in a busy airport, people rushing by all around him in a flurry of jackets and suitcases. He hurried toward his gate, only to find he had to wait in a mile-long line. Aiden stepped into the line, tapping his toe and looking at his watch: Twelve-oh-six.

The plane was due to depart at twelve-ten, and he needed to get on the plane. He didn't know why or where was going, but the urgency within him grew, wanting to explode. As he glanced toward the front of the line, he noticed it didn't end. It had no beginning and no end, nor did it seem to move.

An airline worker brushed past him. Aiden opened his mouth to yell at the airline worker, but nothing came out of his throat. Aiden tried to run after the worker but couldn't. Metal cages anchored his feet to the ground. Frantically, Aiden tried to undo the cages around his feet. Twelve-oh-eight.

CHAPTER 16

He was running out of time. The line moved, and people brushed past him to get on the plane. They ran, they pushed, they forced their way in, knocking Aiden around. Twelve-oh-nine.

Aiden tried to move again. This time, he could. The cages were gone, but his luggage was a cinderblock he could lift. He tried dragging it, slowly, across the floor. He needed to get to his gate. He tried to leave the luggage behind and go on his own, but handcuffs connected him to the handle. Aiden kept struggling to the front. Pulling with all his might until he broke a sweat. Finally, he made it to the front. Twelve-ten.

The door slammed shut with a gust of air. Aiden rushed to the window, watching the plane push back further and further away. Aiden pounded on the window. He ran to the door and tried to force it open. Airline workers grabbed him by the shoulders and pulled him backward. A voice said, "I'll take care of it." Then there was an explosion of light.

Aiden woke with a jolt, breathing heavily as cold sweat trickled down his back. He reached for a small canteen and took a long drink and then rubbed the back of his neck and forehead with his handkerchief. What was that all about? Aiden rarely had dreams, and they were never so detailed. Was it possible it was more than a dream?

He pulled himself to his feet, feeling worn out as if he'd just worked out. He tried to push the dream aside, telling himself it was nothing. There was so much on his mind, it was natural to have restless dreams.

Putting the dream out of his head, Aiden grabbed his cell phone and flipped it open. Tonight, he and Mimi were supposed to meet again.

Aiden typed: *Blueprints. 12 disguises.* Then pressed send and waited several minutes. No response.

He closed the phone and slid it into his pocket before throwing on his combat boots and heading to find Mitchum. He didn't expect a response so quickly, but it was still disappointing. Nothing would work if she didn't show.

Mitchum sat amongst a pile of scraps in Dwelling Six. Most people called what Mitchum owned junk, but he called it treasure. An expert engineer, Mitchum could take anything and turn it into something amazing. He'd taught Aiden most everything the boy knew about technology. Given that Aiden had spent his college years in hiding, this was the only college education he received toward becoming a technical engineer. If Teivel hadn't taken over, Aiden was sure he would have gone to college and then worked for Validus Technologies, the heart of the capitol and the hub for all Teivel's evil plans.

Mitchum stooped at a workbench wearing his usual aviator hat, the tassels as scraggly as his long, dark gray hair. He hunched over something, using tools that looked tiny in his large round hands. As Aiden moved closer, he could see Mitchum working on multiple long, slender pieces of metal attached to one another. It looked similar to an arm with a sort of claw at the end.

Aiden stopped beside Mitchum and watched for a bit, admiring his steady hand and intent focus. Mitchum continued soldering. He would take his tool and stick it in the small fire he had going beside him in a small metal bowl, then he'd use the burning tip to melt the metal on his project. Despite not having the usual tools necessary for building and creating, Mitchum still tinkered.

"What are you working on? Is it some new weapon?"

"Not exactly," Mitchum said, still focused on his project.

CHAPTER 16

He put down the scalding hot tool and picked up a screwdriver. He tightened a few screws. After that, he grabbed a wet rag and wiped the metal to cool it off. It sizzled, letting off a small puff of steam. Mitchum smiled and held up his handiwork. "All done."

"What is it?"

Mitchum attached the metal to his right arm like a shield. With his finger, he tapped a button, shooting a long extension with a claw on it. He opened his right hand, spreading his fingers wide, and the claw opened. Carefully, Mitchum moved his arm until the claw wrapped around a tin cup. He made a fist, closing the claw. He pressed the button again to retract the extendable arm, bringing the cup to him. "Pretty neat, huh?"

"You made an extendable arm?" Aiden said, trying hard not to sound too condescending.

"It can go up to ten feet. That's ten fewer feet I have to walk to get something."

Aiden shook his head. Mitchum used to tell him how he was the next up-and-coming robotics engineer in the medical field. Now he was making crude robotic mechanisms with no actual use.

Mitchum took the arm off and set it down. "I have to keep entertained somehow. With everyone either gone or busy training and fighting all day, it gets lonely. But I'm glad to see you here. What can I do for you? You interested in making something?"

"I am actually. Jared has agreed to move forward with my plan."

Mitchum frowned and lowered his chin. "What exactly is your endgame?"

"Taking down the capitol, and give the Notzrim a fighting chance at survival. The Myriad need to be stopped." What else could there be?

"And who's to say Teivel doesn't send more Myriad to keep searching for us?"

"Then we'll take them down, too. I'll take them all down if I have to."

"And then he'll just send more, and it'll be this endless cycle."

"So, what are you saying?"

"I'm saying this won't solve anything, it'll only delay."

Aiden blew out a large breath of air, his muscles tightening. "Look, I already have Jared and Terrance on my side, and we need your help."

"Why not just wait?"

"Wait till what? We're all massacred? Do you want to end up like the Notzrim in that cave? You want to be tortured or watch your loved ones suffer? Because I don't." A lump caught in Aiden's throat and he swallowed hard. If he could wait, and have faith, they were safe, then he would. Aiden nearly laughed out loud. *Faith.* Where had his faith gone? Aiden's head dropped for a moment, and he glimpsed the two markings on the opposite arms. One was the barcode mark of loyalty to an evil dictator, the other, the sign of faith in the coming Meshiakh, who'd restore true peace and righteousness.

"These people are evil and have to be stopped. Are you going to help or not? We need bombs." His voice fell flat.

"I don't know if I can do it."

"What do you mean? Isn't that why you stayed behind? To help the militia?"

CHAPTER 16

"Yes, but with communications and security systems, not weapons. I told Jared, in the beginning, that I wouldn't make weapons. Besides, what's the point?"

"The point is to take down the capitol and hurt Teivel's operations."

"And all the innocent lives that work in the capitol?"

Aiden shoved his hands in his pockets as he shifted his weight. "I have a plan to get them out," he lied. Truth was, he hadn't thought about that at all. Now he would. If he let innocent people die, he was no better than Teivel.

"You really think you can get everyone out safely, blow the place to hell and survive?"

To say yes was arrogant. There was a tremendous risk in everything he wanted to do, and he honestly couldn't say how it would turn out.

When Aiden didn't answer, Mitchum continued, "Why not wait for Meshiakh? He's the one who will wage war against Teivel and win. He's the one who will deliver us from this hell hole we're in. We must wait in faith. He's so close."

"I know you think so, but what you saw in the sky was just another electrical storm. Meshiakh isn't coming anytime soon." *Or ever,* Aiden wanted to say but wasn't ready to admit out loud.

"Oh, my dear boy," Mitchum put a hand on Aiden's shoulder, "how far you've fallen."

Aiden stepped back from his touch. "I haven't fallen. I've wised up. Now, are you going to help me? Tessa and I can make these on our own."

Mitchum laughed. "No, you can't."

Aiden crossed his arms. "This is happening."

"If you do it on your own, you'll kill yourselves before ever getting to the capitol."

"Then help."

"Why should I?"

"Because the Myriad are evil, and because they slaughtered another group."

That gave Mitchum pause. He sat on his stool silent, stroking his beard while his lips moved silently. Aiden couldn't be sure, but it seemed he held back tears, too. He was quiet for so long Aiden thought he'd never respond.

Finally, he spoke quietly, "Alright, let's get to work." Mitchum began rattling off a long list of items he needed as he pulled out a scrap piece of paper and a piece of charcoal. He started drawing out blueprints for his devices and writing notes while Aiden looked through Mitchum's junkyard for everything they needed.

They spent the rest of the day looking for materials and piecing what they could together. By the end of the day, they'd created fifteen shells with detonators. Once they added the explosives, the bombs would be powerful enough to take out a couple of floors. Put enough of them in one building and they'd bring the entire thing to the ground like a sandcastle.

"These are just the shells. I still need the chemicals."

"Do we not have gunpowder?"

"Not enough. We need something stronger. Talk to Jared. He knows people."

Aiden nodded before heading off to find Jared. As he moved his way through the tunnels, his phone buzzed. He grabbed his phone out of his pocket and looked at the text.

"Drop off. Tonight. Usual."

Aiden smiled to himself. He'd planned to go meet Mimi tonight whether or not she showed, but her confirmation

CHAPTER 16

of bringing supplies of some sort was perfect. Things were coming together. Soon, he'd have everything he needed to make this mission a success.

Chapter 17

The next morning, Paxton arrived in the classroom early, hoping to finish scouring through the tablet for information, but to no avail. The tablet was strictly textbooks and old mission files for teaching only. Paxton needed to find another computer.

The door opened, and Frank and another soldier entered. Paxton stood at attention and did his obligatory salute.

"At ease. This is Staff Sargent McGunnins," Frank said, motioning to the man with icy blue eyes and a short, stubby nose standing beside him. McGunnins nodded, barely moving his massive round head. "He'll be taking my place today. I filled him in, so don't think you can get away with anything, Agnelli. This man will report directly to me everything and if there's one slip up, you're done."

"Sir, yes sir," Paxton replied, monotone.

"Good. I'm off then."

McGunnins stared at Paxton, sizing him up, no doubt. Paxton stood waiting for a comment, or at least a grunt, from this goon. He said nothing. Instead, he headed to the back of the classroom. He pulled out a tablet and a small video camera and attached the camera to the wall. He sat and fiddled with the tablet. A red light appeared on the camera.

CHAPTER 17

Paxton turned back to his desk and sat, trying not to show his annoyance at his new situation.

The second day was like the first. He taught what was in the textbook. Avoided anything extra. Skirted as many questions as possible, and was incredibly uncomfortable the whole time. It was not ideal, but at least he didn't have Frank breathing down his neck. Instead, he had a camera to record everything he did and said, along with Igor in the back taking notes. Anytime Paxton tried to read McGunnins' reactions to something he said, he got nothing. The guy probably did great at poker.

At the end of the day, McGunnins collected his things and left without acknowledging Paxton. Paxton prayed McGunnins had found nothing worth reporting to Frank.

The week was mind-numbing. Paxton would teach all day, go to the gym afterwards and then pass out on his bed. He taught two days, did one full day of PT and drills, and then taught two more days before the weekend. He was thrilled when Saturday morning rolled around and he could sleep in. Of course, that meant missing breakfast, but he could last until lunch.

Paxton walked into the mess hall in the main building for lunch and found it packed with soldiers and scientists intermingled together at the long tables. He walked to the counter and through the line, pulling along a plate of spaghetti, salad, and a slice of chocolate cake. There were always so many options at the cafeteria and at first Paxton could hardly eat anything. For one, he'd gone so long just eating the minuscule bread and water that his stomach was too small for heartier foods. But there was also the guilt. The guilt of knowing those in the capitol gorged themselves with a variety of food while the Notzrim scrounged for stale chips, expired canned goods, and any other leftovers in The Beyond—it made his stomach churn. Paxton resolved to eat only what was necessary to sustain his energy.

Paxton grabbed a water and headed to find an open spot, but nothing was available. A hand waving to his right caught his eye. He looked over and groaned when he saw Keetey enthusiastically waving Paxton over to join them. It wasn't typical for high-ranking soldiers to sit with those of a lower rank, especially since at least one of them was a student of his. Keetey was the last person he wanted to see, but he was persistent and there was nowhere else to sit. Paxton reluctantly joined him and his buddies.

It was a small group of four young men with the same buzzed head, shaved face, and eager eyes. For all Paxton knew, they were relatives or clones. Paxton wouldn't put it past Teivel to clone soldiers. It didn't matter. Paxton had no interest in becoming friends, so he didn't need to know them apart.

Keetey introduced the group and as they each said their hellos and greetings, Paxton forced a smile and then ate.

The conversation started typically. The group complained about training, bragged about their strengths, and argued about who in the group would win top recruit. Paxton kept his head down, shoveling food into his mouth, and hoping to get out of there before they took an interest in him.

A young man with more blondish hair than the others asked, "How long have you been with the Myriad, Corporal?"

Paxton groaned inwardly before answering. "Eight years."

"And the whole time you were in the same unit?" The man sitting next to Paxton had more freckles on his arm than the starry sky.

"That's right." Paxton kept his head down and kept eating.

"Did you join on your own, or did they recruit you?"

Paxton didn't respond right away. That was a loaded question. On the one hand, he chose to join, but had a serious organized crime boss not threatened his family, and had the Myriad not promised protected in exchange for his services, would he have joined on his own? "They recruited me."

The fourth young man, sitting across from Paxton with a serious scowl on his face, asked, "So what's your deal, Corporal?"

Paxton looked from his plate, taken aback by the accusatory tone, especially toward someone of a higher rank. Paxton raised his eyebrows, challenging the man to rephrase before there were serious consequences.

Keetey elbowed the kid hard in the ribs. "What's your problem? Show some respect."

"Sorry, Corporal, sir. I just meant, I'd like to hear how you ended up being our AIT teacher instead of running the purity unit, sir." He rubbed at his ribs. His tone was only slightly less aggressive than before

"That's none of your concern." Paxton shoved another bite of chocolate cake in his mouth.

"Were you injured?" Another of the boys asked, clearly examining Paxton's cut and bruised body.

"Or were you demoted?"

Keetey leaned on the table. "Yeah, we're all dying to know how someone like you would end up teaching instead of doing what you're clearly skilled at doing. Unless something happened to you, and you're no longer fit to fulfill your duty."

"Or maybe the rumors are true."

That made Paxton look up. "Rumors?"

"Yeah, that you're a traitor. That you went soft and flipped sides during your last undercover mission and that it's your fault we lost nearly any entire unit during the most recent underground raid."

Paxton stood, his teeth clenched tightly, and his face burned. "We're done here." Paxton snatched his tray and walked off.

If those were the stories going around about Paxton, it was no wonder Frank was doing everything he could to squelch them by making Paxton teach the purity class. He likely hoped that by Paxton teaching the class, he'd change the minds of the youngest recruits and convince them that Paxton was still on their side. You can't have a traitor or a sympathizer roaming around the capitol imposing their lies about the Notzrim. Even if Paxton could share the truth about the Notzrim, he wasn't sure anyone would believe him, anyway.

It was time to find Mimi and speed up his escape plan.

Paxton stepped out of the elevator on level 400 and headed down the hallway toward a lab. He didn't know if Mimi was still working at the capitol, but he hoped someone could give him information as to her whereabouts. They'd only met once before, briefly, when she helped Aiden, Amina, Josiah, and Maya escape a few months ago, but he hoped she'd be willing to help him if she was around.

Paxton walked into the lab, looking around. There was only a balding man with glasses who looked at Paxton, startled.

"Can I help you?"

"I'm looking for someone."

"Oh?" The man pushed his glasses up his nose.

"A young woman named Mimi? About yay high." He held out his hand at about his shoulder. "Super-curly brown hair, big eyes."

CHAPTER 17

The man nodded. "Yes, I know Mimi, but I haven't seen her today. She usually works in lab 422."

When he arrived at lab 422, he stopped just before going in. Through the door's window, Paxton found Mimi, but she was talking to someone. Another woman, taller with dark chestnut hair streaked with gray and pulled into a tight bun. The woman wore military fatigues and her back was to the door, but Paxton was pretty certain he knew who it was. By the look on Mimi's face, it was not a pleasant conversation.

Paxton continued to watch, trying to read Mimi's lips, but she spoke too quickly for him to catch a word. He debated walking in and breaking up the intense conversation, but he couldn't take that risk. The last thing he needed was Frank learning that he was poking around the labs. As he watched the conversation escalate into an argument, he flinched as the Myriad woman slapped Mimi across the face. Mimi's face whipped to the side as she grabbed her cheek. Slowly, Mimi looked back at the woman, her lips pulled tight into a straight line. Paxton read her words, "get out."

The woman turned, and sure enough, it was Cecilia Haddad, Amina's mother. Paxton looked around and bolted through the closest door. The four scientists in the room looked up from their work and stared at him with mixed expressions. He ignored them and stood by the door, listening for Cecilia's footsteps to disappear. Certain she'd turned a corner, Paxton poked his head out and checked the hallway. She was gone.

When he returned to Mimi's lab, she stooped over the table with her back toward the door. Paxton walked into the room and approached Mimi. She was deep in thought and didn't seem to notice him. Paxton stood beside her and waited. When she finally realized someone was nearby, she let out a startled yell and fell off her stool and onto the floor. Paxton helped her up. "Sorry, I didn't mean to scare you."

Mimi pulled the earbuds out of her ears. "Well ya did, nimrod. What are doing surprising people like that?" Mimi smoothed out her lab coat.

She had a bright red welt on her left cheek from where Cecilia slapped her. When she realized another soldier was in front of her, her demeanor changed. She stood straight and softened her expression. He couldn't be certain, but she almost looked scared. "Can I help you with something?" she asked politely. She looked past Paxton as if expecting someone. "I rarely get visits from. . . *you people.*" She clearly didn't recognize him.

"I'm Paxton, we've met before."

She stared at him curiously. "I don't talk to a lot of Myriad, and even when I do, I rarely remember them. How did we meet?"

"I'm not Myriad."

She looked over his fatigues skeptically. Her eyes lit up with recognition. "Oy gevalt, you're alive! But how? And why the uniform?"

"It's a long story. I saw you talking with Cecilia. Is everything okay? Are you in danger here?"

Mimi gently touched her cheek and pulled it away, waving her hand dismissively. "It's fine. She thinks I had something to do with Aiden's escape and she wants me to reach out to him for her. She has no proof or way of making me do what she wants, so she's harmless. Maybe a little desperate, but harmless, I'm sure."

Paxton crossed his arms. Sometimes the desperate ones were the most dangerous. He rethought asking her for help. If she was already being scrutinized by Cecilia, helping him put

CHAPTER 17

Mimi in greater risk.

Mimi sat on her stool and tapped the table with her fingertips as if playing a piano. Before Paxton could say anything, she spoke, "Look, I'm sure you didn't come here to just shoot the breeze. So, why are you here?"

"I came for your help, but I don't—"

"What do you need?"

Paxton opened his mouth, about to speak, when she popped up and moved to the door. She poked her head into the hallway, then closed the door and locked it. She hastened to a side door, waving Paxton to follow.

Mimi closed the door to the tiny closet. "Okay, go on."

"I need to escape."

Mimi crossed her arms and studied Paxton for a moment. "I don't know. I mean, I don't really know you. That's a big risk for me."

"I get your hesitation, but I made a promise to Amina, and I can't keep it without help. You're the only person here I can trust."

"Wow, we don't even know each other. I mean, we met under such dire circumstances. I want to believe you're good people, considering how you sacrificed yourself and all, but can I trust you? How do I know you won't turn me in if it comes down to you and me?"

"I have no interest in either of us getting caught. Please, Mimi. I can't stay here."

Paxton stared at Mimi expectantly. He could see her contemplating, calculating. He hoped she'd convince herself to help him.

"You know you're lucky. I happen to be working on getting some access cards for Aiden. I can make you an extra one that allows you access to any floor in the building."

Paxton grabbed Mimi's hand, elated. "That would be fantastic. When can I get it from you?"

Mimi pulled her hand away. "Tomorrow."

"Perfect. I'll be back." Paxton started out, but then turned around. "Wait, did you say you're working with Aiden?"

"Yes. I'm helping him take the capitol down from the inside."

Paxton's eyes grew wide. "I'm sorry, what? He's coming back here?" It was about the dumbest thing he'd heard.

"Yes, that's usually how you take something down from the inside."

"You honestly think that's a good idea?"

"It's a solid plan. It'll work."

"And then what are you going to do?" Paxton glanced down at Mimi's wrist where her barcode tattoo indicated the microchip embedded under her skin and held her captive in the city. "It's not like you can escape."

Mimi pulled her wrist to her chest and rubbed at it with a distant look. "If I could get it out without losing my hand, I would."

Paxton lowered his chin, his face soft with empathy. "I'll ask again, what are you going to do?"

Mimi dropped her hand and rolled her eyes. "I'll figure something out. Don't worry about me."

"Fine." Paxton didn't want to keep pushing, but he didn't want to see Mimi get hurt either.

She needed an exit plan because once things went down, the Myriad would immediately launch an investigation and pull up backlogs of every employee's whereabouts. If Mimi had been to see Aiden, both she and the Notzrim militia would be found and killed. "When's it going down?"

"That's what—" Mimi stopped herself. "Come back tomorrow. I'll have your card."

"Now hold a minute. Aiden and Amina are my friends. I'm here to help the Notzrim. I have no intention of giving away any information."

Mimi shook her head. "It's not that. People are watching. We've been in here too long, and people will get suspicious." Mimi grabbed a box and stepped out of the room. "I'll see you tomorrow." Mimi waved goodbye.

The abrupt ending to their conversation threw Paxton off, but he said goodbye and left. Once he had the information he needed, he could leave this horrible place.

****

That night, Aiden waited in the usual convenience store for Mimi to arrive. The dim glow of the moon filled the disheveled store with eerie shadows. Even though he couldn't figure out why, he was on edge tonight. Maybe it was because of his unusual dream, or because as they drew closer and closer to executing their plan, he knew it was becoming more dangerous for all of them.

The back door clicked opened and Aiden jumped. To be safe, he hid behind the front counter until he heard a light tapping on the wall. Three taps. Pause. Three taps. Pause. Three taps. It was Mimi.

Aiden stood and came around the counter. "It's good to see you."

She dropped a duffle bag in front of him. "Uniforms and blueprints, like you asked."

Aiden looked from the duffel bag back to Mimi. She stared out the window as she anxiously tapped her foot. Covering her left cheek was a bruise. "What happened? Who did that to you?"

"It's nothing." She waved her hand as if waving off a fly rather than a serious question. "There are blueprints for both buildings and a map of the entire grounds. There are also several business suits and a bottle of freshener to keep them clean. I'll get you briefcases the day of."

"Business suits? But I thought we'd be wearing the gray jumpsuits to blend in?"

"You were, however, as luck would have it, there's a big presentation scheduled with several scientists, investors, and other important people attending. There'll be so many unknown faces. It's perfect. You and your group can walk through the front doors without suspicion."

"Are you sure that's best?" Aiden shifted uncomfortably. Dozens of extra visitors meant a higher risk of casualties. While he wanted to destroy the buildings, he didn't want to kill people.

"Yes. No one will suspect the extra people moving around. As long as we get you through the front gate with visitor's passes, we're golden."

"What about access to the upper levels? I'm guessing these visitors won't be able to go wherever they want."

"I threw in a few jumpsuits you can change into when going onto other floors, along with access badges for everyone. It took a lot of lying and convincing, but my friend finally helped make these badges."

Aiden nodded. "Thank you. What changed your mind?"

Mimi paused and bit her lip. Aiden stared at her earnestly.

"Is it related to that bruise?"

Mimi shook her head. "Not exactly." She took a deep breath and let it out. "There is a rumor that the Myriad found a group hiding in the mountains." Aiden's body tensed, but he didn't speak. Mimi continued, "There's also talk of a new weapon with greater tracking abilities. Once they punch in coordinates with this missile, it will go wherever it's told and there's no stopping it."

"When's it set to launch?"

"That's the thing. I don't know. Part of me wonders if that's why there's this big presentation. They're going to launch a new missile into those mountains, but—I can't let that happen. I won't let that happen. My mother and grandfather are hiding in those mountains. The same mountains your sister is in. I don't know if the rumor is true, but we can't take that chance."

"You're right. We can't. When do we need to be ready?"

"One week. Meet me here, 4 a.m." Mimi pulled a small phone battery out of her pocket. "A new battery for your phone, so it doesn't die." Aiden took hold of the battery. "Don't be late."

"We won't. Thank you."

Mimi stared at Aiden. Something had changed in her. She seemed hardened. "Mimi, please tell me what—"

"Thank you for not pushing me to help. I know I was on the fence, and that worried you. But I'm not the type you can force to do things."

"You're welcome. It was hard waiting and not knowing, but I'm glad you came around."

"Something like that." She gave Aiden a half smile. There was the Mimi he'd hoped to see tonight. "I have to go."

Aiden picked up the duffle bag and headed toward the front

door. It was going to be worth it, wasn't it? If they were successful, hundreds of Notzrim all over the state would be safe, not just his sister and those in the valley. Who knew how many lives they'd save, and saving lives was always worth it.

Stop doing this, Aiden. I've got it. The voice from his dream whispered again, but Aiden pushed it away.

The next day, Aiden delivered the blueprints to Jared. At first Jared was upset he couldn't meet with Mimi, but as he looked over the blueprints, he decided she gave him everything they needed.

"Good work Haddad. When will she be ready to transport us?"

"Next Thursday."

"No way, that's too soon."

"It was the best option." Aiden explained about the presentation and how they'd be able to walk around freely. He debated whether to share the rumor, but he went ahead. Maybe it'd help Jared's motivation. While he was helping, he didn't seem to be in any hurry.

Jared closed his eyes and tilted his head back. It was almost scarier than him becoming outraged, like he often was. He opened his eyes. "Alright, one week. We've got a lot of work to do."

"Don't I know it. We have a problem with the bombs."

Jared raised his eyebrows.

"We don't have enough explosives. Right now, we don't have enough black powder to bring a building down. We need something stronger."

"I'll see what I can do. Anything else?"

Aiden shook his head.

"Good. I need you to find out who is on our team. Let them

know we're going to discuss the plan in two days. Until then, they need to train hard in agility and sprinting. I need these guys to be fast and light on their feet. I'll go talk with my team about reaching out to our contacts for explosives."

Aiden headed down to the training grounds. He found Terrance with who he assumed was the team, though it was much larger than twelve.

"What's going on, Terrance?" Aiden asked, concerned. "We only need twelve."

"Well, right now we have five, because these yellow bellies don't wanna join."

Aiden turned to the group, feeling the heat rise within him. "Why not?" He asked, keeping his voice calm.

"They say it's too risky." Terrance answered for them.

"And it is, but everything we do is risky. Every day we live is a risk."

"Not like this." A man with blond frizzy hair and deep-set blue eyes spoke. He crossed his ghostly pale arms, causing his arm muscles to bulge. He stood with his feet at hips distance, ready for a fight. "We'd be walking into the belly of the beast. How do you expect us to live through that?"

"Sure, I get it. You're scared. I am too. But courage is doing the right thing despite your fear. This is the right thing. Protecting our people is the right thing."

"But we've already been doing that?"

"You've been reacting to situations and trying to stop it before it gets worse. All you're doing is bruising the beast. I'm asking you to cut a leg off. Get them where it hurts and slow them down."

"That's not our job." The man sneered back.

"Why not? It was Moses' job to face Pharaoh and lead the

Hebrews to freedom. It was Joshua's job to lead the armies into Jericho. Sabaoth is not a passive god. He's active, and he uses us to help get the job done."

The man shook his head and walked away, unconvinced. Aiden watched as a couple more walked away. He was losing them. "Wait! What if I were to tell you that our families are in imminent danger?" Aiden swallowed hard, waiting for those few to turn back. His heart quickened as every nerve in his body trembled.

The man turned back around. "What do you mean by that?"

"The Myriad found a community living east of here, and they intend to send a newer and more dangerous missile there. This one is powerful and will wipe out anything in its blast radius." Sure, he was exaggerating a bit, but he needed to make a point. He needed his twelve.

There was a long, pregnant pause as the group contemplated Aiden's words. Aiden looked from Terrance to the others. His mouth was dry like the desert and his throat tightened. He coughed, still waiting for their response. No one looked back as Aiden watched them. No one except the blond man.

"Alright. I'm in. I don't want anything happening to my wife."

Aiden sighed with relief as another person agreed to help, and then another. By the end, he had nine. Counting Jared, Terrance, and himself, that made twelve. Aiden grinned. Terrance slapped Aiden hard on the back and smiled back at him.

Chapter 18

After their conversation, Paxton sensed Mimi wanted to leave the capitol for good. He spent the rest of his day trying to contact his veterinarian friend Heather, whose side job was black market medical procedures on humans. He called at least a dozen times, but she never answered. Eventually, he took the risk and went to her office. He was free to leave the capitol if he signed out at the front gate.

When Paxton walked into the front office of Heather's veterinarian clinic, her face immediately dropped. She was not happy to see him. Heather rushed over to the front door, flipped the closed sign, locked the door, and pulled the blinds shut. She looked at the security camera in the corner when she faced him. Her eyes bulged and a small gasp slipped through her lips. She dragged him through the back door, down the hallway, and into an examination room.

"What's with the secrecy?"

"What are you doing here? Do you realize last time you were here, I was nearly arrested?"

Paxton's head jerked back as his mouth dropped. "What? Why?"

"Your friend I helped. Did you know she was wanted by the Myriad? That she's one of them?"

Paxton rubbed the back of his neck. Unanswered questions about the day, coming to light. "Yes, but since when did you care who you treated? You've treated worse criminals."

"Maybe, but not more notorious."

Paxton placed his hands on Heather's elbows. "I'm sorry. If I'd known they'd—"

"You still would've brought her, and I still would've treated her." Heather sat on the counter in the center of the room.

"You're right. I guess we're just good people, you and I," he said, partly joking. He leaned against the door and crossed his arms casually. "How'd you escape arrest?"

Heather let out a half laugh. "Somehow, I convinced them I was just about to call and report her. That'd she'd come in asking for my help with her leg. When I realized who she was, I helped her, but then locked her in my basement so I could report her."

"And they bought it?"

"The Myriad are pretty gullible," she said with a sly smile.

Paxton stood and placed a hand on his chest. "I'm offended. We're not all that stupid." He gave her an exaggerated look of hurt and then cracked a smile.

Heather laughed. "Sure you aren't. Now, why are you here?"

"I have a question and you weren't answering my phone call."

"It said it was a capitol number. I try to avoid those."

"Makes sense. Anyway, have you ever removed an identity chip from someone's wrist?"

Heather raised her eyebrows. "That's quite the question."

Paxton nodded. He knew the procedure was more dangerous than a Notzrim. "Have you?"

Heather answered slowly. "Once. It was a pretty rough

CHAPTER 18

surgery. I was able to save the hand, but it had some nerve damage, leaving it partially paralyzed."

Paxton's stomach somersaulted with excitement. "But you can do it?"

"I can, and I think I could avoid some of the same side effects if I did it again."

"Perfect. I don't know when—"

Heather jumped off the counter and put her hand out to stop Paxton. "Now hold on. I said it was an extremely dangerous surgery not just for the person I'm removing it from, but for me too. You need to make it worthwhile for me."

"Would three million be enough?"

Heather sucked in a quick breath as her hand splayed on her chest. "Ummm. . .Yeah, I. . .I guess so. You have that much?"

"They paid me a lot, but I never spent much. I've accumulated a lot of money over the years, and I won't need money where I'm going."

At that comment, Heather crossed her arms and stared hard at Paxton.

"It's not what you think?"

"You're not leaving the city and going after that Amina girl?"

Paxton laughed. "Okay, it's exactly what you think. Will you help?"

"Alright, I'll do it. Just tell me when."

* * * *

Paxton practically skipped into Mimi's lab. He was tremendously giddy. He had a way to get her out of there, and he couldn't wait to see the look on her face when he told her. As he approached the door to her lab, Paxton slowed and took a deep breath. He needed to appear calm and professional for the cameras.

Paxton found Mimi typing away on a computer. The door clicked closed, and she glanced up. "You're here."

Paxton looked around. Was she talking to someone else? "Wasn't I supposed to?"

"Yes, of course, I just. . .Never mind, come on." Mimi stood from her seat and headed to the tiny closet. After the door was closed, Mimi handed a plastic card to Paxton. "As you requested. Access to all floors in building one only, which I'm guessing is all you need, right?"

Paxton took the card and slipped it into his pocket. "Right. Thank you."

"And you plan on leaving soon?"

"That depends."

"On?"

"You."

Mimi tucked her hair behind her ear and fussed at her lab coat while avoiding eye contact with him. "Why me?"

Paxton didn't take Mimi for the flustered type, but she certainly wasn't comfortable at this moment. "I found a way to get you out." He paused, waiting for a reaction. She looked at him but didn't speak. He continued, "I know you want to help Aiden. So, I can't leave until you're finished helping him."

"What makes you think I want to leave?"

"I don't know anyone who wants to take down the place they work and then stay. Do you?"

Mimi puffed her cheeks out and held up her wrist with the tattoo. "You found a way to get rid of this and keep my hand?"

Paxton nodded.

CHAPTER 18

Mimi slowly lowered her arm.

"It's risky and you might lose some function, but it can be done. So?"

Mimi ran her fingers behind her ear, even though her hair hadn't fallen, and then crossed her arms. Paxton waited silently, though he wasn't sure what the delay was? He had a way to free her from this prison. Why wouldn't she want that?

Mimi looked Paxton in the eyes. "I'll do it. You know about the big presentation happening soon?" Paxton nodded knowingly. "Be ready."

* * * *

The wind started in the middle of the night. Amina was still awake at that point, trying to relax her mind and yet unable to stop thinking. Unable to put out of her mind the mysterious person trying to ruin their town. Who was he? Or she? Why were they determined to ruin the Notzrim and for what purpose? The Notzrim meant no harm. They just wanted to live in a safe place away from the Myriad. Then why did Amina not feel safe or welcomed in this place? If she could just capture them, then they could put an end to this all.

Amina tried to convince herself she was doing this for the Notzrim and not for her own vendetta, but that wasn't completely true. The fact that this person made Emily and several others sick, nearly killing some of them, enraged her. How could someone be so heartless? Amina needed to stop them for good. Though, the one person Amina could depend on to help find this person...she'd turned against. She didn't mean to yell at Salome, but the stress had gotten to her and she'd overreacted.

Amina let out a deep breath and turned to the window. A cool breeze pushed into the room and swirled about like a fan. Outside, the wind rustled the bushes and trees. Somehow, the sound of nature calmed Amina, and she did her best to only focus on that noise until it lulled her to sleep.

A couple of hours later, Amina woke again to a loud rumbling noise. Still half-asleep, she looked around. Was someone in the room? She couldn't see anything. The clouds were thick, blotting out any moonlight. The wind howled outside while a tree branch banged on her wall. A bright flash lit the sky, blinding her. Next came the thunderous boom that rattled the cabin. The storm was closer than anything she'd ever experienced. She did her best to ignore it by throwing a pillow over her head. The thunder continued to sing, crescendoing and decrescendoing like a church choir. The constant sound should've lulled Amina back to sleep, but just when her nerves would settle, an enormous crack of thunder would hit, startling her out of sleep all over again.

Constant thunder and wind shook the walls. A bright flash of light shot veins out of the clouds and toward the earth with an ominous sizzle. Amina wondered where the thunder to follow was, but nothing came. No thunder meant one thing. The lightning was right above them. Amina shivered as the lightning storm continued to dance. The thunder was its accompaniment. There was no way Amina was going to sleep until the storm was gone. After putting on her boots, Amina looked out her window and noticed Paul and Mo's cabin had a candle lit.

Amina looked at the flashing sky, uncertain, but then risked the short distance to her aunt and uncle's place.

Inside, Mo and Paul sat at the table whispering and drinking from their small clay cups. Emily still lay in bed with the blanket pulled tight around her chin.

Mo looked over at Amina startled, "You all alright?"

"I'm fine. Just can't sleep with all the noise."

More lightning and thunder struck. Emily yelped and covered her head with the covers. Amina moved to Emily's side and hugged her. "It's okay, Emily. It's just a bit of thunder. Nothing to worry about."

Emily poked her head out from under her blanket. "Are you sure?" she whispered. "Because it sounds angry."

"It's not angry, just powerful. We'll be okay, though." Amina rubbed Emily's back, reassuring her as she looked over to Paul and Mo.

"You're welcome to hang out here until the storm passes," Mo offered.

"Thanks."

Paul walked to the front door and watched the sky. "Such a bizarre storm. It's close but hardly any rain."

Another bright white bolt of lightning flashed in the sky and seemed to touch the village. A loud sharp sizzle followed by a burst of sparks shook Amina. She looked at Paul, whose eyes were as wide as her own. A sinking feeling inside Amina's gut grew.

In the distance, someone shouted, "Fire! Fire!"

Paul rushed out of the cabin, and without thought, Amina followed toward the shouting. When they rounded a corner, an engulfed cabin came into view. People were running out of the building coughing from the smoke or running toward it with buckets of water. Amina and Paul jumped into action. Amina ran to the building, making sure no one else was inside while Paul went for more water buckets. Surely the sky was about to burst open, quenching the angry flames, but how long and how much damage would occur before then they didn't know. Nor did they want to take the risk.

Amina drew closer to the cabin. Hot flames seared her cheeks as the smoke constricted her lungs. She pulled her handkerchief out of her pocket and held it to her mouth and nose.

"Anyone in there!" Amina shouted as loud as she could. The smoke invaded her lungs, and she coughed. A black curtain of smoke spewed out the windows and doors. Amina ran to the next room and shouted again. Each time, no one responded. Amina was sure everyone was clear from the cabins until a woman screamed from outside the cabin. "Helen! Helen, where are you?"

Amina ran to the woman, crying and screaming. The portly woman grabbed Amina by the shoulders and shouted. "My Helen is missing. I don't know where she is."

"Which cabin are you in?"

The woman pointed behind Amina. Amina turned and ran toward the cabin door. Just as she reached the front door, sparks cracked and a piece of roofing slid off. A clump of flames was about to fall when Amina jumped back.

"Amina, what are you doing?" Paul yelled from behind. "Get back out here. It's too dangerous!"

The portly woman shouted at Paul. "But my Helen is in there! She must go get her!"

Amina didn't wait for anything else. She tied the handkerchief around her face, dropped to all fours, and crawled across the threshold. Inside, Amina couldn't see a thing. The smoke was too thick and the fire too bright, creating an eerie red glow. Amina coughed. She thought she'd stop breathing from the amount of smoke being inhaled. *Sabaoth give me strength. Help me find this little girl.*

Amina continued crawling around, feeling her way around in every direction. The heat seared her face and eyes. She closed her eyes tight, trying to wet them, but they were too dry from the smoke. *Sabaoth, where is she!*

Another loud crack came from above Amina, and something crashed beside her. Amina screamed but didn't move. It took a moment for her to regain composure. She couldn't let fear freeze her.

She moved again, blindly sliding her hand around. Nothing but hot coals of debris and emptiness. Cautiously, she crawled. A weight came over her like a ton of bricks. All she wanted to do was rest. *No, you can't, or you'll die.* Amina swept her hand out as far as she could and touched something soft. She grabbed at the blanket and under it was a lump that felt like a human body. *Oh, thank Sabaoth.*

Amina scooped the child into her arms and stood. Her legs wobbled underneath the weight. She felt dizzy. Another crack and more debris fell. Adrenaline surged through Amina, and she hurried. If she didn't, they'd both be dead. Smoke hung about her like a curtain, blinding her. *Where's the door?*

Up ahead, however, the smoke swirled like a mini tornado. Amina prayed there was a door or a window there. She moved toward the smoke and that's when she heard voices shouting. Amina kept moving, her legs weighed down with lack of oxygen until she stepped into nothingness. Amina tumbled forward, down the stairs, and out of the cabin. As she fell through the air, Amina curled into a ball and turned onto her side to protect the child in her arms. She fell hard onto her right arm and rolled onto her back.

Amina couldn't see, but someone grabbed the child out of her arms. There was sobbing and choking. Amina was disoriented, she didn't know whether the sounds were coming from her, the child, or the mother.

"Amina," Paul's voice sounded distant. "Amina, are you okay?"

She lay on her back with her eyes closed. Fat plops of rain pounded on her skin and face. She welcomed the wet cold.

Paul lifted Amina to a sitting position and pressed a cup of water to her lips. Gladly, she drank, needing something to soothe her burning throat, but the water tasted of dirt and ash. Amina choked on the water and spat it out. Smoke clogged her throat, and she couldn't swallow.

"Take it easy there. Come on, let's get you over to the medical ward." Paul assisted Amina to her feet. She went weak in the knees as she tried to stand, but Paul instantaneously caught her.

Paul supported Amina's weight as they made their way to the medical ward. The rain now poured down, washing the soot off Amina's face and body. Amina leaned her head back a moment and opened her mouth, drinking in the rain. She swallowed and this time the water stayed down.

A young man, likely in his teens, rushed to them. "Paul, the fence broke, and the animals have escaped. We need your help."

"Shoot. Okay, I'll be right there. I need to take Amina to the medical ward."

At the sound of more trouble, Amina perked up. "I'm okay. We need to get over there and find the animals."

"You are in no condition to help. You need to get checked out. There was a lot of smoke back there.

CHAPTER 18

"Honest, I'm fine." Amina tried to stand without Paul's help. She felt weak, but she was upright. "See." Amina tried to walk toward the barn but promptly went weak in the knees again. Paul caught her.

"You're not going." Paul looked at the young man. "Please assist Amina to the medical ward and then meet me over at the barn."

"Yes, sir."

Amina put her arm around the teen's neck and let him help her to the medical ward. Inside, several people ran about, placing buckets to catch the water from the leaks in the ceiling. Not only that but several beds were filled with patients from the fire. When Vanita saw Amina, she looked around for an open bed.

"Put her over there." She nodded toward a bed in the middle of the rows. "I think it's dry."

The teen helped Amina over to her bed before leaving.

"Wait."

He stopped and turned.

"You better come back and give me a full report of what happened at the barn. Got it?"

He answered, uncertain. He had no reason to come back, but she hoped he would. She might not be an elder, but she was more involved than most people with the goings on of the village. And considering she was the one to find them in this place and her uncle was part of the elders, that had to mean something to people, right?

Amina leaned back into the bed and closed her eyes. She hated waiting, but that was all she could do. Fatigue took over her body and her eyelids grew too heavy to keep open. Amina lay in the medical ward bed with her eyes closed. It was nice to rest in such a cozy bed. However, her lungs were heavy and her throat scratchy. No one came by to check on her, and she really needed something to drink.

* * * *

When Salome heard the crack of lightning, she knew what had happened. Lightning often came close in the valley. Only once before had it hit something, but that was only a tree. Salome put on her shoes and ran toward the commotion. Sure enough, a cabin had caught fire and the flames were illuminating the sky.

Salome turned to those closest to her and started barking orders. Those around jumped into action, looking for jugs to go fill with water.

Salome rushed to the group of onlookers. "Hey, if you're not going to help put it out, then get out. Get far away, go toward the medical ward and the teaching space, now!" It took everyone a moment to process what she was saying, but as Salome repeated herself and physically guided people away from the fire, they moved. "Go, come on, get out of here!"

"Helen! Where's my Helen!" a desperate mother cried.

Salome turned just in time to see the woman clinging to Amina. Amina turned and dashed toward the cabin. What was she thinking? There was no way she'd be able to find anyone in that fire. The mother followed, and Salome dashed over to stop her.

"Ma'am, it's okay. Please stay back."

"But my child."

"I know. Amina is going to find her. But we don't need you getting hurt as well."

CHAPTER 18

The woman clung to Salome while her body shook. Tears mingled with soot ran down the woman's cheeks as they watched Amina disappear into the smoke-filled cabin. *Sabaoth, get her out safely.*

They waited for what felt like an eternity. All around them, people were grabbing buckets of water and dousing the cabin. They extinguished one section, just to have a new flame take over, larger than before. What they needed was for the rain to come fast and heavy.

Salome stared at the cabin door where Amina had disappeared and watched anxiously. Her body tense with anticipation. Where was she? She'd never forgive herself if something happened to Amina before they could make amends.

A body tumbled out of the cabin door and onto the ground. Salome let out a sigh of relief. The woman ripped herself away from Salome and over toward Amina and her daughter. Salome's eyes stung with tears, relieved that Amina was safe.

"There you are."

Salome turned as her father ran toward her.

"We need to get to the barn. The fence broke and the animals are loose."

Salome looked at Amina one last time as Paul helped her up. She was going to be okay. Salome turned and followed David to the barn and pasture.

At the barn, several people ran into the field looking for the scattered sheep, pigs, and horses. Salome wasn't concerned about the horses; they would find shelter and then return when the storm was over. As for the sheep and pigs, she wasn't sure how they'd react. Sheep were timid creatures and often would run themselves into more danger if let out on their own. They needed to find the sheep before they wandered into the river or into any thorny bushes. And the same with the pigs. Salome sprinted over to the fence to see if someone could easily patch it. If they didn't enclose the space, there was no use corralling the animals.

Why were the animals out?" Salome asked Henry as they inspected the fencing.

"It started as a pleasant night. Unseasonably warm, which is why we let them out to sleep in the field," Henry said.

Salome shook her head. "That kind of weather is the first sign of a storm coming."

"How are we supposed to know that? No one told us."

"Never mind that. We need to fix that fence and find those sheep and pigs."

Salome continued to inspect the fencing with David and Henry's help.

"Salome, look at this," David said, motioning for her to come closer. As she did, she noticed the way the fence broke. The securing rope was severed, but not in the way you'd expect. Then there was an issue with the posts and the holes in the ground. If the wind had knocked them over, there would be a longer mud mark on the ground. Salome bent down and inspected the scene. An eerie feeling came over her.

She stood and looked at David and Henry. "I don't believe the storm caused this. Look at the way the fence fell compared to the way the wind is blowing."

"Agreed."

Henry dragged a hand over his face. "Oh geez. Are you saying someone did this?"

"I think so."

Henry yelled in frustration. "Why do these things keep happening? Why haven't you found them yet?"

"We're working on it, but they're sneaking."

"Well, try harder, unless you aren't interested in stopping them."

"What are you getting at?" Salome shouted back over the wind.

"I'm saying maybe you want this to happen. Maybe you're allowing things to go wrong because you want us to leave."

"How dare you." David jumped in. "Salome risked everything for your people. She wants the same thing as everyone else here. To find and stop this person."

Salome and Henry glared at one other, wondering what new storm had formed.

The wind continued to whip around, smacking the rain into the face. Salome's hair was coming out of her ponytail and strands whipped across her wet face.

"Please, Henry," David said. "This is not the time. We need to focus on fixing the fence and getting those animals."

Salome pushed her hair out of her face. "He's right. We can discuss this later. Let's get this fence figured out."

Salome bent and grabbed a post just as Paul approached with a toolbox and a long, skinny shovel. Salome was grateful to see him. They went to work on the fence while directing the rest of the villagers to look for and herd the animals back to the pasture.

With the fence repaired, Salome and the others spent the rest of the night looking for the animals. They found most of the sheep and gathered them back into the barn. While two women corralled the pigs into a nearby cave and stayed with them till the storm passed.

Eventually, the wind stopped, the rain gave way to a small drizzle, and the clouds thinned out, allowing the early morning sun to poke through and say hello. Salome sat on a soggy barrel of hay along with David. She leaned her head on his shoulder, completely exhausted from their crazy night.

"I'm glad that's over with."

"Me too. But you know, we still have a bigger issue to deal with."

Salome closed her eyes, dreading what was coming next. "I know."

"What issue is that?" Paul inquired.

Salome lifted her head. "The fence was purposely broken."

Paul sighed and ran his hand through his hair. "Salome, I know you don't want to hear this, but I think we need to try a different strategy. And I think it's time we have a town meeting and build that wall."

Salome groaned, but she knew he was right.

Chapter 19

A soft voice called Amina's name, gently pulling her out of sleep.

Amina opened her eyes to find Maya standing in front of her. Amina smiled as she pushed her stiff body to a seated position. "Hey Maya, what are you doing here?" Her voice was scratchy and foreign.

"I am assisting the nurses. They needed the extra help with all the many coming people. I have been helping here quite a lot."

"Oh, really?"

Maya's face lit up. "Yes. With no need for scavengers, I put my time into research. Me and the other scientists want to improve our medicines. We make good progress with the limited items we have."

"That's great. I'm really glad you're putting your skills to work."

"Thank you." Maya handed Amina a small cup filled with a thick, black liquid. "Drink this. It will clean your lungs."

Amina investigated the cup and wrinkled her nose. It smelled like dirt and went down like sludge. It took all her willpower to keep the foul-tasting liquid from coming back up and onto the floor.

"Good." Maya took the cup back and held it to her abdomen. "I heard what you did. That was a feat, saving Helen. Her parents are in your debt."

"It was nothing. Someone was in need, and I jumped into action."

"Yes, but few would do such a thing. You are the bravest of us Amina Haddad."

"I guess." She leaned back and looked out the window. The sky was bright blue without a cloud in sight. A very different picture from earlier. And when did she fall asleep?

"Get rest. I'll be back later to check on you." Maya turned and walked away.

Amina lay back in her bed and closed her eyes again. She must've dozed off again at some point because she jumped at another soft voice calling her name.

Amina opened her eyes to see a timid boy standing by her bed wringing his hands. He looked distressed, and Amina's stomach churned at the inevitable bad news. "What'd you find out? Is everyone okay?"

"No one's hurt, and we found most of the animals. It's just, I heard the fence was not an accident, that someone pulled it apart, like, on purpose. I don't know, but you told me to report what I found out."

Amina sighed. She was afraid that was the case. It was too good to believe the culprit was done with their destruction. The storm was a perfect opportunity for misdirection. Get the Notzrim to believe it was a storm, but this person underestimated them. "Thank you."

The boy turned and left. Amina clenched her fist and pounded the bed as she let out a muffled grunt of frustration. This wouldn't have happened if she'd caught the person the

CHAPTER 19

previous night. She was angry at the person for being cruel, but also angry that she couldn't catch them. They were within her grasp not too long ago, and yet she failed. But she needed to not fail again. She needed to find them and stop them for good. But how?

Amina leaned against the pillow and thought. They already had guards in place to keep an eye out. But this person was sneaky. They knew how to be invisible.

A loud moan interrupted Amina's thought. When she opened her eyes, she saw a man standing at the entrance of the medical ward, holding his hand up. Blood trickled from what looked to be a small metal hook on his thumb.

"What happened?" the nurse asked as she guided him to an open bed.

"I went to check on my fish traps and caught my thumb on the hook."

All Amina could see was the agony in the man's eyes as the nurse worked. He seethed, trying to hold back a yell. Eventually, she poured something on the wound, and he couldn't hold it back anymore. He let out a loud yell that echoed in the small room.

Amina's face twisted, and she looked away. The fish trap, though, gave her an idea. She could set her own traps around the perimeter of the village. That way, if anyone saw the culprit, they could chase them into the trap. Maybe they could add some nets that swooped the person up into the tree when stepped on. Those always worked best and didn't hurt the person. The only problem was Amina didn't know how to build these traps. Not to mention she was stuck in the medical ward until given an all-clear, but she didn't have time for that.

Amina looked around the room. One nurse still worked on

bandaging the man's bloody finger while the other two seemed to be missing. Amina slowly sat up and swung her legs to the edge of the bed. She slipped on her shoes and stood. The floor creaked beneath her, and she froze. When the one nurse didn't turn around, Amina headed toward the back door, away from the nurse. A few of the patients stared at her suspiciously but said nothing. As Amina reached the last bed, inches from the door, a nurse entered, blocking Amina's exit.

The large woman put her hands on her hips and knit her brow. "Where do you think you're going?"

"I'm leaving. I have things to do, and I'm feeling just fine. Really."

"Mmm hmm." The nurse placed a hand on Amina's chest and back. "Take a deep breath," she commanded. Amina did as told. As the nurse felt and listened, she shook her head. "Yep, that's what I thought. You're not going anywhere. Go back to your bed." The nurse kept one hand on Amina's back and guided her toward the bed.

"No, you don't understand. I really need to go. It's about the person who's been causing all the sabotages in the village. I know how to stop them, and I need to go talk to someone about it."

"That's the elder's job, not yours. Your job is to get better." The nurse crossed her arms and stared at Amina until she complied.

Amina slipped her shoes off again and crawled into her bed. "Please, I need to talk to someone about this."

The nurse took Amina's arm and pressed two fingers to her wrist, checking Amina's pulse. When she finished, she let go of Amina and said, "How about you tell me who you want to talk to, and I can go get them for you? Will that work?"

CHAPTER 19

Amina leaned back in her bed, thinking about who she needed to talk to. She didn't actually know who could help her. She knew Salome's job was to find the culprit, but would she be willing to come see her? It was doubtful after their argument. Who else knew how to build traps? Then it clicked. "Josiah Smith. Can you send for him?"

The nurse looked at Amina skeptically as if wanting to change her mind. Why offer the help if she didn't intend to follow through?

"Oh, alright. I'll have someone go get him for you."

"Thank you."

The nurse walked away as Amina leaned back in the bed. Her heart raced, and she felt as if she a heavy blanket pressed on her chest. If such little excitement could get her heart pounding this hard, maybe it was a good idea to rest a while longer.

At some point, Amina dozed off again. When she woke, Josiah sat by her bedside. Amina smiled and pushed herself to a seated position. "You came." Amina took a deep breath with greater ease than before. She let it out slowly.

"Of course, I came. I'm always here for you. How are you feeling?" He placed a hand on Amina's.

Amina smiled and casually pulled her hand away. "I've been better, but I've also been worse. I think whatever sludge they made me drink is helping."

"Good. Geez, Amina, you gave us one heck of a scare when you ran into that house."

"You were there?"

Josiah nodded. "I'm glad Sabaoth protected you."

"You and me both. What's the damage?"

"On the cabins? Just the main one burned to the ground and the two surrounding it have minor damage. It's fixable."

"And no one was seriously hurt?"

"A few people with burns and the little girl you saved had serious smoke inhalation." Josiah motioned over to another bed. The mother was asleep on a stool with her head leaning against the wall while the husband sat holding his little girl's hand. His head was bent, and his eyes closed as he prayed.

Amina smiled, hopeful that the little girl would pull through. While her lungs were smaller than Amina's, she was sure the girl was healthy and strong.

"Anyway, why did you want to see it?" Josiah asked, changing the subject.

"I have a new plan."

"Oh?" Josiah looked at her skeptically. "For what?"

"For how to catch this person and finally stop them from ruining our village."

"You know the fire wasn't their fault."

"I know that, but the destroyed fence and letting all the animals out was."

Josiah's eyes grew wide. "I hadn't heard about that."

"Yeah, it happened last night during the commotion of the fire."

"How do you know the storm didn't cause it? You've been here the whole time."

"I have my sources. Anyway, I want to set traps around the village, hoping they'll fall into one."

Josiah pondered her idea for a minute. His face was unreadable, but Amina hoped he'd agree.

"What kind of trap?"

"Something with a net that flies into the air when stepped on. Nothing too dangerous."

"And what if one of our people falls into it?"

"We'll check them. Or we'll tell people about them. I don't know. All I know is we need to find this person. We've had enough issues happen and I can't keep letting this go on. People are going to catch on and they'll either retaliate or they'll want to leave. I can't let either happen. We're here because of me, and I have to make sure they stay safe."

"Okay, I'll help."

"Thank you." Amina leaned over and hugged Josiah. "This will work. I'm sure of it."

* * * *

For the next several days, Aiden hardly slept. He was busy mapping out a plan with Jared, honing his combat and weapons skills with Evan, and building bombs with Mitchum. With each passing day, his anxiety grew. While he was excited to get going and finally see his plan succeed, he was terribly nervous.

Everyone knew the risk—that death was a possibility—yet Aiden felt responsible for everyone's life. They were trusting Aiden to get them out safely. They wouldn't say it out loud, but Aiden felt the pressure. He felt the prowling eyes of failure waiting around each corner, ready to pounce on him and tear him to bits like a wild animal.

All the while, his dream kept creeping back into his mind. The looming feeling that it meant something more. And that voice kept insisting, *I've got this.* If this voice wasn't his own inner confidence, if it was Meshiakh telling him to wait, then why were things going flawlessly? Aiden couldn't believe how quickly Jared got a group out and they were able to bring back explosives. They'd somehow gotten their hands on a chemical called RDX. Aiden had never heard of it, but when he told Mitchum, Aiden thought he was going to faint.

"What are they doing bringing that stuff down here? Do they know how dangerous it is?" Aiden shrugged. Mitchum carefully took the crate of materials from Aiden and moved it to his workbench. "This stuff had better be mixed properly or we're in trouble."

"Jared said it was from a Myriad armory, and all it needed is a detonator."

"Okay good. That's what we want. I'm no chemical engineer. If I had to mix this stuff, I'm not sure we'd make it to Thursday." Mitchum sat at his bench and pulled out a long cylindrical paper tube from the box. It didn't look dangerous, but Aiden knew better. It was military grade. Nothing he wanted to mess with.

"What do we do?"

Mitchum motioned at the box of bomb shells they'd been creating. "We take those and attach them carefully to the dynamite and program the detonators. By the time we're done, there will be one detonator button for each set of five. Whoever sets the dynamite in the building needs to activate the bomb, that way the detonator can pick its signal up. Once everyone is clear of the building, push the button and cablooey. Down goes the building."

"Are these things stable?"

Mitchum laughed as he grabbed the first bombshell. "As stable as a scared dog. If you handle it right, you'll be fine. Mistreat it and it'll go off before you intend for it to."

"Oh." Aiden sat beside Mitchum. For all his excitement and enthusiasm for this mission, he was feeling dumb about being naïve to the real danger of it all. Sure, he knew these things weren't safe, but it had sunk in. His anger had blinded him toward Teivel, Frank, and the Myriad until now.

Mitchum glanced at Aiden sideways. "You know it's not too late to back out." His voice softened, like a concerned father. "We can go to Jared together and tell him you changed your mind."

Aiden stared at the crate of dynamite. This box only had the fifteen they needed, but how much more were in the armory? How many other explosives and weapons did they have just so they could wipe out those who stood for Sabaoth? Aiden shook his head. There was no backing down, not now.

"Tell me what to do to make these bombs ready to go."

Mitchum sighed, his shoulders sagged, but he didn't argue. Instead, he went on to reluctantly teach Aiden what he needed to know. After that, the two of them worked in silence, getting the bombs ready. It was already Tuesday night. They needed to finish and show the team how to activate them properly before it was time to go.

* * * *

Aiden and the team stood awkwardly inside the convenience store in their business suits with their access visitor's badge clipped to their lapels. Just before leaving, everyone cleaned up as best they could—they showered in the lukewarm water, combed their hair, shaved with their dull razors and knives, and did everything they could not to look disheveled. Despite their preparation, everyone still looked completely out of place. How were they ever going to pass as businessmen and women? No one had been in any sort of business setting for almost a decade. Some, never in their life. And yet they were about to walk into the busiest professional ground of their lives. They needed to blend in, and right now, Aiden doubted that was possible.

An hour after their arrival, three large black SUVs with blackout windows pulled up to the convenience store. Aiden's heart skipped a beat. How did the Myriad find them? Then, Mimi hopped out of the front seat of the first SUV and Aiden audibly sighed in relief.

"Tense morning. You good?" Jared asked, slapping Aiden on the back.

Aiden nodded as he watched Mimi. She wore a navy-blue straight skirt that stopped just above her knees and a blazer to match with a pop of red from her frilly shirt. Her thick wavy hair was tamed, with a rhinestone clip on one side, keeping it out of her face. Mimi moved around to the trunk of the SUV and pulled out a stack of briefcases before heading to the front door. Aiden opened it for her and took the cases.

"Put your explosives in these. There's a lead box inside to hide it when you go through security. All they'll see are the random papers and pens we stuffed inside."

Aiden passed out the briefcases and everyone did as they were told. Mimi went back to the car to grab the last of the briefcases. Once everyone was situated, she split the group up. Two would go to the two main buildings while the third driver headed to the airport on site.

"How did you persuade them to come here?"

Mimi pointed to three identical SUVs out in the road with flat tires. "I told them your cars got flats, and you were already irate about having to hire your own drivers for this momentous event. The event coordinator immediately got me three new SUVs with the highest security." Mimi smiled, proud of herself.

CHAPTER 19

"You ready then?"

"As ready as I'll ever be."

This was it. The moment they were all waiting for. They had their plan drilled into their minds, memorizing blueprints of the building, activation steps for the bombs, and escape routes. They could conduct the mission in their sleep. Even so, there were numerous unknowns.

They made their way through The Beyond and the Outer City with no hiccups. Before leaving, Aiden warned the others not to look shocked by the extraordinary changes to the Inner City. There was no need to make the drivers suspicious.

With traffic, checkpoints, and several turns, it took them about two hours, but they finally made it to the capitol. The first SUV stopped at the gate and the driver handed the security guard his badge. The SUV rolled through and down the main street toward the airfield. Aiden's SUV pulled up and stopped next. Same thing. The driver handed him his badge and waved them through. They didn't have to drive very far to their destination. They were heading to building one, and it was right up front. The driver pulled into the circular drop-off out front and stopped.

Aiden grabbed the handle of his briefcase, slick with the sweat from his palm. He gripped the handle tighter, not wanting to let it fall out of his hand. He stepped out of the car and a wave of memories and emotions flooded him. Reminders of his imprisonment, beatings, forceful compliance, the moment when he almost gave in, and the embarrassment of it all. No one knew the truth. No one knew he'd lived half of his time here in comfort. Or that he'd enjoyed himself for a time.

A hand squeezed his shoulder. "You good?" Mimi asked.

"Yeah." Aiden glanced back, looking for the third SUV. It

arrived at the second building across the way. He turned back to the entrance and headed through the sliding glass doors.

Inside, the lobby appeared the same. A circular receptionist's desk sat just to his left. In the middle was a large sitting area with fancy modern furniture, a decorative rug, and a massive lighting fixture hanging above with sleek curves twisting around one another to create a tornado of metal with refracting light.

The difference was the metal detectors and x-ray machines for their bags. With the high volume of visitors coming and going for their big presentation, it made sense to have tightened security. Myriad soldiers stood on both sides of the security stop with their AR-16s in hand. Aiden tried not to make eye contact. While it was unlikely anyone would recognize him, he didn't want to take the chance.

He gently set his briefcase down in the belt and walked through the metal detector. He stood on the other side, beads of sweat forming on his forehead as he waited for the briefcase to clear. His whole body shook, and he was certain people could see his fear. Aiden glanced at the Myriad soldier looking at the small screen, inspecting his briefcase. The conveyor belt stopped, and so did Aiden's heart. What was wrong? Did the lead box not work? Aiden grew faint. He glanced at the others in his group who stood beside him, also waiting for their cases. Finally, the conveyor belt started again, and Aiden grabbed his briefcase and took off.

They were all on their own. They each had their own location to get to and drop off their briefcase. Tessa was in charge of the detonator, so she stayed in the lobby with Mimi. Once she saw the rest of the team clear the building without their cases, she and Mimi would leave and detonate the bombs. Two of

CHAPTER 19

the teams had five minutes to get in and out to ensure both buildings went off about the same time. The commotion at the front of the property would allow for the airfield team to set off their bombs and evacuate with everyone else.

Aiden stepped into the elevator and hit the number eight. As the doors closed, he watched Terrance enter the elevator across from him. They both nodded at one another before the doors slid shut.

Thankfully, Aiden was alone, giving him a moment to breathe. His body still trembled. He tried to calm his nerves by breathing slowly in and out. Things were going according to plan. There was no need to be worried. Soon he'd be out and heading back home. Except there was still the issue of everyone in the building. They had no idea that in just five minutes, their lives would end. Aiden couldn't risk killing all these people. He knew some of them. He actually grew to like some of the scientists he worked with.

The elevator dinged, and Aiden stepped out. He just needed to pop into one of the inner offices, leave his briefcase there, and get out. Aiden looked up and down the hallways. The coast was clear. He headed down the inner hallway. As he approached the first room, he jiggled the door handle. Locked. He tried his access badge. Still locked. He went to the next door. Still didn't work.

He was on the floor with the military offices. It was likely his badge wouldn't work at all. He'd have to leave his case in the hallway. As he approached the next door to try again, he passed by a fire alarm. Aiden slowed and backed up until he was in front of the alarm. He looked around again, but still no one. Aiden set the briefcase down, kneeled, and opened the case to reveal the lead box. Gently, he opened the lid to the box. The dynamite was attached with wiring to a metal plate with a switch. Once he flipped the switch, it would send out a radio signal to Tessa's detonator.

By his judgment, he'd been in the building about three minutes. He had little time left. Aiden's hand shook as he placed it on the switch. He took a deep breath and flipped the switch. Nothing happened, but Mitchum said that was normal. They didn't have the parts or tech to add an indicator light. Aiden had to trust it was on.

He closed the box and briefcase back up and stood. The fire alarm stared at him. All he had to do was pull it and everyone would have a fighting chance. He could save them, too. Aiden placed his hand on the alarm and pulled down. Immediately, a loud beeping noise and flashing lights went off throughout the building. Aiden turned, ready to run back to the elevator when a door opened, and out walked Frank. They made eye contact, and a slow malicious grin spread across Frank's face.

"Well, look who it is." Frank stepped further into the hallway. He wore a black suit and held a tablet in his left hand. "I was hoping I'd find you here." Frank looked from the briefcase, to the pulled alarm, and back to Aiden.

"It's too late. You can't stop this from happening."

"Think again, kid. You've failed." Frank walked toward Aiden slowly. "You see, we knew you and your team were coming, and we've already confiscated their briefcases. You're all going to wish you'd never come here."

"That's a lie."

"Why would I lie about something this fantastic?" Frank stopped, inches away from Aiden. He slowly lifted the tablet in his hand and showed a video image of Myriad soldiers arresting several of Aiden's team, the team that was supposed to go to the airfield. Aiden did his best not to react to what he watched, but inwardly he crumbled.

"Did you really think you could pull this off? Blow up the most secure building in the world?" Frank laughed. "You're more of a fool than I thought. And that little curly-haired friend of yours—"

"What'd you do to her?"

"It's more like what she did for us."

Aiden's jaw dropped as he tried to justify in his mind what Frank was implying.

Seeing the look on Aiden's face, Frank continued, "Oh it's not as bad as you think. She's just not a good liar. One of your drivers suspected something and tipped us off." Frank smirked. "It's rather fantastic if you ask me. On the cusp of the war, you and your team thought you could what—defeat us? Cripple us? You of all people should know how big this war is going to be, and your tiny attempt to do something is futile."

For just a second, Aiden's confidence in his decision faltered, but he narrowed his eyes at Frank, the fire in them nearly blinding him. *What does Frank know? He's evil and a liar.* Aiden swung his right fist fast and hard at Frank's face, getting a good clean hit. Frank stumbled, thrown off by the force, but he quickly recovered. He shoved Aiden hard into the wall. Aiden bounced off the hard surface, disoriented. A sharp blow stung across his cheek and another in his stomach.

Frank was fast, and Aiden did his best to compose himself. He blocked his face right as Frank threw his next punch and kicked him in the knee. Aiden wildly threw punches of his own. Some landed. Most Frank blocked. Over and over, Aiden punched until Frank punched back. Frank continued to throw his own blows, one of which landed hard in Aiden's tender ribs. He felt the wind rush out of him and he gasped for air.

"Face it, Aiden. You screwed up. This was not your war to fight and yet you tried anyway. Now you and your entire team are going to pay for it." Frank punched Aiden again in the ribs. "You should've just stayed home."

Chapter 20

Paxton finished packing his backpack and zipped it up. He had everything he needed for a two-week trip. He hoped it wouldn't take that long, but in case he had to lie low somewhere, he wanted to have enough food and water.

Paxton threw on his boots and laced them up nice and tight. He grabbed his military jacket and patrol cap before performing a final sweep of the room. He needed everything to be in order and look as if he'd only stepped out for a while, not indefinitely.

Paxton lifted his mattress to reveal a hole. He shoved his hand into the hole and pulled out a handgun. He put the gun in his waistband and retrieved a box of bullets before replacing the mattress back on the bed. The box of bullets went into the front of his backpack before he slung it over his shoulder and pulled his other arm through the hole. He clipped the strap securing the backpack, and walked out of the room and toward building one.

His plan was to leave the same way he came in, through the underground tunnel that connected with the subway system. He knew the path well and after Mimi made him a temporary access card, he'd easily be able to get down the elevator and where he needed to go. Now he just had to do it without looking suspicious. At this point, Frank still had no reason to believe Paxton wanted to leave. Paxton had made it clear to him that he had no reason to escape and nowhere to go. Since then, Frank seemed to back off of his surveillance of Paxton. He still had his babysitter during class, but that was it. Paxton was free to move about the capitol without worrying about someone spying on him.

Besides a few early risers or night owls sitting and drinking coffee, the lobby was empty. The receptionist looked as if she was ready for her night shift to be over and whether she noticed Paxton, he couldn't tell since her bright pink eye-shadowed lids drooped too low. The only Myriad, he noticed, were the two women across the way, heading in the opposite direction from him. Paxton turned away from them just to ensure they didn't take notice.

As he passed the couches in the center of the lobby, he saw Mimi sitting there with another woman he didn't recognize. Paxton and Mimi made eye contact briefly, and she nodded at him. He kept moving, not acknowledging her. He needed to hurry. Their plan was to meet at the underground parking lot at 0700 and he needed to make a put stop before then.

At the elevator, Paxton pressed the up button. Before leaving, he needed to get his father's compass back. The thing was old and didn't work, but that was beside the point. It didn't belong to Frank, and Paxton was tired of Frank taking what wasn't his. He knew it was a risk, but it was important to him. It was the last and only thing he had of his father. When he joined the Myriad, they'd taken all his belongings, and he thought he'd lost it forever. But seeing it in Frank's office, sitting like a trophy, both irked and pleased Paxton. He could finally get it back while also making one last dig at Frank's

CHAPTER 20

failure.

The elevator dinged, and the doors slid open. Paxton stepped out and froze. There in front of him was Frank, locked in hand-to-hand combat with Aiden. Frank had the upper hand as he wrapped his monstrous hands around Aiden's neck and squeezed.

Paxton unclipped and threw his backpack onto the floor before rushing to Aiden's aid. Frank turned just in time to see Paxton tackle him to the ground. Paxton sat on him and threw several punches to Frank's face before Frank caught Paxton's hands and wrestled him to the ground. Frank lifted Paxton just enough and slammed him onto the hard tile. His head hit fiercely, and pain shot through his skull. His vision clouded over with black dots. He tried to blink them away just as another swift punch landed on his cheek, likely reopening an old wound. It wasn't long before Aiden pulled Frank off.

Paxton was about to jump in and help Aiden but stopped when he saw the gun. Paxton's hand instinctively flew to his empty waistband. It wasn't there. Paxton grimaced.

* * * *

Frank grasped Aiden in a headlock while he firmly pressed the cold barrel to the side of his head. Aiden's heart drummed in his ears, muffling the sound around him while his stomach roiled. He was about to be sick.

"Oh, look here, a two-for-one deal. It's my lucky day."

"Let him go, Frank."

"Or what? You have nothing over me. I own you."

"No one owns me, Frank. Now let him go." Paxton held his ground, but he needed to leave. There was no point in both of them dying.

A loud explosion went off somewhere outside. The building shuddered, startling Frank just long enough for Aiden to wriggle out of Frank's grasp and reach for the gun. Frank's grip was too tight. They wrestled back and forth, with Frank holding the gun in the air and Aiden holding Frank's arm. All he had to do was knock it loose. He smashed Frank's hand as hard as he could against the wall. Frank's grip loosened around the gun. It fell to the ground and bounced but didn't go off.

Aiden kicked the gun as far away as he could and sprinted toward Paxton. "Run!"

They sprinted down the hallway. Aiden didn't know where to go. All that mattered was to put enough distance between them and Frank, then they could find the stairwell.

A loud gunshot echoed through the hallway as something pressed into his back. He skidded to a stop, uncertain what just happened. He and Paxton locked eyes, Paxton's eyes widened. A burning sensation penetrated through Aiden's body like a scorching fire as the building around his spun. His legs shuddered and he crumpled to the ground.

Paxton dropped to his knees and turned Aiden over. He drew in several sharp breathes but nothing filled his lungs. Instead he tasted metal in his mouth.

"Aiden, Aiden, can you hear me?" Tears brimmed Paxton's eyes and spilled over, dropping onto Aiden's cheek.

He looked at a blurring image of Paxton. "You need to go, Paxton," he wheezed. It was becoming increasingly difficult to breathe.

"I can't leave you. I gotta get you help."

"No, go. . ." He tried take a breath, but his body felt weak.

CHAPTER 20

"Save yourself. . .tell Amina. . .I love her."

Aiden closed his eyes. This was it. He wasn't walking away from this. This wasn't worth it. Why hadn't he waited? The voice of Meshiakh kept calling to him, telling him to wait, and he ignored it. *I'm sorry. Forgive my impatience. Forgive me for not trusting you.* A warm glow filled Aiden's vision as an overwhelming peace hugged him, soothing his troubled heart. In the light, an image of a face appeared, smiling at him as it said, "It's time to come home."

* * * *

Aiden's body went limp in Paxton's arms. He was gone.

Tears stung his eyes, and his body shook with fury. He looked at Frank again, who was still standing there, with a sadistic smile spread across his face. Paxton had never felt such intense rage and hatred for one person. With a loud warrior cry, he jumped up and charged Frank.

Frank tried to shoot, but the gun didn't go off. Paxton hadn't loaded the gun. There was only one bullet in the chamber. That's it. One bullet. The one that killed Aiden. The one that took away the most important person in Amina's life.

Paxton's rage engulfed him. All he could see was Frank's terrified face as Paxton threw him to the ground and started punching him repeatedly. Blood splattered with each punch. Frank tried to fight back, but Paxton's hits came too fast to block them all. And even when Frank's body went limp, Paxton still punched, wishing the punching would make the pain in his heart stop.

In the distance, Paxton heard someone scream, pulling him out of his rage. He looked behind to find Cecilia folded over Aiden, her body heaving with tears. Paxton got up and lumbered over to her.

"What happened?" Cecilia sobbed into Aiden's shoulder.

"Frank got a hold of my gun. We tried to get away but. . ." Paxton couldn't finish the sentence. "I'm sorry."

Cecilia looked at Paxton, still clinging to her son's limp body. "Frank did this?"

Paxton nodded slightly as he swallowed hard. Something in Cecilia's eyes changed. Her nostrils flared as her whole body shook.

"I'm sorry I couldn't save him," Paxton whispered, slowly backing away.

Cecilia didn't respond. Instead, her eyes locked on Frank's motionless body. Every muscle in her body strained against her skin. Paxton could only image the rage surging through Cecilia. Despite her own issues, she loved her children fiercely. He couldn't be sure what would happen next, but he couldn't stay. Slowly, he turned toward the elevator, grabbed his backpack, and left.

As he stood waiting for the elevator doors to open, he heard a gunshot echo around him. Paxton didn't flinch, he didn't even turn to look. He knew Frank was finally gone for good.

Chapter 21

Paxton rode the elevator to sublevel one. The doors opened, revealing Mimi waiting. She stepped into the elevator, and they headed to sublevel two and their way of escape.

"Building one is down," Mimi said matter of fact. "This one's due to come down once everyone's clear."

Paxton flinched at her words. *Not everyone.* He wanted to tell her about Aiden, but he had no words.

The elevator dinged, and the doors slide open, revealing a long tunnel. They ran. It was the same tunnel he'd entered just a few months ago with Amina. The same woman he'd fallen in love with. And the one he wanted to return to now but wasn't sure he could. As soon as he'd reach her, he'd have to tell her about Aiden, her twin. How could he possibly tell her he was there when Aiden died but couldn't save him? She'd blame him for Aiden's death and never want to see him again.

Paxton noticed he'd slowed his running, weighed down by his thought. He didn't have time to think, he just needed to get as far away from the capitol as possible before anyone caught up with him. Paxton pushed his thoughts aside and picked up his speed, racing through the tunnel and around a few corners. His heart rate sped up, and he struggled to keep his breathing even, more from the fear and adrenaline than the actual running.

Eventually, he made it to the end of the hallway and to the stairs. Paxton paused a moment and looked around. On the ground, about two feet away from the foot of the stairs, was a dark crimson stain. That was where Paxton had caught Amina. She'd stepped on a sensor. In a desperate attempt to save her from the unknown booby trap she'd set off, he'd forced her to jump. Paxton had caught her, but she didn't go unscathed. A nasty ravenclaw dart shot out of the wall and pierced her thigh. Paxton winced at the thought.

Paxton heard footsteps running toward him from behind. He listened and counted the sets of feet. *One, two. . .six.*

Paxton rushed up the stairs, down the tiled hallway in the subway system, leaping over the string sensor that likely had another booby trap with it, and through the door that led him into the subway tunnels.

By the sheer number of people darting up and down the hallway and around corners, Paxton guessed it was morning rush hour. This was good. Paxton could use the crowd to disappear. Paxton jumped into the sea of people and moved deeper into the subway tunnels. He weaved his way around the slower commuters and turned as many corners as possible before he came to a stop at a platform with fewer people. Looking at the sign, Paxton determined the train wasn't due for another five minutes. Perfect.

Paxton walked to the edge of the platform and jumped onto the tracks. One person tried to call after him as he ran into the tunnel, but most people ignored him.

"There he is! Paxton, stop!"

The Myriad found him. He didn't haven't much time before they caught up. They needed to get ahead, and they needed to hide. Paxton willed himself to run faster, hoping he wouldn't lose his footing. The subway tunnel kept straight, nowhere for them to turn. The Myriad could see him, but he kept going.

A loud shot echoed and ricocheted off some metal. Paxton instinctively ducked but kept running. He needed the tunnel to open up. He needed to make a turn somewhere.

The wall to his left gave way to the next platform, bustling with people. Not exactly what Paxton wanted, but he'd make do.

"This way." Paxton jumped and caught hold of the edge of the platform and hauled himself up. He turned to help Mimi, but she was already on the platform. Several people around gasped and backed away from them. He didn't bother to go around. Those who got in his way, he pushed aside as he took off again toward the hallway and away from their pursuers.

He heard the Myriad shouting after him again and people screaming, Paxton turned a corner and ran directly into a large man, giving him pause. The Myriad yelled, "Stop that man!"

The large man wearing a trench coat and hat set his suitcase down and tried to grab Paxton. Thankfully, he was slow, and Paxton ducked and got away, only to be stopped by another man who grabbed Paxton and twisted Paxton's arm behind him.

"I've got him! Over here."

Paxton kicked backward as hard as he could and connected with the man's leg. The man yelled in pain, letting go of Paxton. He continued forward. Anyone who got too close to him was pushed hard out of his way until he could get around another corner. Every so often he'd look back to make sure Mimi was still following. She was, and it impressed him. He continued to weave his way through the people and maze of tunnels until he found another platform and jumped onto the tracks. This time he didn't look to see when the train was due, but he hoped it wasn't soon. Paxton ran into the darkness but stayed close to the wall. Usually, there were maintenance closets along the edges, and he hoped to find one and hide in it.

A distant whirring noise and a soft wind picked up. Paxton swore.

"Paxton, the train!" Mimi said in a high-pitched voice.

A dim light came around a corner in front of them. Paxton continued to run toward the light, toward the oncoming train.

"What are you doing, you lunatic!?"

"Trust me."

Frantically, he checked the edges of the walls, hoping to find a door. Then, across on the other side of the tracks, he saw it. A maintenance door. Paxton looked at the oncoming train. It was rapidly approaching. Paxton held his breath as grabbed Mimi's arm and rushed across the tracks toward the door. His hand firmly gripped the doorknob. It was stuck. He pushed. He yanked. He shook the door and yelled as he used all his force to try and open it.

The train horn whistled loudly as a gust of wind swirled around them. The door swung open. Paxton shoved Mimi through and dove inside, falling hard on his shoulder. Without time to close the door, the train slammed into it, ripping it off and dragging it along. Paxton instinctively wrapped his body around Mimi to protect her from any debris.

When the train passed, he rolled off of Mimi, holding his chest. He breathed heavily and looked over at her. "You okay?" he asked.

Mimi nodded, unable to get words out between gasps. She pulled herself up and sat leaning against the wall.

CHAPTER 21

Paxton took a deep breath and let it out. Laughter bubbled from inside and burst out of him uncontrollably. He looked at Mimi, who stared at him bewildered before she also erupted into laughter.

After several minutes of laughing, they slowly regained their composer and sat silently in the closet's dark. By Paxton's estimations, he had about ten to fifteen minutes before the next train. That should be plenty of time to find another closet or a platform.

Paxton stood. "You ready?"

"As ready as I can be."

Paxton and Mimi took off again, looking. This time, they found another door and secured themselves inside before the train came whirring by. Inside, the closet was empty except for the fuse box on the side of the back wall. Paxton looked, hoping to find a ladder leading to the street level. Nothing. If they stayed, they'd be sitting ducks. But if they left, they risked the Myriad catching up again.

"So now what?" Mimi asked. "We can't get to your friendly safely if the Myriad knows you're running."

"For now, let's catch our breath."

"How did they find us so quickly?"

Paxton shook his head. The Myriad had their way about things. It was possible they weren't even looking for him, but if he ran, he'd make himself a suspect.

Paxton threw his backpack to the ground and sat with his back against the wall. He closed his eyes and drew in a slow, deep breath, held it for a couple of seconds, and then let it. He did this again and again, trying to calm his nerves. After the third breath in, Paxton erupted into a sob. He let the tears come. His whole body shook as the emotion from the day took over. His mind wanted to process it all but couldn't. He'd lost a dear friend and nearly died himself. And he wasn't in the clear yet. How had it come to this? All his life, he was a rule follower. He didn't get into trouble. He didn't question authority. But now, his life was upside down. He was now one of the criminals he used to defend the city against. And yet he didn't regret any of his decisions. For once in his life, he followed and was doing what he wanted to do, not what he was told to do.

"Woah, hey, shhhh," Mimi tried to soothe Paxton. She scooted next to him and rubbed his shoulder, though it felt more like she was shaking him. "You okay? I know it's been a crazy day and all."

Paxton composed himself and wiped the tears and snot away. "Not really." Paxton looked at Mimi with dry puffy eyes. "I'm sorry to tell you this, but Aiden won't be making it out of the building."

Mimi froze. The blood drained from her face. "What happened?" Her voice was barely audible.

Paxton didn't want to relive the scene. The wound was too fresh, but she deserved to know. He told her—explaining everything, including Cecilia showing up and the gunshot.

She didn't cry, but Paxton could see the pain in her eyes. Mimi stood. "We've been sitting too long. We need to go."

"I agree." Paxton grabbed his backpack and poked his head out the door. The coast was clear and as he listened, there were no sounds of footsteps. Paxton and Mimi stepped out on the track and continued down the tunnel. The ground and everything around them shook like an earthquake. Paxton braced himself, looking around to make sure nothing was coming toward them or about to fall on them. The shaking didn't last long before everything was quiet again. Paxton waited a moment longer and then continued walking. He knew what that was. One of the bombs detonated. He smiled to himself, hoping it had taken down the entire building.

"At least they're getting what they deserve," Mimi said, and Paxton agreed.

He was completely disoriented underground and didn't know in which direction he was heading. He needed to get to another platform and find a map. No sense in running in the opposite direction from where they needed to go.

It wasn't long before Paxton and Mimi reached the platform, jumped, and moved toward the intricate subway system map on the wall. According to the map, they'd been moving south, but they needed to move east. Paxton studied the map, putting the images and letters to memory as quickly as possible, a skill he'd acquired as a detective a lifetime ago. Once they were confident of the route they needed to take, they took off down the subway hall and toward Platform P on the purple line. They moved quickly, but not fast enough to draw attention. The crowd had thinned out as well, allowing them to maneuver around the people with greater ease.

Eventually, they made it to the exit they'd wanted and meandered to the street. Outside was chaos. Sirens whirred as emergency vehicles sped toward the capitol. When Paxton and Mimi looked toward the capitol, billows of smoke rose into the sky blocking the sun. Two helicopters circled the area, dropping blue liquid toward the burning buildings.

"We should keep moving," Paxton said, though he also had a hard time ripping his eyes away from the scene.

* * * *

The surgery took three long hours. Due to the nature and location of this secret procedure, all Heather could do was numb Mimi's arm, but otherwise, she was awake the entire time. Heather set up a sheet to hide Mimi's view from her arm and Paxton did his best to distract Mimi. Every so often, when the conversation would lull, Paxton could see the fear in Mimi's eyes. That's when Paxton would come up with another story about himself to distract her.

"Did I tell you about the time my grandmother and I tried to make ice cream?"

Paxton launched into a story about how hot the day was and how his grandmother wanted nothing more than a large bowl of chocolate ice cream with whipped cream on top. They'd pulled out an old recipe book and an ancient-looking ice cream maker and went to work. After two hours of waiting for it to freeze, they pulled it out of the freezer, and it was anything but delicious. First, it never fully froze, and second, they'd put way too much salt into it. It made both their lips pucker when they tried it. "It was the worst thing I'd ever tasted. To this day, I still can't eat chocolate ice cream."

Mimi laughed. "You and your grandmother were close, weren't you?"

"She helped raise me. She was the only mother I knew. Mine died in a car accident when I was a toddler."

The smile melted off Mimi's face. "Oh geez, I'm so sorry."

"It's okay. My grandmother more than made up for me not having a mom. What about your mom?" Paxton asked cautiously.

Mimi straightened her back, breathing life back into her. "She's actually with Amina. Her name is Salome."

Paxton smiled. "No kidding? We better make sure we get

you back to her in one piece."

"I'm doing the best I can," Heather retorted from the other side of the sheet.

Heather finished the last stitch, took off her gloves, and came around the sheet. There was a sink where she promptly washed her hands. "All finished."

"What's the damage?" Mimi wrinkled her nose.

"We won't fully know until the local anesthetics wear off, but as far as I can tell, no paralysis. You might have some numbness that could be permanent, but that's it." Heather grabbed a paper towel and dried her hands.

Mimi sighed.

Paxton shook Heather's hand. "This means so much. Thank you."

"What are you going to do with the chip?"

"Melt it in acid. It looks like it's already deactivated somehow, but we'll want to be safe and get rid of it altogether."

"Yeah, my friend built a device that can fry the GPS and temporarily disable the chip without triggering anything," Mimi said.

Heather raised her eyebrows. "Really? Do you have it with you?"

Mimi nodded. "It's in my bag. Do you want it?"

"It could come in handy, considering the type of people I help."

Mimi reached into her back with her good hand and pulled out the small device that looked like a flashlight. "It's all yours."

Heather thanked Mimi and gave her some pain meds and instructions on how to keep her wound clean. They said their goodbyes, and Mimi and Paxton made their way back to the subway system and toward the outer city.

Getting through security to the outer city and to The Beyond was a lot easier than Paxton expected. Since he was still in a military fatigue, he could drop Frank's name and make up some lame excuse for needing to go out there with Mimi. The soldiers didn't question it.

Paxton and Mimi walked silently for a good three miles out in the Beyond, heading toward the mountains. They kept an eye out for drones or patrol vehicles. Although they freely made it out to The Beyond, being out in the middle of a field was cause for suspicion. They were close to hiding in the tree line. From there, they could make their way to the valley and finally be free. Never to worry about the Myriad again. Paxton didn't want to risk getting caught when they were this close.

As they continued their way toward the mountains, Paxton slowed at the hidden entrance to the tunnels. He wondered if he should go down there and see if the others had made it back. He knew at least two of the bombs went off, but that didn't mean they survived. And what if those left behind wanted to come with him to the valley? This would be their only chance.

A scuffle caught Paxton's attention, and he spun around. He stopped as an older woman with caramel skin, dark brown hair, and deep hazel eyes—red from crying—stepped out from behind a large boulder.

She put her hands up. "They're not down there."

Paxton took a step toward her, his fist tight. "What did you do to them?"

"I didn't do anything to them. They were already gone when I went down there."

"Then what are you doing here?"

"I could ask you the same thing, but I already know."

CHAPTER 21

Paxton eyed her suspiciously. The last time they'd spoken was before he'd gone under. She was the captain in charge of the raid. Once Paxton had given Frank the necessary information, she was to lead the team down into the tunnels and take the Notzrim out. Only Paxton didn't go through with it. Instead, he turned and helped Amina and the Notzrim find a new place to escape and live safely. He was certain Cecilia knew this by now and was not pleased with Paxton's choices.

"Everyone knows. You're all anyone talks about these days in the purity unit. But what they really want to know is what us officials are going to do about it. I thought you could be given a second chance, and yet, here you are." The tone in her voice wasn't menacing or accusatory. It was soft as if something had finally broken inside her and she no longer had any will.

"Here I am." Paxton tried not to look surprised at her confession. "So I ask again, what are you doing here?"

"I was hoping to find you or someone who could help me. I need my daughter to know something."

Paxton swallowed hard, not wanting to ask his next question, but he forced himself. "Who's your daughter?"

"Why Amina, of course. The one you got close to."

Paxton's stomach dropped. "I'm not helping you."

Cecilia put her hands up in defense. "I don't want you to take me to her. We don't need to be together. She's made her choice. I don't agree with her, and I think she's insane for holding on to this belief so hard. I also know I can't force my children to do anything. I just want her to know I'm sorry for what I did to her, and I'd like to see her one last time to officially say goodbye. Maybe in a week, she can come here and see me. After that, I'll stay away, and do whatever I can to keep her location hidden."

"And how do you expect to do that?"

"You let me worry about that. I've already lost one child, I don't intend on losing another, even if I can't have her with me." Cecilia sniffled, holding back more tears she undoubtedly had for Aiden. "Will you tell her?"

Paxton gritted his teeth. What good would it do to tell Amina? They would never see each other and if Paxton told her, would Amina even believe Cecilia's words?

"We'll tell her," Mimi answered for him.

Cecilia looked at Mimi as if seeing her there for the first time. She gave a half-hearted smile. "Quite the mess you made at the capitol."

"What are you talking about?"

"I'm assuming you were working with those Notzrim scum we arrested after they blew up two of our buildings? There's no other way they could've gotten in that easy." Cecilia took a step forward, causing Mimi to step back.

Paxton stepped between the two women. "I think you should go now, Cecilia."

"That's fine, but she—" Cecilia pointed at Mimi, "needs to come with me."

"Not a chance."

"I still have a job to do, Paxton. Don't get in my way."

Paxton looked her in the eye. He was done with her games and manipulations. All he wanted was to be free of her and any other Myriad. "You take her, and I don't tell your daughter a thing. You'll never get the chance to make your peace with her. Your choice."

Cecilia stared at Paxton. Her jaw tightened and her hands curled into fists. Paxton couldn't read her. Part of her expression seemed to indicate pain, but mingled with complete rage.

CHAPTER 21

He wasn't going to back down from her, and he was ready for whatever she was going to do next. Finally, Cecilia turned and walked away. It was the right move.

Once Paxton was confident Cecilia wasn't coming back, Paxton turned to the tunnel's entrance and pulled open the fake rock to reveal the manhole with a keypad underneath. He punched in a code and the keypad beeped and dropped open.

"Woah," Mimi said with her mouth hanging open behind him.

Paxton smiled. "C'mon, let's go see if Cecilia was telling the truth." Paxton lowered himself through the hole and descended the ladder into the dark tunnels. His boots slashed in the muck below, sending off unthinkable odors. Once Mimi was inside, Paxton punched numbers into another keypad, which closed the manhole and reset the rock in place, securing them inside. Beside the keypad was a switch to turn on the string of lights hung above, but nothing happened when Paxton flipped the switch. He tried it a couple times, but still nothing. Giving up, he headed down the tunnels toward the main hall. It'd been a while since he'd been in the tunnels and even then, he never fully memorized its layout. He hoped he was moving in the right direction.

After winding through several dark tunnels, one opened into a large dome-shaped area with water running through the center and a catwalk high above them. Paxton descended the ladder into the main hall and wandered toward the center. The last time they all thought everyone was missing, they were actually hiding in a shelter hidden under the water. Paxton prayed that was the case now.

"This is where they all lived, huh?"

"This is it. Well, part of it. There are several other areas like this one all interconnected to make their own city."

"Where are they now?" Mimi asked while staring at the tall ceiling.

"Most left to the valley, where we'll be going, but the militia hung back. I don't know where they are now, though. I'm hoping they're hiding around here somewhere." Paxton continued to the other side and up another ladder. Just as he reached the top, a gun clicked. Paxton froze as he slowly looked into the abyss. He couldn't see anyone, but he knew they were there. "I'm not here to hurt you," Paxton said calmly. "It's me, Paxton, the Hebrew, friend of Amina and Aiden Haddad."

From the shadows stepped Tessa, still holding her gun aimed at Paxton's head. Her head tilted slightly as her eyes narrowed at him, studying him. She moved to the edge of the tunnel, still keeping her gun on Paxton, and peered at Mimi. Her eyes lit up, and she dropped the gun. "Mimi, you're alive!"

"Yeah, I made it out."

Tessa stepped aside and let Paxton and Mimi climb to her. Standing there, Paxton could get a good look at Tessa's red puffy eyes and tear stains streaking through the dirt on her face. Once they were all standing together, Tessa raised her gun again and pointed it at Paxton. A second person stepped from the shadows: Terrance. He aimed his gun at Mimi.

Mimi put her hands up. "What is this all about?"

"That's what we'd like to know," Tessa said. "The entire mission went to shambles after you disappeared. We blew two of the buildings while trying to escape, but only five of us made it out. The rest were arrested. Tell me, Mimi, what happened?"

"I promise, it was not me. Paxton had a way to remove my chip, and I went with him. I told Aiden, but. . .he didn't make it out."

"How'd they know where to find us?"

"I don't know. I'm very sorry, but you all had to know going into this was a dangerous mission. The odds of escape—minimal." Tessa and Terrance didn't respond. "Do you honestly think I'd come here if I had turned you in?"

"Maybe you're here to finish the job," Terrance said, while still holding his gun aimed at her head. "For all we know, there's a cloud of Myriad above us right now."

"We came to get you and take you to the valley where the others are," Paxton explained. "Mimi is on your side."

Terrance looked at Paxton, confused. "Who are you again?"

"Paxton, the Hebrew who took Amina to the valley." He hated to lie anymore to them, but telling the truth wouldn't help their situation. Thankfully, Mimi was keeping quiet as he spoke.

Terrance lowered his gun. "Oh yeah. I thought you looked familiar. Why aren't you in the valley, then?"

"Long story, but I'm heading there now, with Mimi. Come with us. You and whoever else are still here."

Tessa also lowered her gun. "Thanks, but we still have work to do. There are other Notzrim still out there and though we weakened the Myriad temporarily, they're not going to stop. Until Meshiakh returns, we need to do what we can to help protect our fellow Notzrim."

Paxton smiled inwardly. It was a noble cause they were fighting for, and he appreciated, despite their loss, they wanted to keep going.

"What about the others here? Do they all want to stay?" Mimi asked.

"Most likely, yes, but you can ask them."

"Was it worth it?" A scratchy voice spoke behind Tessa and Terrance.

Tessa turned around. "Was what worth it?"

Mitchum stepped out of the shadows, his eyes swollen with tears. "All the arrests, all the sacrifice? What good did it do you?"

"We weakened the Myriad, slowed them down."

"No you didn't. I took down two minor buildings in a sea of thousands. This war is not ours, it's Meshiakh's, and you should've had more faith." He took a ragged breath before continuing. "Nothing ever turns out the way we expect or happens in our timing, but that doesn't mean Sabaoth isn't working. If he says something is going to happen, then it'll happen. He's proven that time and time again and yet, you all forgot that. Now, Aiden is dead, the rest arrested, and for what?" Mitchum eyed Paxton. "Can I come with you? I'm done here. I should've never stayed in the first place."

Paxton nodded. It pained him to a reflection of his own grief in Mitchum.

Tessa bit the inside of her cheek as she stared at the ground, unable to answer.

"I'll take you to the others," Tessa mumbled.

She led Paxton and Mimi through the tunnel and into another dome-shaped sector. This one was smaller and had a large fire pit in the center instead of a water canal.

After introductions and explanations, no one agreed to go with Paxton and Mimi. It surprised Paxton. He expected a few to want to walk away from the danger, but they all seemed even more convinced of what they were doing than ever.

Tessa and Terrance loaded Paxton, Mimi and Mitchum with supplies before saying goodbye and sending them on their

CHAPTER 21

way.

Chapter 22

It took four hours, but Paxton, Mimi, and Mitchum finally made it to the mountains. As the sun fell low in the sky, Paxton reoriented himself and headed in the right direction toward Amina. The only problem was, he still didn't know if he was actually going to go. Was going there and facing her, and telling her how he couldn't save Aiden, the best option? She'd forgive him, right? He wasn't sure he could forgive himself or that he deserved forgiveness. He'd done so much already, and it was a wonder how Amina got past his first betrayal when she discovered he was Myriad and a Notzrim murderer no less. But there had to be a breaking point. A line drawn where she could no longer look past his mistakes.

Paxton noticed the darkening sky as night drew near. They needed to make camp. It was easy to find a clearing, build his fire, and get situated. Once he'd done so, he rummaged through his backpack and pulled out the two MREs he'd stolen. One was macaroni and cheese and the other two were beef stew. He tossed Mimi and Mitchum the beef stew packets. He was happy with the macaroni and cheese. It was simple and comforting. Paxton placed the foil pouch on a rock near the edge of the fire to let it heat.

The MRE wasn't tasty, but it filled him, and it somewhat

resembled macaroni and cheese. It hadn't occurred to Paxton how quickly his memory could forget the cardboard taste of an MRE.

When he finished, he took the empty pouch and tossed it into the fire. Though they'd never figured out how to improve taste, they at least learned how to make pouches that could disintegrate in a fire.

During dinner, no one talked much. Just a basic introduction and a few comment about the food, but that was it. Paxton figured they were still processing the day as much as he was. He laid on his back with his hands behind his head and stared up at the sky. Light sounds of creatures sung in his ears. Crickets chirping, an owl hooting in the distance, and the scurrying of claws across a rock.

As he observed the sky, he spotted a single cloud flickering with lightning. While a storm cloud wasn't unusual, this particular cloud swirled with colors of blue, gold and red. The more Paxton stared at the lightning show the more his heart raced. He no longer believed it was a lightening storm, but if not, what was it?

Paxton closed his eyes and took a deep breath, trying not to worry himself about some cosmic haze. It took him what felt like forever, but eventually he relaxed himself enough to fall asleep.

The dark night sky enveloped Paxton. No matter where he turned, there was nothing but darkness. He tried to escape, running frantically in no particular direction, trying to seek the light. The darkness grew thick and clung to him like a toxic sludge. Paxton wiped it off and when he looked at his hand, it was crimson. Stumbling backward, Paxton tripped and fell into a pile of something hard. He looked down and picked up the broken piece, a bone. Paxton dropped it and looked around. He was on a massive pile of bones. He scurried down it. Bones, slipping and sliding as they gave way under his weight.

Finally, he escaped the pile. In front of him was a white door bordered with more bones and skulls all about. A black gas seeped from the edges of the door, releasing an odious smell of death. Paxton crinkled his nose. While the door terrified him, it also piqued his curiosity. An inexplicable curiosity drew him closer. Slowly, cautiously, he stepped toward it, stopping just short, yet close enough to touch. He stuck his hand out and paused. He swallowed hard. Tiny beads of sweat formed on his forehead. What would happen if he opened the door?

Paxton lowered his hand, fighting the urge to go through the door. Nothing good could come from this door. He tried to walk away and yet something held him there. Staring. Wondering. Paxton placed his hand on the doorknob. It was cold as ice. He turned to the door about to push it open.

A host of high-pitched screams pierced his ears. He clutched his ears, trying to muffle the sound while he looked around. Where was it coming from? There was no one. The scream grew louder and almost seemed to say, "open the door." The more Paxton resisted the door, the louder the scream became, ripping through his brain and crippling him. He fell to his knees and cried out audibly. Make it stop! Make it stop! Oh, Sabaoth, I beg of you to make it stop!

Another voice broke through the screams, like a hissing snake. "Why should Sabaoth listen to you? You who caused all this pain? You who murdered his people. You don't deserve him."

"You're right, I don't, but Sabaoth have mercy!"

"There is no mercy for the wicked. Come with me instead. Come

CHAPTER 22

through the door to your destiny. Get what you deserve."

Paxton looked around but still saw no one, just the door. Paxton pushed the door open. Beyond was a black hole, thick as velvet. The scream still pierced his ears, but as he looked through the door, a sudden overwhelming feeling of emptiness grasped his heart.

"No Sabaoth, please, have mercy. Forgive me! I'm sorry. I'm so sorry."

Paxton fell prostrate, still mumbling to himself. He was caught up in his agony that he hadn't recognized that the screaming had stopped until someone placed a hand on his shoulder. Paxton flinched and was about to turn to see who it was when he woke up from his dream.

Paxton looked around his campground, trying to ground himself in reality. Chills ran over his sweaty body from the cool night air. The fire beside him had died to a gently glowing ember. His boots were beside him and his backpack served as his pillow. Nothing else around him seemed out of the ordinary.

The night sky gave way to the dawn. The few stars left were fading as the sun peeked over the horizon. As his heart returned to normal, a calm wash over him. The dream was terrifying and confusing and yet whoever or whatever had touched his back, lingered even now. He'd never experienced this much love from a single touch. Paxton smiled as a light breeze wafted over him and whispered, *I forgive you.*

* * * *

"Aiden!" Amina jolted out of sleep, gasping. Her vision blurred in and out of her dream. Flashes of white-washed hallways and metal doors. Fear and pain pierced her heart, and she clung to her blanket tightly. The wooden walls and surrounds came back into view as the confusion subsided. She was back in her cabin, safe. It was only a dream and yet it seemed real.

She couldn't remember any details about it, but she felt it. She felt the hate and the pain. She felt his death. Tears sprung to Amina's eyes. *Aiden.* Though she couldn't be certain, something inside vanished. A piece of her soul, missing. Amina drew her knees to her chest and wrapped her arms around them as she let the tears fall. *It was just a dream.* A dream she'd had for the past four nights in a row. *It was just a dream.* She tried to convince herself. It wasn't working. It was too real. The more she tried to push it away and ignore it, the more intense her dream the next night would be. Maybe if she just accepted that it was real, accepted that she was too late, and her brother had gone too far, then maybe it'd go away.

Eventually, the sounds of movement and life grew louder outside, cluing Amina into her need to get going. It was Sunday morning, and Amina needed to meet Mo, Paul, and Emily for worship. Slowly, she dragged herself out of bed, feeling the weight of grief leeching her energy just like it had when she first arrived in the valley. Only this time, Amina was not going to let it suck her dry. She wasn't even certain it was real. *It was only a dream.* It was her mantra for the morning and would be for the rest of her life if need be. Amina pulled on her moccasins and ran a comb through her hair. After pulling it into a quick ponytail, she grabbed a peach and headed out.

It was a cool morning, but not a cloud was in the sky. The fall leaves were in full effect and rained down into the village anytime a breeze blew. It made for a lot of work to clean them, but also a lot of fun. Adults would sweep the leaves into massive piles, allowing the children to jump and roll around in the crunchy leaves. Fall time was Amina's favorite.

At the center of town, the amphitheater was already filling up with chattering people ready for the morning's worship. Amina scanned the crowd and found Mo, Paul, and Emily sitting toward the back of the amphitheater.

Before she could reach them, Josiah appeared at the edge of the amphitheater with Matthias. He held onto Matthias' elbow, guiding him toward a nearby bench. Amina smiled as she watched Josiah. It hurt her to see Matthias weak and sickly, but she was glad he was out and about. Amina bounced her way over toward them.

"How are you doing today, Matthias?" Amina asked.

Matthias turned to face Amina. He had deep bags under his eyes and cracked skin all over.

Matthias forced a smile. "I've been better, but Sabaoth has given me energy today to get out."

"I'm glad to hear it." Amina looked from Matthias to Josiah, trying not to appear worried. This couldn't possibly be from the baneberry poisoning, could it?

Josiah led Amina further away from Matthias. He turned and looked at Amina, his brow wrinkled. "It's not looking good for him."

"What do you mean?"

"I mean, he's not getting better. He's been to see Vanita several times and they think it's something more. Possibly cancer."

Amina's hand flew to her mouth. What do you say in a moment like this?

"It's okay. He's taking it well."

"And you?"

Josiah looked up at the sky, his eyes filling with tears. "I will be."

Amina reached out and hugged her friend. They'd known one another for over a decade, and Josiah was there for her after her father's death.

"Anyway, have you checked the traps this morning? It's been a week since any commotion. Maybe they've wised up?"

"Doubtful. And no, I haven't checked today. We can check after worship."

Off in the distance, a man's voice laughed, and it sounded eerily like Aiden's. Amina gasped, and the tears sprung to her eyes again. This time, she held them back. *It was only a dream. Trust Sabaoth. Even if it wasn't a dream, he's home with Sabaoth. It'll be okay. Everything's okay.* Amina let out a slow, shaky breath.

"I'm fine."

He stared at her longer without a word, but she didn't want to tell him. He had enough worries of his own right now. No reason to bring up bad dreams.

"I'm going to sit with Mo and Paul. I'll see you after the service."

Josiah looked at her one last time, giving her the chance to share, but when she didn't say anything, he left to take his seat.

Amina made her way to Mo and Paul. An uproar of chatter pricked her ears and she saw Salome walking toward the amphitheater. The surrounding crowd cleared out of her way, staring and whispering as they did so. Amina grimaced and bit her lip. While she didn't blame Salome for causing the sabotages, she felt guilty for adding to Salome's distress.

Mo put her hand up and waved to Salome. "Over here."

CHAPTER 22

Heads snapped in their direction, shooting glares of annoyance and disgust. Amina was excited for Salome to sit with them, but there was no need for all the evil eyes.

Salome sat between Mo and Amina.

Amina's chest tightened, and she rubbed at it. Amina still needed to apologize for her outburst. After the storm, she'd thrown herself into helping with the traps and the wall, justifying that she didn't have a moment to speak with Salome.

"Thank you," Salome said to Mo. "People aren't very happy with me still."

"Ignore them. They'll get over it."

Salome turned and looked at Amina. "Good morning."

"Hi." Amina shifted uncomfortably, hoping Salome wouldn't bring anything up. There were too many people around for a serious conversation.

When Salome realized that she wouldn't say anything else, she turned and faced the stage. Amina winced. She needed to stop making excuses. Amina turned to say sorry to Salome just as the music from the stage began and everyone stood to sing along. About a minute into the song, Salome excused herself from the group. She scooted her way out of the seating area and headed to the far side of the amphitheater. As Amina watched her curiously, she noticed her approach a group of Hebrew families.

* * * *

"What are you all doing here?" Salome asked, shocked to see this many Hebrews at the Notzrim village.

"We wanted to hear Father Stephen speak. Some of us were here before, but we had to stop because of Aryeh's warriors.

Now that they're gone, we thought we'd take our chances. Many of us want peace just as much as you do Salome. And we'll help in any way we can to get it."

Salome hugged the woman who'd spoken. "I'm glad to hear that. Please come sit." Salome brought the group over to sit on the benches.

As more Notzrim arrived, there were several stares and some whispers, but no one confronted Salome and her group outright. Some of the Notzrim even came over to say hello. Salome was thankful and hoped that they would all be accepting of the newcomers.

The small group of musicians on stage ended their first song, but immediately started a new one. Salome knew all the songs and sung along, but noticed many of the Hebrews looked lost and stood awkwardly listening. A familiar Psalm of David began. The Hebrews wouldn't know the melody, but they knew the words, and they tried to sing along:

As the deer panteth for the water, so my soul longeth after thee
  You alone are my one desire, and I long to worship thee

Salome's heart soared as she sang to Sabaoth, glorifying him with her words. Knowing that both Hebrew and Notzrim stood together united was exhilarating, and she only hoped more would come too. Maybe this was it. Maybe now was Sabaoth's way of saying, let's have that party. Salome looked in Mo's direction and when she caught her eye, she smiled. Mo gave her a thumbs up as if understanding.

During Father Stephen's story, Salome leaned in closer.

CHAPTER 22

"Two men went to pray. One was a highly regarded religious man, and the other was a despised swindler. The religious man stood by himself and prayed, 'I thank you, Sabaoth, that I am not like other people—cheaters, sinners, adulterers. I'm certainly not like that swindler! I attend worship weekly, and I give you a tenth of my income.'

"But the swindler stood at a distance and dared not even lift his eyes to heaven as he prayed. Instead, he beat his chest in sorrow, saying, 'O Meshiakh, son of Sabaoth, be merciful to me, for I am a sinner.'"

Father Stephen paused, looking out across the crowd while his words sunk deep into Salome's heart. Somehow, she felt guilty. As if she'd been doing things wrong all this time. All her life she focused on the outer actions to be good, but was that not enough?

Salome leaned closer, her fingers gripping the edge of the bench. What was the point of this story? Was Father Stephen going to share more, or was that it?

Finally, he opened his mouth and continued. "I tell you, this swindler went home forgiven, not the supposed religious man who did things for show. My brothers and sisters, if you walk around with your nose in the air, thinking the things you do make you more religious, you're going to end up flat on your face. Anyone who exalts themselves will be humbled, but those who humble themselves, doing things with the heart of Meshiakh, will be exalted for Meshiakh came to seek and save those who know they need forgiveness, not those who think they're already perfect. Let us pray." Father Stephen bowed his head.

Salome did the same and tried to listen, but her mind wandered. Was it true? Was salvation really about confessing sins and believing in Meshiakh who came to save? The battle raged within. Everything she learned growing up fighting against this learned information from the Notzrim's. *I need clarity, Sabaoth. Give me your truth.*

A faint smell of smoke tickled Salome's nose. Her first thought was it was someone cooking, but the smell was not of food but of burning pine. Something tickled her hand. She opened her eyes to find a small piece of ash. Salome's heart quickened as her breath caught in her throat. She looked up and saw another piece of ash floating in front of her. Visions of her dream rushed in, and heat rose into her face.

In the distance, someone yelled, and though she couldn't quite make out what they were saying, she knew. The voice drew closer and people in the crowd turned, looking for the disembodied voice. No one needed to know what they were saying. Salome and the others turned to find black smoke rising above the trees, thick and menacing.

"Fire! At the edge! Come quickly! The village is on fire!" A man broke through the brush and halted. He waved for others to follow and then disappeared again.

A loud frenzy of disarray burst from the group. Salome needed to do something, and fast. She ran to the stage. "Everyone who can, get buckets of water! Others take the children and disabled to safety. Back near the cave."

The crowd rushed around like swirling wind as they jumped into action. Parents grabbed their children by the hand or picked them up and rushed in one direction while several ran in the opposite direction to find buckets.

Salome ran to the man and asked, "where is it? Where's the fire?"

"By the hospital."

CHAPTER 22

Salome's hand flew to her face. "We need to evacuate them." She turned to the crowd again and yelled to help evacuate the medical cabin. She ran with them until they reached the fire. Salome stopped as she saw the looming fire engulfing the trees and creeping its way toward the medical cabin. It hadn't caught fire yet, but it was only a matter of time.

The fire spread along the tree line, forming a perimeter around the village. If they didn't stop this soon, they'd be trapped. Her dream flashed through her mind. It was coming true. But did that mean Aryeh was, in fact, behind this fire and potentially all the sabotages like her dream portrayed? It didn't matter. Salome needed all the help she could get.

She could see that things were under control. Several ran into the cabin to pull people out, while others had water buckets and were dousing the flames.

Salome took off. She needed more help. She needed Aryeh and the other Hebrews.

Salome sprinted as fast as she could through the village, across the open field, and toward the Hebrew's village. Smoke engulfed the air and constricted her lungs while her muscles burned. She pushed faster.

As Salome approached the main building in the Hebrew village, she heard Aryeh yelling at someone inside. Salome stopped before entering and listened.

"What is wrong with you!" Aryeh growled. "Do you realize what you've done?"

"I thought you'd be happy. Weren't you the one who wanted the Notzrim gone?"

"Not like this! You've jeopardized not only them but our people as well."

Salome crept forward to see who he was speaking with. Then

she saw him — tall, black hair, it was Camden.

"I thought you'd be happy about this. After all, you said you wanted them gone."

"Not like this! I don't want them dead!"

"Oh please, they'll be fine. Maybe a few causalities, but it'll be enough to convince them to leave like you've always wanted."

"This is not what I wanted, and you know it. You went too far when you took this into your own hands, Camden."

Camden poked a hard finger into Aryeh's chest. "You encouraged it."

"I encouraged separation."

"And hate. Your hate for the Notzrim is evident. Everyone sees it. I did it for you because you were too feeble to take action."

Aryeh put a hand over his face and dragged it down. "And I suppose you're the one who vandalized our own village and framed the Notzrim."

"I needed more people on my side."

"You're banished, Camden. Gone. Goodbye. I never want to see you in this valley again."

Camden let out a haughty laugh. "You can't banish me."

"I just did," Aryeh spoke slowly and calmly, but there was a deep anger seething in his tone.

"But—"

"No, that's final. You have brought shame to your people and to Sabaoth. Eloina!"

Eloina came out of the back room. "Yes?"

"See that Camden gathers his things and leaves the valley in the next few hours."

Eloina glanced at Camden and back to Aryeh. "Yes, sir."

CHAPTER 22

As Eloina escorted Camden out of the building, Salome stepped in and rushed over to Aryeh. She couldn't believe what she'd just heard. Aryeh wasn't responsible. In fact, it appalled him. There was hope for him, after all.

"Aryeh," Salome called after him.

Aryeh turned around, startled. "Salome. I was just about to gather everyone to join and help. How bad is it?"

"It's bad. That's why I had to get over here. Oh Aryeh, thank you. I'm sorry I suspected you. It's just—"

"It's okay. You had every right to think it was me. Let's focus on getting that fire out before it's too late."

Chapter 23

Amina had no time to process what was happening as she watched Salome run off. She wanted to give her the benefit of the doubt, but she wasn't sure. Amina turned to the medical cabin and dashed inside to help finish evacuating everyone. The fire was getting dangerously close and one stray ember could quickly catch the building on fire.

Inside the medical cabin, men and women were already hard at work lifting patients who couldn't walk onto stretchers and gathering supplies into crates in order to save as much as possible. They all knew the fire was coming. There'd be no saving the cabin.

Thick smoke seeped into the cabin and constricted Amina's lungs. She grabbed her handkerchief and tied it around her face before rushing to the closest patient. It was an elderly woman Amina recognized but didn't know well. The woman's eyes were closed, and her breathing was soft. How could anyone possibly sleep at a time like this? Amina gently shook the woman, but she didn't budge. She tried again.

"Ma'am, you need to wake up. There's a fire!" Amina spoke with urgency as she shook the woman again. She still wouldn't wake.

Amina looked around for a nurse and flagged down one lady

CHAPTER 23

who was rushing by. "She won't wake up?"

The nurse looked at the elderly lady. "She just took her meds recently and they make her extremely tired. I'll grab a stretcher."

Soon, the nurse returned with a stretcher. She and Amina worked to slide the stretcher underneath the unconscious woman and then carry her out of the cabin. The woman was incredibly light, as if they were carrying a child. They made their way out of the cabin and toward the center of the village.

"Why are we going toward the center? We need to get out of here."

"There's nowhere else to go. The fire has us surrounded."

Everything around Amina seemed to freeze as her body went limp. The stretcher and Amina both hit the ground. They were doomed. The fire would continue to grow until it consumed everything.

"Hun, are you alright?" The nurse asked, with her hand on Amina's back. "Do you need some water?"

Amina shook her head but couldn't find the words. After all her work, after all the Notzrim sacrificed over the past nine years, this was how their story ended. Burned alive in the flames of hatred. *No!*

Amina stood. She couldn't give up now. She couldn't let Aryeh win. There had to be a way to stop this fire. A way to put it out.

Oh Sabaoth, we need you now more than ever. We need this fire to go out.

Amina picked up the stretcher and she and the nurse finished bringing the elderly woman to the center of town. Then Amina sprinted, not toward the medical cabin, but toward the supply cabin. There had to be something there besides tiny buckets that could help them put out such a large fire.

Nearing the supply cabin, Amina found dozens of people rushing in and out, grabbing buckets and crates, anything to hold water. Amina ignored them and ran into the cabin to look for something else. A hose of some sort. She felt completely lost as she looked around. Even if there was a hose, there was no running water to squirt out of it. There was no way to get a fast jet stream to put out the fire. The only thing they could do was use buckets and douse the fire.

In the corner, Amina saw a pile of shovels and rakes, which got her thinking. Once before, she'd seen firemen purposefully burning brush in order to clear it out and help prevent a large wildfire. Maybe they could get a large enough cleared barrier around the village to stop the fire from consuming anything new. Eventually, it would burn itself out.

Amina turned around and shouted to anyone around to grab shovels and rakes. The people just glanced at her oddly and kept grabbing buckets.

"I'm serious right now! We need to create a fire barrier. Clear as much out of the way so the fire can't consume anything else!"

"We have too many structures and trees. There's no time for that!" A man, who'd actually stopped long enough to listen to Amina, shouted back at her and took off again.

Amina refused to believe him. Instead, she grabbed a shovel and took off toward the center of the village. She ran as fast as she could down the hill, letting gravity propel her forward. It took everything in her not to fall over. Her chest tightened and her body shook all at the same time. Desperation and fear kicked into full gear and drove her actions.

At the center of the village, Amina looked around to determine where the best place to start was. The fire was still on the edge of town, but it was only a matter of time before it burned through the trees and drew closer. Amina ran to the edge of the clearing, where the first bush appeared, and started digging it up. She needed the clearing to be larger. There needed to be as much dirt between them and the fire that it couldn't keep moving. She was desperate. Her body surged with adrenaline. Sweat rolled down her face and her eyes burned. She worked frantically. She had a mission. Stop the fire. She didn't care who helped her anymore or who listened. She knew what she needed to do, and she wasn't going to stop.

"Amina!" Josiah shouted from behind her. Amina kept working. "What are you doing?"

"Trying to stop the fire from getting any closer." She grabbed the bush and pulled it out of the ground. She threw it onto a small wagon nearby. Once she had enough debris cleared, she could wheel it toward the fire and away from safety.

"By digging up bushes?"

"I'm trying to create a barrier of just dirt. That way, the fire can't keep burning." She rushed over to the next bush and started digging.

"There's no way we have time for that. We need to evacuate people instead."

Amina stopped. A lump in her throat. "To where? There's nowhere to go, Josiah. We have a cliff on one side of us and a raging fire on the other."

Josiah stepped closer to Amina, and she collapsed into his arms, letting the tears flow. She let out a loud scream, her heart splitting in two at the thought of them all burning alive.

* * * *

The trek through the mountains and toward the valley felt easy. Paxton hadn't experienced this much excitement in a very long time. Knowing that Sabaoth had visited him, or he thought he had, filled him with an immense joy that he thought would burst. He needed to tell Amina.

It was surprising how easily the memory of traveling to the valley came to Paxton. Before he worried, he wouldn't be able to figure it out, but as each major landmark appeared, it reminded him exactly which way to go. He was going to get there in no time.

The hours passed quickly as he hummed to himself and kept up a soldier's pace. Mimi had no problem keeping up, but Paxton found himself having to slow down or take breaks for Mitchum. In the past, waiting would've irritated Paxton. He didn't like to be slowed down, but today, it didn't bother one bit.

They followed the river as Paxton had done all those months ago, and he knew he was getting close when he really started climbing in elevation.

About mid-day they stopped to have a snack and pull out their ponchos. In the distance, dark storm clouds ominously made their way in his direction. It was only a matter of time before they dumped on the three of them.

As they sat eating freeze-dried apple slices, Paxton looked in the direction they were headed. That's when he noticed it. Smoke. And not just a small stack from a campfire. This was a large black cloud that fanned over the sky. How had he not realized that before? Paxton's stomach sank. Was that coming from the valley or beyond? And if beyond, how close was it

CHAPTER 23

before it reached the valley?

Moving quickly, Paxton grabbed his things and raced toward the smoke, toward the fire. Who was going to stop it? There were no firemen out here. No hoses or airplanes to drop water. He needed to warn Amina and the others if they didn't already know about it. Or if it was in the valley, he needed to get them out.

"Hey, where are you going?" Mimi shouted after him. Footsteps followed behind.

Paxton ran faster, and with every step, his fear grew. There was no way he'd get there in time. How could he? Paxton glanced at the clouds still moving toward him. *Hurry with those clouds already!*

He came to a screeching halt when he reached the edge of the cliff at the edge of the valley. He'd made it, confirming his fears. In the valley, a massive fire raged. The black smoke blocked all of Paxton's vision. *No, no, no, no, no!*

* * * *

Salome and Aryeh arrived on the outskirts of the village. A gust of wind whipped Salome's hair into her face. She pulled it back as her mouth fell agape at the sight. She couldn't believe how quickly the fire spread. How it enveloped the village. The only opening she saw was to her left, where the farm and barn were located. If people could get over there, they could escape, but did they even know there was an opening? Being down in the flames must be terrifying.

Salome looked to Aryeh, who was shouting out orders to his people. Dozens of Hebrews carried buckets of water, dirt, and some other sort of white liquid. They worked together like a well-oiled machine, passing buckets and tossing the water into the fire.

A couple of men had a large hose attached to a manual pump and a trough. One man was pumping the lever for the pump while others dumped the water and white liquid into the trough. As the man pumped, the liquid moved through the hose and out the other end with such force that it sprayed toward the top of the giant flames. The impressive machine worked well to help dampen the flames, but it would take some time before the fire was completely out. Salome wasn't sure they could work fast enough with just the one hose.

Soon, in the distance, Salome saw a second hose fighting the fire. The hoses worked to put out the flames while other Hebrew villagers used smaller buckets.

"We need to get people out." Salome looked back at the farm. The Notzrim's only hope of escape was quickly closing. "Over there, there's an opening. How do we stop the fire from closing that off?"

"The hose." Aryeh ran toward the hose operators who were carrying the hose contraption over toward the farm. Salome followed. Once they had it reset, they worked at putting the fire out in that area and keeping the area open. Salome took that as her cue to run back into the village and tell people about the escape route.

Salome flew down the hill toward the row of cabins and toward the center of the village. She was sure people were there somewhere. As she moved about, the wind did its best to push her over, but she kept running. The smoke thickened, and Salome gagged. It was thick enough to chew on. Just as Salome reached the edge of the market, she halted. The once lively food market was now alive with dancing flames, breaking apart the tables and booths, engulfing the canopies, and tearing everything down like a raging lunatic. Salome didn't stop long. She cut to her left and ran toward the cliff, following the edge of bushes, trees and cabins, looking for an opening into the center of the village. There was nothing. The fire had created a wall where the trees and bushes once stood.

"No! How can this be?"

Salome ran until she was just a hundred yards from the cliff when she saw dozens of people throwing buckets of water onto the fire's edge. There was an opening. There was still a chance.

Approaching the group, Salome shouted, "Can I get to the center here?"

"Yes! But I wouldn't if I were you."

"We need to get people out. There's a way out!"

Salome ran past the group before anyone responded and darted into the center of the village. Hundreds of women, children, and the elderly sat huddled together. Their heads bowed and their eyes tightly closed. Tears streamed down faces as their wails of fear and desperation floated above the crackling of the fire.

Salome stopped at the edge of the group. "I have a way out. Hurry!"

The people looked at her with confusion and disbelief. No one budged.

"Please, we must go toward the cliffs. Now! Before the fire completely engulfs us."

A few people stood but were still hesitant. Amina stood, and the two women locked eyes. A plea for help and a sign of solidarity were exchanged between them silently. Amin turned to the others. "You heard her. There's a way out. Get moving!"

People stood, picking up those who couldn't walk, or grabbing stretchers, and they followed Salome toward the cliff and toward their only route of escape. As they neared the opening, a large gust of wind blew and a loud crack made several shout. Just to their left, a large tree crumpled to the ground, ablaze. Those who were close ran out of the way as it crashed, sending embers bouncing toward the group. Those who'd been working on putting out the fire in that area ran to avoid getting pinned under the fire-blazing tree. Salome winced as she watched the tree fall, closing off their one and only way out.

Those who still had buckets tried to get back to work using dirt to smother the fire on the tree hoping to reopen the path and get people out.

"We're trapped!" a voice sobbed in the group, stirring everyone into a terrified frenzy.

Salome looked at the group and then back at the fire. There had to be a way out. A way around the fire. But even if there was, these people were too terrified to do anything. And some couldn't even walk on their own.

Then Amina shouted through the crowd, "We might be trapped, but we're not doomed. We can't lose hope in Sabaoth. He can save us. He's worked miracles before, and we must believe that he can do one now. We must pray and we must believe with our whole being. If ever there was a time to have faith, it's now."

The group quieted to an indistinct murmur of agreement.

Amina closed her eyes and prayed aloud. Salome watched as others followed suit, lifting hands to the sky, their faces either lifted to Sabaoth or bowed in reverence. Some kneeled while others stood swaying from side to side. The murmurs of

CHAPTER 23

their prayers grew and something within Salome bubbled. A bubbling of hope. It was inspiring to see these people putting their complete faith and truth in Sabaoth. In his ability to do miraculous things. Certainly, as a child, Salome had heard the miraculous story of Hananiah, Mishael, and Azariah, but to not see it happening in real life, her faith wavered.

Salome continued to stand, looking around for a way of escape. The group with the buckets was still working hard at putting the fire out, and Salome decided to help. There was no way Sabaoth would answer this prayer if Salome prayed, too. Her faith was too weak. So, she did the only thing she could. Help douse the fire. Since their source of water was blocked, they had to use dirt.

Salome grabbed a bucket and scooped mounds of dirt into it. Dust and smoke mixed in her nostrils, and she sneezed. But she kept working. Once her bucket was filled enough, she ran to the fire and threw it on the fallen tree. It spread all over but did nothing to help extinguish the fire. Salome turned and went to gather more dirt. She had to believe this would help.

As Salome continued throwing bucket after bucket of dirt into the fire, the prayers of the Notzrim grew louder in earnestness. All around her, she sensed the power of not only the fire but of the prayers within her. A supernatural power that seemed to light up the surrounding air. Salome thought she was imagining things, that it was only the fire growing brighter as it grew in size. But then Salome looked. She wasn't imagining the light. The light was real, and it was blinding. Salome covered her eyes and fell on her knees as the bright light from the sky cascaded down to the ground like a glittering waterfall, creating a barrier between the people and the fire. There it stayed, protecting them. Salome tried to peer up at the light and glimpse at whatever was causing this supernatural barrier around them, but she couldn't see. It was too bright. However, she could feel it. With the light came a calming peace. Salome's fear dissipated, as well as the wind. Salome couldn't be certain what was happening, but there was something deep within her that told her this was Sabaoth. He was performing a miracle. He'd sent an angel or Meshiakh himself to protect them. They were going to be okay. Salome stopped digging up dirt, and she bowed her head. Though she didn't have the words, her heart gave thanks.

"I believe." Was all she could muster. "I believe."

It was uncertain how long the dome of light shone around them, but when it finally subsided, so did the fire. Blackened remnants of a village were all that remained. Salome shivered.

The Notzrim too slowly opened their eyes, gasping at the surrounding village, now decimated into a pile of char. Salome was overwhelmed with joy, and she didn't know whether to laugh or cry. Her hand clasped over her mouth as she laughed, utterly shocked at what had just taken place.

It wasn't long before she arms wrapped around her. "He did it," Amina said.

"He sure did."

All around people shouted with joy, they clapped and jumped around, and a song of praise rose loudly to the sky:

> *Sing to Sabaoth with thanksgiving;*
> *make melody to our God on the lyre!*
> *He covers the heavens with clouds;*
> *he prepares rain for the earth;*
> *he makes grass grow on the hills.*
> *He gives to the beasts their food,*

CHAPTER 23

and to the young ravens that cry.
His delight is not in the strength of the horse,
nor his pleasure in the legs of a man,
but Sabaoth takes pleasure in those who fear him, in those who hope in his steadfast love.
Praise Sabaoth!

This was all Sabaoth. He'd come through for them. He delivered a miracle that saved them from the fire. Salome would never doubt him again.

Chapter 24

Paxton looked around for the staircase he'd used once before. As carefully, but as quickly as possible, he descended into the valley. There was no plan. Just save the people. The rain came down harder, making the steps slippery. He lost his foot and skidded down several steep steps before catching himself on a bush. He bounced back up and kept going. The rain picked up, soaking right through his poncho.

At the bottom, Paxton stopped and tried to wipe the rain out of his eyes only to be blasted again. He was breathing heavily and stopped to catch his breath. As he rested, he looked to find the smoke and the flames dying out until they were no longer noticeable. The rain had put the fire out. Sabaoth had put the fire out. A new flood of emotion washed over Paxton, relief, and thanksgiving. They were going to be okay. This valley was special. It was protected by Sabaoth. And they were going to be okay.

"Whoa," Mimi breathed.

Paxton looked at Mimi, who stared in awe at the valley's landscape. Even for someone who hadn't spent nine years in a cement city, the views were breathtaking.

The river rushed away from the waterfall through the bushes and trees. Beyond it was wide open fields. The grass had

CHAPTER 24

turned from a deep green to a vibrant gold. The leaves that still clung to the trees, refusing to descend upon the earth, were all shades of orange, yellow, and red. Even as the rain fell, dampening the autumn valley, there was such beauty. And that was just the beginning. Mimi still had to meet any of the wonderful people that lived in the valley. She and Mitchum were in for a real treat.

"Welcome home."

* * * *

Amina stayed frozen to the ground in her kneeling position, staring at the sky. Her throat was still tight, and a light breeze chilled her wet face. The same angel that Amina experienced years ago when she received the mark of Meshiakh had appeared again. This time to protect them. When the light grew around them, the same overwhelming feeling of peace filled her, just as it had in that tiny basement years ago when she and Aiden were fleeing their hometown. Meshiakh had sent an angel to protect them, to deliver them from the fire. He was the one who put it out. It wasn't anything anyone had done or could've done. In that moment of complete surrender, Amina trusted and was at peace.

It took her a moment to pull herself out of her daze, but when she did, the village was a sight to behold. She didn't notice the charred trees or the collapsed buildings she knew were there. Instead, she saw smiling, laughing faces. She saw families reuniting and hugging, and the elderly sobbing with relief. Men and women alike were shouting songs of praise. It was an impromptu party of celebration and Amina couldn't wipe the smile off her face, even if she'd wanted to.

Amina looked around and spotted Salome with a group of Hebrews. She, too, had the biggest smile as she hugged those around her and spoke to them.

Finding her legs, Amina stood and headed in Salome's direction, feeling a little guilty for thinking Salome was abandoning them. She knew the thought was unjustified in the moment, but her fear made her project blame on someone she was already upset with.

As soon as Salome and Amina made eye contact, Salome rushed over and hugged her.

"Did you see that? Did you see what Sabaoth did?"

"Yes," Amina laughed. Amina stepped back from their hug. "Salome, please forgive me for being so hostile against you. I was upset and wanted to blame someone for—"

Salome placed a hand on Amina's forearm. "I forgive you. These past months have been very stressful. We all said and did things we shouldn't have. But let's put it behind us. You're my friend Amina and I want nothing getting between that."

"Thank you." They hugged again, feeling the weight of guilt being lifted.

Amina watched as the crowd rejoiced with one another. There was cheering, hugging, and jumping for joy. Nothing could make Amina happier at that moment than knowing that they were safe. Amina looked to the sky and allowed the light drizzle to wash over her face. *Thank you.*

"Amina!" Mo's voice broke through the crowd's cheering. Amina spotted Mo, Paul, and Emily and ran to them. "Thank Sabaoth you're okay."

"We're all okay. Everything's going to be okay."

"Yes, I think so."

In the distance, the crowd's murmur turned angry. Amina

looked and there she saw Aryeh and several of his warriors coming toward the crowd. Salome met him and they started talking. Amina scowled. How could he dare show his face here? Amina turned and rushed over to Aryeh.

"How dare you come here! After all you've done! You nearly killed us."

Aryeh threw his hands up in surrender.

"Amina, stop! Aryeh helped us. He wasn't the one who caused the fire, and the one who did is gone. Banished. He won't be coming back," Salome said.

Amina paused a moment, taking in what she'd just heard. How quickly things can change. "Are you sure?"

"Yes. I heard the entire conversation."

Aryeh lowered his hands. "Amina, I'm very sorry for all this. It has gone too far, and it's my fault. I see that now. My prejudice against you and your people caused others to act out. I never intended for it to get this bad. You have to know that. I was just trying to do what I thought was right by keeping our people pure. But this is not the way. Sabaoth is not about prejudice and segregation. He wants us to live in harmony together and from now on, that's what we'll do. We're here to help you rebuild. We'll even teach you everything you need to know. It's time we have a united community. How does that sound?"

"Music to my ears."

"And you forgive me?"

Amina bit her lip, thinking. She knew it was the right thing to do. And he was trying to make amends. "Yes, I forgive you. And hopefully, with enough time, everyone here will too. Come on, let's go tell the others."

Amina led Aryeh and Salome to the main stage, where they

told the entire village what was happening. They assured them that there would no longer be any sabotages but rather unity between the villages and a community that worked together as one. The Hebrews dedicated themselves to helping the Notzrim get back on their feet and thrive in the valley.

After their little meeting, Amina left the stage and went back over to Mo and Paul. Josiah and Maya had joined the group as well and Amina gladly greeted them, thankful they were also okay.

"What a day, huh?" Josiah said.

"You could say that again. I'm completely overwhelmed right now. I don't even know what to think," Amina replied.

Maya smiled. "Much has happened to be grateful to Sabaoth."

The group looked around, at a loss for words for the moment. No one in the village seemed to disperse. There wasn't anywhere to go.

"Now what do we do?" Josiah asked.

Mo put a hand on Amina's shoulder and looked at Josiah. "Today, we rest. We've been through a lot, and we don't need to solve every problem right at this moment."

"But we do need to solve the problem of dinner tonight." Paul grabbed at his stomach. "I'm oddly hungry, despite everything going on."

The group chuckled at Paul's comment and discussed where to get food.

As they were chatting, someone shouted from across the way. "Amina!"

The voice was familiar and yet deceiving. It couldn't be. Amina turned and looked. There, at the edge of the village center, stood Paxton, grinning ear to ear. Amina's heart leaped, but she stood frozen. It was a ghost. He said he'd escape, but she didn't want to believe it. To move forward in life, she had chosen not to believe it. And yet, there he was.

Paxton moved closer. Amina found her legs and sprinted toward him until they met in a longing embrace. Amina's eyes filled as she breathed in his earthy scent. It was him. Solid, real, and alive. Tears sprung to her eyes and brimmed over onto her cheeks.

"You're alive," she sobbed.

"I'm alive."

"How?"

"It's a long story, but before I tell you, I have something else to share."

Amina stepped back and looked at Paxton with concern. His face was sober and his eyes red. Somehow, she knew what he was about to say. She knew he was going to confirm her worst fear. The feeling she already had deep in her soul, that Aiden was gone.

"I'm sorry to be the one to tell you this, but—"

"Then don't," Amina cut him off. "I already know."

Tears slid down Paxton's face. "I couldn't stop it. I tried, but—"

Amina grabbed Paxton into another hug and gripped him. "It's not your fault. He made his choice. I don't agree with it, but it happened. We'll see him again one day. Just—" She couldn't talk anymore. The tears broke into a sob, as they held one another tightly, happy to be together but heartbroken from their loss.

"Never leave again, okay?" She said.

"I won't. You're my family now."

After another long moment, they broke away from their

embrace. Amina spotted Mitchum chatting and hugging several people as well as Mimi standing awkwardly off to the side. Her bandaged arm crossed over her abdomen and her frizzy hair blew in all directions with the wind. Amina looked at Paxton for reassurance. "Is this safe? Her being here?"

Paxton nodded. "It's been removed. No chip. She's safe."

Amina smiled as she crossed to Mimi and hugged her. It took a moment, but Mimi wrapped her good arm around Amina. "I'm glad you came with him."

Mimi stepped back from their embrace and froze. Her eyes looked past Amina and filled with tears. Standing across the way, Salome stood with her hand clasped over her mouth.

"Hi mama," Mimi said, breaking the silence.

Salome smiled as the tears welling in her eye broke free. "Ruth!" She ran to her daughter and embraced her, not wanting to let her go ever again. Amina stepped aside, letting them have their moment. A reconciliation that no one ever expected, and a reunion only Sabaoth could orchestrate.

Paxton wrapped his arm around Amina as they watched the mother and daughter. "I saw your mother before coming here," he said. His tone seemed burdened as if he didn't want to tell her this truth. Amina looked at Paxton quizzically. "She wants me to tell you she's sorry."

Amina leaned her head on Paxton's shoulder and sighed. She had an unexpected aching in her heart for her mother. Cecilia was wicked. She did and said terrible things that weren't worthy of forgiveness, and yet, Amina had compassion for her mother.

"She also wants you to go see her for closure, but I don't think you should. I don't know if she's capable of letting you go fully. She might try to take you again. I don't want you getting hurt."

Amina agreed. It wasn't safe for Amina to go. If Cecilia lied to Paxton, who knew what she had planned for Amina? For everyone's protection, Amina would stay. She'd never have the chance to tell Cecilia she forgave her, but in her heart, Amina let the pain go. Let all the hurt and anger wash away. It was time for a fresh start. It took a while, but Sabaoth had renewed her strength and her hope. Meshiakh would return and this nightmare on earth would be over. Until then, Amina resolved to trust. Trust Sabaoth, that'd keep them safe until the day Meshiakh returned.

* * * *

The sun slowly dipped behind the cliff, leaving a dim white glow over the charred village. A faint smell of smoke still lingered in Amina's nose as she and Paxton walked hand in hand up the hill and toward the open field at the edge of the village. The one area nearby that wasn't destroyed.

After the fire, Matthias and Aryeh had decided the two villages needed to have dinner together to celebrate their union. It was a sight to behold. Hundreds of people sat spread around the field, Notzrim and Hebrews intermingled with one another as they sat sharing bowls and plates of food. The general conversation was quiet and pleasant as people asked questions to learn about one another.

Nearby, Amina spotted her family and friends. She and Paxton made their way toward the others, who greeted them with boisterous hellos and giant hugs. Each of them had to share their excitement again with Paxton, even though they'd done so just a few hours before. Paxton didn't seem to mind. He politely smiled and shared his gratitude. There was something different about him that Amina couldn't quite pin. He appeared more at ease and, dare she say, new. Then she saw it, under Paxton's sleeve, the same glow that emanated from her own skin. The incandescent cross and seal of Meshiakh. Tears sprung to her eyes, and she grinned. Paxton looked at her, and tilted his head. She pointed at his arm. He pulled back the sleeve, revealing the entire cross now permanently tattooed onto his skin. His eyes rounded.

"Hey look." Emily pointed at Paxton's arm. "He's like us now."

The others stared and this time everyone erupted in celebration, but for a new reason. The group swarmed Paxton with hugs and words of affirmation. Amina couldn't help but laugh.

Josiah and Matthias joined the group and Amina stopped laughing. Josiah and Paxton did not part on good terms. Amina shifted uncomfortably, wondering what Josiah would do.

When Paxton spotted Josiah standing there, arms crossed, he walked toward him.

Josiah eyed Paxton before speaking. Amina held her breath. Now was not the day for an argument.

Josiah cracked a smile. "I'm glad you made it back safe."

"Me too."

"And," Josiah paused. "Forgive me for being judgmental toward you." Josiah looked toward Amina and back to Paxton. "You're a good man, and Amina is lucky to have you."

Amina let out the breath she was holding. "We're all lucky to have him," she said, walking toward them.

"Are you eavesdropping on our conversation?" Josiah asked with one eyebrow raised.

"Of course I am. I had to make sure you two boys didn't start

CHAPTER 24

a fight."

The rest of the evening, everyone ate and conversed. There was even an impromptu music group that played instruments brought by the Hebrews.

Most of Amina's group spent their time filling Paxton in on their adventures in the valley as well as drilling him about his time in the capitol. They needed to catch up on everything. It was perfect. Amina couldn't ask for anything more.

Though, when the conversation turned to the subject of Aiden, Amina's stomach twisted into a massive knot. After the nightmare she'd had about a week ago, she'd been dreading the truth.

"Have you heard from Aiden?" Paul inquired.

Paxton stared at his plate a moment, unwilling to speak. Amina grabbed his hand and squeezed. He looked at her and at the others. "Yeah, I ran into him." He took a deep breath before going on. "When I was escaping, he was there in the capitol. I don't fully know why, probably to destroy it, but..." Paxton swallowed hard, and Amina squeezed his hand again, encouraging him to keep going. "He didn't make it out." Tears filled his eyes and spilled onto his cheeks. "He was shot, and I couldn't do anything about it. I wanted to, but he told me to go. He told me to tell you all that he loves you and that he'll see you again when Meshiakh comes to bring you home." Paxton sniffled and wiped his tears. "I'm sorry for your loss."

Everyone in the group was silent. They had no words for the pain they felt. Aiden had been the breath of fresh air, the ever-cheerful problem solver. They each loved him tremendously and would miss him.

"He's right," Amina spoke softly. "We'll see him again soon. I'm sure of it." She had to cling to that hope because if she didn't, she'd never recover from his death.

Mo took a deep breath and exhaled. "Well, who's ready for some dessert?"

The group agreed and Mo and Maya proceeded to pass out small raisin cakes to the group.

The rest of the evening, they spent laughing and enjoying one another's company.

The last several months had been hard. Harder than even that last nine years, and yet, they'd made it. They were finally at peace and where they were meant to be. For now, they could wait in peace, knowing that they were only days away from their true home. Leaving the tunnels and coming to the village was exactly what Amina and likely everyone else needed, to rekindle their hope and faith that Meshiakh was coming back. He was going to establish his kingdom and take them there.

Epilogue

Seven Months Later . . .

The sun radiated in the sky, warming the earth as the trees swayed in the gentle spring breeze. Winter had brought much-needed moisture to saturate the valley, and when spring and the resurrection of new life rolled around, it was vibrant with color. Bright green grass, and brilliant red, purple, yellow, and pink flowers blanketed the field and filled the air with a sweet aroma. The farm burst with the early harvest of lettuce, broccoli, cabbage, and more.

Both the valley and the village sprung to life. It was a surprise how quickly the Notzrim and Hebrews banded together to rebuild the Notzrim village. They were living and getting together the way Amina had always intended it to be. Teaching one another. Learning from one another. And creating a unified community. Amina was in heaven. Or as close as she could get until the real heaven came.

And though she knew a war was brewing, there was still significant evil beyond the valley, she was safe and at home. The only thing missing was her brother.

"You alright?" Paxton asked, breaking Amina out of her daydreaming.

"Huh? Yeah, I'm fine."

"Then let's finish getting this lumber where it needs to go."

"Right, sorry." Amina grabbed the handles of her wheelbarrow and followed Paxton down the hill and toward the far end of the village, where the last set of cabins was under construction.

"This is the life, isn't it?" Paxton said.

"It really is. And I'm glad you're here to enjoy it."

"Me too. This place is better than the city. I've always preferred the outdoors."

As Amina and Paxton approached the build site, Josiah and Paul helped them unload the lumber.

"With the way things are going, we're about finished building the homes for everyone," Paul said while grabbing several pieces of lumber and hauling them toward the current build.

"No kidding, I can't believe how fast it's going," Amina replied. "We've already built a dozen cabins and half of them are furnished."

"It's incredible what happens when people work together," Paxton said.

They finished unloading the lumber.

Paul examined their haggard faces. "Why don't you three take a break? We've got things covered here and you've all been working hard this week."

"Are you sure?" Amina asked. She picked up a leather canteen and took a swig before passing it to Paxton.

"Yes, I'm sure. And I believe the lake water is refreshing this time of day." Paul smiled knowingly.

Amina, Paxton, and Josiah all looked at one another and nodded in agreement. It was time to have some fun.

At the lake, a small crowd of people gathered around, enjoying the sunshine and water. Amina spotted Mo, Salome, and Maya sitting at the edge of the water chatting while Emily

EPILOGUE

swam in the crystal-clear lake with her friends.

While the weather wasn't unbearable, the hard work made the lake look even more inviting. She and the others headed over to the women and greeted them.

"How are you off work duty?" Mo asked.

"Uncle Paul insisted on it."

"Oh, did he now? And I don't suppose he'll be joining us here too?" Amina shrugged. "Of course not. That man works too much."

"Did you three come to swim?" Salome asked.

"You better believe it." Amina stripped to her undergarments. She made her way over to a large rock and climbed.

At the top, she looked over the edge and her stomach fluttered. She made sure the area and water were clear of people before taking an enormous leap. Her body fell through the air until she splashed into the ice-cold water. The cold shocked her, constricting her lungs for just a moment as the water enveloped her sweaty body. She slowed down enough that she could swim her way back to the top.

She let out the air she was holding in a loud sigh as she flung her head back and floated. Spreading her arms and legs wide, she closed her eyes and let the sun warm her face. The water below cooled the rest of her body. Her world was at peace, and she realized she didn't need to be in charge to have influence. The Notzrim was a beautifully built body, each with unique abilities that made up one unified whole. Amina had her own abilities, and she used them every day to help the village thrive. She was a part of something exquisitely crafted by Sabaoth and she needed nothing else.

Amina moved her arms up and down and fluttered her feet to move toward the center of the lake.

As she did, she heard Paxton shout, "Geronimo!" followed by a loud splash. Amina chuckled to herself. Having Paxton around made up for her brother being gone. While this was not the life she'd expected, it was the life Sabaoth had given her, and she found contentment in that.

A tug at her foot promptly sucked her under the water. Amina started flailing anxiously, trying to escape from her captor. It didn't take long before they let go and both she and Paxton rose to the surface. Amina spat the water out of her mouth and gasped. Paxton laughed.

"Paxton, you punk!" Amina splashed him playfully. Part of her was a little annoyed, but mostly she thought it was funny.

"I'm sorry, I couldn't help it," he said through the laughter.

Another splash came. Amina looked and saw Josiah's head pop up and swim over to her. "Man, the water is cold."

"But it feels good," Paxton said. "I'll race you back to the rock."

"You're on." Josiah took off, swimming to the edge of the lake.

Paxton took off after him and caught up. He was a much stronger swimmer than Josiah. As he approached Josiah, he grabbed his leg and pulled him backward, using the moment to propel him forward. He reached the edge before Josiah resurfaced.

Josiah recovered and, as he caught up with Paxton, he grabbed his arm and flung him back into the water.

Amina laughed, watching them be boys before she returned to her floating. She closed her eyes and filled her lungs with fresh air.

It wasn't long before the sun seemed to grow bright beneath her eyelids. A familiar feeling of peace overflowed within

EPILOGUE

Amina, just like she had during the fire. As the light brightened and her heart swelled, Amina smiled excitedly. She opened her eyes and saw a curtain of sparkling gold replace the sky. Amina gazed into the spectacular light as it grew in brilliance.

The sound of horse hooves caught their attention. The sound grew louder and, in the light, Amina could see horses galloping in the sky. Amina's eyes rounded. The horses drew closer and on each horse was a soldier wielding a sword and dressed in ancient armor that glittered gold. The one who led the charge, however, was the most magnificent. His hair shone white, and his eyes were flecked with fire. Power emanated from his features, and he wore a dazzling white tunic and a purple robe. As he drew closer, Amina studied the familiar face. Had she met him before?

A loud trumpet blew, echoing throughout the entire valley as the voice spoke. "It's time to come home."

THE END

About the Author

Britney Farr loves to create suspenseful and dangerous worlds from the safety of her home. There's nothing more exciting than watching her characters thrust into impossible situations, forcing them to grow despite the surrounding threats. Through grit and perseverance, Farr challenges her characters to find hope and strength in something greater than themselves—God.

Beyond writing, Britney Farr is a social communications manager at her church in the north metro Denver area and serves as president of the Thornton Community Chorus.

Britney Farr is an avid reader, devout Christian, and former English/Theatre teacher. She loves crafting her creativity and skills to bring readers an emotionally engaging, nerve-wracking, faith-filled story.

Farr has a bachelor's degree in English, but first began creating other worlds and characters as a young girl and she's never stopped. Whether she's building a character through her acting, creating emotion with singing, or putting pen to paper,

Britney loves the creativity. When she's not being creative or watching others' creativity, you can find her enjoying the outdoors. She loves hiking, camping, traveling the world, escape rooms, and enjoying the company of her friends and family.

To connect, discover fun bonus readings, and stay updated on Britney Farr's most recent writing projects, subscribe to her mailing list.

You can connect with me on:
- https://britneyfarr.com
- https://www.facebook.com/BritneyFarrAuthor
- https://www.instagram.com/BritneyFarrAuthor
- https://www.goodreads.com/britney_farr

Subscribe to my newsletter:
- https://landing.mailerlite.com/webforms/landing/h5d1g6

Also by Britney Farr

Searching for Refuge
First came the natural disasters, then the world war, and finally the impossible decision: conform to the new world order or die by the faith. Twins Amina and Aiden are forced with this impossible decision.

For nine years they survive, but when a mysterious newcomer appears in their underground hideout, Amina realizes they are on the verge of being discovered and killed. Now, they must make another impossible decision: stay and risk their lives along with hundreds of others or escape to a new location that may hold more enemies than before.

Either way, the clock is ticking.

Searching for Direction
Just as the pieces start to come together, they are shattered again.

Amina Haddad returned home victorious and proud. However, after discovering the mysterious disappearance of her twin brother, Aiden, her world quickly shatters again. Convinced he's still alive, Amina heads for enemy territory, determined to rescue her brother, no matter the cost.

Before leaving, Amina charges the Hebrew newcomer Salome with the daunting task of safely guiding the Notzrim people to her home in the mountains. Further complicating matters, the Notzrim people are not welcome among the Hebrews, and Salome knows it. Will Salome follow through with her promise to Amina, or will the fear of banishment prevent her from completing such a courageous task?

Meanwhile, Aiden—still alive but held captive in the capitol—is surprised to discover the identity of his captor and the extraordinary lengths they go to entice him to stay. The only question that remains is whether Aiden will give up everything he believes in for this new and unexpected opportunity.

Made in the USA
Las Vegas, NV
01 February 2023